THE FORBES FAMILY

I0692778

Settling The West Series
The Forbes Family

Copyright © 2012 by David Dodge

ISBN 1-890548-24-3
Masair publications

Published in the United States of America
October 2012

Printed By

Southwest Direct Inc.
southwest direct.com

Cover Design By
Isaac Munoz
isaacmunozsr@yahoo.com

Revised Edition

Special thanks to
Maryanne Chambers Gilmore,
writer, editor and good friend,
for struggling with me on this project.

Settling The West Series

Strong men and women from all parts of the world, looking for a way to a better life, settled the West. Families, like the Forbes, broke apart when the yearning for change filled their souls. Each had a goal in mind, that often changed when reality set in. Those changes were the forerunners of the development of this country.

Some lives were improved . . . Some were lost, but the settling, and the expansion of this country continued through the hardships to give each American the opportunity to live a better life.

This is the story of The Forbes family, five sons and a daughter, and how their lives unfolded as they settled in the West.

The Forbes Family

Chapter 1

In the early 1800's, Richard Albin Forbes with his wife, Iona and his brother Ivar Findly Forbes, and his wife, Brenda, often dined together. They were decended from families with holdings in the rail business, and had followed their ancestor's careers.

On this cold night in northern Aberdeen Scotland, in the Parish of Tulleynessle and Forbes, at least one member wanted to make a move.

Richard Forbes excitedly spoke up, "Yes I mean all of us . . . move to Ireland and buy enough land to raise the thoroughbred horses we want to breed. We know people that will buy from us. I hear that the land is filled with limestone, and the moisture is high. It's ideal there, on the southern coast. Besides, the climate is milder there."

Ivar Forbes exclaimed, "I believe I could enjoy that!"

The wives sat speechless for a short while, just looking at each other. But when they realized that the men were serious, Brenda asked, "What about our friends?"

Richard quickly spoke up, "We'll make new ones!"

"We could raise potatoes there, and I hear they do very well," laughed Iona.

Brenda looked at Iona, unbelieving. "You didn't say 'raise potatoes' did you? Grub in the dirt like a farmer?"

"I think it would be fun . . . like raising flowers," responded Iona.

Brenda, her face twisted in thought, replied, "I suppose . . . since you put it that way."

Rising, Richard said, "It's settled then. We can start making plans immediately."

He turned to Ivar. "We can take both our studs, and buy thoroughbred mares when we get the land!"

Together, they bought land on the southern coast of Ireland, in Wexford County. The Forbes brothers bred horses until 1845, when the potato famine brought down the horse business, for the Forbes brothers' families.

The two Forbes Families, now a bit larger than before, planned another move together.

Richard Forbes had three sons at the time: Delbert, Charles and Matthew. The families decided to make the jump of their lives, by going to America.

Months later, in October of 1846, they stood at the rail of their ship, as it sailed into New York harbor. They marveled at the size and height of the buildings on such a small island. Their first stop was Ellis Island for processing, as all immigrants were required to do in those days.

The two Forbes families soon purchased land in Virginia, where the borders of Virginia, West Virginia and Kentucky come together. There, they began their required period of time of living in America for naturalization, to become citizens of their newly adopted country.

The two families built their homes near each other, and became known for their fine thoroughbred horses.

After a few years, in Virginia, Iona became ill and died. Her body was buried in her beloved Scotland.

Not long after his mother's death, Delbert Forbes, the oldest son, returned home from college wanting to go 'West'. His enthusiasm spread among his four brothers.

During an evening meal, when all the Forbes family was gathered, their father, Richard Forbes, spoke to his five sons. "I know that you boys have been craving adventure in the West. Delbert, I credit you for most of this, what with all the stories you've heard back east. I really can't blame any of you, for wanting to get out in life, even though I had wanted you to stay here, and raise horses.

If your mother was still alive, Lord rest her soul, I would say 'no', because it would break her heart. I see though, that you are each determined, so, go with my blessing. But you had better keep me informed as to where you are . . . I guess Mary Elizabeth and I will keep this place going."

Eventually, they each left home, to find their fortunes in the American West.

The five Forbes sons Of Richard and Iona were Delbert, Charles, Matthew, Bryan and Benjamin. Each chose their own time, and direction in their pursuit of a life in the 'West'.

Delbert Forbes

Chapter 2

Delbert Forbes, the oldest of the boys, was the first to leave their father's home in Virginia. His wanderlust led him to the fascinating state of Texas, where he learned the ways of the west. After years of cowboying, he had wound up in Montana. This morning, as the sun was coming up, he sat on his blue appaloosa, with his leg over the pommel of his saddle. His green eyes gazed lazily from his perch on a low butte. At this time, Dell was well over forty, handsome by ladies standards, about six feet three, with sandy hair. He had a small scar over his right eye, from one of his many battles.

The lacy clouds in the sky were a brilliant rose color, from the rising sun. There were sweet smells of early morning in the air, the kind of smells that come with fall. The cattle he watched belonged to his good friend and employer, Thomas Sneed. It was a small herd, part of a larger group he had brought up from Texas back in '85. Dell Forbes had been with Thomas Sneed for over twelve years, and had been his foreman for ten of those years.

It was warm in the Montana sun, after a cold night watch that he had volunteered to take. His bones were beginning to soak up the sunshine that the morning had brought. Fall always started that way in Montana, cool nights and warm days. He knew that soon the days would be cold, and nights would be intolerable. In his younger days, it didn't bother him much, but lately, he found it hard to face the fact that winter is coming on.

As the sun came up, the warm breeze off the sun-filled valley caused his mind to drift back to the time he had spent in the 'Hill Country' of Texas. There, much like here, a buzzard was always circling, in unrewarded anticipation. The Blanco River rushed in its banks near by. A fish would jump out of the water occasionally, in a backwater pool along the edge. Squirrels would be running up and down the trees, transporting pecans to a hide-a-way for winter. And there, he would have a warm sun most any time!

Suddenly, Delbert Forbes was jerked back to the present by a voice from the valley below. "Dell, you gonna stay up there all day? Wesley's here to relieve us, and I'm hungry." The voice was Thomas Sneed's young nephew, Jay Sneed, his brother's son. He had started to attend college back East, but was stricken by the romance of the "West", as described in the dime novels that had begun to circulate in the East. Also his uncle's letters gave a lot of praise to his foreman, Dell Forbes. He came here to his uncle's, much to his mother's objections, to learn the ropes of being a 'cowboy'.

As Jay topped out the hill from which Dell watched, he asked, "Didn't you see our relief come into the valley?"

Dell answered. "Naw, I was miles away in Texas. Now that you mention it . . . seems like I recall it's about time for some chuck. Hope I'm luckier than that ole buzzard up yonder."

Jay smiled and said, "When he rode in to relieve us, Wesley said that Cookie had some great steaks for us, if we don't fool around. Suppose we get after it."

"I'm right behind ya!" Dell responded.

Riding together, back toward the ranch, Jay's curiosity got the best of him, and he asked, "What'd you mean, you were in Texas?"

Dell didn't answer immediately. "For a long time, I've been thinking about hanging it up, and going back to Texas. I lived there, on the Blanco River for a little while, and the weather was just what my ole bones need now. I may even want to be further south than that."

"You don't mean you want to leave now, do you?" Jay asked. "I don't think Uncle Tom could get along without you!"

"Sure he could," Dell responded, "I think he's got some great hands here, and they've been with him long enough that he knows each one and what he can do. Wesley would make a good foreman. He's got the savvy it takes, and he's been with Tom almost as long as I have. He can handle cattle better than me."

Wesley Holt was what you would call 'El Segundo', the second in command to Dell. He had been with Tom for seven or eight years.

Wesley was tall, with black hair, thick, but not long. His dark eyes seemed to move constantly, surveying everything that moved. He had proved to be a good hand for Tom. He was younger than Dell, and plenty 'wiry'. He was as good with a gun as Dell.

"When would you be leaving, then?" Jay asked.

"Well, I was thinking, before it gets cold again."

They rode along, lost in deep thought. Neither had anything to say, listening to the gentle clopping of the horses hooves.

After a while, Jay asked. "How did you wind up in Texas anyway?"

"Well, Gordon Weaver and I were getting ready for our second year of college, in Virginia."

Jay interrupted. "You went to college?"

"Yep, for 'bout a year. Anyway, Gordon and I, kept reading about how Texas had won it's independence from Mexico, and how all those heroes, like Bowie, Austin, and Houston, from our part of the country, had gone to Texas. And it being the biggest State in the Union, we decided we wanted to see it. Besides, there were two fellers, a Pointing and Malone, as I remember, brought a hundred or so of Texas Longhorns to the Hundred Street Market, in New York. Gordon and me were there to celebrate the fourth of July, in '54, as I recall. We were just kids, and the longhorns from Texas were a sight to see. They had horns half again as long as these. Well, we could hardly wait; we sold some stuff, and bought a couple of extra horses from Papa, packed up and moved. You talk about a learning experience, we got that all right!"

Jay let that soak in a minute, and then asked, "What did you do, when you got there?"

"For a long time we moved from ranch to ranch, getting' work where we could. There were a lot of small ranches that needed help, from time to time. Why, I even cooked for a while, for one ranch. We stayed alive by shuckin' cattle out of the mesquites, and selling them. Then we met your Uncle Tom. He had bought, and rounded up out of the brakes, thirty five hundred head of cattle out of Mexico and south Texas. He needed to move them up here. Well, Gordon and I had starved about as long as we wanted to, so we jumped at the chance and hired on, and brought the cattle up the Bozeman trail . . . took nearly four months. That was our first meeting with Tom. I made a couple'a trips for him after that."

"What happened to Gordon? Did he go back to Texas?"

"No, on our second trip up here, we ran into a storm in the Nation, right after we crossed the Powder. The lightening and thunder was bustin' the skies wide open. The cattle got started running, and we like ta not been able to stop 'em. When it was all over, we found that Gordon got caught up in the middle of all that, and he and his horse both went down. We buried him about half way between the Powder and the Tongue Rivers."

"It's been a while since you brought cattle up from Texas, hasn't it?" Jay asked.

"Yeah, a lot of people move cattle west to the mining towns now days. So, Tom decided to just build up his herd, with good breeding. He could make more money with better stock, so he bought a Shorthorn bull from a Scotchman that had come over to buy ranch land," Dell answered.

Jay, seventeen, tall for his age, with sky blue eyes, and a shock of blond unruly hair, was new to the west. And he had a lot of information to process. He was, however, getting the hang of a lot of what goes on in ranch life. Some of the changes taking place were still a bit hard to stretch his mind over, and he was never bashful when he had questions to ask.

Jay's attention to his thoughts was interrupted when Dell pulled up quickly, and brushed a hand toward Jay, as if to halt him.

"What is it?" Jay asked.

Dell was standing high in his stirrups, sniffing the air. After a minute, he answered. "I got a wiff of smoke, only lightly, but smoke. I don't see any yet. We need to keep an eye on the horizon though.

"When you smell smoke, you need to check it out at that very moment. Smoke smells different. Grass has a distinctive smell, as does wood. When they are burning, pine, cedar and oak smell different. So you need to learn the difference. If it's wood, be careful, as you may ride up on a campsite that's not friendly. If you know about a camp ahead of time, you can ask the campers if it's all right to come in. A grass fire could mean you are going to lose your grazing. So you see, smells can tell you lots of things."

"What kinda smoke did it smell like?" Jay asked.

Dell thought a minute, and then answered. "It was scrub wood, Jay. I think I'll have a look around. Stay right here. I'll be back." As he spoke, he eased his spurs to Blue, who was ready to move out. Looking around, he saw a whisp of smoke. He slowed Blue to a walk, and stepped down near a shallow canyon that was used as the border between Tom's Bar T Ranch and Raffe Haskell's Box RH Ranch. He saw where a calf had been roped, and dragged down into the canyon, and he could hear his bellowing.

11

In the canyon, a small fire was heating an iron, and the calf was tied nearby. The man with the branding iron was Rusty Davis. Dell knew him well. He was acting foreman for Raffe Haskell, after Raffe's foreman had been dragged to death a few months ago. Rusty was a young man. His sleeves were rolled up, showing strong arms, and sweat rolled down his face. He had a small mustache and dark black hair, that when he ran his fingers through it, the waves would return. He was alone.

"I wouldn't run a brand on that calf, if I were you Rusty. I can see where you picked him up, and dragged him into the canyon," Dell said.

"And just why not? He's one of Raffe's," Rusty responded.

"Because, it would look funny if that calf that's still nursing had a different brand from its mama! I expect you had better cut him loose, and bring him back up here."

Rusty Davis considered the situation; he had seen what happened to men that drew a gun on Dell. Besides, his rifle was leaning on a tree, and his revolver hung over his saddle horn. He began to untie the calf.

Dell watched a minute, and then said. "Rusty, lets just let this be between us. I think that Tom Sneed and Raffe Haskell have bigger problems that you and me, as their foremen, need to consider."

"What'a you mean?" Rusty asked.

"I'll let you know later. Tell Raffe I'll come by the ranch tonight and lay out what I'm thinkin'," said Dell.

Rusty was bitter, but he kept his jaw clamped, to not show it. He wasn't sure just what Dell had in mind. *"Does he know more than he let on? Guess I'll find out later,"* He thought to himself.

Rusty watched Dell ride away. Then, half out loud said. "I'll be ready for whatever you've got, Dell Forbes."

As Dell rode back, Jay asked. "What happened in the canyon, Dell?"

"Ah, Rusty Davis was noonin', and had a small fire going. Made me hungry. I guess we'll miss the steak and eggs."

"Not if we hurry, we won't," Jay Sneed called back, as he spurred his horse into a run, "At least, I'll get mine!" he shouted.

Gentle spurs in Blue's side were the only signal he needed. That sense of going home, that is in the heart of every horse, took over, and soon Jay was in Dell's dust.

'Cookie' had seen the two racing toward the ranch. Since he had a good fire going for wash water, he slipped a couple of steaks on, and heated up the skillet. 'Cookie's' name was James Spence. Spence was the name his grandfather had used while he was a slave, for the Spence family. James had kept the name when Tom Sneed gave him his 'free' papers, years ago, and had stayed with Tom ever since. The hair he still had was in ringlets along the sides, and mostly grey. He walked slightly bent forward, from getting on in years. No one knew how many.

When Dell and Jay came in, Cookie asked, "What took you fellers so long to get here? Mista' Wesley done left hours ago!"

Jay was eager to answer. "Well, Dell smelled smoke, and had to check to see what was burning."

Cookie looked puzzled, and asked. "What wus on fire?"

"Oh, it was just Rusty, over on the Box R H, near Little Creek, a noonin'." Jay responded.

Cookie was serving the steaks, and sliding the eggs onto their plates, when he mused, "That seems kinda strange, Mitsa' Rusty a cooking that close to headquarters. Ole George Beck come back with Miss Belle, and has been cookin' for three o'foe weeks."

Dell was taken by surprise. He nearly dropped his fork. "You mean Belle has come back to the ranch?"

"Yes suh, she done got tired o' city life, and George tol' me she come home to stay," Cookie continued, "an' I think mist'a Raffe ain't feelin' too good, neither."

Dell took a sip of coffee. "I told Rusty that I would be coming over this evening, to talk about this rustling' that's been going on. I never thought I might see Belle," Dell paused in thought, and then went on, "It's been a long time. I expect she's grown up by now."

"Yes suh, I reckon she has, and Rusty thinks he got his rope on her, I speck," mused Cookie with a smile.

Jay had been working on the steak and eggs. Finally, with his mouth half full, he managed to ask, "Who's Belle?"

"Belle is Raffe Haskell's daughter. She left their ranch several years ago, to go to Kansas City," Dell explained.

Before long, Jay and Dell were patting their bellies, and relaxing on the front porch, when Bar-T owner, Tom Sneed, walked in from the barn. Tom's hair was mostly grey, and his face reflected the years of riding in the sun. His grey eyes shined bright and clear and he seemed younger than his years. He and his wife Judy had lived most of their lives in Montana. She died from the flu, not too many years after they married.

Tom stepped up on the walk, and cleaned his boots on the scraper. "You two look like the pigs that got into the corn crib," he said. "James feeds pretty good, doesn't he?"

Dell smiled in agreement then related his plans to go to the Haskell ranch.

Tom broke in. "You sure you don't just want to see Belle?"

"I didn't even know that Belle was in these parts, 'till Cookie just now told me!" Dell objected. "By the way,

Tom, I think I'll come back by the old line shack in the north pasture. If it's still standing, I'll stay there tonight. I want to check the grass. We may have to sell some of the old beef, if they are over-grazing that short grass. You're welcome to come along to talk about this rustlin', if you want. I thought I'd see what Raffe's thinkin' is."

Tom declined, saying he had things to do. He felt that Dell could take care of these matters. "Do what you can, and tell Raffe we'll get together, and take care of this problem. You just be careful, staying up at the line shack."

Jay asked if he could go along but was told that he was expected to do his job in the morning. "Besides, Tom couldn't get along, if two of his best hands were gone at the same time!"

Dell loaded up food, which Cookie put together for him, and all the gear that he would need for a couple of days. He drew a horse that he had packed before. He thought about saddling Blue, but since he had worked him the day before, he decided to take Patrick, a speckled grey that he often rode.

Dell was looking forward to getting away for a while. It would give him a chance to think.

As he rode along on the trail to the Box RH Ranch, he was not sure just how he would approach this rustler business. He had no idea how many cattle the ranches had lost, but it had to be looked into. As he rode, he enjoyed the warm weather, no sounds except the squeak of the saddle, and soft repetitive sounds of his horses' hooves on the dusty trail. Dell had forgotten about moving back to the warm climate of Texas. The thoughts would return, when the evening cold would begin to settle around his back.

Other thoughts ran wild in his mind. *"What possessed Belle to return to the ranch? She must be close to twenty-five or six. Is she going to stay, or go back to Kansas City? What about Rusty, is she really involved with him?"* Softly he said to himself, "Hey, you are going to talk about rustling', not the lady's social life!" His mind then began to search out places that stolen cattle could be held and not found, until there were enough to be sold.

He had ridden just about every foot of this ranch, or at least he thought he had. "*May be a good idea for me to look again*".

It was getting late in the day, when he reached the Haskell ranch.

Rusty Davis came out to meet him. Dell watched him carefully.

Out of the corner of his eye, he noticed one man that he didn't recognize, leaning on the bunkhouse porch rail, and another in the shadows by the granary. He couldn't see the face of the man in the shadows. He didn't like the situation, because he figured there might be more strangers around that he couldn't see.

Other thoughts came to him. "*I wonder where the new men came from, and where are Robert, Jesse, and Alverez, men that have been with Raffe for years?*"

He dismounted. "Howdy, Rusty. Is Raffe here?"

"Naw, he ain't here. They went into town, and ain't got back yet."

Dell thought a minute, and then said, "I understand that Belle has come back to the ranch."

"Yeah, but she ain't here neither. She went with her paw."

"Is Jesse or Robert here?" Dell asked.

"Naw, they done quit last week."

"I see you got some replacement hands okay."

"Yeah, they're a little green, but they'll do."

Dell took the reins, and mounted up. "I guess I'd best get to movin' on. It'll be dark 'fore long. See you later, Rusty."

"Yeah, Dell, another time I reckon."

Dell rode off in the direction from which he had come. The man in the shadows stepped up to Rusty. Ed Landros, a big burly guy, with a scraggly beard on a poc-marked face. He had hard dark eyes, shaded by heavy brows. He wore a low-slung gun, with the holster tied down, for gun-play. "Where you reckon he's going with that pack horse? I don't 'speck he'll go back home, since he's all loaded up with supplies."

"Ed, maybe you'd best see where he's going. I shore don't like him poking around."

"What should I do about it, Boss?" Ed asked.

"Whatever you think, Ed. Just don't tell me! Take Dustin with you. You might need some help," said Rusty.

Dustin Davis was Rusty's 'little' brother, tipping the scale at two hundred and forty five pounds. At first glance, it looked as if his head was way too small for his huge muscular body. His hair looked greasy, giving it a dark golden color, nearly to his shoulders.

As Dell rode along, he wondered, *"What was that all about? All the old hands quit, and have been replaced with strangers, wearing tied down guns. I don't like the looks of that. I asked Rusty to tell Raffe I would like to talk to him. It's not like Raffe at all to not be there. Things didn't look right, and I was probably lucky to get out with my hair. I wonder what Rusty is up to? I'll go on up to the cabin. I can think there."* Dell was looking forward to being alone. In the cool evening, going back to Texas kept popping into his mind.

Chapter 3

The day was beginning to loose light, but Dell could see that the grass here was an excellent stand of Bluestem, and would support a good many cows and their calves. The few cattle he saw were in good shape, with a few that could be culled out.

17

Not a lot of dust here, as the rain would sprinkle a bit each afternoon, another reason the grass was so good.

As he rode through the trees, he walked Patrick slowly. He didn't want to approach the line shack directly, until he was sure that it was clear.

Thoughts kept running through his mind: *"I wonder if rustlers have been using the camp . . . naw, it's too rundown . . . I can remember many a night spent here. Sometimes the snow was so deep I couldn't get the door open for days. That reminds me, I was going to get back down to Texas, where it's warm, and here I am getting ready to spend the night in a rundown shack with the cold fall night poring down my neck.*

I still can't figger Rusty; maybe he has something to do with this ruslin' . . . Naw, surely not! He's always seemed happy at Raffe's. Now that Belle is there, he seems happier. But . . . who are the men he has around now? I couldn't see their faces, so I don't know if I've seen them before. I guess they've been around since his hands quit . . . if they did quit! . . . reckon he ran them off?"

The cabin was in sight now. He stopped the grey, and studied the situation carefully. He listened for any strange sounds that didn't fit the natural ones. Then he approached, and dismounted. He dropped the reins, eased the thong off the hammer of his Colt, and walked to the cabin and eased the door open. It was nearly dark outside, and even darker inside. He struck a match, and shadows flickered all around the room. Then he turned to the small table, and lit the kerosene lamp. With the warm glow of the lamp, Dell surveyed the room. All seemed to be in order. The bunk in the corner had a mattress that wasn't full of rats . . . a good sign.

"Boy this brings back memories; I've worn out several decks of cards playing solitaire right here."

He went outside, placed the horses in the corral, and stripped his gear from both. He softly talked to them, as he rubbed them down, and pitched some hay, stored in the small shed at the back of the corral. He took a small can, and poured a bit of coal oil from the large supply, to take inside for his lamp.

The early evening was quiet. A gentle breeze drifted down from the mountains, stirring the leaves on the big cottonwoods. Dell tugged his collar up tighter, as he began to shiver a little. "Doggone it, what am I still doing here? I should have left this country years ago, an' I will soon, before I freeze to death!" he heard himself say emphatically.

Before he carried his stuff in, he looked around slowly and very carefully, listening to every sound. Back inside, he pitched his soogan on the bed, and then he stoked a fire in the small stove. Wood was always left for the next one to stay at the cabin, so there was plenty for the night. He slipped off his boots and hung them upside down on the bedposts to keep the 'varmints' out. He realized then, he had been up for two days. Sleep came immediately.

An hour or so later, consciousness slowly returned from his deep sleep that was caused by exhaustion. Usually he woke up instantly at any small disturbance. As his mind began to work again, he realized that he smelled smoke, and that it was the first time that he had been warm enough. At that moment, Dell realized that the cabin was totally engulfed in flames! He quickly grabbed his boots, his Winchester and other gear. He opened the door in the floor to the root cellar, pitched in some of his gear, and then pulled the rest in behind him. He struggled to pull everything through the narrow area to the exit door. He pushed on the outside door. It didn't give, and he tried again, with no luck. Grass, tree roots and years of blowing dirt had packed around it. The small cellar was beginning to fill with smoke. He turned around, placed his feet against the door, and finally forced it open. He was out into the fresh air again,

19

looking back at the cabin that had burned nearly to the ground.

The big cottonwoods growing right around the cabin were beginning to catch fire. As he watched, he thought of every thing that could have caused the blaze, but nothing came to mind. Suddenly, by the flickering light, he saw two riders as they were disappearing into the dark of the night! He raised his rifle, but didn't fire. It was then he smelled the coal oil that had been spread around the cabin.

He pitched his stuff on the hay from the small shed, and layed back on his saddle. He was still tired, even with all of the excitement. His thoughts began to race again over the situation. *"Was Rusty responsible for this? Neither rider looked like him. It was only a glance, before the riders disappeared into the darkness."* He then realized that the riders thought that he had burned with the cabin. He half spoke out loud; "Well, they're sure they got rid of me. I'll just stay that way, 'till I can find out what's going on!" He once more was overtaken by a deep sleep.

When Dell finally awoke, the sun was well up into a clear blue sky, but at least he was well rested. He sat for a few minutes, and stared at where the cabin had been, still smoking. With the cabin gone, he now had a clear view down the hill, and across the valley. He gathered some small limbs that had fallen from the trees, and made a fire. He felt that no one would notice his campfire smoke, since plenty of smoke was still coming from the cabin. He got his coffee pot started, then took a small can from the pack, set it near the fire, and placed a few of Cookie's biscuits in it to warm. He cut a few slices of bacon, and waited for his skillet to get hot.

"No reason not to have a good breakfast! I'm gonna have to figger this mess out. Here I am again, living outside cold and lonely . . . I got'a get out of this country, before I freeze to death!"

As he tipped his cup to take another gulp, he saw movement in the edge of the trees. He set his skillet off the fire, and reached for his Winchester. He hammered back, as to not make noise that would give away his position when the rider got closer. He then leaned back on his turned up saddle and waited. He could watch every move from his location.

As the rider came closer, he saw neither a gun drawn nor a rifle scabbard on the saddle. The rider sat quietly and starred at the rubble. After a few minutes Dell spoke out. "Quite a mess isn't it?" Having not noticed Dell, the horse jumped and stepped back. As he did, the rider hollered, "Whoa!" It was a woman's voice.

Dell immediately apologized. "I'm sorry, if I scared you, ma'am."

She replied. "You didn't scare me, but you gave my horse a start."

He rose and walked toward her. "You must be Belle."

"And you must be Dell Forbes," she replied.

"That I am. What's brought you out, on such nice morning?"

As he walked, he carefully set the hammer down on his Winchester.

Seeing him hammer down, she asked. "You weren't going to shoot me were you, Dell?"

"No ma'am!" he replied. "But two men rode away last night as the cabin was going up in flames. I wasn't too sure that they weren't coming back."

The closer he got to her, the more surprised he was at the change from the last time he had seen her. He was amazed at her beauty. Her hair was pushed up under her hat, but he could see the redness of it. Her eyes were blue that seemed to look right through him. He hoped that she could not hear his heart, as he could.

"You never said why you rode out this way," he reminded her.

21

As she eased off her horse, she replied, "I heard Ed tell Rusty that Tom's old line shack had burned, and that you had burned to death with it!"

"I wonder how they knew I was at the cabin. I didn't say where I was going . . . kinda makes me wonder about Rusty . . . this, and the fact that I caught him trying to run a brand on one of Tom's calves. I'm sorry, Belle, I heard that Rusty sorta had his rope on you. But I still wonder."

"Who told you that? Rusty is nothing to me," she objected.

Dell was still struck by her beauty. What she said made him wonder if maybe he had a chance. The more he thought about that, the more he realized that he had nothing, and she probably thought he was too old for her.

"Pardon my manners. How about some breakfast? I was just putting on some bacon." He set the skillet back on the coals. "The coffee is ready, and so are the biscuits. They're in that warming can by the fire. Help yourself." After a moment he asked, "What else did they say?"

"Nothing else that I heard, I was just leaving to ride for a while, and was at the other end of the barn. I don't think they even knew I was around."

"I sorta decided to stay 'dead' a while, to look into the rustlin'. Now, I wonder who wanted me dead and why?" he mused out loud, as he poured her a cup of coffee.

"As far as I know, no one knows you're still alive. They didn't know that I was coming up here.

"I just remember having been to this cabin many times, when my brother, Marvin, was alive and worked for Tom, before you brought the cattle up from Texas. Marvin went to the gold fields around Denver, or somewhere, and we never heard from him after that. I think he got into some shady deals. We think he may be dead. I just wanted to see the cabin again." She paused, and then asked, "Dell, was it Ed and Dusty that were here last night?"

"I don't know Ed or Dusty, and I couldn't see that well. But who else could it be? They probably followed me, when I left the ranch."

"You were at the ranch?" she interrupted.

"Yes, I came by yesterday afternoon to talk to your dad. Rusty told me that your dad and you were in town. I couldn't wait for y'all to return, so I left. I had told Rusty that I wanted to talk to Raffe about this rustlin', but I guess he forgot."

"We didn't go to town! We were down at the spring. Dad loves it down there, and we were just passing the time. We weren't gone but a little while. We happened to see a cow bogged down, and we had to pull her out."

"The lies seem to keep coming. What really happened to Robert, Jesse and Alverez? Rusty said they quit. "

"Rusty ran them off! He had brought those toughs in, a few at a time, and Robert, and Jesse couldn't get along with them. Finally they told Dad they couldn't stay."

"What did Raffe do about that?"

"Not much he could do. He needed hands to work and Rusty seemed to be his only hope, after Ben Gerard was dragged to death. You see, Dad had a stroke a while back, and hasn't been able to do much since. That's why I came back. I still don't know how Ben could have gotten dragged like that. Now, I kinda wonder about that, too."

"Since I'm going to stay 'dead' a while, to find out what's going on, when you are at Tom's place, take him aside, and let him know what is happening . . . just Tom and your dad, no one else!"

"Yes I will. I will also listen for any information I can pick up around the ranch. I had better get back so they won't get suspicious! I've been gone about as long as I usually am, on my morning ride. As she started to rise, he caught her arm and said, "You will be all right there, won't you? If you feel any danger at all, go to Tom's. Someone there will take care of you!"

They walked together, to her horse, and Dell helped her on. She didn't ride sidesaddle, since she wore britches, and wore them well, in his opinion! Her perfume floated gently down to Dell. It was like the smell of the spring wild flowers. His mind raced once more to the thought that he just might have a chance with her.

He stood still, his hat in his hand, and watched as she disappeared into the trees.

When Belle returned from her ride to the cabin, Rusty began to question her. "Where you been, Belle?"

"Oh, just on my usual morning ride. Is Dad in the house?"

"Yeah, he went in awhile ago. You better be careful where you ride from now on! It may get dangerous out there."

"Oh, why is that?"

"Well, we think we've seen strange riders out there," he replied. "Anyway, you'd best be careful. I don't want anything to happen to you."

"Well, thank you, Rusty, but I think I can take care of myself."

"Just don't go too far, anymore!" he instructed.

Belle went into the house, and found her dad sitting on his bed. "Are you all right, Dad?"

"Yes, a little tired though, and a bit worried about the cattle. I'm not sure about Rusty. I can't get any straight answers from him."

She filled him in on what she had discussed with Dell, and how they had begun to suspect that Rusty was involved in some sort of unlawful action. "Dad, Rusty thinks that Dell burned to death in the old line shack. Dell wants everyone to think so, except you and Tom. I'll let Tom know later. Dell needs to look around without any interference. He thinks that Dusty and Ed burned the cabin. He saw two riders leaving, while it burned."

"I always thought that something was going on, by the way the hands have acted since Robert and the others left. I just couldn't put my finger on it."

"Well I'm sure that Dell will find out something, and let us know. Just don't worry, in the meantime," encouraged Belle.

The morning was gray, and brisk. Dell had loaded the packhorse, saddled Patrick and mounted up. He sat looking at the remains of the cabin, and then made sure none of the coals could blow to start a fire on the pasture. He rode off north to continue looking around. As he rode along, Belle kept flashing through his mind. "Boy Patrick, I sure didn't remember Belle like that! She was just a youngun, or she was to me anyway. Now she's the gal for me, if she'll have me!"

After a day's ride, the sun sank low in the sky, and Dell realized that he needed a place to make camp. When the light had just about gone, he rode up to a shelf of rock that had a good overhang for protection, in case it should rain. He unsaddled Patrick, unloaded the packhorse, and made his bed. A small fire got his coffee going, and he ate a cold biscuit, with a piece of jerky. Then he crawled into his blankets. He was tired from a busy day, and was soon sound asleep.

Before the dawn brought much light, he fixed his breakfast. By the time he had finished, it was light enough he could study the terrain. So far, nothing looked like a place to take cattle off the range. The mountains rose in front of him, and the canyon was to the right, too deep to even think about going down the sides.

He walked up to where the mountain seemed to meet the canyon, and paused. When he started to take another step, out of the corner of his eye, he saw movement on the top of the butte. He stopped still, and watched.

Soon he saw a man with a rifle on the far side. He then looked toward the other side. Sure enough, there was a rifleman there, too. *"Guards on the canyon! Why?"* He began to move to the edge of the canyon, shielding himself from their view by the rocks. Suddenly, there it was! A wide shelf with a gradual slope downward! It was wide enough that cattle could be taken down into the canyon. It could not be seen until you were right on the edge. The trail was rock that left no tracks.

Dell thought, *"How come I haven't seen that before? Now they couldn't get cattle to start down that slope, unless . . . unless they had an old mossback longhorn leader that would lead them anywhere. That must be it, guards and a way down. Somehow, I must get down there to see what's going on. I don't think I could get Patrick to go down in the dark, so I guess I'll go afoot."*

He went back to the horses, and sat down. In the quiet of the morning he listened to the birds. A rabbit ran from bush to bush. Soon the wind shifted and he noticed that he was hearing the faint bawling of cattle, barely perceptible. Cattle were being held down in the canyon, somewhere.

His thoughts went to the night. *"It's clear now, but will it be tonight? The moon has been out lately; maybe it will give enough light to get down into the canyon. Maybe I can get past these guards, if I'm on foot. All I can do now is, wait till dark."*

Before he unsaddled Patrick, and unloaded the packhorse, he rode a mile or so to a spring. He let the horses drink their fill, and also filled his canteens. Then he rode back and picketed the horses where they could get plenty of grass.

Chapter 4

Tom Sneed leaned on the corral fence; Jay Sneed was putting out grain for the horses.

"I'm concerned about Dell. He should'a taken another hand with him," said Tom.

"Aw, he'll watch priddy good, since he's trying to find a place the rustlers could'a taken stock off our place," Jay surmised.

The two of them gazed toward the setting sun. Birds were searching for the last few grains before heading for the trees. A horse whinnied in the barn.

"Well, I guess we'll know when he gets here. S'pose we head in, and see what James has cooked up for supper."

Back at Dell's camp, he sat waiting for the sun to go down. The sky was changing. Clouds were drifting. He thought that might be a good thing. Moving shadows, cast from the clouds passing across the moon, would cover his movements as he went down into the canyon. It was a long walk down, and would not be easy in boots. So he got his moccasins from his saddlebags.

The canyon didn't widen out quickly, and the strata had washed out different amounts, by the water rushing through, leaving overhangs that Dell was able to get beneath to hide from the lookouts. He could no longer see anyone on the upper sides of the canyon, but he was sure they were there. He walked quietly, as fast as he could.

The further down he went, the louder the bawling of the cattle became. He knew that he would have to watch for the night wranglers that would be circling the herd all night.

"So far, so good," he thought, *"Now if I can just get close to the stock to check the brands on a few,*

27

without disturbing them too much, I can maybe find some answers."

He finally reached the floor of the canyon, and checked for riders. Then he circulated in among the cattle, pushing them just enough to see a few of the brands in the moonlight. He saw those of Tom's, Raffe's, even an XIT brand from up at Miles city, and others of ranches not too far from here. Apparently, this holding was located centrally to several ranches, and they had not had time to change the brands.

Eventually, he heard a night wrangler coming. He decided to take a chance. "Hey young feller, which one are you?"

Startled, the young man answered. "I'm Jimmy."

Dell asked, "How many are we on watch tonight?"

"Me, Jeff, Dave and Juan," Jimmy answered.

Before the boy knew it, Dell had pulled him from his horse, and with one blow, he was out like a light. Dell pulled him away from the cattle, and leaned him against the side of the canyon. "Sorry Jimmy, but I need your horse for a little while!"

Dell mounted up, and slowly began circling the herd. He could see the lights from their main camp, and was careful to circle on the opposite side. As he continued along, he soon came to another night wrangler; and spoke first. "That you, Juan?"

"Yeah," Juan answered. "Things are pretty quiet so far."

"Well, keep after them! See you at breakfast," Dell said, and then rode on.

He was pleased that this was going well, and he rode on as quickly as he thought would be safe. Soon he was able to check out the opposite outlet of the canyon. It was wider and slower decent than the side that Dell had come down. *"So this is how they work it: bring cattle in both ways, hold them on this heavily grassed area, and move out when they have a profitable number of cattle."*

Dell turned to return to the other side, saw another rider, and thought, *"Well why not try once more?"* Then aloud, he said, "That you, Dave?" The answer came. "No, I'm Jeff."

"Things going okay, Jeff?'

"Yes, Sir, going great!" Jeff answered.

"Good, I'll see you in the morning," said Dell, as he quickly rode off.

Returning to the other side of the grassy area, Dell expected Jimmy to be gone, or at least up and around by now. But much to his surprise, Jimmy was still leaning against the wall of the canyon, asleep. Dell tied Jimmy's horse to a small bush, and proceeded up the narrow canyon wall. When he was far enough away, he took a small rock, stepped behind an outcropping and tossed it at the boy. Jimmy was immediately awake, mounted up, and began to circle the cattle, not sure what had taken place.

Chapter 5

At the Raffe Haskel Ranch, George Beck, Raffe's cook, had fixed a small evening meal just for Raffe and Belle, after he had fed the hands in the cook shack.

He was setting the table when Belle rose up from the rocker in front of the fire. "Thank you, George. I'll go get Dad."

"All right, Miss Belle," he answered.

George was going into the kitchen when Belle cried out for him to come to her dad's room. "George! I think Dad may have had another stroke. I can't raise him!" They checked for a heartbeat, and found none. Raffe was dead.

"George, I know that you have no idea what I've found out the last few days, and now I'm really scared. Do you think that you can keep Rusty, or anyone else, out of Dad's room until I get back? I will probably be gone less than an hour. Please don't say anything until I get back."

"I won't, Miss Belle. You do what you have to do, and I'll see they don't go in there."

She slipped out the back door, quickly saddled her horse, and was gone before anyone noticed. She pushed her horse as hard as she dared, and headed for Tom Sneed's.

It was still early, and Tom was seated on the front porch, and as Belle rode in, he rose to meet her. "Hey young lady, what's the big hurry?" he asked.

As she stepped off, both she and the horse were heaving for breath. "Tom, Dad has had another stroke, and this time he didn't make it."

"I'm so sorry, Belle! What can I do?"

Belle spoke rapidly, "I need to get back as quickly as possible, before Rusty or any of the hands find out that dad is dead." She then explained what had happened to Dell at the line camp cabin, and their suspicions about Rusty and his hands he had brought to the ranch.

"Dell wants everyone to think he's dead, until he can look around, without worrying about being followed. He wanted you and Dad to know what was happening. I told Dad before he died."

"Again Belle, I'm so sorry about Raffe. He was a good friend. If there is any thing I can do, let me know!"

"Thanks, Tom. I'll send someone to tell you about Dad's death again, so they won't know that I was here. Rusty has already warned me, more or less, to not leave the ranch."

"Will you be all right?" Tom asked.

"I think so. If I doubt that I am, I'll come here." She rode off, hoping that the short break had been enough to rest her horse.

When Belle rode into the headquarters yard, Rusty was standing by the corral gate. There was nothing she could do, but ride up to where he stood.
"I thought I told you not to not ride off!" He shouted to her. "Where've ya been?"
"Dad's sick again, and when I couldn't find you, I was intending to ride to get Doctor Clark, but about the time I got to lost creek, the moon went behind a cloud, and I thought better of it. I came back thinking one of the hands should go, and I should stay here with Dad."
This seemed to satisfy Rusty, and they went to check on Raffe. After Rusty examined her father, he told Belle, "There was no need to go after Doc. He's gone!"
Belle could hold it no longer. She finally broke down and cried.

In the meantime, Dell had positioned himself in a secluded camping area, to observe the entrance to the canyon. *"As many brands as they'll have to blotch there ought to be a lot of comin's an' goin's,"* he thought.
He was right: Soon a couple he was sure were Rusty's hands came to the hidden entrance and went down into the canyon. After waiting a short while, he went to the edge of the entrance, to check on them, but the guard was still watching. So Dell returned to his campsite.
At his camp, a few minutes later, he saw three riders coming across the slope from the south. As Tom, Jay Sneed and Wesley Holt approached, he stepped from behind the large rocks that hid him from their view. "You fellers going somewhere?" he asked.
"Doggone you Dell! You could scare a body to death, and get yourself shot! Where in blazes you been?" Wesley Holt asked.

Dell didn't have time to answer before Tom sadly reported, "Dell, I'm afraid we have bad news. Belle rode over to tell me about your situation, and that Raffe had another stroke that killed him. He had been worried about Rusty's handling of the ranch. I'm not sure what went on over there, but I think Belle is afraid of what might happen. She wants to stick it out, if she can. I told her if she has any trouble, to come to us with it."

"I guess that's why a couple of riders came in here awhile ago." Dell replied. "They were Rusty's men, and I guess there is someone down in there, that they needed to tell about Raffe. I wonder what Rusty's plans are now."

Dell filled them in on the layout of the range, where the stolen cattle were being held. He gave them the position of their camp, and the outlet, where the cattle could be taken out the other end.

Jay interrupted. "Dell, a couple of riders are coming out of the canyon now."

"Maybe we should check, to see what's going on," said Tom.

Dell mounted up. "Tom, if you and Jay will back us up, Wesley and I will get to the bottom of this."

Dell and Wesley Holt rode out in plain sight, and the two riders pulled up, surprised at seeing them.

"What'ta you two want?" Asked Ed Landros, one of Rusty's hired gunmen.

Wesley answered. "Why, we thought we'd ask you the same thing."

"Hey, you're Dell Forbes, ain't ya?" Ed asked. "I thought you wus dead!"

"Apparently a lot of people did!" Dell responded. "What's your business on Tom's ranch? Did you get lost?"

"Ain't none of your business," replied Ed.

"I'd say, since Tom is here, it is our business."

Dusty Davis, the other rider, was partially blocked from view by Ed and his horse. He started to ease his hand to his gun, when a shot rang out from behind the rocks. His gun flipped into the air, as he was lifted from his saddle by the shot from Tom's rifle. Ed's eyes widened, as he watched Dusty hit the ground.

"Look, you got'a understand," Ed began to reason, "I'm just doing what I'm told!"

"That's exactly what we want to know! What were you told?"

"Rusty said for me to come here, and tell them that the time is now, that Raffe is dead," answered Ed.

"The time is now for what, and tell who?" asked Wesley. "You're not making any sense."

"I don't know who the message was for. I just passed it along to one of the hands to tell the boss . . . I don't know who the boss is. Only Rusty knows that! I guess that 'the time' means it's time to move in to the ranch, since Raffe died.

Dell spoke emphatically. "I'd say there's not a time to move in for anyone, but Belle. The ranch is her's now!"

"I don't really know," said Ed, "and what am I going to tell Rusty, about Dusty? He ain't going to like your killing his brother."

"Well, Ed," said Dell, "I reckon Dusty shouldn't have gone for his gun. I told you Tom was with us, and he doesn't like his hands bushwacked. Tie Dusty to his horse, and we'll all go tell Rusty what happened! I'll take your gun and rifle. Better wrap your partner in his slicker. It looks like it might rain before we get there."

The rain came, whipped by the wind, cold and sharp, against their faces. It made the ride to the Box R H seem longer. When they got to the ranch, no one was outside. They rode into the barn, and tied the horses in the dog run. The wind was blowing the rain sideways by now. Rusty had heard them as they rode by the bunkhouse. As he entered the barn, he called out, "Ed, what's going on here?" Then he saw the body on the horse, wrapped in a slicker.

Ed answered. "It's Forbes and Holt, and they killed your little brother!" Rusty's anger came to a boil. "That does it, Forbes, you should'a died in that fire!" He dove at Dell. They both hit the dust, and rolled under Dell's horse. Patrick was used to cowboys walking around and under him, but the suddenness of the attack caused him to high step, and pull on his reins. His hoof hit Dell's shoulder with a glancing blow. The shoe edge still cut a gap on his arm. Dell managed to shake Rusty's grip, and rose to his feet, only to be hit again by a flying tackle. The force caused them both to break through the boards into a stall. Dell got to his feet before Rusty could recover, and smashed his face with a powerful right that sent Rusty across the stall. His nose and lip started to bleed profusely, and his eyes began to swell.

"This can end right now, Rusty! I didn't come to fight. I came to talk," Dell breathlessly reasoned.

"I'll let my fist do the talking, Forbes!"

He lunged at Dell, and swung with a right, followed by a swift left that sent Dell into the dog run again. Dell rolled, as Rusty leaped for him. Missing Dell, Rusty plowed a furrow in the dust with his face. Dell reached down, grabbed Rusty by the collar and jerked him to his feet, then landed a firm left to the jaw. Rusty was sent out of the barn door, rolling in the mud. He lay there, too exhausted to move. Dell pulled him back into the barn, out of the rain, and placed him against a stall.

"Ed, how about you gettin' a little water and a rag, and clean Rusty up a bit? I bet he's having trouble breathing, with all that blood and mud on his face! Wesley, if you don't mind watching these two for a bit, I'd like to check on Belle. I expect Rusty will be out for a while, and I'd like to talk to him before we go back up the canyon."

"I got 'um covered," said Wesley.

Dell walked quickly to the ranch house. As he stepped up on the porch, Belle opened the door.

"Are you all right?" She asked, "You look a mess! What have you been doing?"

"Well . . . Rusty and I had a little run in. His brother Dusty was drawing down on us, and Tom shot him. Needless to say, Rusty was bit upset. I came to see if you were all right. I guess you know you are in charge now."

"Rusty informed me earlier that I wasn't, and wouldn't be. I guess he thought he would be in control."

"Rusty is out of the picture now. He's been working with rustlers up the canyon. I'll come back by, after I find out what's happenin' up there."

"Dell, I wish you wouldn't go. I'm not sure I can take over right now."

"I'm sure you can. We'll talk about it when I come back."

"If you do come back," she said, turning away, to hide her tears.

Dell eased close to her. He was touched by the fact that she was truly concerned about him. He took her by the shoulders, and turned her toward him, looking into her eyes. He had feelings he had not had before. He knew this was the only girl for him. While he stood there, she stepped toward him, and kissed him. He looked at her sweet face a moment, then pulled her into his arms, and returned her kiss.

"I've got to go, to get things straightened out." He went out into the rain, but now, he didn't seem to mind.

Thoughts raced through his mind, as he walked back to the barn; *"She really does love me! Or . . . does she just need me, to help with the ranch? She has the ranch now, so I couldn't expect her to move to Texas, but I've got to get out of this cold climate. I'm just too old . . . my bones can't stand another year like '86. Forty-six below zero, even the trees exploded . . . But I made it through that one! For Belle, maybe I could make it through . . . nah not again."*

He arrived back at the barn. "Everything all right, Wesley?"

"Yeah . . . Rusty is still a little groggy, but he can talk now."

"Rusty, we need to know what's going on at the canyon, and you can tell us! Ed said that he didn't know anything, not even who was in charge," Dell insisted.

Rusty looked up, trying to see out of an eye almost shut, the other one completely swollen shut. "I don't know nothin', really. I was ridin' up there by the mountain one day, and found that trail leadin' down into the canyon. I wus just ridin', not payin' a lot of attention, when I seen them cows, and the closer I got, I realized that there wus riders on all sides. Well, this one feller I'd never seen before wanted to know where I wus from, and where I wus going. I told him, nowhere in particular. He asked me who I rode for, and I told him. Then he asked me how I'd like to run the Box RH. I said, I wus already foreman, and he said, 'I mean 'run the ranch!' Well, I told him I'd like that! Then he said, 'Ride back, don't say nuthin', and we will talk later.' I wus just to keep him informed, about the ranch. Well, when Raffe died, I sent Ed and my brother to let him know. That's all there wus to it. Honest, that wus it!"

"If that's all there was, why did you try to kill me at the cabin?"

"Well, Belle was my gal, and I got tired of her askin' about you, all the time. Besides, I didn't like you a buttin' in, the other day. I wus jealous, and lost my temper. I just told Ed and Dusty to watch what you wus doing. They thought it would be fun to burn the cabin. That wus their idea."

While untying Dusty's body from the saddle, Ed slipped a small, four shot Colt House Pistol from his saddlebags, into his shirt. He continued to move Dusty's body from the horse, and place him in a stall. Then he noticed Rusty trying to get up, but slowly dropping back down.

Ed realized that Rusty was distracting Dell and Wesley, and pulled out the house pistol. Wesley saw the move out of the corner of his eye. It was like his gun jumped from his holster into his hand, roared and spouted flame at Ed. Though twisted by Wesley's bullet, Ed was still able to get off another shot that caught Dell in the shoulder. He cocked his gun again, but was already dying. On his way down though, he squeezed off a third shot that accidentally caught Rusty in the temple. Rusty fell over into the dog run dust.

Wesley watched Rusty as he slipped into the dust. "Now ain't that a fine kettle of fish! We've got three bodies to bury, and a canyon full of stolen cattle to see about. You all right, Dell?"

"I'm all right, but I'm not going to be much help diggin' graves," said Dell. "Let me see if Belle can stop the bleeding, and I'll be back to help. There's an old family graveyard behind the smoke house. I reckon the ground will be soft after this rain."

Chapter 6

The sky was just turning a light grey as Dell Forbes and Wesley Holt were riding toward the mountain again. It was not raining, but the air was so thick with moisture that water dripped off the brim of their hats. The wind seemed to have an edge like the knife that Dell carried on his belt. Dell grumbled constantly, not out loud, but under his breath. It was just enough that Wesley kept asking what he was saying, only to have him answer, "Nothin', nothin' at all!" Then, he would sink further down into his coat. It seemed to help him keep warm by thinking of Belle. He didn't like leaving her alone . . . though George was there. He was the only one left at the ranch, as the hands that Rusty had hired were gone, probably down in the canyon.

They swung a few hundred yards to the south, so they could reach the rocks, out of sight, if anyone came up. When they reached the campsite, Tom and Jay had a small fire going. They had brought in dry wood, so that the fire wouldn't smoke much. Dell edged as close as he could to the small fire . . . so close, they were sure he would catch his clothes on fire. "Thank you Boss, for having this fire going. I haven't been warm in days. Has there been any action since we've been gone?"

Tom looked up. "Nope, nothing has moved. We will probably have to go down in there, to see what's going on, and that won't be easy, with the lookouts."

Dell turned to warm his front side. "I've been thinking about that. It will take me a while, but I think I can get up there, at least on this side, and knock out that guard. Come to think of it, I'll be on an even keel with the other side, and maybe can take him out too. If you hear shootin', go on down the trail, but be careful. They may take me out!"

"Can I go with you?" Jay asked.

"Best not, Jay. It will take a while for me to get back. You'll be needed to go down with the others."

"Dell, while you and Wesley were gone, Jay rode to the ranch and told James to let the hands know they are needed here, and they should be along by the time you can get back around here."

"I don't suppose he'll give them any food to bring," quipped Wesley.

Since he had been down in the canyon, Dell explained the set-up. "I kept to the south, but the headquarters, if you can call it that, is on the north. You'll have the cattle between you and most of their men, if you go that way

"We'll wait for your signal, or when the firing starts." Jay, Wesley and Tom checked all their rifles and side arms, as well as their ammunition, then saddled their mounts, and stood ready.

Dell headed south to an area with which he was familiar, where there was an Indian trail used years ago by the Crow and the Sioux. Small bands ranged through after the wars, hunting deer and buffalo, mostly. The trail turned west and up the mountain.

After a few switch backs, he was out on top. The terrain was rising, and the trees were beginning to get a bit thicker growth, as he rode upward toward the canyon rim. The sky was still overcast, but bright. He approached a thick grove of trees, and knew that he was getting close to where the guards were stationed. He dismounted, and tied Patrick a little long, so that he could graze. He checked his Colt again, jacked a shell into his Winchester and eased cautiously, from one group of trees to the next.

He soon came closer to the canyon's edge, where the trees became fewer. He walked slowly now, being careful where he stepped, so as to not make any noise. The ground was thick with Conifer needles, and a few Aspen leaves that were easy to see and avoid, not giving away his position. Not seeing a guard yet, he continued to move silently forward.

He had the feeling that someone, or something, was very close. Too late to move, he heard the 'swoosh', as a tree limb was swung at his head. But the feeling had caused him to raise his good arm enough to soften the blow to his head. He was knocked off his feet, but sprawled on his back. He instinctively raised his rifle and shot from the hip. He saw where the bullet struck the guard's shirt and dropped him on the spot.

"I was lucky he decided to use the tree limb, instead of his six shooter. I guess he wanted to find out why I was up here. Now he knows!"

Dell had no idea if there were any more guards on this side of the canyon. He rolled onto his stomach, silently listening for footsteps. None came, so he used his rifle to help himself up, again listening, while getting his balance back.

Dell saw that the man he had shot had no side arm or rifle. His belt was unbuckled, and the top button of his pants was undone. He then knew why the man used the tree limb.

Dell walked to a spot where he could see the other side, still staying behind the trees, until he could size up the situation.

Across the canyon, he caught a momentary glimpse of a reflection off of a rifle. Looking closer, he located the other guard, who was trying to see what was going on. He realized the guard saw Tom, Wesley and Jay starting down the trail, and was moving closer to the edge to get a shot at them. As he came out into the open, Dell took the man out, with one shot of his Winchester. Then he waited until he was satisfied that no one else was there before he returned to Patrick, tightened his cinch, and rode down the mountain to join the others.

Tom and the other two knew that the shots would alert the men with the cattle, so they rode on quickly to the clearing toward the herd. Reaching the level floor, they turned immediately to the left, toward the large rocks that had fallen from the sides of the cliffs.

"Jay, take the horses behind that tipped shelf, and then find a protected place to shoot from. I see about six riders a comin' this way. If they don't have their guns drawn, I'll try to talk to them. Otherwise . . . well, we'll see. Maybe they just thought the guards were hunting. I don't know if they've seen us or not. Just be ready."

A tall straight backed fellow with a sandy mustache, and scar on the cheek of his sun-baked face, led the riders. His outfit was all black, saddle and all, with a lot of silver. He gave the appearance of being the leader. He rode in toward the rocky area where Tom, Wesley and Jay had taken cover. As he came near he asked, "You fellers looking for something?"

Tom stepped out from behind the rock. "I've been given to understand, that some of these cattle might be carrying my brand. So, before I sent word to the Montana Stock Growers Association, I thought I'd look for myself. No use fellers gittin' hung 'till I was sure . . . and you know that's what they do."

All ranch hands were aware that the Montana Stock Growers Association was organized for the purpose of stopping cattle rustling . . . and it did, generally with an immediate hanging!

The man in black was just smiling. "And I hope you brought your army, 'cause the cattle here are mine. I don't aim to let you look at any of them!"

"I have my army and more a comin'," Tom said confidently. "They'll be here soon."

In the meantime, Dell was coming down the narrow trail. "Boy, Patrick this is a lot easier in the daylight than it was when I came down on foot the other night." He was moving about as fast as he thought he should, since the trail was rather rough. His thoughts were still of Belle. He didn't know why, since he had never had serious thoughts of a woman before. *"I need to clear my head . . . I need to concentrate on the task at hand . . . besides with all this killing, even if it was to keep from being killed, I can't count on Belle even wanting me around anymore."*

A shot echoed through the canyon, and Dell pulled up sharply. "The guys must be in trouble, Patrick, let's move!" He spurred him gently, and they trotted quickly down the trail.

The shot came from the man in black. So quick was his draw that it was as if the gun was already in his hand! He spun his horse at the same time, and sped away. Tom had taken one in the thigh, and was down. No more shots were fired immediately, as the strange riders rushed toward the herd. Then Jay raised his rifle, took aim, and fired. One of the riders went down. A cloud of dust rose up around him. His stirrups were flopping, and the reins were flying in the air, as his horse continued to run. The others disappeared among the cattle.

Dell reached the scene too late to see the action. He dismounted on the run to help pull Tom back behind cover. Then he went to work on Tom's wound, while Wesley filled him in on what had happened. Jay led Dell's horse behind the rock shelf.

"Tom, we need to stop this bleeding. Do you think you can handle a bit of pain?"

"Hell man! What do you think I've been doing?" Tom answered.

"I mean real pain, 'cause this is going to hurt!" Dell then took out his knife, and carefully dug the slug from Tom's thigh. He removed a bullet from his belt, bit the lead out, and sprinkled a little powder on the wound. He then struck a match to the powder. There was a quick, bright flash, and a puff of smoke rose up.

"I forgot to give you a bullet to bite on, Tom. Hope it didn't hurt, too much!" Dell chuckled. "Anyway the bleeding stopped."

"Just you wait! I'll get you back! Now wrap it up, and let's get on with this. I knew I should have sent someone to get the Montana Stock Growers Association out here, and let them hang those damn fools."

"When do you think the other hands will get here, Tom?" Wesley asked.

"If they weren't spread out too much, they should get here pretty soon," Tom answered.

Jay spoke up. "They were all working together in the far south pasture, so they were told at the same time. It was pretty far off. They took the chuck wagon."

"If they come straight here, and don't go back to the ranch, they should be here soon. Right now, let's get a plan together." Dell took a stick and drew in the sand. "If we ride far enough south, then west around the livestock, we can keep the sun at our backs, and not have to look into it when it gets late. Their main camp is on the north side of all the cattle.

Tom said, "Jay, if you don't mind, stay here out of sight 'til the boys get here, and let them know the plan."

"Yes, S ir."

After they helped Tom onto his horse, the rest mounted up, and started their move. The sun was still pretty high, but they needed to get into position before dark. They rode as close to the trees as they could, slowly, in order for the other hands to catch up.

At the rustler's camp, the man in black was giving orders. "These yokels are trying to see if any of their cattle are here. I've worked too hard putting this herd together, and I don't intend letting any of them go. They are all going to the Box RH, and I guess the brand changes will have to wait 'till we get them there. You men get your guns and plenty of ammunition. There ain't but two or three men over there, so it won't take long to get rid of them. I don't want any left to talk about this. I think I got one of 'em as I left. Let's move back into the rocks. They may be here soon."

The man beside him was Jose Bonito, a big man, not much taller then he was wide. He wore a wide brimmed sombrero that covered a dark skinned face, with a bushy mustache. He held the reins of a horse that stood higher than his head. The saddle was a Californian style that was covered with leather that hung in squares down the sides.

The man dressed in black was getting his ammunition ready, and didn't notice that three of his men were mounted, until they rapidly rode off. He took a quick shot with his Colt, but they were already out of range. He cursed a bit, and then said. "Good riddance, I couldn't count on those kids anyway!" They all began to move toward the rocks.

Tom's men were carefully watching the camp from a distance. Wesley Holt observed. "There go three we won't have to kill."

"That looks like the three I saw the other night. I'm glad they left. I wouldn't want to kill them. They're just kids," Dell replied.

Tom asked, "How do you plan to get close to these fellers, Dell?"

"I figger the best way is after the sun goes down, we'll spread out, and ride up to the edge of the cattle, then walk from there right through them, keeping them between us and the camp. If cows are shot, we'll use 'em just like the army trains their horses, to lay down for cover."

The sun was hanging behind a cloud, just above the southwestern horizon. A few brilliant beams of light escaped and danced along the treetops. It would soon be dark. They watched a ground squirrel flit from one hole to another. "I think I'll have a look around, while we wait for the boys. I need to find out where these men and all that livestock are getting' water. If we're here very long, we'll need some too. My canteen is gettin' low." Dell stepped into his saddle, "I'll be right back."

He headed toward the trees that were growing up against the side of the canyon wall. He kept an eye out toward the rustler camp. As he rode closer to the wall, he heard gurgling before he could see the water. The creek had cut down pretty deep, over the years. "Well Patrick, looks like we've got water! How about a drink? I know I can use one." He led Patrick down, and both drank their fill of cold, clear water. Dell filled a couple of canteens, with thoughts running through his mind. *"I see now, how they can keep so many cattle in this canyon. There's plenty of grass and also this water. It looks like it's coming out of the wall, back there. This would make a good place to finish out some stock. There's lot of protection from the wind. Just need to build a line shack, so someone could stay with the cattle, and take care of 'em . . . Boy! What am I thinking? I'll let Wesley worry about that!"*

As Dell started to mount up, he heard a rustle in the grass, near the edge of the stream. Patrick's ears went forward, and his head went up. Dell dropped his reins, and quietly spoke to Patrick. "I think I'd better see what that was, Patrick." He drew his Colt, and advanced cautiously, along the bank. He soon heard the movement again, and what sounded like a moan, from a pocket in the bank of the stream.

Then he heard. "Don't shoot again! I can't run anymore!"

He walked closer. "I don't want to shoot you," Dell assured Jimmy, the boy he had knocked out the night he came down into the canyon. "What happened to you?"

"They shot me! 'Cause I let somebody snoop around the other night. I couldn't help it; I thought the guy was one of us. Then he hit me, and I was out like a light. I hadn't slept in two days, so I was out a long time. Anyway, when I tried to leave, they shot me," he groaned.

Dell confessed. "Well kid, I guess it was my fault. I was the one that came down in here, and I'm sorry about hitting you, but I had to find out just what's going on." Dell set the kid upright, so that he could examine his wound.

"Do you think I'm gonna make it?" The boy asked.

"Jimmy . . . you did say your name was Jimmy, didn't you?"

"Yes Sir."

"Well, you'll probably live a long time, if you're careful. Now, do you think you can ride?"

"Yes Sir, but I ain't got no horse."

"You'll have to ride behind me. It's not far." Dell helped the boy up behind the saddle, and mounted.

The ride back to Tom and the others was short. Wesley helped the boy off, and laid him close to the small fire they had going to make coffee.

"What happened to you?" Wesley asked.

Jimmy repeated his story, as Dell removed the boy's shirt to bind up his wound. The bleeding had stopped some time ago.

"Think you'll be able to man a gun, Jimmy?" asked Dell.

"Against them guys? You bet I can! I don't hold with back shooters!"

Tom asked. "Jimmy, who's the guy in black?"

"I don't know. They kept us out with the herd."

"Well then, who hired you?" Tom followed up.

"A big Mexican hired me. He 'us about the only one of 'em at the camp I seen." Jimmy answered.

"Okay, get a little rest! We'll be moving in soon." Tom's cowhands were riding in with some extra men, making a total of fourteen.

"Tom, looks like we've got a few extras coming in with the boys," Dell observed, "got any idea who they are?"

"I can't tell from here, Dell."

As the men got closer, they could tell that Raffe's former hands, Jesse, Robert and Alverez were with them.

Dell walked toward the riders as they dismounted and asked, "You fellers planning to join this fight?"

Alverez was the one that spoke up. "Si, we do it for Miss Belle."

"Well, with your help, we ought to be pretty even. Near as I can tell, they have twelve or fourteen now, since three rode out a while back. They are in those rocks, just behind the trees. I imagine they are all hired guns."

"Look here, men," said Seth, one of Tom's hands, "what Cookie sent you." He pulled a pouch from the packhorse, and walked to the fire. "There's biscuits and jerky, and when we git time, a lot of other stuff."

While they ate, Dell laid out his plan of attack, and told them that they would start at dark, so they could ride across the open area without being seen.

"Wesley, you and Jesse take a couple, and go around to the east. Tom, if you feel like it, you and Jay take a few, and go around to the west. Seth and whoever is left will go with me right up the middle. Just watch out for each other, and remember where everybody is."

Dell paused, and then said, "I'd like to take the man in black alive. Ed Landros said he planned to take the cattle to the Box RH, so he must have had something in mind. I want to find out what."

"By the way, there is running water over there, better water your horses, before it gets too dark."

Some of the men followed Dell's advice, and left to water their horses. The fire was dying down a bit. So Dell put a few more branches on it, to keep the coffee warm. Then he sat gazing into the fire.

Dell's thoughts were on the man in black, wondering how he expected to take control of the Box RH. After a short while, he heard rapid hoof beats. "Are the guys coming back already? They haven't been gone long enough to . . ." Suddenly, he realized that the sounds were coming from the east and west. "We're being attacked!" He shouted. "Take cover!"

He was too late; shots rang out before they could move. The rustlers were attacking from both directions. The sky was not yet totally dark and the rustlers could be sky-lighted for a better shot. Dell took aim, and fired each time a man could be seen against the dulling sky. He reached for his spare side arm, and continued to fire. He lined up another rider, and was following him, when he saw by the light of the fire, flashing silver on the saddle. He knew that it was the man in black!

Convinced that the man in black couldn't see him well, he stood up quickly, and swung at him with his rifle. The man was moving so fast, that the impact stopped him in mid air, and he crashed to the ground. His breath was knocked from him, and he lay still on the ground, face down. Dell grabbed a piggin' string from his saddlebags, and quickly tied his hands behind him.

Dell shouted. "Check to see if any of our men are down!"

As soon as they heard the shooting, the men that were watering their horses joined the fight, surprising the rustlers, causing them to retreat. The battle was over, as quickly as it had started.

"We have the man in black, so they probably won't come back. At least not right away. Make this man secure, while I check on our men," Dell said. "Anyone know how many of them are down?" he asked.

"Skinny and Hoyt both took a hit, not too bad. I think that's all," answered Robert.

Tom asked. "What about the rustlers?"

"I expect several went down. I shot at every flame I could see!" said Jay. "I walked around out there and decided that we will have to wait 'till tomorrow to see anything."

Dell kicked a couple of branches back into the fire. "Okay, build up the fire, but keep a good lookout! And get somebody on the outskirts to watch . . . At least the coffee didn't get spilled."

Now, mister 'Man in Black', what should I call you?"

"Blacky, I guess," he answered sarcastically.

"Well, if your plan was to take over the Box RH, you shouldn't have shot Tom Sneed, 'cause he would have been your neighbor! Or did you plan to take over his ranch too?"

"I didn't know who he was . . . he thought I had some of his cattle, and I wasn't going to let him call me a rustler and get away with it!"

"Well, we'll see about the cattle in the morning, and find out just whose they are. We can tend to the fallen men at first light. There's no way to do anything tonight.You men get some rest. I'll take the first watch." he said to the ranch hands.

Dell ran over the facts in his mind, trying to figure out just what this man was doing. *"He obviously took cattle with other brands, strays maybe, but at least some had brands, because I saw them. He had some sort of connection with the Box RH, and led Rusty to believe he could run the ranch, even before Raffe died. What about Belle? Did he plan to get rid of her? Or did Rusty not tell him about her, planning to keep her to himself?*

Dell was up early, shook out his boots and rolled his bedding, He eased to the fire that Seth had going, where the coffee was already made.

"I'll have some bacon purdy quick," said Seth.

"That's okay, Seth, I'll just take some jerky now, and breakfast up later! Fill this ol' cup about three quarters full for me." It was an old habit, taking his tall cup made from a section of bamboo, so he could drink another cup of coffee as he rode. He did pretty well, without loosing much, as long as his horse took it easy. The cup had a leather thong, so when he finished he could hang it on the saddle horn. It came in handy to dip water from the creek. That way, he didn't have to lie down and get cold from being wet.

Dell rode out to check on the cattle. The stock brands were about what he expected. He had seen many of them the night he circled through them on foot. He also saw that a few of Tom's Bar T brand, and others, had been changed, to the Box RH.

He decided to move on through, to see if any of 'Blacky's' men were left in the camp. He took the thong off his revolver, made sure that it was loaded, and jacked a shell into his Winchester, then slipped it into the gun boot, before he rode to the north side of the canyon. His approach was from the east, to keep the sun to his back. He saw no smoke from the fire ring, and no movement, so he slowly started in. Patrick's ears were alert, as if he too, was watching for movement.

The camp looked deserted, even though pots, pans and a coffee pot were still near the fire ring. An axe was embedded in a log.

Dell stepped down and started to look carefully around the camp. Something seemed to bother him. Maybe it was too quiet. That was it, too quiet! No birds were singing, even the leaves on the trees seemed not to move. He noticed too late! He turned quickly and drew his gun. At the same time that he heard the shot, he fired in that direction.

The shot had creased his head, and he staggered and dropped to his knees. As he fell, he saw that the Mexican, Jose Bonito, was knocked back on his rear, and was slowly getting up.

Blood was running into Dell's eyes, and he wiped it away on his sleeve. He knew now, it was up to the man that acted the fastest. He fired another shot, but it didn't seem to slow Jose at all! He fired again, and Jose kept coming.

"Dang, this man has so much fat, I may never be able to stop him!" said Dell, as he put another slug into the advancing man.

"Señor take *mas* keeling." Jose remarked, and shot at Dell again.

Mockingly, Dell responded. "Well Señor, I think I have just enough left to do that!" He fired, this time the bullet creased the bottom of the brim of his sombrero, flipping it off. The bullet entered his forehead. Jose dropped to his knees, and fell forward on his face. Dell counted five bullets had entered the man.

He looked around, holding his revolver ready. No one else appeared, so he loaded his Colt, then got an extra neckerchief from his saddlebags, and began to dress his wounds.

When he finished, he walked up the hill a short distance, and found the big bay horse, with the California saddle, that had been Jose's.

"I'll just bet that Jimmy would be proud to have you and that saddle, since they shot him in the back, and killed his horse." commented Dell. He was unfamiliar to the horse, so it took a short while to approach him, and put a lead rope on him. Then he struggled on to his own horse, and led the bay back to his camp.

As Dell was approaching the camp, Tom Sneed, and some of the others, were coming in, too. A column of soldiers was coming down the trail. They met at the campsite.

"Hello Colonel. Won't you get down and have some coffee, and maybe a bit of breakfast?" invited Dell.

"I don't imagine you could feed this entire bunch! Besides, we bivouacked not too far back, and had a good breakfast. I will take a cup of that coffee though. I'm Colonel Theodore Blevins."

"Good to meet you, Colonel. I'm Dell Forbes, foreman of the Bar T. How did you find this trail?"

"We've known about the trail into the canyon for years. We chased renegades in here during the wars, and we also get water here when we are riding this way from the fort. Matter of fact, we're headed west, looking for a few young bucks that fancy themselves as warriors."

Dell shook his head. "I've been around here for a long time, and I can't understand how I missed this place!"

"We only found it by accident."

Dell asked, "You out from Fort Custer?"

"No sir, we're out of Fort C. F. Smith, south of Custer," Colonel Blevins answered.

"How come a Colonel is out riding with the troops?"

"A man's got to get out occasionally in this part of the country, and stretch his legs. Besides I don't like paper work that much."

The Colonel approached, and greeted Tom. "Howdy, Tom! Good to see you again." They had met years ago, and had seen each other over the years since. "Dell said you got a little nick in your leg. I'll have my Doc look at it, and look at Dell, too."

"Thanks Theo! It's good to see you again, too."

The man in black had been snoozing. When he woke up, and saw the soldiers, he engaged the Colonel, "Sir, these men are rustlers! They shot up my men, tied me up and are trying to take my cattle! Just look: Most of those brands are the Box RH; the others are strays and mavericks."

The Colonel looked him in the eye. "Nice try young man, but I've known Tom Sneed and Raffe Haskel for years, and I know who owns what ranch."

"But I own the Box RH now! I'm Marvin Haskell, Raffe's son. He died of a stroke, a few days ago!" argued the man in black.

With that, Tom took him by the shoulder and turned him so he could see his face. "By golly, it could be Marvin. It's been a long time, but it kinda looks like him. He worked for me years ago, when he was just a kid. I'm not sure . . ."

"Well, Tom, if you think he's a rustler, would you like for me to take your prisoner with us? I'll see that he gets his day in court," offered Colonel Blevins.

Dell spoke up. "No Colonel. Marvin here has a sister he needs to meet. After all, she too is an heir. I'll take him to Miles City later. Thanks anyway."

"What do you mean, a sister?" Marvin blurted.

"Your sister Belle! She used to ride behind you when you worked for Tom. You mean you don't remember?"

"Oh . . . Yeah, I . . . I do remember . . . It was so long ago."

His answer didn't set well with Dell or Tom. Something just wasn't right.

The Colonel gave the order, "Lieutenant, let's move'em out!"

Dell sidled close to the Colonel, so the others couldn't hear, and asked. "Colonel, before you leave, I'd like to ask, do you know of any telegraph office not too far away?"

"Well . . . let's see, there was a station about fifteen or twenty miles south of here, in a little town called . . . Lindsey, or something like that, but I'm not sure it's still there."

"I think I know the place you're talking about. It's called Linholf," agreed Dell, "I didn't know that it had a telegraph station. Well, I'm much obliged Colonel."

They watched the column move out across the expanse, toward the other outlet of the canyon.

Dell looked back at Marvin . . . if he was Marvin. Things had been said that caused doubt in his mind. Then he said, "Wesley, suppose you and some of the boys take this feller to Tom's. We can let him meet his sister later. Secure him in the corncrib, 'till I can take him to Miles City. That crib's built like a fort.

They put 'Marvin' on his horse. When he saw the Bay with the California saddle he asked; "What happened to Jose?"

Dell smiled. "Well, Jose decided to donate his horse and saddle to Jimmy, since your bunch shot him and his horse. Matter-o-fact, Jose seemed quite willing, since he didn't need it any more." Dell tightened the girth on Patrick. "Well I hope you got enough rest ol' feller! At least we won't be draggin' a pack horse where we're going." He loaded his saddlebags with some food and coffee.

"Tom, why don't you and a bunch of the fellers take this herd to your place? We'll separate 'em later. I'll be back in a couple of days to help. Don't take Marvin to Belle's just yet. I've got to get a bit more information. You do feel okay, don't you?"

"Shore, I'm doing good! Just a burned place on my thigh where some whippersnapper played doctor. You go on, and get back as soon as you can! We'll take care of the stock. I hope there are some good horses in the bunch!"

Dell rode up the trail, and out of the canyon. He headed south, toward what he remembered as the town of Linholf. His mind was going over all that had occurred. Some of what 'Marvin' had said didn't jibe.

"Patrick, I'll rely on you to help me look out for renegade Indians. The colonel might be going the wrong way, and we might ride right up on 'em."

Chapter 7

Dell had ridden several miles, and the sun had settled into the west. There were a few trees close to the hills, and Dell rode close to them, so as not to expose himself too much. *"Doggone it! Here I am chasing shadows! At this rate, I'll be here when the snow gets so deep I can't leave this country! And there is Belle . . . I think she likes me, but I don't know. I can't think straight with so much going on."*

He reached down to pull his spur up on his boot heel. Just then, he heard the 'swoosh' of an arrow that passed over him about where his head would have been, had he not bent over. "Dang Patrick, I guess we were both asleep!" He gigged the spurs into Patrick's ribs, and was on the run.

Dell looked around, as Patrick ran at top speed, to see how many were chasing him. His Colt repeatedly belched flames toward the source of the arrows. One went down, and as far as he could tell, there were three more.

Dell reined Patrick to a grove near a water source where dead driftwood had caught in the trees during a heavy rain. It made a fair shield for both himself and Patrick. He stepped down, pulled more ammunition from the bags, and reloaded the revolver. The Winchester and the Colt revolver both shot the same ammunition. He had time to load the weapons because of the lead that Patrick had gained.

The Indians had split, hoping to squeeze him from both sides, but Dell was able to get off a couple of shots that didn't miss. The odds had been cut to one! He looked for the remaining man, but lost him while concentrating on his other shots.

He felt the burn in his shoulder before he heard the splashing hooves coming up out of the creek! An arrow had glanced off his shoulder, just leaving a cut. The Indian was moving too fast to notch another arrow, so with a loud yell, he dove from his horse. He was on Dell almost before he could turn. Dell had seen the sun flash on the knife soon enough to grab the Indian's wrist. They both rolled down the hill and into the water. Dell had been shaken lose from both firearms and was struggling to hold onto the wrist. He knew if he let go, the knife would be in his belly.

Each time he turned loose with the other hand to get in a blow, the Indian would land one also. Dell's nose was bleeding, and he had opened a wide cut over his foe's eye. Dell managed to pull his knee up to get a foot in the stomach of the Indian, and pushed him sprawling into the water. There was enough distance gained for Dell to recover his gun. He turned and fired. The Indian had run so fast that he fell on top of Dell. The whole skirmish took only a few minutes, but seemed like the whole afternoon.

Dell slowly rose to look up over the dead wood to make sure that there were no more Indians.

"Once again, I'm patching myself up! This can't become a habit, at least I hope not! You didn't get hurt did you, Pat?" He looked for any injury on the horse, but found none. They both needed rest.

Dell decided to make a camp right there. *"Maybe with the dead Indians around, others won't approach."* So he tethered Patrick, and built a small fire just as the sun was sinking over the hills. He crawled into his blankets, thinking about all that had happened in the last few days.

The next thing he knew, the sky was gray with dawn. Birds were singing, a deer watered a few hundred yards down stream, and all seemed well with the world. Dell stirred the fire until a few coals appeared, and soon he had the coffee on.

After a hurried breakfast, he saddled up and headed out. "Patrick, I hope that we can make the rest of this trip without any more trouble. I'm about all in!"

As Dell rode in to what had been the town of Linholf, he stopped and took in the scene. There were three buildings on the west side of the street that had not totally collapsed. Two were still standing on the east side, with a couple that had caved in. Tumble weeds had blown onto the walks, and sand had drifted against the walls of the buildings. A small church stood on a hill at the edge of town. The steeple, like a big arrow, had broken off and was sticking out of the roof.

"Looks like I might have trouble finding a key man to send any correspondence from here. I'm a little rusty, but I think I can remember enough to get through."

Dell rode on to the other side of the town, searching for an abandoned set of rails and a depot where a telegraph would be present. He could see the poles and the wire. So he followed them to what used to be a depot.

He walked into the office carefully, as to not fall through the floor. He glanced around the room. Everything was covered with dust from what seemed to have been years of neglect. There on a small table was the key. He blew on it, filling the air with dust. He gave a couple of coughs, and fanned at the air with his hat. Battery jars to power it up were there, but they were low on water and acid. He checked and found the liquid below the contacts in the jars. He searched the back room, and found a jar of acid to add.

"A little water in this and we should be in business!" He murmured out loud. "Let's see now, is it add water to acid, or acid to the water. Since it's probably the water that has evaporated, I'll add that." He carefully poured a bit into the jars from his canteen. Then he checked the wires. One had come loose at the pole. Fortunately the pole had climbing pegs, so he began to climb up to connect it again.

Back in the shack, he clicked the key and the relays worked. *"Now if I can remember the code, to get a message through and if all the wires are still connected from here to somewhere . . ."* He slowly tapped out "Is anyone there?"

He began to think it was all in vain, because it took a while for anyone to answer. When they did, he asked them to bear with him, as he was pretty rusty. When he had sent his message, he was asked to wait an hour for an answer.

In the meantime, he walked through the streets of the ghost town. *"I wonder if the folks that lived here left because of the cold weather. I guess that their dreams for the future just collapsed."*

It was late when his answer came. The operator on the other end took it slow, so that he could comprehend the code.

Patrick had been enjoying the tall grass that was growing in the area and had gotten much needed rest. Dell saddled him, and cinched it up gently on his fat belly and commented, "I'll be glad when I can fill mine!" He mounted up and rode north.

On his way to Linholf, he had spotted a sheltered place where the rocks had dislodged and left a small half cave. There was a spring nearby, with plenty of grass. He planned to camp there for the night.

He arrived at the planned campsite about sundown. *"This should be a good spot for a fire to cook some of that bacon that I brought."*

When he had cleaned up after his meal, he stretched out his blanket. He didn't have time to think before he drifted off to sleep.

It was a good camp, and Dell slept soundly. He was well rested, as was his horse. After breakfast he saddled up and was on the move again. He avoided the open valley and kept close to the trees.

After a few miles he saw Colonel Blevins and his troops coming through the valley. He didn't think they saw him, and rode toward them.

"I guess if I had been Indians you would have been in trouble!"

"I'm sorry to disappoint you Mr. Forbes, but my scouts told me you were coming an hour ago!" said the Colonel.

"Well, I'll be doggone! I thought I'd been watching mighty good," admitted Dell. "By the way, how many renegades were there in that bunch you were hunting?"

"No more than three or four. Why?" asked the Colonel.

If they were Sioux, I reckon you can go back to the fort. They attacked me yesterday. I'm sorry, I killed them all." said Dell.

"It's too bad they attacked you. I'm sure that you had to kill them." The Colonel agreed, "They were bound and determined to show that they were real Indian warriors."

"Yes sir, it was a matter of life and death . . . my life and their death! I have the wounds to prove it!" answered Dell.

"Well then, let my doctor have a look," offered the Colonel.

"I would be much obliged if he would. I'm shore tired o' having to patch myself up," said Dell. "I'll also take you up on your offer to take along our prisoner, if you have time to stop by Tom's ranch to pick him up.

"Well, since you've taken care of our renegades, we'll have time," agreed the Colonel. "I guess you learned he is not Mister Haskell."

"That's right! You can stop over, since it will be late. We've plenty of hay and water. It will give your horses a chance to rest before heading back. And I bet that Cookie will have enough food to go around. Everybody says he cooks enough to feed an army!"

"Sounds good to me! Lieutenant, we'll move out as soon as Doc gets through with Mr. Forbes."

As they rode along toward the ranch, Dell offered, "By the way Colonel, that town of Linholf's not a town any more. It's all falling down, abandoned, apparently years ago."

"Oh? Then you didn't get to contact your party?"

"Yes, I did get through. It took a while though. I found the old batteries almost dry and a bit of water and the doggone things came alive enough. I hooked up the wire, and before long I got a man in Denver. It took most of a day. But the feller in Denver rounded up the information for me. I found out our man claiming to be Martin Haskell is actually John Talbot. He served time with the real Martin Haskell, who told him a lot about himself, and Raffe's Box RH ranch. But he failed to mention his sister to him. That's what caused me to

59

doubt him. They were released at the same time, and John Talbot killed Martin in a bar fight. Since they looked very much alike, this feller Talbot decided he could take Martin's place, and take over Raffe's ranch. That's what he was planning, until we got in the way. Anyhow, he's wanted for murder in Denver, but I imagine your circuit judge at Fort Smith can get the facts and try him there at the fort."

The Colonel thought about that a minute and said, "The judge from Miles Town is due to come to the fort next month. I'm sure we can take care of it, with no problem. Our stockade is a good one!"

At that moment, the loud blast of a Sharps rifle echoed through the valley. The men and horses jumped, even though it was a distance away.

"What in tha . . .!" exclaimed the Colonel, as he turned in his saddle to see.

"It's all right, Sir," said the sergeant, as he was riding up. "The Scout, Little Bear, couldn't resist bringing down a buffalo in the draw over there. Said it was his heritage. He had seen it for miles back, just grazing away. I guess the young bull got separated from the herd."

"All right Sergeant, take a detail and prepare it to go in the wagon. Well now, we won't lack for a good bar-b-que tonight! Save the liver for Little Bear and tell him he did well!"

Dell and the Colonel carried on a conversation about the Indian wars, and how the buffalo were becoming scarce. Dell talked of going back to Texas where it was warmer. And the Colonel expressed thoughts of going back to Ohio to see his family. "I have two children, a boy and a girl. The boy is not much younger than you. He served in the Army for a while and then was medically discharged. He's teaching school now and doing very well. How about your family?"

"I haven't seen my family in years. Tom and all the hands at the bar T have been my family. My folks

60

are back east. Mom died while I was in college. I haven't seen my brothers or little sister since I left for Texas years ago. Oh, we wrote letters and all for a while. But after I moved here to Montana, I lost touch. It's a long way to Virginia. I don't know where my brothers are for sure . . . I think a couple are in Texas or New Mexico, and maybe another in Kansas." Dell answered.

Soon the ranch house came into sight. The troops began to look for a place to set up camp. The first thing they did was erect a spit to get the buffalo cooking. There was enough wood cut for a while, but Seth had a wagon ready to get more.

Dell walked into the house to talk to Cookie. "Sorry Cookie, hope you don't mind . . . I brought an army along, since you always cook enough for an army!"

"No sir, Mister Dell, I don't mind! They's gonna be plenty of meat left over. Ev'a body can eat buffalo for few days. I'll get some 'taters from the cellar, and we still got greens growin' out back. I'm gonna make up some more o' that sauce you like. We'll make out okay!"

"Thanks James . . . I mean Cookie. The Colonel is doing me a favor by taking a prisoner back to the fort. By the way Colonel, this is James Spence, but we call him Cookie. He's a free man and has stayed with Tom ever since he got his papers."

The Colonel extended his hand, "Good to meet you James! I hear you are a mighty good cook."

"Yes'sa mista Colonel, I does my best. It's nice to meet ya."

"Where's Tom?" asked Dell.

"He done went ta lay down, said his leg was hurtin'."

"Colonel, do you suppose you could have that Doc of yours take another look at Tom's leg?"

"Sure he can! Corporal, call the doctor in to look at Mister Sneed's leg."

61

Dell and the Colonel went into Tom's room, to find him lying on the bed with a chair laid back-side-up in the middle, with his leg propped on it.

"Come in gentlemen, and have a seat!" invited Tom.

"We just wanted to see how you were doing, Tom," said the Colonel, "My doctor is coming in to have another look. Dell told me how he fixed you up."

"He fixed me up all right! Liked to 'uve burned my danged leg off! How come you can travel away from the fort and bring a doctor anyway?" asked Tom.

"Well, we are lucky enough to have two doctors at the fort right now. It doesn't happen often . . . Doc's replacement decided he would come early."

The doctor walked in about then. "Doc's going home soon and wanted to come along with us for the last time. Doc, take a look at Mister Sneed's leg, if you will."

Tom removed his trousers so the doctor could have a look at his wound.

"Well, Mister Sneed I couldn't have done better myself! It's healing very well. Cauterizing it the way Mister Forbes did, was the only thing to do. You would have bled to death if he hadn't!"

"See there Tom, I saved your life!" joked Dell.

"And you dang near killed me doing it!"

Chapter 8

The sun had just sunk below the hills. A few birds were beginning to roost in the Cottonwoods that grew around the ranch. A large cut of buffalo was soon turning on the spit. Some of the men were singing songs, while Alverez played his guitar. The men sat and watched the sun go down, as the sky turned a fiery red.

Lanterns were lit, and the fire burned brightly. Some of the men stared into the fire, as the plaintive songs were sung. Others rolled smokes and watched the cooking buffalo slowly turn on the spit. 'Cookie' brushed his special sauce on it, while juices dripped into the fire with a sizzle, causing tiny sparks to rise and disappear into the night.

"Wesley, the Colonel has agreed to take our prisoner to the fort for trial. He's wanted in Denver for killing Martin Haskell. His name is John Talbot. Ever heard of him?" asked Dell.

Wesley rubbed his chin, "Naw, I never heard of that name before."

"Sheriff down there said that Talbot was a dead ringer for Martin Haskell. I reckon that's why he tried to take Martin's place, after he killed him. Sheriff said they were locked up together for some time. By the way, where did *you* lock him up?"

"We put him in the corn crib. Those logs are about the most solid thing we have around here," answered Wesley.

"I guess we'd best take him a little food and coffee."

"I'll get some, and meet you at the corn crib." Wesley went inside, filled a plate with buffalo and all the fixings, he poured a big cup of coffee. When he stepped outside, the whole place was lit up by the fire the men had going. Dell was swearing, as he came from the back of the corncrib.

"What's the problem Dell?" He asked.

"That son-of-gun punched the chinking out and kicked a couple of logs loose, enough to squeeze through," answered Dell.

"He can't 'uve gone far. We ought'a be able to find him, with the help of all these soldiers here!" said Wesley.

"I checked the corral. He took Ruby and a halter. He's lucky she works as well with a halter as with a bridle. He couldn't get into the tack room, so he's bareback . . . so maybe he won't go too fast. We'll have to wait 'till there's more light. Old Ruby will be easy to track, with those corks on her shoes. Let's get some grub. I'm hungry!" said Dell.

As they approached the fire, Cookie was bringing more food out for the men.

"Colonel, once again I gotta thank you for your offer. But our prisoner has escaped."

"You want my men to look for him, Dell?"

"No sir, he took one of our horses, so he's long gone. I'll track him in the morning. Did you get plenty to eat?"

"That I did! James is every bit the cook you said he was. You're mighty lucky to have him. I might try to recruit him before we leave!" joked the Colonel.

The sky was still grey when Dell slipped into his boots and quietly eased out carrying his coat and rifle. Then he buckled on his Colt. In the the corral, Patrick turned and trotted toward him. His ears were perked up and he gave a gentle snicker.

"That's okay old man," he whispered to Patrick, "You've been giving a lot lately. So I'll let you rest and give Blue a chance to do a little work." He swung his saddle on Blue and cinched it up. While tying his gear on behind his saddle, the only sound was the click of the bit in Blue's mouth as he continued to work on a mouth full of hay. Dell mounted and began tracking John Talbot.

It was cold out. Dell had noticed a thin sheet of ice on the water trough. He tightened his coat collar, and pulled his scarf around his ears.

"I don't know about you Blue, but I hate these cold mornings more and more every time I have to get out in it!"

Dell could see that Ruby's tracks went behind the ranch house. They joined the road that headed north. He followed them, even though he lost them now and then, as the tracks went along the rock shelf along the creek.

"He's following the creek, Blue. That'll take him toward the Box RH."

Realizing that, he started to ride as fast as he could, and still follow the tracks. Dell sunk down deep into his heavy coat. His collar was turned up and his hat pulled down. He peered through the small tunnel between his hat and collar.

He soon noticed a few flakes of snow. "This is all I need: snow! The tracks will cover and I won't be able to follow," He mumbled under his breath, "I know I'm going to get caught in another winter up here!"

The snow only lasted a few minutes after the sun came up and warmed the air, changing it into a fine mist, not quite heavy enough to need a slicker.

Suddenly Dell smelled smoke and the thought passed through his mind, *"This must be where Talbot camped last night."* His thoughts diverted Dell's attention, and he didn't see the large tree limb that had been tied back. As he passed by the half dead fire, the rope that held the limb back was suddenly cut! The force knocked Dell backwards over the tail of his horse. He lay where he fell, as the breath had been knocked out of him.

John Talbot walked up to Blue, with a satisfied look on his face. "Well now Dell, I expected you last night. It got mighty cold out here waitin' for you! I do thank you for the loan of your saddled horse. I got mighty sore riding bare back. Oh, I let your other horse go; she may be around somewhere." said John Talbot. He mounted and rode off on Blue, leaving Dell still out of breath and lying on his back.

It took a while for Dell to recover from the spill he took. When he got to his feet, he whistled for Ruby. He had at least three of his favorite horses that he had trained to come when he whistled. Ruby was one of them. Sure enough, she came wandering out of the thicker part of trees where she had been cropping the tall grass.

"Well Miss Ruby, I hope you've had enough to eat because it may be a while before you graze again." He pulled her near a log, stepped up and mounted. "Looks like he is still headed for Belle's ranch, Ruby! Give me all you've got, and I'll try to hold on."

Dell followed the trail that Talbot had left, as he didn't seem to mind being followed. Dell didn't need the trail; because he was convinced Talbot was headed for the Box RH. So he proceeded to head that way.

As he approached the ranch house, he paused a few minutes to see what moved. Then he eased the thong off the hammer of his Colt. He looked for Blue, but couldn't see him in the corral. He eased Ruby slowly toward the house, paused again in front, then rolled off the horse and headed toward the door. He knocked gently and waited. Shortly the doorknob rattled and opened, and there stood Belle.

"Oh Dell! Come in! You'll never guess who was here!"

Dell stepped slowly into the room. His eyes scanned each corner, expecting John Talbot to be there. "Who was here?" He spoke cautiously.

"My brother, Martin! I was thrilled to see him. I thought he was dead!"

"Belle, I'm sorry. Martin is dead! That was not your brother. It was a man named John Talbot. He was in prison with Martin. When they got out, he killed your brother. He's wanted in Denver for Martin's murder."

"But . . . he knew about me . . . about when I rode behind him."

"I told him about that, Belle. I began to suspect him when he didn't know about you.

"Dell, I gave him money and Dad's gun! He said he had cattle for the ranch and was going to get them."

"The cattle wore a lot of other people's brands."

66

He looked into her troubled eyes, *"Here I am giving her all this bad news. All I want to do is take her in my arms, and tell her I love her!"*

"I'll need to borrow a horse and saddle. He ambushed me on the way over here, and took Blue. I got here on Ruby. He stole her from our corral when he escaped, and left her when he got Blue. She's not a strong horse. I'm really sorry to destroy your happiness. I'll be back as soon as I can. I have some things to talk to you about."

He turned and hurried out the door before she could speak, and went to the corral. He spotted a roan gelding that Raffe rode all the time, and quickly saddled up.

The trail was still plain. It looked as if Talbot might be headed for the hidden mesa where he had bedded down the stolen cattle. Dell talked to Raffe's horse, so that he would become familiar with his voice. If they were to go down that narrow trail into the canyon, he would need to be able to assure him that he could make it.

"I wish I knew your name . . . seems funny, but it makes a difference. I like to think of you as a friend, and it would be nice to know a friend's name. I'll expect your help along the trail, because this guy ambushed me once. I can't let that happen again. You'll probably know where Talbot and Blue are before I do. So don't whinny, just perk up your ears and if you just have to . . . snort a little."

Colonel Blevins stepped up on the porch and went in where Tom was resting. "Tom, we will pass very close to Raffe's Box RH on our way back to the fort. So I think we'll check to see if they caught that Talbot fellow, and we can take him back with us. By the way, is that leg of yours going to be okay?"

"Yeah, Theo, your doc bandaged it again and fixed me up fine. I appreciate you takin' the time."

67

"I wouldn't a missed this blow-out for nothing. It's not often we have a bar-b-que with all the fixings like James laid out!" The Colonel turned and left the room.

Three men had been waiting outside until the Colonel came out, before they went in to see Tom. Robert spoke: "Jesse, Alverez, and me thank you for taking us on, Tom, but we think that Miss Belle will be needin' some help at the Box RH. And if it's all right with you, we'll go back there. And Tom, we'll be back to help with separatin' that bunch of cows real soon, and take her's back to the ranch."

"Sure! You boys go on over there and help Belle. She'll certainly need you now." Tom responded. "We'll get after that herd in a day or two."

They saddled up, and joined the troops that were headed to Belle's ranch.

"Thank you, Colonel, for letting us ride along with you. We all worked for Raffe 'till some outsiders came and ran us off. Since their plans went astray, we want to go back, 'specially since Mister Haskell died."

"You boys are welcome; I know that Miss Haskell will appreciate it," said the Colonel.

The dust rose from the column of men. The sounds of the horses' rhythmic hooves and the squeaks of leather were enough to make a fellow sleepy. This melody caused most small animals to scurry off long before they could be seen. The flags popped in the wind, and the column proceeded at a walk. It would be a long dusty ride to the ranch.

"You boys been with Raffe long?" the Colonel asked.

"Yes sir, I reckon nigh on to seven years . . . Alverez about nine."

"That tells me you've been good hands. Drifters don't stay that long anywhere."

"Yes sir, it's a good place to work."

When the troops reached the Box RH, they found that Talbot was still on the run, with Dell continuing to go after him.

The Colonel asked Belle for permission to camp nearby, because it was late, and there was water close.

"Yes Colonel that will be fine. Maybe Dell will be back tomorrow," said Belle.

"We'll see. I don't have to be in a hurry, since Dell took care of the renegades for me. We might even send out a party to look for those two, if they don't get back," assured the Colonel.

Dell was still following the tracks left by John Talbot. It led to the trail down into the canyon. As he descended, the roan gelding became nervous. His ears twitched as he listened, first to the echo of his own hooves on the rocks, then to Dell trying to settle him down. "Take it easy fellow! You're going to do just fine. You need to look ahead, 'cause with your ears twitching like that, I won't know if Talbot is ahead or not." Dell gave him a pat on the neck, and he seemed to settle down.

The rocky trail made it hard for Dell to tell if he was gaining on Talbot or not. So, he slowed his pace, and stopped completely when the trail opened up into the flat land. He squinted and scanned the entire area before moving again. The tall grass was gently blowing in the wind. It reminded him, once again, how well cattle would do here. He saw nothing of Talbot.

As he rode toward the trees that grew along the stream, he saw movement. He paused to watch the area more carefully. He saw the hindquarters of a horse move, without a rider. He carefully headed in that direction. As the sun struck across the rear of the horse, Dell saw that it was Blue! He dismounted quietly, He walked slowly. He stayed under the trees, close to the brush growing there, so he could duck, if necessary. He was leery of the situation, because of what had happened on the trail to the Box RH. He slipped behind the brush, slowly taking a step or two, then stopping to listen. He watched Blue, who saw someone or something down in the stream. His ears would flick forward, then back.

Dell was sure that Talbot was down in the stream, and that Blue had his eyes on him. Dell made his way to where he thought Talbot would be. He stepped beside Blue, where he could see down into the stream. "Doggonit Blue! You're watchin' a beaver!"

He heard the familiar sound of four clicks . . . the cocking of a Colt six-shooter.

"Yep, he's been watching that beaver work on trees quite a while now," said Talbot, with his gun on Dell.

Dell turned slowly. "What now, John?"

"Well, first drop your gun, Dell. Then we'll talk. You've messed up most of my plans for some time now. I think it's time to put a stop to it!"

Dell's mind began to search for a plan. He knew that Talbot had nothing to lose by killing him. He wasn't sure he could draw his spare gun behind his back, and get a shot off before Talbot could fire. He knew one thing: this man had plans to kill him!

"Step back away from your gun." Talbot ordered.

Dell stepped back. Talbot advanced and kicked the gun away, keeping his eyes on it and briefly away from Dell. At that instant, Dell jumped for him and caught his gun hand. The gun fired into the ground and they both went down. The force was so great that Talbot lost his gun, and they both rolled down into the stream.

Blue jumped back, while the beaver slapped the water in a warning and hurriedly ran for the other bank.

Both men rose, at the same time. Talbot got the first lick in, and Dell was back in the cold water. He came up with an uppercut that laid Talbot on his back against the bank. His face was bloody, from a smashed lip, and a cut tongue. Talbot used the bank of the stream at his back, to shove both feet into Dell's stomach. Once again he was in the cold water. He recovered quickly, catching Talbot by the foot, as he tried to scamper up the bank to his gun. Two blows, one to the chin and one to the stomach, and Talbot lay still on the bank.

Dell turned him over on his stomach, and reached into his chaps' pocket for a piggin' string, to tie his hands. Then he marched Talbot up the bank, to where Blue stood. Blue quizzically looked at Dell, who was wet and cold. "Fine friend you are! If you'd been watching what you were supposed to, I wouldn't be cold now!" Blue continued to just look at Dell with those big, dark eyes.

Dell helped Talbot on to Blue, and then got more leather string from the saddlebags to tie his hands to the pommel, and both feet to the stirrups.

"It would be a good idea to make an effort to stay upright in the saddle, 'cause if you fall off, Blue might drag you all the way to the Bar T." Dell mounted the roan, and led Blue back toward the Box RH.

Even though it was getting late, Dell didn't want to stop. It was getting colder, a slight wind was beginning to wrap around both riders. Even though it wasn't dark yet, the moon was beginning to rise. "Well, it'll be clear tonight, and the trail will be easy to follow with this big ole' moon, so we'll keep moving."

"Have a heart Dell! We need to stop and build a fire. I'm still wet." Talbot insisted.

"We'll see. I'm not takin' any chances with you. I've had just about enough. Besides, thanks to you, I'm just as wet as you are! If we make good time I might stop and fix us some coffee, but not right now."

They rode on, with neither speaking for what seemed to be an hour. Actually it had only been a few minutes. The sun was behind the mountains, but it was still bright. A few rabbits were out looking for something to eat. A lone wolf called to a mate. The breeze was light and cold.

"Dell, don't you think it's time to make that coffee?" Talbot asked.

"Nope, gotta get on to the ranch. Besides, I'm beginning to warm up these wet clothes." Dell responded.

They rode on in silence.

Chapter 9

At the BoxRH, the troops set their tents and fixed a meal. A few sat by a big fire, singing and telling about sweethearts back home.

Belle was beginning to worry about Dell. She expressed to the Colonel, "Do you think there's a chance that neither will come back?"

"From what I've seen of Delbert Forbes, I think he'll be back with his prisoner. If I were you ma'am, I'd go right on to bed, and let us worry about them. Remember, we're staying around 'till we know something!" said the Colonel.

"Thank you, Colonel. I think I *will* go to bed now."

Also worried about Dell, Tom had reluctantly given Jay Sneed permission to ride to the Box RH. He arrived at the ranch just a few minutes before Dell and John Talbot.

"Well, we were beginning to worry about you." Jay said.

"Not too much I guess, since you didn't come to help!"

"When a feller rides off by himself, a body'd assume he don't want any help." retorted Jay.

"I think I'm gettin' to a point where I need more help than I used to. This ridin' for the brand is about to get the best of me!"

Dell turned to Robert, who had just walked up, "Robert, would you or Alverez please take Raffe's horse and Blue, and give 'em a rub down for me. They've had a hard day . . . maybe a little grain too. I want to take care of my prisoner."

The Colonel heard that Dell was in, and was headed toward the fire. He had slipped on his pants, no shirt, just his long handle top, with his suspenders hanging to his sides. He approached Dell who had backed up to the fire to warm himself.

"You'd best let Miss Haskell know that you're back! She was worried."

"I don't want to wake her, Colonel."

"Well, you'd better or you'll likely regret it tomorrow! Go on. I'll take care of your prisoner."

"I hope you don't get me in trouble, disturbing her tonight!" Dell commented as he walked toward the house.

He stepped upon the porch and slowly walked toward the door. Two gentle taps, and the door swung open before he could finish his knock.

Belle had heard all the talking, and the horses moving about and was at the door. She threw her arms around Dell's neck. He was embarrassed for the men to see them, so he lifted her, and walked her inside and closed the door behind them.

"Oh, Dell, I've lost so much, I didn't want to lose you too! I've been on pins and needles since you've been gone."

Dell stared into her eyes, spellbound by her beauty. She was in her nightgown, and it was like a husband holding her on their wedding night. He could hardly get a word out.

"You won't lose me Belle! I'm yours, and I couldn't be anyone else's. I've loved you since I saw you ride into my life at the cabin!"

He held her close. They kissed as they had never kissed before. Finally, she pushed back and asked; "What about what Jay told me?"

"And what *did* Jay tell you?"

"That you were quitting and going back to Texas!"

"Wouldn't you like to sell to Tom, and move with me?"

"What for? We have a perfectly good ranch here, cattle and all."

"But Belle, this is your's, lock, stock and barrel. None of it is mine!"

"It's ours! You saved it or it would all be gone. You'll have help with the work, with all the hands we have now. And we can hire more, since you got Daddy's money back! Stay, please."

"Belle, the reason I was going was . . . I really have trouble with this cold weather here."

"I'll see that you stay warm! Dad also had a great cold weather coat that you can have."

"In that case . . . looks like I'll still be ridin' for the brand . . . It'll just be a different brand!   I guess . . . I guess I won't be hangin' it up anytime soon!"

Charles Forbes

Chapter 10

Meanwhile, a thousand miles south, at the border of Texas and the territory called Oklahoma, Charles Forbes sat astride his roan mustang. Charles was the second child of Richard and Iona Forbes. He was staring south across the Red River, into Texas. He prided himself on having safely crossed the Indian Territory, which more than twenty tribes called home. He crossed it alone and had arrived still in one piece at the Red River Station.

Doan's store was just across the river, on the Western cattle trail. Spring rains had filled all the watersheds, and the river was filled to the banks. He thought of all the cattle that had crossed, right here. The red ribbon of a river stretched as far as he could see in both directions. His dog Chip sat quietly gazing at the water before them. "Well Chip, it looks pretty rough. Think you can make it across by yourself?"

Chip looked up at him, and back at the water. It was running fairly fast, and was bright red from all the mud it had stirred up. Chip turned and started to trot back up the bank, his tail between his legs. Charles Forbes laughed, and asked, "You're not going with us?"

Chip was a medium sized, mixed breed mongrel that had attached himself to Charles sometime back. Chuck, as he liked to be called, thought that the dog had been with the Indians, and had gotten separated during one of their moves. He was an active dog. He had learned to jump high enough for Chuck to catch, while in the saddle. He rode behind Chuck when having to cross places he couldn't maneuver alone. It looked as if this would be one of those times.

"Okay, Chip, up you go!" said Chuck. Chip ran and jumped high enough for Chuck to catch him on his knee, and place him behind his saddle. "Now, you know that you may have to swim a little."

The roan hardly flinched, as he had gotten used to this procedure. Chuck called the roan 'Sonny', because his temperament reminded him of a friend he had, called Sonny. He was a kid that would just stand there, until he was told what to do. Then he would do what you asked, and would do it well. He just had to be convinced that it needed to be done. Chuck had traded for the horse from some Indians passing through the ranch where he worked in Kansas. Sonny was a mustang, with stamina and speed. When it was needed, he would give a little extra.

The mustang that he was using as a packhorse, he called 'Flip'. He was always flipping his ears back and forth, listening to every sound. He was a paint, mostly brownish; in paint horse terms, a tobiano. Chuck would alternate Flip with Sonny, to carry the pack load.

"Well guys, maybe we can get a meal here at the crossing and some supplies too."

Chuck then touched the roan lightly, and started across the Red River.

Charles Forbes was a young man, about six feet tall, a hundred and sixty pounds of muscle. He had brownish hair with light streaks from bleaching in the sun. It was long enough that when he removed his hat, the sides fell to frame a handsome face. He had a small scar on his right cheek that his little sister, Mary Elizabeth, had accidentally given him. His face was smooth, and tanned, which made his gray eyes shine. His broad shoulders and narrow hips were accented by graceful moves.

Chuck had been working in the tall grass country of Kansas for about a year. There was no place to his liking to spend his money, so he had saved quite a sum! He decided to go south and look things over. He had originally come from Virginia, where the Forbes family had settled after leaving New York. However, as beautiful as it was, he had no desire to return there. His plans were to follow the railroad, as soon as he crossed into Texas, to find land for a business and a home. As they were crossing, the water became so deep that the horses had to start swimming. Chip started yapping, to encourage Sonny along, because he didn't want to have to swim.

There was not much at Doan's Crossing, except a store or two, and of course a livery stable. Doan's big store was the main business, and would sell everything that a cowboy might need, as well as some things they didn't!

Chuck rode up to a man standing by a mule loaded with supplies. "Where's a good place to get a meal and some supplies here?" he asked.

The man shifted his cud, spit and then answered, "You can get a meal at that place with the blue sign out front. But I'd move further south, maybe to Fort Griffin, to get many supplies."

"Thanks a lot!" Chuck responded, realizing that the man meant supplies would cost a lot at Doan's store.

He rode on down the street toward the building with the blue sign. Even when he got close, he couldn't make out anything but the word, 'FOOD'. "This must be the place, Chip. Watch our stuff, and I'll see if I can find you a bone." He tied both horses to the hitching rack, stepped up on the porch, while rubbing as much water from his clothes as he could, and then went inside. It took a moment for his eyes to adjust to the darkness, after the bright sun outside. There were a couple of men at a table near the back, but no one seemed to be concerned with him. They hardly looked up.

After he had a good meal and fed his dog, he led the horses down to the livery stable. Then he gave Sonny and Flip, some oats and hay.

"That'll be two bits fer the grain, Mister," said the stable owner. He paused and looked Chuck over, then asked, "I ain't seen ye in these parts a'fore, have I?"

"Nope, I'm just passing through! Been up in the tall grass country."

"That's the case with most folks I see here! 'Just passing through', they say," the owner replied.

"Any herds come through lately? I didn't pass any on my way from Kansas."

"None lately, and they don't bring as many through here as they used to. They's a couple o' fellers started some trails further out west, called the Goodnight-Loving trail. Most all the cattle come from the same place, so don't as many come through here as they did," said the stable owner, "Ye gonna stay the night, or move on?"

"Not much to keep me here," answered Chuck. "So I think I'll move on. But I think I might just pick up another horse and buy supplies from Doan. It would be out of my way to go as far south as Fort Griffin. By the way, doesn't a railroad go out of Ft. Worth, west to Denver or somewhere?" asked Chuck.

"Yep. I think the crew's about forty or more miles southeast o' here . . . 'corse it ain't finished yet, so it won't take ye nowhere, if'n that's what ye're thinkin'."

"Nope! I heard they were sellin' plats in town sites along the railroad. I thought I might find a good location, and buy a plat to set up a gunsmith shop."

"Ye fix guns, do ye?" The stable owner asked.

"I sure do, and I'm kind'a itchy to get started somewhere." Chuck answered.

"I'd swap ye them oats, yore horses 'er eatin', and some to take wi' ye, if ye can fix my pistol fer me."

Chuck had been fortunate to have a friend in Kansas that taught him the art of gunsmithing. He had been willed the old man's tools, when he died. They were part of the load that Flip carried.

"What kind'a pistol do you have? He asked.

"Well, thar wus a British feller through last year. A lot o' the ranches around here are owned by British fellers, and I traded for a forty-five caliber, Tranter, center-fire. The firin' pin keeps slidin' out. It ain't got a claw on the hammer like most guns."

"I know the revolver, and they do tend to get a loose pilot pin, that lets the firing pin slide out. Sure, I can fix it. Where is it?" asked Chuck.

"It's here where I stay. I gotta place in the back."

Chuck removed the pack from flip and unsaddled Sonny. "No use you fellers standing around with that load," he said to the horses. He separated the tools he would need to repair the revolver.

Chuck had designed his own pack like a large canvas saddlebag, a little different from the normal pannier. It had several pockets, so his things could be arranged to even the load of the pack. His tools and equipment fit right on top. The pack fit on a leather frame, with a double cinch that made it easy to remove, like a saddle.

The stable owner came out of his back room with the Tranter revolver, and handed it to Chuck. "It shoots pretty good, but I's afraid I'd loose that pin, and then it wouldn't be no good no more."

Chuck looked the gun over carefully, checking the action and agreed, "You're right. It sure wouldn't be much good anymore, but you could throw it at somebody! Tell me again, how'd you come by this gun?"

"Well it's kinda long story. The BarX out southwest of here belongs to an English bunch, and it was losin' money. So, this feller, named Balfour as I 'member, came in one day all the way from England, and went into Doan's store. He bought overalls, neckerchief, boots and the works, then went out there and applied for a job . . . and he got it. Well, he stayed about ten days, found out why it was losing money, then came back and got back in his fine English clothes. He called the foreman in and fired him. They said he saved the ranch," said the stable owner.

"That doesn't tell me how you got the gun."

79

"I tole ye it was a long story, so be patient! This feller Balfour didn't think that this English gun would look right, when he went out to the BarX to apply for a job, so I traded him my ol' six shooter fer it. Anyway, he didn't come back fer this one."

Chuck did some 'pinging' on his small anvil, and replaced the pilot pin, which set the firing pin. The stable owner watched him insert a rod into the barrel, and asked, "Ye goina to clean it too?"

"I will, but this isn't a cleaning rod, it's a pilot rod! The pilot tip is the size of a forty five shell, and it tells me if your cylinder is in alignment with your barrel."

Soon he returned the gun. "Don't think it'll give any trouble, until you wear it out again. These guns were converted from cap and ball to center fire pistols for the British army, and they're pretty good weapons."

Chuck looked up at the sky, and picked up his tools. "It's getting pretty late to start out now. Mind if I spread my blankets in the hay?"

"Why, shore! It'll be better'n sleeping out there on the prairie."

"Well, I'm much obliged to you . . . what'd you say your name was?"

"I didn't, but it's Sam, Sam Edgers. I came from Virginny twenty years ago. Been right around here ever since," he said.

Chuck remarked, "I lived in Virginia years ago. My Dad and sister still live there."

"It's a purdy place. I'm gonna heat up some beans and cornbread. Ye interested?"

"Maybe in a little while. I ate pretty good at that 'blue sign' cafe."

The early morning sun spread bright yellow and pink rays across the sky. Chuck rolled his blankets, and saddled Flip. He put the pack on Sonny. It seemed no one was stirring on the street. A rooster crowed, and a dog barked, which made Chip's ears stand up, but he didn't respond. Chuck turned and saw Sam Edgers coming from his room in back, pulling on his suspenders.

"Don't ye want any breakfast 'fore ye go?" he asked.

Chuck placed his gloves in the pommel of his saddle. "I don't mind if I do. You sure you have enough? I'll pay you."

"Won't be necessary, I got enough bacon fer that dog o' yorn too."

"He'll appreciate that . . . you do have coffee, don't you?"

"Does a goose go barefoot?" Sam laughed, and led Chuck into his room.

As they were finishing breakfast, a man's voice rudely called from outside, "Edgers, where's the feed I ordered for Mr. Sanders?"

Sam put his cup down. "That's Paul Temple. He thinks he runs the town. Works fer James Sanders, always pushing people around. Sanders owns a place out close to the Bar X ranch that them British fellers own . . . I'll go out and talk to him. Ye finish yore coffee."

He got up from the table, and went out into the stable. "The feed shipment hasn't come in yet, Paul. I told ye it'ud be Friday, at least."

"I rode all the way in here for feed, and I ain't leaving without it!" His face was turning red and twisted. "I can see some feed stacked in the back there, and I'm going to take it . . . you just load it in my wagon, NOW!" growled Paul Temple.

"No! That feed belongs to Jim Taylor, and he's already paid fer it."

"He can wait 'till Friday. I'm not!" demanded Paul.

Chuck, hearing the commotion, came out of the room. "I think you heard the man, Mr. Temple. The feed's not here yet."

"Just who the hell are you?" asked Paul Temple.

"I'm the man that said I think you heard the man, the feed's not here yet!"

As Chuck walked closer, Paul Temple said, "I'll show you not to butt in where you ain't concerned." He swung at Chuck with a roundhouse blow. Chuck blocked with his left, and punched with his right. Temple went staggering back, into the stable boards that stopped him from falling. His nose began to bleed, and he wiped it with his sleeve. When he saw the blood, he made a move for his gun. He was fast on the draw, but his accuracy was way off. His first shot went into the ground, and he didn't get a second chance. Chuck stepped in close, and cracked Temple's head with his revolver. Temple was out cold.

"Ye go ahead and get on the trail. I'll take care of Paul," said Sam.

Chuck helped Sam put Paul into his wagon, then slapped the horses on the rump and sent the wagon home. They watched the dust swirl up from the road, and the wagon bounce from side to side. Chuck observed, "He'll be sore by the time those horses get him home. I can stay, if you think you'll be in trouble."

"Nope. Ye go right ahead. Mr. Sanders knows Paul. He won't let nuthin' happen. Besides, I got my revolver back, thanks to you."

"Sam, can you sell me a horse? I got a packsaddle with my supplies. I've got to pick up all that stuff up at Doan's, and pack it. I don't want to run short of supplies, 'cause I don't know when I might run across another place to buy them?"

"I do have a horse fer sale, dang good one too! She's even packed before! . . . Ye know yo're invitin' somebody to come and take yore stuff away, by taken three horses out there on the trail, don't ye? They's Indians that just luuuv horses!"

"I'm willin' to take that chance. I'll need supplies, and I'm going to carry them along with all my equipment."

Chuck went to Doan's store to pick up all the supplies he had bought. In addition to the one on Sonny, he put a packsaddle on the horse he bought from Sam. Sam watched as Chuck tightened the cinches, and mounted up. Flip's ears were checking all the noises, by moving back and forth. Chip's nose was twitching, sampling all the smells in the morning air. They were ready for the trail again.

"By the way, Sam, what do you call that horse?"

"I call her 'Sugar', but ye can call her anything ye want to."

"I reckon 'Sugar' is good enough. It'll be nice having a lady along! Okay, Chip, you lead the way. Go east and angle south. Just so's we hit that railroad 'fore too long."

Chip trotted off, and it almost looked like he trotted with his head held a little higher, as the leader of the pack. Chuck left plenty of slack in the lead ropes, so each horse could see where he or she was stepping.

The trail they were taking was not marked, but if the railroad was not too far south, they would come to it before long.

Charles Forbes always talked to his animals, mostly to keep himself company. "When we find a place to camp tonight, it's got to have a lot of grass for this crowd, and wood too. Can't go without my coffee!"

After a good many miles, he came upon a creek with plenty of water and cottonwood trees. Chuck decided to let the horses rest awhile. He removed the saddles and packs, and stretched a rope fence around a large area of tall lush grass for the horses. He then gathered up small branches for a fire to fix lunch. After his clean up, he flipped his saddle over, leaned back and took a nap. Chip decided to investigate the area and headed off toward the creek.

It didn't seem more than few minutes, but had actually had been an hour, when Chuck was awakened by the sound of a running horse. He quickly slipped out his revolver, and thumbed the hammer back. He stood, and faced the man as he reined in his horse.

The man breathlessly said, "Quick! Let me trade my horse for one of yours!"

"Now why would I want to trade for a horse that's rode out?"

"I'm being chased by Indians, and they've taken my pack horse, and this one's run out! I could take one of your horses, and lead them away from you."

"You must not know Indians! You've already led them to me. You just as well get down and help me. I don't plan to let them get *my* supplies!"

It suddenly dawned on Chuck that Chip had not awakened him as usual, long before any rider got as close as this one had. He began to worry, "What's going on, Chip should . . ." Then he shouted loudly; "CHIP! . . . CHIP! Come on boy!" But Chip didn't come.

"How many Indians are there, and how far away are they?" asked Chuck.

"Not more than three or four, and they're not more'n a mile behind me."

"Well, let's get these horses and supplies behind those rocks, and see if they'll come close enough to be in rifle range . . . you do have a rifle don't you?"

"Yes, I do," answered the stranger.

They quickly took the packs and horses back out of sight. They each steadied their rifles on the big rock, and waited. Chuck's eyes scanned the area constantly, along the flat and along the creek. "There, along the creek . . . something moved."

Chuck knew that Indians could crawl silently along the ground. And if you weren't careful, they could get very close. He shifted his rifle toward where he had seen the movement. Soon he was able to see Chip struggling up out of the creek, and he was hurt bad. Blood covered his front leg.

"I thought them Indians killed that dog. They were shootin' arrows at him when I accidentally rode up on 'em."

"He does range pretty far out; maybe he'll stay a little closer after this! Come on, boy."

Chip half hopped, half crawled to Chuck. "Just lay down boy! I don't have time to do much now. We're expectin' company any minute!"

The four Indians rode into the clearing at once. They were too far south to see where Chuck had camped. They continued on without stopping.

"Wheeyu, that was close!" Relieved, the stranger started to rise.

"Best hold on! They'll be right back, when they see that you didn't go the way they thought. They're awful young. It's a shame to have to kill 'em, but they should be on their reservation, instead of out killin'." mused Chuck.

After a few minutes, the Indians returned, slowly now, looking every direction, bows at the ready, arrows notched. The stranger shifted. When the young wishful warriors saw him, they whooped and hollered, and split up. Two stood and loosed their arrows, with one arrow catching the stranger in the shoulder. Their effort was too late, as Chuck swung his Winchester '73 from right to left, firing, then cocking as his sights bore down on each. It was over as soon as it started. All four had fallen to Chuck's rifle.

"Better try to catch the horses, and remove all the gear. That way, the horses will look like wild ones. Then, maybe no one will come looking for these bucks. Here, let's take a look at the damage you got from that arrow." He looked through the hole in the man's shirt. "Best leave it uncovered. It'll dry out pretty quick," instructed Chuck.

"You sure worked that rifle fast. I didn't even get a shot off!"

"Yep! Handling guns, that's my business." said Chuck, as he examined Chip's wound, and cleaned it with water from his canteen.

"Mind if I travel along with you? My name's Robert Chesterson."

"I'm Charles Forbes, and yes sir, I'm afraid I do mind. You see, I like to travel alone. If I were you I'd go look for your pack animal, before he wanders off too far! I have a shovel, and I'll take care of the Indians."

"That's a good idea, thanks . . . thanks a lot, Mr. Forbes."

Chesterson tightened his cinch, mounted and rode off to catch the Indians' horses to remove the hackamores, and blankets, before setting them free. He rode in the direction from which the Indians had come, to find his packhorse.

Charles Forbes took a short handle shovel from the pack, and headed toward the fallen Indians. He pulled them to the creek, dropped them into a wash down stream, and then pushed more dirt over them. He covered the area with flat rocks hoping it would keep the varmints away.

"Well, Chip, I guess you'll have to ride atop the pack. It ought to be soft up there. I reckon you won't be able to smell anything else, 'cause I put some coal oil on that bandage, so it won't take long for you to heal." He made a nest in the top of the canvas, and gently put Chip in it. Chip, lay still, and licked Chuck's hand, as he lifted him. "I'd best take one of my shirts and tie you in, so you won't pop out when we cross that creek! I think you'd better start staying in sight of camp from now on."

Chuck went over everything in his mind: "*Canteens are full, everything's tied down. I guess we're ready to move on, as we've got a little time before the sun goes down.*"

"Flip, I reckon it's up to you now, to watch out for Indians and uneducated travelers, while Chip is laid up.

86

And don't get carried away with flippin' them ears unnecessarily!"

The three horses, loaded with man, dog, and equipment, headed once again toward the southeast in search of the railroad. Following the rails would lead them to locations where towns would be platted, and maybe some settlements would already be established.

Chapter 11

Charles Forbes steadily headed away from the Texas sun, bound for . . . well that wasn't totally known at this time. He wanted to locate somewhere near the railroad, in one of the newly established townships, near enough that he could have parts, guns and ammunition shipped to the gunsmith shop he hoped to establish. Few towns had been incorporated, because the railroad was not complete.

One settlement that old cowboys talked about was Henrietta, Texas, that had settlers as far back as 1857. It suffered many Indian attacks, was burned and abandoned several times. After a battle between about 50 soldiers, and the Kiowa Indians in 1870 in the ruins of Henrietta, settlers came back and stayed. Chuck knew that a town that had folks living there for fifteen or twenty years would have a few ready-made customers for gun repair, as well as new guns and ammunition. He might consider Henrietta. There may be other towns along the way.

It had been a long day. The sun was to the point where it would seem to sink faster. Chuck surveyed the area, and seeing a few mesquites and some cottonwoods in the distance, that indicated there might be water, he headed that way. He found a good place to make camp, beside a creek that did have water. Grass was growing well, after what seemed to have been a rainy spring. "Well, looks like we might stay here a couple of days Chip, and get you back up and running."

Chuck took a ground sheet and placed Chip on the piece of canvas. "Stay here while I take care of the horses." He took the loads off of the horses, and led them to the creek to water. He brushed each one and splashed a bit of water over the areas where the load was carried. He put a rope corral around a good grassy area to hold them, before he went back to take care of Chip.

The sun was almost gone, so he gathered wood on his way back from the creek. As he turned back and forth, picking up wood, he kept noticing something yellowish and bright. It was at least two hundred yards down the hill from his camp, and it only lasted a few seconds, as the sun disappeared. *"What do you reckon that was . . . sun, bouncing off something, maybe a campfire?"* By the time he got back to the camp, he could no longer see it. "I'll check it out in the morning. Well Chip, how about some dinner?"

Chuck got his lantern from his pack, and added some coal oil, lit it, and took care of Chip before he built a fire. "Looks like you will be up and around pretty quick! I think that ride today gave you a chance to heal." He got a lick and tail wag from Chip, showing his appreciation.

After a leisurely dinner of beans and heated biscuits, Chuck set up a tarp cover to sleep under. He planned to stay at this camp for a couple of days. He spread his bedding, Chip by his side, and relaxed, still wondering what he saw at sundown. Within a few minutes he was asleep.

When morning came, Chip was up and stiffly moving around. He woke Chuck, who responded, "You're up early this morning! You must be feeling pretty good. I slept like a log."

He shook out his boots, rolled his bedding, and stretched a bit. He headed for the creek to bathe and shave, as it had been a while since he had cleaned up. He watered the horses before starting a fire to get his coffee on.

"How about some bacon this morning, Chip? You're not able to chase a rabbit yet, and I've not even seen a deer." He went about his breakfast, cleaned up his utensils at the creek, then mused about the bit of light in the distance last evening.

"I'm curious about what I saw last night. A little hike will be good for me." He took his rifle, told Chip to stay and watch things, and then headed toward where he had seen the light the previous night. He first saw the bed of the railroad, then saw that the tracks had been put in place. "So the railroad has passed this place, and we've overshot the crew. Time to move back west now, to find them. Lucky I saw the sun reflected on the shiny part of the tracks last night, 'cause I could have traveled miles and never come any closer to where they were working."

Chuck turned back toward the camp when Chip started barking, frantically! "What's Chip sounding the alarm about, now?" Then he saw two young Kiowa braves who had ridden up and were dismounting, with tomahawks in hand.

It was mostly open ground between Chuck and the camp, with just a few low bushes and young mesquite trees. He traveled most of the way without being seen. When he got close, he shouted, Sa-tan-ta! The only thing he knew about any Kiowa, "'White Bear' was a coward!" He yealed! He knew that they wouldn't understand what he was saying unless it was, Satanta, 'White Bear'. He thought how the Kiowa leader, White Bear, slashed his own arteries while in prison. It was just something to say to get their attention. They turned when they heard him shout, ready to attack.

He fired at the same time, and one of the braves died on the spot. The other threw his tomahawk at Chuck, hitting him in the forehead. The force knocked him over backwards. He was only stunned, as the tomahawk had struck him with the flat side, instead of the sharpened edge of the fluted rock.

He shook his head to regain his senses. As he looked up, the brave had retrieved his tomahawk and was about to straddle him to take his scalp. Chuck quickly raised his rifle to meet the on-coming man, and pulled the trigger. The blast caught the Indian just below the rib cage.

Chuck dropped back a moment to get his breath. Thinking there might be more Indians; he rose and hurriedly checked the area. Chip had stopped barking, so he was sure no others were around.

"I'm glad to see that you are back on duty!" he said to Chip. "I found the railroad, so we are going to move back west this morning, to see if we can catch the crew that's building the thing. Maybe I can get some more information as to where these rails will be laid down."

He stripped all signs of 'Indian' from their horses, and placed the blankets and other things in the grave with the braves. He decided to take the horses with him, so he made halters and lead ropes for each.

Chuck cleaned his rifle, checked his revolvers, replaced everything into the packs, and then loaded them on the horses, before he saddled Sonny. He put Chip behind the saddle, to give him a little more time to heal.

Once they got started, the going was easy, along the right-of-way that had been cleared by the railroad crew. At every water-crossing and springs, he filled canteens and water bags, never knowing when they would ride upon a stretch without a water source.

As he rode westward, the steady sound of the horses' hooves and the gentle swaying back and forth were enough to put him to sleep. He did snooze, occasionally. As he brushed against sagebrush the pungent smell rose up on a gentle breeze.

After about two days of riding, he thought he saw signs of life in the distance. He rode well away from the right-of-way, staked out the horses and reminded Chip, "Stay here Chip, and watch things." The dog found a shady spot and curled up for a rest.

Then, with rifle in hand, Chuck went ahead on foot, staying behind the brush and mesquite trees. Getting closer, he could hear men working, so he knew that it was not an Indian camp, but the railroad crew. He continued on into the camp. Some of the men were carrying rails and placing them on the cross-ties. One man looked up and saw Chuck. "Lord 'o mercy man, where did you come from?"

"Well, a while back, from Kansas. But a few miles back, I rode north of here, past you somehow. Then I found the tracks and followed them back here." Chuck answered.

"You afoot?" The man asked.

"No. I have horses a way back. I wasn't sure who you were, so I staked them out."

"Well, you better go look out for 'em, or they'll be gone!" advised the man. "They's Indians in and out all the time!"

"I'll do just that. By the way, where is the head honcho around here?"

"He's in that yeller box car on the temporary sidin', a tall feller with a wide handlebar moustache."

"Thank you kindly. I'll look him up," said Chuck.

"His name's Shannon." The man watched Chuck head toward the boxcar, and then shouted after him, "Pat Shannon!"

Chuck Forbes stepped up into the open doorway. It took a minute or two for his eyes to adjust to the dark interior. He spotted a man with the outstanding moustache and approached him with out-stretched hand. "I'm Charles Forbes."

The man looked up and responded, "And I'm Patrovic Shovenowski, but to the guys here, I'm Pat Shannon. What can I do for you?"

"That's a good Irish name you've picked. I wanted to find out more about the township plats along the road. I thought I'd set up a business in a town along the railroad. Maybe get a small ranch, but I didn't know where a good location would be."

"Well, right now this will go to Henrietta, and that will be the terminating point for a while . . . If we can make it that far, then it's supposed to join up with the Colorado and Southern. That little town has really had trouble over the years, and we're having trouble getting there." Pat Shannon informed him.

"Yes, I know about the little town's past. But I thought there might be others, too."

"Right now that's it," said Pat. "There are other towns planned, but I don't know where they'll be."

"What did you mean, you were havin' trouble?"

"We've been raided by both white men and Indians, I'm low on supplies for the men, my hunter was killed during the last raid, and tracks have washed out somewhere along the route. They can't run a train until they can get some 'gandy dancers' in there to line up the rails again. Wagons can carry fishplates and spikes, but they can't carry rails! We need the work train to get through. I bet we didn't make a mile this whole week!" Pat Shannon explained.

"I see . . . that kinda gives me an idea what to expect," mused Chuck.

Pat Shannon looked Chuck over, noticing his rifle and his six guns, "I see you carry a '73 and Colts. If you know how to use them and if you'd be interested, I could hire you to hunt, and maybe scout for raiders until they send me men and supplies. Wagons should come in a week or so, that is if they don't get raided."

"Guns are my business, Mr. Shovenowski. They aren't for hire . . . but I just might be." said Charles.

"But we need meat, and someone to help the men know how to protect themselves and our supplies."

"I just meant I'm not a gunslinger. Hunter yes, and I've been a lawman before. I could be of help that way. I'll give it a try for a while."

"Good! You're hired then. There's an empty bunk in the second car there, if you like."

"That's all right. I have my own set-up, but I would like some hay and feed for my horses." Chuck thought a minute then added, "I thought the Rangers were up around these parts."

"They were, a time back, but with outlaws and Indians they've had their hands full. They no sooner take care of some of the Kiowa than they are called to go south because of rustlers! That's where they are now, I think." explained Pat. "There's plenty of horse feed in the car next to the cook car."

Chuck left to get his gear and when he returned, he put his extra horses in the temporary corral with the railroad horses. Then he saddled Flip. The weather was nice, so he only put up a fly to sleep under.

He explained to Pat that he wanted to ride the area to check out the game. "Chip, you're doing pretty good! How about showin' us the way? You can ride back, unless we bag a deer."

Chuck rode west from the camp, and then turned south. The area was open land with patches of live oak that offered cover for game. Cottonwoods and pecans grew along the creeks that had water. Chuck rode in the trees as much as possible, to conceal his movement and to watch for game. Chip stayed close to Chuck. He had good instinct, and when Chuck was hunting, he was quiet. There were lots of signs of deer, but he rode a long distance before he actually saw any. Then he took a shot, and bagged a good-sized buck.

"Well, Chip, looks like you'll have to walk back! I don't have room for the both of you."

He field dressed the deer near a stream. While he was washing up, he noticed something carved on a tree trunk. He took a closer look, and realized what it was, and that he had seen it before. "Look here, Chip! It's Basque arbor glyphs, like I saw in Idaho years ago! There's gonna be a sheepherder around here somewhere, but that will have to wait for another day. We need to get this meat back as soon as we can."

At camp, he rode directly to the cook car. The cook was sitting on the steps taking a smoke break, and rose to meet Chuck. "Looks like you had a bit of luck! Just drop him down here on the grass, and I'll take care of it."

"Okay, but I'd like to have the hide when you're through. I need some new moccasins, and I can start the tanning tonight. By the way, do you have some extra salt?"

"I do, and I'll sack you up some. You can pick it up when you get the hide."

"Thanks! The name is Charles Forbes . . . just call me Chuck."

"I'm Ben Whitaker. Good to have you aboard."

Whitaker was a burly man, red faced from facing a hot stove all day. He was wearing a white apron, and a cook's cap.

"Say, will this crew eat mutton?" Chuck asked.

"They'll eat most any thing."

"Good, 'cause I may have to ride a ways, but I think there's a shepherd somewhere in this area. I'll have a look tomorrow."

"Sounds good! A little variety will go well with the men!"

Chuck rode over to the car where Pat Shannon stayed, dismounted and stepped up to the entrance. He turned in the doorway and spoke to Chip. "You've been a good dog today, Chip. You know when to be quiet, but you better go lie down and get off that leg awhile."

Chip stood with his tongue hanging out, looking up at Chuck. He seemed to know what Chuck said, and trotted over to their fly to lie down on the grass.

Chuck went inside, and saw Pat at his drawing board. "Pat, do you have any money to buy food?"

"A little, why?"

"Well, I think there might be a sheepherder somewhere up the way. I saw where some Basque had put his mark on a tree recently, like they do. I thought maybe I'd see if I could buy a few sheep. Whitaker said the crew would eat mutton." He paused then added, "I'm not real sure where they are, so I may have to ride a bit to find 'em."

"Mutton would be a good change for the men. If you've got money, I'll reimburse you."

"That sounds good enough. I will have ta send a wagon back for 'em, if I make a deal. No way am I gonna try to carry 'em on my horse!"

"Since we've used up supplies, we've got an empty wagon we can send." said Pat.

That evening, Chuck took care of his horses, and rubbed Flip down before turning him into the corral. He then worked on the deer hide. He scrapped it thoroughly, then rubbed it smooth, and salted it down, rolled it and put it away.

After the evening meal, both Chuck and Chip curled up on the blankets, and were soon sound asleep.

Chuck was awakened well before daylight by the breakfast bell. He shook out his boots, got dressed and preceded to the wash rack to splash cold water on his face. As he washed up for breakfast, he could already smell the coffee.

When he went in to eat, Pat and the crew were just sitting down. Pat spoke up, "Men, this is Charles Forbes. He'll be hunting and scouting for us until we can get another train in here. You can thank him for the venison steaks you're having with your eggs this morning. He says his friends call him Chuck."

In unison, everyone said. "Howdy Chuck." A few also added, "Thanks."

"Maybe I'll get to know a few names. If I don't, let me apologize now." Chuck responded.

After eggs and a good-sized steak, Chuck got ready to leave. Ben Whitaker, the cook, handed him a package and said, "This is for Chip, since he can't chase rabbits for a while."

"Well, thank you Ben! He'll be much obliged."

Chuck fed his dog, and saddled Sonny while Chip was eating. All together they rode off, roughly in the direction of the carving on the trees.

Chuck had been riding for about two hours, still no signs of sheep. He came to a small spring that ran into a creek, where he filled his canteen and watered his horse. He sat down and leaned on a tree. Sonny was cropping grass nearby, and Chip was stretched out and about half asleep. Suddenly, Chip jumped up and started a low growl, which brought Chuck to his feet.

"Okay, Chip, I see 'em." Two riders were passing a few hundred yards away. He watched them as they continued to ride on by. They never noticed they were being watched. *I wonder why a couple of cowboys would be riding in here. They have no traveling or camping equipment at all. Maybe it would be a good idea to follow. We'll stay pretty far back."*

Hours passed. Nothing happened, and Chuck was about to give up when he heard the bleating of sheep in the distance. "Well, thank you gentlemen! This is just what I was looking for." He started to advance, and then stopped, as he heard one man shout. "Come on out old man, and say your prayers! You know this is cattle country and we don't allow no sheep around here. Our Boss says you go, or else. But we think you deserve killing, just because."

The door of the shepherd's wagon opened slightly, and a shotgun barrel stuck out.

"This is free land! My sheep weel stay. Please, you go!" the shepherd shouted.

The two started to fire into the wagon and the shotgun blasted. The men took cover behind rocks on the creek and continued to fire.

Chuck unshucked his Winchester from the saddle holster and shouted. "You men had better ride on! This man has a right to be here!"

"Who are you to tell us move on?"

"I'm the one that said you had better ride on."

"Well, here's your answer," shouted the man from behind the rock.

They both began to fire at Chuck. Before he could get down, a bullet clipped his shirtsleeve. Sheep dogs were under the wagon barking. One ran out into the open, and suddenly a young boy came out from the wagon door, past the older man.

Chuck shouted, "Go back . . . stay inside!"

There were sheep all around. As long as Chuck was down, the men could not get a good shot at him. The older man followed the boy, and blasted a couple of shots at the men. He tried to get the young man to go back inside. Just as the older man reached the boy, a bullet from the men behind the rock hit one of them. Chuck couldn't see which. It had caught the young man just below the ribs, and the force splattered blood. Chuck watched as if in slow motion, the bright red blood splashed across the white sheep by the boy's side.

One man rose up to see his kill. Chuck's Winchester blasted the rock just in front of him. The rock chips were like buckshot, and peeled the man's head, as an Indian would with a tomahawk. When the man stood up, Chuck managed another shot.

Chuck shouted, "Have you changed your mind yet?" There was no answer. He got up carefully, and slowly checked the old man and the boy. He then

97

advanced to where the other shooter had been. Somehow the second man had managed to get the wounded one onto his horse. Both men and their horses were gone!

Chuck returned to find the old man cradling his son in his arms. "I'm sorry sir."

"You did what you could do to protect us. I'm sorry that you were hurt." the man said.

From the wagon a woman's voice, "Is it safe? What happened?"

The old man answered, "It is safe now, but Ormano was shot."

"Please Señora do not come out," said Chuck, but she didn't listen.

"It's Señorita, sir." She ran toward the old man holding his son. "Oh, Papa is Ormano . . ." The words would not come. She put her arms around them both, and they cried helplessly.

The old man slowly looked up at Chuck, blood covering his face, "You came out of nowhere to us."

"I'm just sorry that I could do nothing for your son."

"He was young and foolish to run out, but he thought he could help you, and he feared for his dog. I tried to stop him." The man looked Chuck in the eye and asked. "Sir, why did you come . . . did GOD send you?"

"I'm afraid not. I came to buy some sheep for the railroad crew. They are in a little trouble for food."

"You may have as many as you need."

"We will pay you, after I send a wagon to carry them." He paused a moment, "I'm Charles Forbes."

"I am Juan Francisco Borda, and this is my daughter, Emilia."

Chuck looked up and saw Francisco's daughter. She was very close, looking at him. He stared deeply into her dark tear-filled eyes, and marveled at her beauty. Suddenly, he saw his reflection in her eyes, and realized this was not the time to think of such things.

"I'm glad to meet you." He turned back to the man, "Let me help you with your son, Señor Borda."

"Thank you. He liked the hill over there."

They carried the boy's body to the hill, and buried him. A crude cross was placed on the grave. After a prayer, they all slowly returned to the wagon.

"Señor Borda, perhaps I should come back another time." said Chuck.

"No, it eez all right, you stay for supper. My daughter Emilia was starting it when zis all happened. Stay please."

"Very well, if you insist."

"I do, Señor Forbes."

"I knew that you were in the area, I saw your fresh markings on a tree a ways back."

"You know zee marks, Señor?"

"I know the marks, but I don't know the code."

"No code Señor . . . just a longing for home."

"I saw markings like that in Idaho, years ago."

"Yes, my brothers that came before me went there. But I like it here."

"You know that you probably haven't seen the last of those men that would kill you." said Chuck.

"It eez true, but we will watch next time. We weel move farther north, too," replied Francisco.

Emilia lowered a table, on the shady side of the wagon, and began to bring food. "The wagon is too small to be comfortable. We will eat out here."

"You don't seem to have much of an accent, Emilia." Chuck remarked.

"I went to school for a while, after we came to this country."

Chuck was a bit embarrassed because he found himself staring at Emilia a lot more than he should. When they finished the meal, he helped clear the table and take in the benches. He walked down by the creek and sat under a tree. Francisco joined him, stoking his pipe. He struck a match and puffed a few times. Sadly, he said, "It's a lonely life for a young girl out here . . . sometimes I think I should send her away to a town somewhere."

"Francisco, I'm very sorry about Ormano, I'm sure Emilia would not leave you now."

Changing the subject, the old man said, "You know Señor; they come to find you, too."

"I can handle that! It's you and Emilia that I'm worried about. How soon will you move north?" Chuck asked.

"Mañana, I guess. We will see."

"I will bring a wagon tomorrow and start here. If you are not here, I will look for you north of here."

Emilia had finished cleaning up, and joined them in the shade.

Chuck could hardly keep his eyes away from her, even though the time was wrong. Her beauty attracted him more than any woman he had ever seen, and he had seen many. Her figure was outstanding, but no more so than others. Her hair was raven black. Her skin was dark and smooth. The way she looked at him with her beautiful dark eyes, and the way she moved held him spellbound. Realizing his situation, he rose quickly and said, "I'd best be going back! It will be dark before I get there. If either of you should need me for anything, Francisco, you know where the railroad camp is, and you can tell Emilia."

He returned to where he had left Chip, who was sleeping as if nothing had occurred. Sonny was standing on three legs, also asleep. He woke them both, tightened his girth, and headed back to the railroad camp. His thoughts were of the Borda family . . . especially of Emilia. *"Will the cattlemen return before Francisco moves out? I just don't know! I'll return as soon as I can."*

Chapter 12

After Chuck arrived at the railroad encampment he and Pat Shannon sat in the cool of the evening, around a small fire.

"The coffee is extra good tonight after that long ride."

Chuck related what had happened during the day at the sheep camp. Pat told him,"They are probably the ones that raid us from time to time. I don't think these men are from any ranches around here. We have had no problems with the people that live and ranch along the railroad. As a matter of fact, they seem glad that it's here." said Pat.

"Are there many, when they raid?"

"Sometimes six or eight; sometimes just two or three."

"I was wondering, 'cause I shot one, and may have wounded another. Maybe, if they are getting fewer in numbers, they will be easier to control," said Chuck. "Oh, I'll need that wagon tomorrow, to pick up the lambs."

"That will be fine. By the way, we had a rider come in today with some news. A train should be here in a few days with plenty of provisions, so we won't need too many of those lambs."

Chuck got up and stretched. "I think I'll turn in! It's been a rough day. Goodnight Pat."

"Yeah, goodnight, Chuck."

After checking on the horses to make sure they had a bit of grain, hay and plenty of water, Chuck stretched out on his bed. Chip curled up beside him. His thoughts about the demanding day soon drifted to the Bordas. *"I really hate the fact that they are in danger. Maybe Francisco moved on."* Thinking soon faded into a deep sleep.

The breakfast bell awakened him once again. *"I can't get used to waking up to a bell. If I did, when I leave here, I'd probably sleep 'till noon."*

He quickly dressed, rolled his bed, went to the cook car and washed up. All the men came in for breakfast.

"Pat, who will drive the wagon today?" Chuck asked.

"Chris Jenkins volunteered . . . said he could use the distraction. He also has worked with sheep before."

"That's great! We'll leave as soon as we finish here."

After breakfast, Chris and Chuck met at the corral and got acquainted. Chuck saddled Flip, and then helped Chris hitch up the team to the wagon. They both got ready to move out. Chuck told Chris, "I don't think the wagon will have any trouble. It's pretty smooth travelin' . . . well most of the way."

"Good! We shouldn't have any trouble. Our wagons are all made up extra strong to handle heavy equipment and the trails we have to go on." informed Chris Jenkins.

Chuck tied a lead rope on the back of the wagon and hooked it to Flip's halter, then crawled up on the seat next to Chris. "Okay Chip, up you go!" He indicated the direction to head out, and they rumbled west, with the glow of a rising sun behind them. There wasn't much of a breeze, and the dust from the wheels and horses rose up and surrounded everything.

"Suppose we get over closer to the creek, out of this dust. There's a little grass there near the water." suggested Chuck.

"We should get a breeze when the sun comes up." said Chris.

"We can hope," said Chuck, half in thought. "Pat said you had worked with sheep before."

"I worked with my dad before I went to work for the railroad. We had a few hundred that we kept."

"Did you have trouble with cattlemen where you were?" Chuck asked.

"Not a lot. They didn't like us, but we kind'a got along."

"Pat told me that the cowpokes that gave most of the trouble at the railroad camp were just drifters between jobs. Is that the way you see it?"

Chris thought a minute. "It does seem that way. Their horses were not wearing a ranch brand that anyone noticed. They wanted supplies, and that's what made us think that they were not ranch hands from near here."

"Seems logical." Chuck ran all the information through his mind, then said, "The men that raided the sheep camp the other day must be some of the same kind of drifters, but I'm not sure. Have you noticed a lot of men traveling through this area?"

"Not a lot, but occasionally we see a few here and there."

"I shot one . . . may have wounded another. Somehow they were both gone by the time I could check on them. I hope they were just passing through." He paused, struck by a new thought. "You know, now that I think of it, I heard one say something about 'the boss' not likin' sheep', when they rode up on the old man's wagon. I reckon renegades would have a boss, too."

Chris was silent for a minute before he spoke. "It does sound like someone around close maybe sent them out."

"That's what bothers me. Not liking sheep and my having shot them . . . they could return and raise havoc. Maybe even bring more with 'em. I've asked Señor Borda to move north, away from that area. I hope he has. It may mean we have ta go further to find them. But at least they might be safer."

When Chuck and Chris came to the creek with water, fed by a spring, they stopped to water the horses and rest for a while.

103

"Chuck, you hungry? I got some jerky in the wagon, or we can build a fire and have some coffee . . . maybe heat up some beans."

"Some jerky will be fine. I want to get moving as soon as I can. I'm a little bit afraid that Francisco may not have moved on. That grass was good where he was, and he may not want to leave his son right away."

Chuck crawled back up beside Chris, they continued their journey. It was warm with clear skies. The dust wasn't as bad as before. The trees along the creek were throwing a bit of shade that covered half the wagon. Game was sighted at a distance, running from the noise of the trace chains jingling, and wheels creaking, as the wagon rolled on west.

Chris was sitting on the creek side of the wagon, and began to see tracks of shod horses. "Chuck, when were you along here?"

Chuck wondered why he asked, but answered, "Yesterday. Why?"

"Well, I'm seeing tracks that look like they were laid down this morning. I'm not close enough to tell for sure. You want ta stop?"

"Yep, let's take a look." Chuck jumped down and examined the tracks. "There's only one set, and it looks like he went somewhere ahead, and then came back."

"You reckon he was scouting the sheep man?"

"I don't know. I hope they will be on up the trail by now. Let's move on." Chuck crawled back up on the wagon seat, and they started off again.

They had been traveling about an hour when they began to hear the bleating of sheep in the distance. They soon saw the familiar Shepherd's wagon, and Emilia on the hill where Ormano, her brother, was buried. A light breeze was blowing her long black hair, and her dress fluttered with the wind, seductively showing her beautiful figure. Both men stared at her.

"I see you didn't just find sheep when you came out here!" quipped Chris.

"She really is beautiful, isn't she?"

"Buenos Dias, Señor Forbes," greeted Francisco Borda, as he walked toward them from his wagon.

"Howdy, Señor Borda. I thought you would be on up the trail by now."

"It has been hard to leave my son, Señor."

"I'm sure it is, but I fear for your safety." He tossed his thumb toward Chris. "This is Chris Jenkins. He works for the railroad, and has come to take a couple of lambs back for the men. We don't need as many as I thought, 'cause they're finally gonna get a train through."

"Con mucho gusto, Señor Jenkins. I have a few young sheep gathered . . . take what you need."

"Like I said, we'll pay you for them. You may need the money later."

They loaded the sheep into the wagon. Then they rolled to the creek to fill the water bags and water the horses. "I'll stop along the way to give the sheep some water. You goin' back with me, Chuck?"

"Nah, I'll be along directly. You go along now, so's you'll get there before dark." He untied Flip from the back of the wagon.

Chris grinned knowingly at Chuck, then pulled out and headed back down the trail to the camp. Francisco had taken the dogs to bring back a few strays that grazed a little too far. Chuck left the halter on Flip, so he could munch a bit of grass. Then he walked back to the wagon, where Emilia was standing by the steps.

"Would you like a cup of coffee, Mr. Forbes?" asked Emilia.

"Just call me Chuck! Everybody does, and yes I would like that very much. We didn't stop to make coffee on the way."

Chuck sat down on the steps and waited for Emilia to return.

"I'm sorry Chuck, but you will have to move, so I can get the door open."

"Sorry! I guess I'm tired. I forgot that I'd be in the way when you got the coffee. Here, let me help you." He jumped up and took both cups, while she stepped down.

She looked at him with sad eyes, and asked. "Will we ever see you again, Chuck?"

"I sure hope so Emilia, but I don't know. I'll be leaving the railroad camp some time tomorrow. If your Dad moves on northwest, I just might catch up with you . . . and I do hope he will move the sheep from here. I saw tracks when we were coming here, that might mean someone is checking to see if you have left yet."

"It's hard to leave a loved one behind," she explained, with tears in her eyes.

Chuck put his arms around her, as she broke down and cried.

"I'm so sorry that this had to happen." Chuck said, trying to comfort her.

She finally regained her composure, and apologized to Chuck.

"Think nothing of it. I understand. I guess it's time for me to get on back to camp. I've got a lot of things to put together before I can leave."

"Must you go so soon?" she asked.

Chuck was embarrassed about the fact that he *liked* what was happening. Digging his toe into the ground, he put his hat on and answered. "Yes, I think I better leave now."

He walked to Flip, who was dozing, Chip was sitting in the shade, both waiting for Chuck. He tightened his cinch and mounted. Flip turned and Chuck was facing Emilia. Tears welled up in her eyes again, and the sight affected Chuck deeply. "I know that it gets lonely out here, and I'll make every effort to find you and your father after I get my stuff, but for now, I have to go." He turned and loped down the trail, afraid to look back.

When he arrived at the railroad camp, Chip ran to the lean-to where there was shade. Chuck took Flip to the corral, stripped the saddle, and brushed him down. "You'll all get a workout soon, 'cause we're pulling out tomorrow." He put out feed for each horse, with a little extra for Flip, and tossed them some hay. Then he retrieved the deer hide that he had tanned. "Well, that turned out nice and soft. It'll make a nice pair of moccasins."

Chip had revived, and was standing at Chuck's feet. "Come on Chip! Let's see if we can talk that cook out of some eats." Chip gave a small yelp, and ran toward the cook car. Chuck watched him go. *"It's amazing to me that he seems to understand what I tell him."*

Ben Whitaker, the cook, met Chuck at the door. "Saw you come in! There's a bit of food set on the table and a little something for Chip."

"Thanks Ben! Don't know how I'll make it out on the trail after all this special treatment!"

"You headed out?"

"Yep, probably tomorrow. Pat said a train and a new hunter are on the way. They won't be needin' me, so I'll be moving on."

"Chris brought the lambs in a while ago. They'll do nicely." said Ben.

"I'm glad you're happy with them."

It was late when Chuck had finished eating, so he spread his blankets, and made himself comfortable. He was pondering the day when he was overtaken with sleep.

Morning dawned cool and clear, and after breakfast Chuck stopped by Pat's office to receive his pay. "It's not much, considering you kept us in meat," said Pat.

"It'll be plenty, Pat. I enjoyed the distraction, as Chris would say."

"We enjoyed having you here for those few days. Do you need anything else?"

"Nothing but a little grain. I think I'll make some moccasins before I go. They're good for sneaking up on someone, if'n you need to."

"Well, so long then, and help yourself to the grain."

"Yeah, so long, Shovenowski . . . excuse me, I mean Shannon, you old Irishman!" said Chuck, laughing as he stepped out of the office. Chuck gathered his things together, rolled his tarpaulin, and sat down to cut out his moccasins. He was cutting strings to lace them when he heard someone yell, "Indian coming!"

Chuck grabbed his Winchester and quickly ran to the men who were watching. The morning sun was shining from behind the rider, making him hard to identify. "How many's out there Chris? Did you see 'em?"

"Looks to me like one, and he's ridin' a mule."

They all stared at the figure in the distance. Several had their rifles ready. Someone said. "I can hit 'im from here!"

"Don't shoot . . . It's not an Indian! I know her, it's Emilia Borda. She's the daughter of the man we got the sheep from," said Chuck.

Most of the men went back to work. Chris and Chuck stood and watched as Emilia approached. She rolled off the mule and ran to Chuck's arms. He didn't know exactly what to do. Chris walked away when he saw what was happening.

"What is it Emilia? What happened?" asked Chuck.

"They killed papa! Then they killed the dogs and the sheep! And they burned the wagon!" She could barely talk between sobs.

"The same men, Emilia?"

"I don't know. They just rode in and started shooting. I was at the creek with the mule. I don't think

108

they ever saw me. . . . I hid there until they left, then I ran to check on papa . . . he was dead! I didn't know what to do, so I came here."

"You did the right thing, Emilia! Are they following you?"

"I don't know. I didn't see them.

"Which way did they go when they left?"

"They went south," she answered.

"I'm packed and ready to go. We need to get away from the railroad camp; I don't want them to get pulled into this." Then he hollered. "Chris, help me get saddles on a couple of my horses, and we'll get out of here. I'll put the packs on. Those guys may come hunting me, 'cause of that last run in."

They finally had everything ready. Chuck looked at Chris, shook his hand and thanked him for his help.

"Chuck, several of us have free time until the train comes. I know where Borda is. We'll go over and take care of 'im. We'll put him with his son."

"I'll tell Emilia. She'll be relieved to hear that. Thanks again, Chris. By the way, the mule is your's. She's a little too slow for us to take along." He helped Emilia onto a horse, and handed her the lead rope that was tied to the other horses. "Hang on to it tight." Then he mounted up, and they rode off with all the horses that Chuck had acquired.

They first went north, hoping they could avoid any meeting with the killers, by not riding toward them. They rode on the sandstone as much as they could, to leave as few tracks as possible. Later they turned west again, and they soon dipped into a shallow canyon. The bottom was soft sand, which would make it hard to tell how long it had been since they passed. The Indian ponies had no shoes, and Chuck hoped they would be confused.

"We need to be looking for a water source and some good grass, to make camp before dark," commented Chuck.

"Do you think they will find us, after all this time?" Emilia asked.

"I doubt they'll do anything else, after what they did to your father. If they decide to attack, we'll be ready. You can sleep well. Chip will be on duty."

Without looking, he knew she was still crying, and that it would take a while for her to deal with the deaths of her brother and father.

Chris Jenkins had come alone to the site where Francisco Borda was gunned down. He figured that he would bury Señor Borda, and let the scavengers have the animals. He had just finished the burial, and was erecting a cross, like his son's, when riders came up out of the creek.

"Where's the girl that was here?" shouted the man in front.

Chris looked up and answered. "I don't know! I work for the railroad and when I found this mess, I buried the old man."

"Well, there wus a girl here, and a man that killed two of our men! I aim to find them."

"Don't you think you've done enough here to even the score?" asked Chris Jenkins.

"What we've done is none of your business! Now where's the man and the girl?"

"Like I told you, I don't know!"

The man on the horse reached down and struck Chris across the face with his quirt. "Now where are they?"

Chris quickly reached up and grabbed the quirt that was around the man's wrist and jerked him out of the saddle. He fell into the fresh dirt from the grave. "I still don't know where they are."

Another rider spurred his horse into Chris, knocking him down. The first man then began to kick him.

"Where is this railroad crew you are supposed to be working for?"

Chris said nothing. Then the man started to kick him again. Chris caught his leg and jerked him down, but before he could strike a blow, he was hit from behind and knocked out.

The man mounted his horse again, "We don't need this guy! Get Finny over here! He can back-track him to the railroad camp. We'll see if they are there, . . . and leave a good trail for the boss. He'll be comin' along tomorrow."

Finny headed out toward the east, back-tracking the trail that Chris had made. The others followed, looking for the railroad crew, to see if the girl and Chuck were there.

Chuck and Emilia continued on a faint trail, probably made by the Kiowas in the past. If it was an Indian trail, he knew that water would not be far away. After another hour, cottonwoods came into sight. Chuck looked for water first, and then he would find a place to make camp.

Soon they found a spring coming from a wash in the hillside. It formed a small canyon, wide enough to corral the horses where they would have plenty of grass. Large rocks, some flat and others round, had fallen away, hiding the entrance to the narrow canyon. Chuck decided it would be a good place to camp. He dismounted and placed the horses in the small wash, with a rope across the entrance. He diverted a part of the stream so it would cross into the corral for the horses. He and Emilia brushed them, and gave them a double hand full of grain.

While examining the water source, Chuck found that the spring ran to a wide opening where the water fell about fourteen feet down into a small, deep pool, with ferns and water flowers around the edges. Large, flat limestone ringed the edge that gave clean access to the

111

pool. Chuck filled the canteens and water bags. From above, the ground sloped downward to the level of the pool, giving easy access.

"If you like, you can bathe while I fix something to eat. Just go down the hill. There's a pool at the bottom, under a nice waterfall."

"I'd like that very much. Do you have anything to dry on?"

"Yes, I'll get something for you. I have some lye soap too, but it might be a little strong."

When Chuck brought the cloth and soap, Emilia was already disrobing. He left them on a rock by the pool, turned quickly and retreated. He gathered wood along the way, moved into the cove and built a fire.

Shortly Emilia came up the hill drying her hair. Chuck was speechless seeing her beauty.

"I'll set up my small tepee for you to sleep in. I hope it will be all right."

"It will be fine. Where will you sleep?" she asked.

"I always sleep out here under the sky. I have this thing about counting the stars. It's usually bad weather, if I sleep in the tepee."

"Thank you very much. Now what's for supper?"

"Well, Ben put in some dry venison before we left. I'll heat it with a strip or two of bacon. I think the coffee is ready. I have some biscuits, too. That's it!"

"That sounds good to me. I'll pour the coffee."

She sat with her coffee cup in both hands, balanced on her knees that she had drawn up almost under her chin. It was hard for Chuck to not stare.

"Have you ever married, Chuck?"

The question took him by surprise, and it took a while for him to answer. "No, I haven't, Emilia; I guess I've never had time."

She looked at him for a long minute. "Have you ever thought about it?" she quizzed.

"I believe this is ready," he said quickly, to change the subject. "Hold your plate over here, and I'll fill it." He carefully placed the hot meat on her plate. "Careful now, it's hot!"

"Thank you," she wouldn't let her question go, "But . . . you didn't answer me."

"Well Emilia, not many gals would give me a second look." He blushed and looked down.

"I don't believe you. You're quite handsome."

"Well . . . thank you ma'am! Now you'd better eat, so we can get some sleep."

They ate silently for a long while, each with their own thoughts. Chuck didn't know it, but he was falling in love. Emilia smiled, as if she knew.

They said their 'goodnights', and Emilia went into the tepee. Chuck stretched out and leaned on his tilted up saddle.

Her thoughts were of her family, now that it was quiet; Chuck's thoughts were of her, until he drifted off to sleep.

The birds that always seem to stir things up before it gets daylight sang life into Chuck. He put on his hat, shook out his boots, and tugged them on. Then he picked up his clothes and went to the pool to wash up and shave.

On his return, he heard sobbing coming from the tepee. He listened a moment then asked, "Can I come in Emilia?"

"Yes, you may," she answered, as she sat up and wiped her tears.

"I know it's been hard on you, but you must try to put it behind you," he insisted.

She slipped into his arms. He was comfortable having her there. She looked into his eyes. "It's so hard to forget."

"I know it is, but a little time will help." He reassured, as he stared down into her moist eyes. He could hold out no longer. He kissed her. She didn't resist.

113

Chapter 13

At that same moment, Chip began to bark, and a loud voice cried out: "Forbes, if that's your name, I know you're there! I seen your fire. Send out the girl, and come out with your hands up!"

"And who are you?" Chuck shouted back, "What do you want?"

"Never mind who I am. I want you, and the girl! You killed two of our men, and you're gonna hang fer it."

"Oh? . . . and who's going to do it?" he yelled back, stalling for time, as he got guns and ammunition ready. "How'd you find us?"

"I quizzed your grave digger and followed his tracks."

"He didn't know where we were!"

"No, but he became willin' to tell us he worked for them railroad folks. I followed your trail from there. Now come on out!"

By then, Chuck had his rifles, revolvers, a Sharps Carbine and plenty of ammunition ready.

"Emilia, keep these things loaded, and we will do okay."

He picked up the Sharps first, and eased out from behind the rocks in front of the tepee, and mumbled, "I believe at this close range, this ole Sharps will cut right through that tree he's behind. It's worth a try." He took aim, fired, and the bullet nearly cut the tree in two. The splintering tree filled the man's stomach and chest with wooden projectiles. The man folded as if the bullet had hit him. Chuck followed with a six-shooter shot, and the man stayed down. Then the shooting broke out.

Chuck turned to hand Emilia the Sharps to reload just as Chip started barking at something up behind them. A man with a rifle was moving toward the edge of the small canyon, where he could look down on them. Chuck drew his Colt from its holster so fast; the man was falling almost at the same time!

"That's two down! I wonder how many more are out there," he commented, as he turned back and picked up his Winchester rifle. Chuck kept watching the flash and smoke to determine the location of the shooters. He then raised his rifle and brought down two more. He liked the Sharps, because it was powerful and very loud. It would put fear into any man, so he took it up again.

"Are the rest of you ready to die today?" he shouted, and got no response.

While stabbing shells into the Winchester, Emilia looked out to the right and saw a man moving to a position where he could see them behind the large rock. She racked in a shell and watched. Chuck was preoccupied with other shooters. Suddenly he heard a shot directly behind him. He turned quickly, only to see that Emilia had taken down the man that was advancing on them.

There were fewer shots now, and Chuck yelled again, "You know you can ride away, or die here and let the buzzards pick your bones!" No response. His eyes were constantly surveying the entire scene. Nothing seemed to move. The only sounds were those from the waterfall. Little or no breeze was blowing. A few birds were flitting here and there, flying from a large oak tree. And then the branches on the large live oak began to move.

A man was climbing the tree, hoping to get high enough to either shoot directly, or to ricochet a bullet in on them. Chuck let him climb a little higher. Then, with the Sharps, he let go, right where the branches were moving. The sound of the shot, and the crashing of branches as the man fell, interrupted the quiet.

"I don't know who's the leader out there, but you can't have many men left . . . If *you're* even alive!" He listened for a response, but got none. He decided to

115

show himself a little, and watch for movement, if anyone decided to take a shot. One man reacted. Chuck swung the Winchester and shot, without taking a good aim. It didn't matter because his shot was right on, and the man dropped on the spot.

"I sure hope that's all of 'em. I'm kinda tired. You okay, Emilia?"

"Yes Chuck. Do you think it's over? I mean, will more come?"

"I doubt they have anyone left to send out. We will stay here a day or two. It's such a nice place. Then we should be able to ride into a town before too long." While he was speaking, he once again raised up to show a little of himself, just to make sure no one was left. This time, no one shot.

He proceeded to reload the Winchester, and checked his Colt. He eased toward the men lying around, to check if any were just wounded. All were dead.

"Emilia, keep an eye out for any still alive that I might have missed, that would want to take us on. I'm going to check their horses for a brand." He moved back into the brush, and found they had picketed their horses all together. He moved among them, looking at each one. Not all had brands. Some had initials, and one had a year brand. "These fellers must be a bunch of renegades. I don't see any indication they came off a ranch," he mumbled.

"I guess we can take these horses with us. They could bring a good price, and make it worth our while. Man, it's gonna look like we've got a whole remuda! I only hope there'll be enough grazing along the way. They have good saddles. But it'll look kinda funny, this many horses and all with saddles. It may look like we stole 'em."

Chuck continued to clean up the area, pondering just what to do with all those saddles. "They probably stole them! If so I don't want them." He finally decided to put the best saddles on the two horses that had no brand, and bury the rest with the bodies.

"Gonna be lot's a diggin'. I better get started."

When he returned to camp, Emilia asked: "After that, do you think it's safe for me to bath again?"

"Yes, I think it's safe. I'll still watch . . . I mean I'll . . . I'll watch for anyone! You go ahead." He walked off, to keep her from seeing his red face.

She smiled coquettishly, as she walked toward the waterfall.

"I'll be all right. You have given me a feeling of justice here today, and I thank you."

"Okay then, but you did your share! I'll get wood and see if I can stir up some grub."

Charles Forbes built up a good fire to get plenty of coals going. As he went through his store of supplies, he ran across some potatoes that were beginning to sprout. He decided to use them and not let them ruin.

At the stream, he scooped up enough mud to cover each potato. He then returned and placed them in the coals. He sliced some bacon, and pulled enough coals out to the edge to heat his skillet. The coffee water was boiling, so he put a double handful of coffee in the pot. When all was going to suit him, he began to daydream of Emilia, trying to figure her out.

"Does she really like me, or is she just grateful? I swany, I can't tell."

The coffee pot began to boil over, and the sizzle was loud. Emilia was approaching and asked, "Are you so lost in thought that you can't watch your cooking?"

"I suppose I'm sorta tired," Chuck dodged, covering what he was really feeling. "I was thinking that I would go out in the morning and see if I could get a deer, or at least a squirrel. While I'm gone, I thought you might like to wash your clothes. So I've laid out a pair of britches and a shirt. Maybe you can roll up the legs and sleeves enough. There's a belt too, if it's not too long. Oh, and I slipped a two shot derringer in the right pocket.

I won't go out too far, but the derringer is just to play it safe."

"Thank you, Chuck."

"We need to find a store somewhere pretty soon, and get you some more clothes."

"I know. But for now, I'll try your clothes, and get mine washed up."

She watched him dig around in the coals with a stick, and as he rolled the two potatoes out, she asked: "What are those?"

"Those are part of your supper: baked potatoes."

"Baked potatoes?" she questioned, "I've never seen potatoes that looked like that!"

"They're wrapped in mud to keep them from burning. You'll like 'em, you'll see."

Chuck had everything else ready. Then he brushed off the dried mud, and sliced open a potato on her plate and offered her a good, warm meal.

"This potato is very good! How did you ever come to wrap a potato in mud?"

"You learn a lot of things when you've been around as long as I have!"

"You must tell me all about your travels sometime."

"I will."

They were silent, while they finished eating.

"That wasn't bad at all! Now I have to clean up and take care of the horses."

"You tend to the horses. Chip and I'll clean up," she encouraged.

Chip jumped up and followed Chuck, looking back at Emilia as if he understood the remark about work. They headed to the horses, to make sure the grass would last them overnight. He had planned to leave before dawn, but decided there was plenty of grass for a couple of days.

The next morning, the sky was still dark except for a light, rose glow, blooming in the east when Chuck Forbes saddled Sonny, and told Chip to stay in camp. Then he rode off to the south, to look for deer along the same stream that came from the waterfall.

Emilia arose just about sunup to a beautiful red and yellow sky. She stood, mesmerized, watching the colors change. "Good morning, Chip! I see we'll have to fix our own breakfast this morning."

Chip barked a small response. They moved to the fire area, and saw that Chuck had left wood, and had banked coals for her. The coffee was still warm, so she placed the pot on a few coals to get it hot. She looked at Chip and said: "This man is too much for words, Chip! He thinks of everything." Chip wagged his tail in agreement.

After eating breakfast and feeding Chip, she put on the clothes that Chuck had given her. She gathered her own clothes and headed to the pool to wash them.

"Chip, hide your eyes! I'm going to get in the pool to wash these things." She giggled, then stripped off her clothes, took the lye soap, and began to wash. After rinsing them, she stepped out of the pool and spread them on a large flat rock.

She was unaware that a stranger had been watching her from above. He stomped down the slope as Emilia was putting on the briches and shirt. The waterfall noise covered his movements until he was at the poolside. As the stranger advanced toward her, Chip growled and ran to attack. He was immediately knocked out by the man's rifle.

"Ya needn't bother with the clothes, missy! I liked it better the other way! I been watchin' the two of ya, til he left. Then I just watched you. It was mighty nice. I'll take care of you now . . . and him later!" he said.

"Who are you, and what do you want?" she demanded.

119

"Who I am don't matter! What I want . . . I think you know."

"Are you one of those men that were here yesterday?"

"They were my men! When they didn't come back, I came to see what kept 'em." He holstered his gun and started toward her. "NOW, suppose you start taken' off them clothes. I tole ya, I liked it better that way."

She quickly turned, so he would not see her run her right hand into her pocket. The stranger grabbed her shirt and ripped it open, exposing her breasts.

"Now, that's more like it!" he said, as he backed away to get a better look. "I like what I see!"

She stood up straight, and said, "You killed my family . . . my father, my brother and all our stock, and I'm glad you like what you see. It . . . it will be the last thing you *do* see!"

His expression changed, as she pulled the derringer from her pocket, and fired point blank. The forty-five slug caught him just below the chin, and cut off his air completely. His face showed total surprise, as she fired the second shot into his left shirt pocket. He dropped lifelessly.

Emilia ran to Chip, as he was beginning to come around. She collapsed of sheer exhaustion on one of the protruding rocks, and began to cry.

Chuck had good luck, and was heading back to camp when he heard the shots. He dropped the deer, and gigged Sonny into a run, and was back in camp shortly. Not seeing Emilia, he called out for her. She couldn't hear him because of the waterfall. He called out again, near panic. He ran to a spot where he could see Emilia sitting with Chip, and the dead man nearby. He raced as fast as he could to the bottom of the slope.

When Emilia saw him coming, she stood and quickly ran into his arms. "Oh Chuck, it was awful! He was one of those men, and he said he sent them! He ripped my shirt open . . . that's when I shot him."

"You're trembling! Are you hurt?"

"No, I'm not hurt. I just have never shot anyone that close to me. He hit Chip with his rifle and knocked him out. He said he would kill both of us."

"Chip looks okay now. I'll check him out later."

Chuck again felt that he should not take advantage of the situation. Even though he wanted very much to hold her longer and kiss her, he suggested that they go back up to the camp.

Chuck made coffee and they sat, slowly drinking it. He consoled Emilia, telling her that she did the right thing . . . this was the man that had ordered the killing, and that her father would be proud of her. He started to go fetch the deer, but she didn't want him to leave just yet. They sat close, and stared into the fire.

"I'm going to saddle Flip, and we'll ride together. I don't want to lose that deer, and the ride will make you feel better . . . at least it does me."

"Let's give it a try. I need something to relax me," she said.

The sun was still high in the sky. Chuck took care of the dead man, and saddled Flip. They rode out together, Chip leading the way.

"It will be a beautiful sunset, Emilia, the clouds in the west will light up the sky."

"I wish we could stay right here, Chuck, it's so beautiful."

"I do too, but we can't, now."

"Why not?" she asked.

"Well, for one thing, you need some more clothes, and we don't know where the nearest town is. Also, I need a place to set up a business."

Chip had been running ahead and was soon barking at the the deer, where it had been dropped. Chuck picked it up, and they headed back to camp.

"We can have a little steak tonight, and I'll have some more hide to make you a pair of moccasins. But tomorrow, we look for a town and maybe a place to locate a ranch."

"Does this mean I can stay with you?"

"For a while, anyway. We'll move on north, and should hit Henrietta before long. I'm pretty sure I caught the railroad crew between Bowie and Henrietta. Not many people in these parts to ask. We'll start in the morning." He cut up some meat to dry in the smoke over the fire. Later he began to work on the skin.

Chuck was up before dawn, getting all his gear ready to leave. Everything was packed, except what it took to fix a good breakfast. When the coffee was ready, he called Emilia. She came out of the tepee in his clothes, and looked even more beautiful to him. Her long black hair fell in ribbons around her shoulders, and her smile came through her full red lips. He couldn't move until she was right up to him and said, "Good morning." That broke his trance, and brought him back to the work of preparing breakfast.

"Good Mornin'! Gee you look . . . well rested." he said, even though he wanted to say that she looked beautiful. He just got tongue tied, when she was around. "We'll be able to leave as soon as we finish our breakfast."

"Do you think we will find a town or store today, Chuck?"

"It's hard to say. When I was out hunting, I saw more signs of people. If they are not of Indians, then maybe they are from folks that live in this area."

After breakfast, they headed toward the direction they thought would lead to a town.

It was a bright morning, although slightly overcast, making for a pleasant ride. Chip ran ahead, occasionally chasing a butterfly, but most of the time running with his nose to the ground. He suddenly stopped, and started to run at right angles to their trail. Chuck decided to follow.

"It doesn't look like he's tracking a rabbit. He's not moving fast enough. It's like he's looking for something. Stay here with the horses, and I'll trail him a bit to see what he's doing."

He followed Chip a few hundred yards off the trail, until his dog sat on the edge of a deep wash. Reaching the edge, Chuck looked down into the gorge, and saw a dog with an arrow in it's' side. An entire family had been killed near a partially burned wagon. He knew it was the work of Indians, because of the arrows and the family had all been scalped.

He dismounted, and slid down the edge of the bank. He checked to see if anything in the wagon had survived the fire that could tell him about the family. Chip sat down beside him. "Well Chip, looks like we've got some work to do! I'll go get a shovel."

As he reached the pack horses, Emilia asked; "What was it, Chuck?"

"A wagon with a family has been attacked a good while back by Indians. They are in a deep ravine. I'll need to bury them. I won't be long."

"I'll come with you. The horses can stand there as well as here."

"It's not a pretty sight, Emilia. After what you've been through, I would think you would want to avoid this."

"What I've been through is the reason why I think I can do it."

"Okay, let's go then."

After the family was buried, they looked around the area. They decided that they had done all they could. "Looks like the Indians took everything." Chuck started to walk to the horses when he stopped. He took a second look at the wagon.

"Emilia, don't the side boards on that wagon look deeper from top to bottom from here, than it did from the top to the floor of the wagon when we looked inside?"

"Yes . . . I guess . . . it seems so."

"Let's have a look." He went back to the wagon, measured, and found there was a difference. He tried to lift the wagon back on its wheels, but was unable to. Finally, he got a rope and tied it to the wagon, took a dally around Flip's saddle horn, and with little effort the wagon sat up right.

He began to examine the floor of the wagon. He pried, tapped and pulled at the boards. Nothing seemed to give. "Maybe I was wrong." He was about to give up when Emilia pulled on what looked like a piece of loose metal, just under the bottom of the wagon. A section of the floor inside the wagon popped open.

"Emilia, you're a doll. You just solved the mystery. This man made a secret box under the floor. I gotta say, he was a pretty smart feller . . . that is, 'till he rode out here with his family, alone. Let's see what all's in here."

He brought out some clothes for a man, a Sunday-go-to-meeting suit and other things. Then he pulled a case from beneath the man's things. When they opened it, they found it contained the clothes of the woman.

"Emilia, it looks like the lady was about your size . . . if you don't mind tryin' 'em."

"I don't mind. They are clean and pretty. I do need a change." She took the things and began to try them on. They fit perfectly.

Chuck pulled out a small box that had a lock on it. After staring at it for a while, he decided to break the lock to see if there were names of kinfolks to notify. In the box were some gold coins and some papers. He unfolded the papers. The top paper was a letter, and he read it aloud.

THE FORBES FAMILY

"Dear Conrad, You are the only relative still
alive since my family died when the flu hit. I am sending
you this deed to my ranch. With the situation here, I feel
I will not be alive by the time you can get here. Molly
died last year. I know that you and Margaret and your
boy will take care of the place. It's been a lot years since
you were here, but I don't think you will have any trouble
finding it. The only road leading southeast out of
Henrietta, Texas, for about five and a half miles will bring
you to the 'Branding Iron Ranch. The name is on the
gate. Good luck and God bless you.
                                    Your Uncle John."

Chuck unfolded the deed. John C. Beckendorf
had signed it, but it was not assigned to anyone. "Emilia,
these folks didn't have any relatives, seems they're all
dead."

"I guess then the contents of the wagon belong
to you."

"What about you?"

"I've got my new clothes." she boasted, as she
turned to model them for him.

They took the contents of the wagon, and placed
it all in the packs. "We'd best move out! The Indians
could come back this way. We need to find a place to
spend the night."

They started out again toward Henrietta. They
thought it to be northwest of where they were. After a
few hours, they found water. They stopped to let the
horses drink and rest. Chuck got out jerky to take the
edge off of their hunger.

"Are you doing okay, Emilia?" he asked.

"Yes, I'm doing fine. These days have been a
new experience for me. Our family traveled some but not
on horseback like this."

After the short break, they were on the trail
again. The sun was hot, but a cool breeze was blowing
from the southwest. There was enough grass to keep

125

down the dust. Chuck had switched out with Emilia on leading the other horses.

The groves of oak trees they saw up ahead had a bluish cast to them, caused by the way the sun hit them. As they marveled at the color of the trees, they looked to their right, and through the trees they saw a few rows of buildings in the distance. Getting closer to the buildings, they saw that they were not all occupied. A couple of false-fronted buildings, and a boarding house sat on the right hand side. Entering the town, the livery stable was the first thing in sight. Chuck watched a man come from a small shack in the back. He had a grey and black scraggily beard, with a bit of tobacco juice running into it. When he smiled, it showed a few missing teeth. Chuck asked the man about bedding the horses.

"You betcha, and I'll feed 'em too . . . say . . . you got a lot'a horses and saddles there ain'tcha?" the stable owner observed.

"Yes, quite a few! I'm looking to set up a business. I'm not sure where yet, but I'll sell horses and used saddles, along with guns and ammunition. I'll also do gunsmithin'. By the way, is there a place we can get rooms and some grub?"

"Why shore, third house down! They got a room or two, and they's the only place in this town you can get a meal. How much you take fer that dog?"

"Sorry, he's not for sale! He's part of the family."

Chuck removed the packs and saddles, and asked the man if there was a place to store things until the next day.

"You betcha! I'll lock 'em up fer ya." The man answered.

"You ever heard of the 'Brandin' Iron Ranch? It's s'posed to be around here somewhere." Chuck asked.

"You betcha! That's ole man Beckendorf's place. It's a few miles up the road there, toward Henrietta. A bunch o' rowdies moved in when ole man Beckendorf died," the stable owner answered.

"Well, thanks. My name's Charles Forbes. I'll see you in the morning."

"My name's Horace Bates. Folks call me 'Stump'."

As they walked to the boarding house, Chuck said, "Sounds as if we may have a little trouble when we get to that ranch. I'll try to find out how many are there tomorrow. Right now I'm hungry and tired! How about you?"

Emilia just nodded.

As they entered the boarding house, a man rose up from a well worn easy chair. Seeing Emilia he said: "She can't come in here. We don't 'low no Indians in here!"

Chuck pushed up in the face of the man." She's not an Indian! She's from the country of Spain. Now, we want two rooms and some supper. You got any objections to that?"

"No sir. I guess not . . . rooms four and five; they're just down the hall. We'll be serving by the time you get cleaned up." The man answered.

"Thank you." said Chuck, a bit sarcastically.

As they were walking away, Emilia whispered, "Actually, Chuck, we come from the Basque Country!"

"I doubt he knows there's a Spain, much less a Basque Country!" said Chuck.

They went to the rooms. Chuck looked around each one, checking the window location. He pushed her bed to the opposite side of the room, so that it could not be seen when the door was opened. Then he gave Emilia a key.

"See you in the dinin' room in a few minutes."

When they entered the dining room, several men were there. Two were at the bar and six sat at various tables, scattered around the room. Chuck held the chair for Emilia as she sat down. She wore a bright dress, one from the chest that they had found, with short ribbons that streamed from the bodice,. Her long, shiny black hair fell about her shoulders. She was very beautiful.

One of the men from the bar walked to the table and asked, "Does your squaw have a sister? If she's half as purty as this one, I'll take her."

"Too much liquor is no excuse," murmured Chuck as he rose. In one smooth move, he drove home a right to the man's face! The man skidded backward to the wall and slowly slid down to a seated position. He was out cold. "Now, maybe we can have our meal," he raised his voice, "unless, of course, there are objections." He paused a moment before he sat down. There were no reactions. A young woman brought their meal.

"You don't have no choice about what to eat here. That's all we got tonight," she remarked as she sat the food on the table.

"This will do fine; I could eat most anything right now."

When they finished their meal, he took Emilia back to her room and told her, "They may cause trouble later. I have loaded the derringer again for you. The reason I moved the bed is that if someone comes in, they will think the bed is opposite the door, as it usually is. That will give you time in the dark, before they realize that you are not where they were expectin' you to be."

She sighed, "Oh Chuck, not again."

"I hope not, Emilia, but it won't hurt to be prepared." He went to the hallway and told Chip to stay with Emilia. Then he went to his room, pushed the bed aside, and laid down.

A few hours passed quietly, with Chuck sleeping off and on. About two in the morning, he was awakened by a squeaking door. He rose up on one elbow, and listened . . . nothing . . . he lay back down. After a moment, he heard Chip's low growl, signaling that something was wrong.

In Emilia's room, a dark figure eased toward where he thought the bed would be. He thought nothing of Chip's growl. Suddenly, Chip jumped into a chair, then sprang, and caught the man in the chest with his full weight, knocking him to the floor. Then he quickly straddled the man's chest, and stuck his barred teeth right against the man's face. The invader didn't move.

Chuck burst into the room, his gun drawn, and carrying a lamp. When he saw Chip on the frightened man, he could hardly keep from laughing. Emilia was still in the bed, blankets pulled up in front of her with one hand, the gun in the other. She did laugh when she saw Chip hovering over the man.

Chuck walked to a window and raised it. Then set his lamp on the table, "Okay Chip, I'll take it from here." He grabbed the man by the collar and the seat of his pants, and threw him out the window. "I'm sorry Emilia, the guy was drunk. Stay with her Chip, you did real good! Will you be able to get a little sleep after all this, Emilia?"

"As long as Chip stays with me, I'll try."

"He will." Then he turned and went to his room, "But I'm not sure I'll get any sleep!" he mumbled under his breath.

Chapter 14

Charles Forbes got an early start. Breakfast was already being served. After he had eaten, he arranged to have Emilia's breakfast taken care of, before he went to the corral to saddle Flip. The sky was just taking on light from a rising sun, which was covered by a layer of clouds that looked like thick buttermilk.

He rode along toward the Branding Iron ranch, staying close to the groves of live oak. When he arrived at the gate, it was open, so he rode on in and kept to the trees.

A thin ribbon of smoke was rising from the chimney of the ranch cookhouse, "Looks like there's someone home." He tied Flip out of sight, and walked toward a small smoke house. A generous supply of wood was piled along the side. The door to the cookhouse opened, and Chuck stepped back behind the shed and watched. The Chinese man was muttering in his native language. He had come to get more wood. Chuck couldn't understand him, but he could tell that he was mighty unhappy.

A loud voice came from inside the ranch house: "Tell that 'chink' ta hurry, I'm hungry!"

Another voice, somewhat placating, answered, "He's gittin' wood for the stove, Jake. He'll be right back."

As the little man came around the corner of the shed, Chuck grabbed him and held his hand over his mouth. His expression was of a very frightened man.

"You with that bunch in there?" Chuck asked softly.

He shook his head no. Chuck released him and he said: "I cook. I cook for Missaw Bekendolf 'till he die! They cause he die."

Chuck thought a minute, and then asked how many are there?

"Six," was his answer.

"You had better get back inside. Expect me later." said Chuck.

The cook nodded his head 'yes', gathered the wood and went back inside.

"It's about time you got back. Get a move on we're hungry!" declared the voice from inside.

Chuck went to the back of the house, where the slanted roof was lower, stepped up on a rain barrel, and on to the roof. He then placed a block of wood from the woodpile on the top of the chimney. When he started to back off the roof, he heard the door open. A man headed toward the privy. He quickly lay flat on the roof. When the man went inside, he stepped back down.

Then he waited, either for the man to exit the privy, or the men inside to get enough smoke to exit the house. The man from the privy was first. Chuck caught him behind the head with his revolver. The man went down. Chuck went to the front of the house, and waited for the others.

From the house came the shouts, "What the hell are you doing? You're fillin' the house with smoke. I told you if you screwed up again, I'us gonna cut off your cue, you dumb Chinaman!" They all came out together, rubbing their eyes and coughing.

"Gentlemen! On the ground! Hands out in front of you!" instructed Chuck.

"What's going on here? Who the hell are you?" asked the man who had been shouting.

"Just do as I say. You men have no business here."

"Watta you mean? This here's our place, and we aim to keep it."

The man at the privy began to come around, he rose up on his all fours. Seeing what was happening, he managed to pick up his revolver and tried to aim. He was a bit unsteady, but his shot caught the tip of Chuck's gun, and knocked it out of his hand. Then he passed out again.

The one called Jake jumped up and leveled his gun at Chuck. But before he could shoot, a booming roar knocked him rolling and he never moved again. The cook had emptied both barrels of a shotgun at once at the man, the force knocked the cook down. He was sitting on the ground. Chuck picked up his revolver and checked it. The front sight was severely bent but the gun was all right.

The other men jumped up and ran back into the house. They had not been wearing guns. Chuck moved behind the smokehouse, motioned for the cook to come with him, "You got any more shells for that shotgun?"

"I have pocket full," he answered.

"Good. Go to the other end of the smokehouse and watch the back door, and the guy at the privy. I'll watch when they come out the front door . . . and don't shoot both barrels at the same time again!"

One man ran out the front door, shooting as fast as he could, hitting nothing. Chuck fired one shot to the man's right side. He took two steps and fell into the dust. Chuck then shouted to the rest, "I don't want to shoot you people! I just want you to leave. I hold the title to this ranch, and you are trespassing!"

A shot rang out from a window where the smoke came boiling out. He heard the shotgun again, and another man was down by the back door. The rest came out with their hands up, without guns. Their faces were blackened from the smoke.

"The three of you get your horses. Get out, and don't come back!"

"What about their horses?" one man asked.

"They won't be needin' them! You're lucky I'm willin' to let you have yours," he answered.

The men saddled up, and rode out in a hurry. Chuck climbed back onto the roof, and removed the wood that had blocked the chimney.

"What's your name?" he asked the cook, "I'm Charles Forbes."

"Missaw Bekendolf call me Chan. My name too hawd fow him."

"Was anyone else here with you before they came?"

"Cecil Johnson. He go to line camp when they come. They not know where is." said Chan.

"Do you ride?"

"Yes."

"Well, then, you ride out and tell Cecil he can come in now. I'll go back to town and get my things. Maybe we can make this a good ranch again."

With a big smile, Chan said; "Okay, Chawly."

Chuck helped Chan saddle up and watched him leave. He went back to Flip, tightened his cinch and rode back toward town. He wanted to make time, so he rode just outside the heavy growth of oaks and pecan trees that grew along the creek.

After having ridden at a good speed for a while, he slowed Flip to a walk, to give him a chance to catch his breath. He hadn't been paying attention; his thoughts were of Emilia and the ranch. Then he noticed that Flip began to twist his ears this way and that, "Flip, what are you listening for?"

Suddenly Flip stopped in his tracks, looked toward the right and his ears stopped moving. They were pointing straight toward the trees. At the same time, a shot rang out from the heavy cover of the trees. Chuck felt a sting in his right shoulder, but was still able to fire his Colt toward where the smoke and flash had come. He heard a yell from the trees. There were no more shots from the cover.

Chuck spurred Flip lightly, and rode to the edge of the trees, from where the shots had come. He saw the man that he had shot . . . it was one of the men who had been at the ranch. He looked around. When he was satisfied the man was alone, he continued quickly toward town.

Soon, Chuck pulled Flip to a walk, so that he could examine his shoulder. But he couldn't tell how bad it was. He placed his neckerchief over the wound and spurred Flip along at a faster pace.

When he arrived at the livery stable, Stump was out front. "Will you unsaddle Flip and rub 'em down for me? I think I need to take a look at this," indicating his shoulder.

"You betcha I'll take care of him. Dang, looks like you done lost a gallon of blood there. You just go on in! I'll see to this here horse of yourn."

Chuck hurried to the boarding house. Chip was waiting on the porch, and followed Chuck as he went immediately upstairs. As he passed by, he checked Emilia's room. She wasn't there, so he went to his room and took off his shirt. He began to clean the wound. It wasn't deep; the bullet had nicked a shallow crease in the skin.

When he had finished and washed up, he put on a clean shirt. As he opened his door and stepped into the hallway, he heard singing. He went on to the dining room. He didn't expect to find Emilia doing the singing, and accompanying herself on a guitar. He sat at an empty table where he could watch her. The room had mostly men and a few ladies. All were mesmerized by a folk song from the Basque Country.

When Emilia had finished, she moved to Chuck's table and sat down.

"Well, aren't you full of surprises! You never sang for me like that."

She smiled, "I guess we didn't have a guitar."

"I guess we were always on the move. I'm sure I would have found out more about you if we hadn't traveled so fast."

Chuck's shoulder had begun to bleed again, and was showing through his clean shirt.

"Chuck, you're hurt! Let's go to my room and see how bad."

They went back up to her room and Chuck removed his shirt. This was the first time Emilia had been close to him with his shirt off. She was fascinated by his muscular physique. She quickly started to take care of the wound.

"Chuck, they've asked me to stay on and sing at dinner time. They think it will bring in more customers. It's a little money, a room and meals."

"Emilia, I don't want to put down your singin', but this place is the only game in town. Where else would folks go? Besides, I want you to go to the ranch with me."

"But it's your ranch."

"No! It's OUR ranch. We were together when we found it."

"I thought I had just been a burden to you. You've always said that you traveled alone. I was sort of pushed on to you."

"I traveled alone until I met up with you, Emilia. Now we will travel together." He took her in his arms and kissed her. Then he pulled back and said: "Ouch! That hurt!" She looked surprised, and he quickly added, "Not the kiss . . . my arm." They laughed together.

"We need to load up in the morning to see what's at that ranch. I can tell you one thing: there's a Chinaman out there that's glad we're coming back. I couldn't think of trying it without your help. Now, let's get something to eat. I'm a little hollow inside."

Morning dawned clear; it was quiet, except forchickens clucking and an occasional crowing of a rooster. Stump helped with the saddles and packs. Chuck was able to do some of the work, but was glad for the help.

"Many thanks, Stump."

"You betcha! Now you folks be sure to come back sometime . . . 'specially you, Miss."

"We won't be too far away, so we'll be back," said Emilia.

Chuck settled his livery bill. They mounted up, leading all the horses they had acquired. The trip to the ranch seemed longer to Chuck than before. Little was said, as they each contemplated where they fit in this new situation. When they arrived at the gate of the ranch, they just sat looking at the overall picture. Chuck had not noticed the main ranch house much when he was here before. He had been looking for a way to surprise the men that occupied the cookhouse.

The wide, low, house was of white plaster over adobe. It looked as if it had been recently whitewashed, as did the trees in the front yard. The roof was made of hand made red clay tiles. It was a beautiful sight. A rise, like the wall of a canyon, lifted behind the house, protecting it from the north wind. After a few minutes pause, they advanced toward the house. There were hitching posts in front.

"Let's tie up here, Emilia. We can take care of the horses a little later. I just gotta see the inside."

She was already off her horse standing, and staring, at the front door of heavy Mexican Pine, with large metal hinges and a metal latch. They lifted the latch and went in through the massive door.

Chuck called out: "Hellooo, the house . . . anyone here?"

Chan answered, "Hello Chawly."

"Chan, I want you to meet Emilia Borda"

"How you do, Missy?"

"I'm pleased to meet you, Chan."

Chan led them into the main room with deer, and antelope heads mounted on the wall. Very comfortable looking leather chairs surrounded a huge walk-in fireplace made of natural stone. As they moved on through the dining area, they could smell food, but the long table was not set. They continued to move through large open doors out into a beautiful garden with large plants, trees and blooming flowers. There before them was another table, spread with food, that Chan had prepared.

"Howdy!" a booming voice came from the opposite end of the table, "I'm Cecil Johnson, I guess you would be the one called 'Chawly'."

Chuck laughed. "That would be right," he answered. "Charles Forbes, and this is Emilia Borda."

"Well, sit down and let's eat. Chan's been whirling a round here all morning a fixin' this meal," encouraged Cecil Johnson.

"How did he know that we would be here today?" asked Chuck.

"I think he has an extra sense or somethin'. He's always comin' up with somethin' sorta odd."

"Chan, if you've finished gettin' everything together, then sit down. 'Cause everything we talk about will concern all of us that are here."

There was a bark. Chuck got up and let Chip in. "This, gentlemen, is the rest of our party, Chip."

As they ate, Chuck related the story about finding the family on the trail and burying them. He told of finding the open deed. "By the way, I telegraphed the land office and found that the ranch was in Montague County. I filed it in my name just so that squatters, like you had, couldn't come in and claim it any more. But understand we're all in this together. How long have you two been here?"

Chan spoke up first, "twenty two yeaws."

Cecil Johnson nodded, "I've been here the same. Chan and I came at the same time. It's a kinda long story."

Emilia encouraged: "Tell us . . . we have the time."

"Well, I was Captain of a ship called the 'Mary Jane'. Chan had signed on as cook. We got caught in a storm, and didn't quite make it inside the outer banks, off the coast of North Carolina. The 'Mary Jane' was crushed on the rocks. Of all the crew, Chan and I were the only ones to make it through. The 'Mary Jane' was the third ship I'd lost to storms around that same place. So, when Chan and I got on land, we decided to give up the sea. We came out west with a wagon train. We stopped here, and decided to become cowboys. We've been here with John C. ever since. He was good enough to hire us, knowin' full well that we were tenderfeet."

"What stock is on the ranch?" queried Chuck.

"We've got about twenty five hundred of purebred Durham," said Cecil, "and about thirty five hundred Durham and Longhorns mixed. We haven't sold off any in a while."

Chuck surmised, "We need to find a market soon, or all the grass will be gone."

"Well, trail herds come through close to here, but they won't give much for them. Still it would reduce the herd and save the grass. Not much has been taken care of since John C. died. A couple of fellows named Johnson, no relation, have started a mining outfit down south in Thurber. The company store there might buy some."

After the meal, Chuck, and Cecil wandered farther out under the trees, enjoying the cool breeze, while Emilia and Chan continued to talk at the table.

"We'll need to hire some men, maybe some that have worked here before, if they were good hands . . . but we can start lookin' about that tomorrow. I've been thinkin', you're a bonified sea captain, aren't you?"

"That's right." Cecil replied.

"If Emilia will just say yes, I allow as how you might just marry us."

"I can do that." he answered.

"I'll let you know, after I ask her. Right now, I'd better take care of our horses . . . by the way; I brought a small remuda of horses with me, and a few saddles that I collected. You can let me know where to put them."

As he went back inside, he reminded them once again that each of them would share in the ranch. The ranch house was large enough to accommodate several families. Even the bunkhouse was one of the wings that surrounded the garden.

Chuck proceeded to care for the horses. His injury slowed him down, so Cecil went with him to remove saddles and the heavy packs from the horses.

"I thank you, Cecil. Just leave those two saddled, and put a little slack in the cinches. Emilia and I will go riding after while . . . I think you know why." Chuck smiled and winked. "I'll help you with that big pack. It has a lot of hardware and ammunition in it. I was going to open a gunsmith shop, but I guess that will have to wait."

"The guys you ran off left a few guns."

"I'll have a look later. I collected a few at the same time I collected the horses and saddles."

Late that afternoon, Charles Forbes, and Emilia Borda rode out to look over the range. The rolling hills were covered with tall green grass that was still in good condition, even though they had thought it might have been over-grazed.

There was plenty of shade from the Oak and Pecan trees, and the cattle were taking advantage of it. Chip, running along ahead of the horses, flushed a covey of quail that caused the horses to get a little nervous. They rode to the top of the tallest hill, just as the sun was sinking low behind the clouds.

"Emilia, it's beautiful, isn't it?" She looked at him, smiled and nodded her head in agreement. He continued, "I would like for us to be able to come here to watch the sunset together the rest of our lives . . . will you marry me, Emilia?"

"Ohhh, yes Chuck! I wasn't sure you would ever ask."

They leaned towards each other and kissed . . . a silhouette of love against the red and gold of a Texas Sunset.

Matthew Forbes
Chapter 15

The third son of Richard and Iona Forbes, Matthew, was appointed United States Marshall by the 21st president of the United States, Chester A. Arthur, for a term of four years. Although he had an assigned district, he was authorized to pursue certain suspected criminals across other districts, territories, or states.

Currently, he had trailed a man across much of Missouri. He had recently lost track of him, and was now at a community called Westport, Missouri, trying to pick up the man's trail again.

Missouri River towns sprang up in the 1850's and 60's to supply wagon trains headed west, either to California, Oregon or to Utah, to join the Mormons. The Oregon Trail had supply landings in several places along the Missouri River. One was Westport Landing, later a part of Kansas City. Riverboats docked there to unload supplies that would be necessary for making the long trip west. The Mormon trail crossed the Missouri, going north through Council Bluffs, Iowa. The old Shawnee, Newton, Chisholm, and Santa Fe Trails all had endings at various markets, including the Kansas City area.

Matthew Forbes sat high on a hill, a few hundred yards south, overlooking the landing at Westport. From this advantage point, he could observe the activity below. He sat in front of a blacksmith's tent while his horses were being shod. The churning paddlewheel gently held a River Boat against the bank, while the gangplank dropped, to unload passengers and cargo.

Matt alternately whittled, and sharpened his knife on the flat rock at his feet. His lean and tanned face showed his rugged life of travel. His auburn hair had streaks of red from the sun, and curled up under the brim of his well-worn gray hat. His clear, blue eyes flashed brightly from his dark face. As he moved, his muscles rippled under his skintight buckskin shirt.

He gazed off into the valley where men, and livestock seemed to be lost in confusion. A few wagons were circled, and had cooking fires going. Some headed out on the trail to get as close to the front of the line as they could. He saw countless tents set up as saloons, cafes, and houses of ill repute. As he watched, in deep thought, he rubbed the flat side of his knife against his two-day growth of beard,

"Smitty," addressing the blacksmith, "whatda you 'spose a man has in his mind that would hook up twenty oxen to a wagon and head out on a trail, with no guarantee of water or food for 'em? Their stock would likely provide food for some Indians along the way."

After a long pause of silence, "Don't rightly know Mr. Forbes," said the blacksmith, speaking in between strokes of his hammer on the anvil, as he shaped the shoes, "Reckon it's about the same thing that brought me this fer: A new land, chance to start a business, just that ole promise of somethin'. . . somethin' better."

Matt mused a minute, "Yeah, I reckon so . . . least they give the grass time to grow in the west before they start."

"Mister?" A voice from behind Matt, and to the right, caused him to turn.

"What can I do for you?" Matthew Forbes asked, as he stood to face the man.

"By your outfit and your guns, you look like a man that might lead a few wagons," the stranger observed.

Matt closed his knife and slipped it into the pocket of his chaps, as he observed that the stranger wore overalls, and had the appearance of a farmer. "I'm afraid you got the wrong man. I been on that trail," he tipped his head in the direction of the landing, "too many graves and oxen bones for me to go again."

"Well sir, I'm not interested in going that way either. What I want to do is head south and west. My brothers and me want to go to a place in New Mexico Territory . . . east of Santa Fe, a settlement called Roswell. We're able and willin' to pay."

Matt looked at the man, who wore a gray beard on a creased face that had seen many years of hard work. "I know the place you're talkin' 'bout, and I can't imagine what you'd want to go there for. Nothin' much there but a store or two, and a saloon . . . I'm sure you have your reasons, and I reckon I'm willin' to talk about it. It's probably growed since I was there. Tell me where you're camped, and I'll come by after Smitty takes care of my horses."

"We're about a hundred yards on up this hill, under a big 'ole tree. Just ask for the Jacksons. I'm Everett, by the way."

"I'm Matthew, Matthew Forbes."

The older man started walking up the hill, "Thank you, Mr. Forbes."

Matthew turned back to the blacksmith, "Smitty, will it be all right to leave my horses in your little corral until I can talk to this feller? I don't want 'em to have to stand with that pack and saddle on 'em while I visit with these folks."

"Sure, I'll put 'em in there when I get through. You go on, and don't worry."

Matt started off up the hill, then paused and asked, "Did I ask you for an extra set of shoes for each one?"

"That you did, and I'll put them in your pack with some extra nails. The shoes with a notch filed in the toe will fit the bay."

"Thanks a lot. I'll be right back. I'm not likely to take on a job like the Jacksons want, but you never can tell." Matthew answered.

He continued up the hill, looking for a wagon under a tree, only to find all of the trees had wagons under them. He stopped at the first wagon, and then saw Everett Jackson stoking the fire under some pots.

"Mr. Jackson," Matt called out, as he continued to approach the fire, "I thought your wagon would be the only one here."

"They're all Jackson wagons. There are four families of us, but we are still all Jacksons. The others are my brothers' families. Pull up a log and sit down. My daughter is fixin' somethin' to eat, and you'll be welcome. She'll be back in a minute. Thank you for coming."

Everett Jackson turned to find a log to sit on. "I guess I was a bit hasty in asking you to lead us. I thought the wagon boss I'd hired wasn't going to show up . . . but he did . . . a day late! He was here when I got back. Stay and eat with us anyway."

"Thanks, I appreciate that." Matthew sat down and watched as Everett Jackson poured a cup of coffee from the big pot hanging over the coals.

Jackson, handing Matt the cup, asked, "So, you've been on that Oregon trail, have you?"

Matt took a sip of the hot coffee, "Yeah, part of it anyway . . . I was coming down the west side of the Wind River Range, from the upper Oregon territory. I got on the trail at South Pass. I came all the way on it from there. I sure don't have any need to go again."

A woman approached from one of the wagons, and walked to the fire while Matt was still talking. When he saw her he stood and removed his hat. Everett turned when he saw Matt stand. He rose and said, "This is my daughter, Jessica, Mister Forbes."

Matthew was silent. All he could do was nod and stare straight into her eyes. She smiled, and looked down quickly to escape his stare. "Pleased to meet you Mister Forbes"

When she turned away, the spell was broken. Matt finally got out a weak, "How do, ma'am." He watched her every move as she dished up whatever she was cooking. He didn't care what it was, as long as he could watch her.

Her golden hair fell in curls from under her bonnet. Her complexion was as smooth as cream, and her eyes were so clear blue he could swear there were lights behind them, causing them to shine. *"How could anyone bring so purdy a girl into country such as this?"* he thought to himself.

Everett Jackson took the dish from Jessica, and handed it to Matthew. Then he began to explain his reasons for wanting to go to New Mexico territory. "We have a brother, Cyrus Jackson, that has a place along the Pecos River and I reckon he's nearing his end, 'cause he has asked us to come and take over before he passes."

Matthew turned toward Mr. Jackson, "I'm sorry that you have to go under such circumstances. I'm sure he'll be glad to see you."

"If'n he's still alive when we get there." Everett Jackson stirred the fire in deep thought.

Matt realized that the conversation had slowed and asked, "What's the feller's name that you've hired?"

Everett Jackson looked up and said: "His name is Floyd Jacobs. He's been down the trails that lead that way many times."

Matthew Forbes stiffened, and then caught himself. "I suppose you wouldn't mind if I tag along behind you, since I've decided to go that way anyhow. Another gun hand across the territory might come in handy."

A voice came from a man stepping across the wagon tongue, "As long as you understand that there's only one wagon boss and that's me!"

"No problem there. I know my place." Matthew rose and held out his hand, "Matthew Forbes is the name."

The man said nothing for a minute and stared Matt in the eyes then took his hand and mumbled, "Floyd Jacobs." He then moseyed over and sat beside Jessica.

Matt sat back down and continued to eat, "This is very good ma'am. Your momma has taught you good."

"I taught myself. I'm eighteen and I been cookin' since I was eight!"

Matt was stunned for a minute by her snappy comeback. "Well it shows, 'cause this sure is good."

Everett Jackson chuckled at the situation that Matt had gotten himself into, and explained, "Her momma died when she was eight, and she's insisted on cookin' fer us ever since."

"I'm sorry for your loss." Changing the subject, Matt quickly added, "I probably won't go that far, but I would like to stay close, if that's all right with you Mr. Jackson. If you have any room in one of the wagons, I'd like to pay you to carry a couple sacks of grain for my horses, and my pack, so's my horses won't have to carry it."

"Be glad to Mr. Forbes. There won't be no charge, and the weight won't matter, since our wagons are extra heavy duty.

Floyd Jacobs gruffly interrupted. "We'll leave early in the mornin'. Be here if you want to go with us!" Jacobs turned to Everett Jackson, "Now you people need to get to cleanin' up and be ready."

Matt scraped out what little that was left on his plate, and handed it to Jessica. He smiled and looked her squarely in the eyes, "It was very good. G'night ma'am." He walked back down toward the blacksmith's tent. She watched him until he was out of sight.

When Matt reached the blacksmith's tent, the hand-pumped bellows was still, and the coals had cooled. "Well Smitty, I'll need you to tack on an overnight stay for my horses, if that's all right. I'll be leaving with the Jacksons in the mornin'."

"Changed your mind did you?" the blacksmith asked.

"Had it changed for me. I been trackin' a feller in eastern Missouri, and lost him somewhere along the river. Lo and behold, he walked right into their camp, and is going to lead them where they want to go."

The blacksmith looked at Matthew, not quite understanding what he had heard, and said: "Life is funny that way, ain't it?"

By the time Matt had gotten his grain and packsaddle loaded into one of the Jackson's wagons, the sun had slipped behind a bank of clouds that sent bright rays like a giant fan into the evening sky.

He pulled his saddle onto some hay in the blacksmith's corral, where his horses were, and flipped it over to lean on. He spread his blanket, then curled up in it and was soon asleep.

Someone's rooster crowing awakened him, even though it was still dark. He fumbled for the stem on his watch, pressed it, and the lid flew open. He still could not see what time it was. So, not having a match handy, he decided it was too early, and rolled over and went back to sleep. It wasn't long before he awoke with a start, and realized what he had done. It was still early but the gray was giving way to a day of bright sunlight.

He placed a halter with a long lead rope on the bay and started to saddle the dapple gray gelding, "Well 'Chico' I'll just bet Mr. Jacobs didn't wait on us, so I'll depend on you to make up the time." He reached into his saddlebags, and got jerky to chew on, and mounted up.

By the time he reached the tree where the Jacksons had been, they were gone. "Like I said, Mr. Jacobs waits for no man. No problem . . . they'll be easy to track."

The Jackson's wagon boss, Floyd Jacobs, had been suspected by the United States Marshall's office of hiring on to lead small wagon trains into Indian Territory and robbing them, leaving no witnesses, and making it look as if Indians had raided them. It seemed that Jacobs had survived these raids too many times. They sent Marsall Forbes to find the man, and to keep an eye on him. *"I'm sure Jacobs doesn't know that it's me that's been trailing him. He thinks he's lost the marshal that was after him. I'll just follow behind a while, and catch up tonight."*

Matt headed along the route that Jacobs was taking the wagons, but it was still too early to determine which of the several cattle trails he would take. Some would have more forts for protection. Others would be shorter.

He took his time and watched the tracks, staying familiar with the wheel patterns and hoof prints imbedded in the soft earth. After a few hours, he noticed a set of strange hoof prints had turned onto the trail, on top of those that he had been following.

"What the . . . new hoof prints! Surely Jacobs doesn't plan to take over the wagons this soon!" Matt swung out to the left and rode a little faster, staying behind the trees in order to observe the new rider without being seen.

When he saw the rider, he noticed that he too, was keeping a distance behind the Jackson's wagons. "Well Chico, what'a you 'spose that feller is trailing the wagons for? I guess we'll just ride out here in the trees 'till we can figger it out."

That evening, the stranger saw that Floyd Jacobs had picked a campsite along a stream, so he rode off behind some heavy brush and dismounted.

Matt watched for a while. Then he decided to come into camp from the east, where he could not be seen by the rider, and could observe from within the camp.

When he slipped off Chico, he tied him and the Bay horse, Curley, on a grassy area outside the camp. He constantly watched the area where the rider dismounted.

"Well, Forbes," Jacobs taunted, "I thought we'd seen the last of you."

"Naw, had some loose ends to tie up."

Everett Jackson walked in from behind his wagon. "Matthew, sit down and eat with us. We have plenty."

Floyd Jacobs dumped the coffee grounds from his cup, "Better watch your food. It may have to last a while." He then walked away.

Matt watched him leave, before he told Everett Jackson, "I'll do a little hunting tomorrow. If I'm lucky, it'll push the food a few days."

"That'll be fine, Matthew. Here, have a cup of coffee."

"Thanks! That'll hit the spot." Matt took the cup, still watching for the rider that disappeared into the trees.

The sun had almost gone down, the grey of evening was beginning to hover over the campsite, and darkness was weaving through the trees where Matt had seen the figure dismount and tie his horse.

It wasn't long until Matt saw a shadow move toward one of the wagons. He rose, telling Mr. Jackson, "I'll be back in a minute." He eased out into the semi-darkness. He could hear a conversation from inside the wagon, so he moved closer.

The voices from the wagon were just a whisper. "Take me with you Michael. Papa has an extra horse!"

"Mary Ann, you know I can't take you right now. I've got to help my folks on the trail."

It was silent for a few minutes. Then with tears in her eyes, "Make love to me before you go, Michael."

"Mary Ann, I can't do that! It would be stealing your wedding night. And besides, anything could happen to me on the trail.

"Don't say that Michael."

"Well, it just might. Lots of folks have died on that trail!"

Matthew walked away, so that he could not hear. As the boy was leaving, Matt approached him and spoke in a low voice, "Michael . . ."

When Michael heard his name, he whirled around, "Good grief man, you liked to 'uve scarred me to death!"

"Sorry! I overheard you talking to the girl. I think you need to know that movin' in the dark like this could get you shot!" cautioned Matthew.

"Yes, Sir, I know, but I had to see Mary Ann before I left." Michael Beck explained.

"You sound like a decent young man. Where are ya leavin' to?"

"My folks want to go to California."

"Well son, take care of yourself. I hope we see you again."

"Thank you, Sir. I hope it will be soon." He hurried to his horse.

Matt watched the young man as far as he could see him, in the fading daylight, and then returned to the campfire. By now several of the Jackson's families were gathered, and Everett introduced Matthew to the group. Again Jessica Jackson dished up their dinner. Matt took his plate and cup, and sat on a log back away from the fire. He still couldn't take his eyes off Jessica. Soon a young girl came near the fire and took a plate. As she moved away from the light of the fire she noticed there was room for her to sit on the log beside Matthew.

"I haven't met you, young lady. My name is Matthew Forbes."

Her eyes were red and tearing, her cheeks were stained, so she looked down at her plate, "I'm Mary Ann Jackson."

They both sat quietly, as the others carried on conversations. Then Matt leaned over and whispered, "Michael seems to be a nice young man."

She quickly turned to Matt, her face red. "How do you know Michael?"

"I met him briefly as he was leaving, told him he could be in danger sneaking around in the dark like that."

"Don't tell papa, please! He forbids me to see him." she pleaded.

"It'll be our secret."

She blushed again and sat quietly.

Jessica looked over the fire toward Matthew and Mary Ann smiling at each other. A tiny bit of jealousy turned her face red. *"What's that all about? He doesn't even know her! Well, it's nothing' to me!"* She busied herself with the cooking, glancing occasionally at the two of them. *"Besides, she's only sixteen, way too young for him."*

Everyone had drifted back to their wagons, except for Matthew and Jessica. She was still putting away things from the evening meal. Matt walked toward her, still holding his cup. She picked up the coffee pot to pour him another.

"Since you've finished here, would you like to walk out where we can see the sunset better?" he asked.

She looked long into his eyes and said, "It's already down, isn't it?

"Well 'spose we go and see." Matt set his cup down and motioned her to follow.

"I'm not sure I should go too far from the wagons. Indians, you know," she gave that coy look as she spoke.

"I'll protect you, ma'am." He laughed, as he took her hand.

She pulled free, teasing, "And who will protect me from you?"

"Do you really think you will need protection from me?"

She laughed and caught his hand again. "Weeell . . . maybe."

They walked to a small pond and stood without saying a word, looking at the reflection of the sky on the water. It was as if they were getting two sunsets of dull pinks and gold, as the evening swallowed up the remaining light of the day.

"I'm glad you asked me. It's beautiful."

"You only saw one vision of beauty. I saw two. Thanks for coming. You know, I've had plans for us ever since the first time I saw you?"

"Oh? And what kind of plans?"

"I can't tell you now, but I think you'll agree, when the time is right."

"You're kind of presumptuous, aren't you? Maybe I have plans with someone else." She started walking back toward the wagons, expecting him to follow. She was not disappointed.

"You'll see, and you need to be getting ready for that day."

Jessica was enjoying his attention, but Matt didn't see the smile on her face. Without another word, they went back to her wagon.

Matt moved close. She didn't back away. *"I had better hold back, for now,"* He thought to himself, reluctantly backing away.

"Will I see you at breakfast, Matt?"

"No. I plan to leave early to hunt, and I'm not sure how long I will be."

"Be careful out there," she offered.

By the light from the stars, Matt could see her face. He could hear his own heart beating. He wanted to take her in his arms and hold her, but she was young and innocent. So he said, "Good night, Jessica," and left.

Matthew Forbes was up and ready to go before the morning grey stretched across the sky. He had his rifle in its boot, and braced a small shotgun across the pommel of his saddle. He rode well away from the campsite to a small creek, to wait for game as it came to water. His thoughts jumped from Jessica to Floyd Jacobs. *"I know he will make his move. I just don't know when. I hate that Jessica and her family are in danger. I'm sure all of the Jacksons have gold in their wagons, since they sold everything to make this trip."*

He leaned against a tree, where he could watch for game. Chico was taking on his morning fill of grass, nearby.

Before long Matthew could see a shadow of a figure riding away from the wagons. "That would be Jacobs, Chico. I might follow him a while, just to see where he scouts, and see what else he's up to. I hope it's just a scouting trip."

Matt waited for a little more light. Then he mounted and rode to his left, toward heavier cover of brush and trees. He kept Jacobs in sight.

After about an hour of following Jacobs, Matt stopped short, as he spotted another rider approaching Jacobs. He couldn't get close enough to hear what they were saying, but he watched the meeting until the rider left. Matt decided to follow him to see where he was staying, and how many others there might be.

The man rode to lose any tracker, twisting, back trailing enough to make anyone dizzy. But Matt trailed near enough behind to watch the whole thing.

It was well past noon before the stranger rode into a camp. Matt tied Chico to a nearby tree, and moved carefully in, close enough to hear the men talking. He counted six men around the fire.

The rider poured himself coffee and reported, "Floyd wants us to move on ahead, and wait for his signal, in about four more days."

Another man quickly stood and poured coffee on the fire, "Hell, I don't want to wait any longer. We been out here a week already, and I'm gettin' tired of waitin'. I say we move in and take their gold today!"

"Sit down Catlin, and listen. The boss has things planned out. He says no Indians will attack this close to the beginning of the trails. So if we wait a few days, we'll be closer to their territory."

"Okay, but I don't like this waiting!"

Matt had heard enough. He eased back to Chico, and headed out to locate the wagons moving along the trail. After several miles, he flushed some prairie chickens. They landed again a short distance ahead. "Dang Chico, I near forgot we were 'sposed to be huntin'."

He eased off Chico, took the shotgun and a few shells, and walked toward the spot where the prairie chickens had landed. He knew they had probably run awhile, after they went down in the tall grass, so he concentrated on the area ahead. Soon they flushed again, and he let go with both barrels. Three of the birds dropped. He scooped them up and returned to his horse. "Well Chico, we won't return empty-handed, anyway." He mounted, and headed toward the place where the camp had been last night.

By the time Matthew returned to the water hole, the sun was dropping in the west, and it was late enough that deer and other animals would be coming to the water. He found a place down wind, behind some brush and waited. It wasn't long before a medium sized buck cautiously approached the water. Matt took aim with his rifle, and with one shot the buck dropped on the spot.

After field dressing the deer, he wrapped it in the ground cloth he carried in his saddlebags. He placed his bounty across his saddle and swung up behind it.

The wagons had pulled together to camp by the time Matt caught up with them. He stopped short of their location, and hung the deer in a tree to skin later. He then went on into camp.

"Howdy Everett . . . 'n Jessica. A few hens are all I got except for a little buck. Maybe they'll help extend the food awhile. Maybe I'll do better tomorrow." He turned to Everett Jackson. "Everett, walk with me." He took a lantern, and they walked to where Matt had hung the deer.

"Looks like you done all right, Matt."

"Thanks for coming with me Everett. I found out something today that you need to know, and also to tell your kin. I'm with the United States Marshall's Office and am here because of Floyd Jacobs."

Everett looked at Matt questioningly, "I don't understand."

"Jacobs has been suspected of leading small wagon trains, like yours, into areas of known Indian activities, and then robbing and killing everybody, and then blaming it on the Indians. Today, I followed Jacobs. He met another man, and they are plannin' to raid you and the other families in a few days."

"We had better take care of him tonight, before he can meet the others!"

"No, Everett. We have to have 'cause' to take him, and we don't have that yet. If we are ready for them, I think we can handle 'em. There are only six of them. You'll have to tell each one of your leaders in secret, and not let the word get back to Jacobs." He glanced back toward the wagons, and added, "I guess we'd best skin this deer, or they'll wunder what we're up to."

The two men skinned the deer, and took it in to butcher. Jessica was preparing the dinner meal. Everett got his saw and began to cut up the deer.

Matt moved to the fire. "Mind if I get a cup of your coffee, Jessica?"

"Help yourself, Matthew. Dinner will be ready soon. If papa will slice a steak or two off the deer, I'll fry them up, too."

Matt watched Jessica as she worked the pots and pans, raking out coals to set the Dutch ovens on. The dress she wore hid her figure from him, but the sharp features of her face, and her piercing blue eyes were enough to tell him he had met the woman he wanted to share his life. Her beauty had him in its grasp. But it was her spunk that sealed the thoughts in his mind.

After he realized he was staring at her, he spoke up, "What do you plan to do when you reach New Mexico territory?"

"I haven't thought about it . . . work with the apples, I guess. By the way, what were the plans you spoke of earlier?"

"Oh . . . I'll let you know when the time is right, Jessica." He looked into his coffee cup, and changed the subject. "I think you should stay close to the wagons for the next few days. Don't go far out, unless someone knows where you are."

"Why, Matt? Are we getting close to the Indians?"

"No, not yet . . . just be careful."

"Matthew, you're scaring me."

"I don't mean to scare you. I just want you to be careful. By the way, when are we going to eat, anyway?"

"When it's ready, that's when!" she snapped.

Matt could tell she was a little miffed at him, so he let it pass. He took his coffee and walked out from the wagons to find Floyd Jacobs. He saw him unsaddling his horse, so he approached and asked, "Well how'd it go today? Does the trail look good?"

Jacobs grunted and looked at Matt with a hard glare, wondering if he was up to something. "Trail looks fine."

"I was wondering if there was plenty of grass for the stock."

"They'll make out all right. Let me worry about those things! I just want to eat right now. My stomach thinks my mouth's laced shut." He walked off, carrying his saddle to a wagon. Matt watched him for a minute, and then walked back to the Jackson's fire.

When dinner was over, Matt returned to the fire. Jessica was alone, and sat near the lantern, reading from her Bible. Matthew stood and watched her for a minute. Then he could hold it no longer. "Jessica, you are an amazing lady."

"Why? Because I can read?" she asked.

"No. Because you can do all the things you do. I think you're special."

"Well, thank you . . . I guess." Jessica was pleased, but embarrassed.

"When you've finished reading, would you like to go for a walk?"

"Yes Mr. Forbes, I would. Matter of fact, I've finished my reading for today."

"You read every day?"

"Yes, every day."

"Good, you can read to me."

"Matthew Forbes, do you mean to tell me that you can't read?"

"Oh, I can read. I just like to listen to you."

She playfully poked him on his shoulder, "Oh you . . ."

He caught her arm and pulled her in close, looked into her eyes a moment, then kissed her. His heart was pounding so loud he was sure she could hear it. But Jessica was also filled with emotions she didn't understand.

"You two better be careful. Papa's right behind me!" Mary Ann giggled, as she walked in and stood by the fire.

Matt took Jessica's hand, and they quickly moved out into the darkness.

This time, Jessica returned his kisses, and they passionately embraced. Matt pulled back and said, "You had better go back to the wagon before I lose control of myself" Jessica didn't want it to end, but he had reminded her that they were much too serious, too soon, and retreated.

Three and a half days passed. Matthew stayed in the brush and trees as he rode a short distance from the four wagons. He watched the white, chalky dust rise behind each wagon, but stayed far enough away that they couldn't see him. He occasionally rode close enough to watch for the men that he was expecting to appear at any time. He noticed that Jacobs had ridden on ahead of the wagons.

Everyone had eaten a light lunch, so that they wouldn't have to stop. The sun was warm, and Matt felt sleepy. When he realized he was nodding off, he knew that the others might be also. He rode quickly to the wagons and talked a few minutes with each driver. He encouraged each one to have someone to keep them awake and watchful.

He rode to Everett Jackson's wagon. "Everett, Jacobs has ridden ahead. I'll be watching from the trees, trying to stay out of sight. It could be anytime. Jessica, keep him awake."

"What is it Matt?"

"We just need to be careful, that's all."

He rode out again, to watch for any riders. Jacobs was nowhere in sight. Matt stopped behind some trees, and checked each of his guns, including the shotgun, to make sure they were ready. He then moved where he could watch the area from which he thought Jacobs' men might come.

Hours passed. The sun slipped slowly behind a few small cotton puffs of clouds. Matt let the wagons advance down the trail before he would catch up. Jacobs still had not returned to check on the wagons, as a trail boss should.

The sun was still bright and low in the west. Matt noticed dust rising in the air, about a mile and half west of the wagons. "Well Chico, looks like the time has come. They are approaching from that direction so that the sun will be in the eyes of the Jacksons."

Matt hit the saddle, and was riding fast toward the wagons. He arrived in plenty of time to warn all the men on the train. "Pull the wagons together and take cover! They are on their way, comin' from the west." Matt rode to the trees on the north, to give a surprise attack

157

from another side. He slid from the saddle and braced his rifle in the fork of a tree, and waited.

The six men had spread themselves into a fan, riding directly toward the wagons, firing as they advanced. When they were quite close, they pulled up sharply, seeing no one on the wagons.

Suddenly, shots from the men hidden in the wagons rang out, and the riders began to drop. Two cursing men turned quickly, their horses looking as if they turned wrong side out. Matt drew a bead on one, and knocked him from his saddle. Then another rider was hit.

When the shooting stopped, Matt headed towards the wagons.

The Jackson men came out to check on wounded raiders. They found five dead, but Jacobs was not one of them. The one man still alive had caught a bullet through to his spine, and couldn't move.

Matt walked slowly looking from one to the other. "Floyd's not here." He walked to the wounded man. "Where's Jacobs? Looks like he left you men to take the heat."

The intense pain caused the man to strain to speak, "I don't know where he is, but he warned us about you."

"Was he watching from somewhere close?" asked Matt.

"I said I didn't know." As he answered he coughed blood.

"Okay, I'm gonna tie you to your saddle, and let your horse take you home."

"Wait! Don't do that. That stupid horse was wild a couple o' weeks ago. He ain't got no home, and he'ud wander fer days. Ole Floyd was on the hill east o' here, said he 'ud back us, but he didn't. You can track him from that hilltop. I seen him when we was ridin' up. Now, what about me? I need help!" He pleaded as he was heaving for breath. Blood trickled from his lips and nose. "I need some doctorin'!"

Matt checked to see how bad the wound was. If the shot had not hit his spine it would have gone clear through. "I'm sorry. Looks like a lot of your insides were stirred up by that bullet." By the time Matt finished his analysis, the man had died.

Matt turned to Everett Jackson, "Is everyone all right in the wagons?"

"They're fine. You go ahead and find Jacobs. We'll take care of the buryin'. Then we'll move on down the trail."

"I'll take you to New Mexico, as soon as I settle this business with Jacobs. This trail we're on has been used a lot, and is marked good for miles. Just take it easy, and keep your eyes open. When you don't feel confident about the trail, find water and camp. I'll come back as soon as I can.

Matt walked toward the wagons. Jessica ran out to meet him. She threw her arms around him. "Oh Matthew, I'm so glad that you're all right!"

"And I'm glad that you're okay, too. I have ta go look for Floyd Jacobs now. If your papa hasn't told you, Jacobs is the one behind all this. We've been looking for him for some time now."

"What do you mean that you've been looking for him?"

He explained, "I should have told you sooner. I'm a U.S. Marshall. My job is law enforcement. Tracking the likes of Jacobs is what I'm required to do."

"When will you be back?"

"Don't know, but his trail is gettin' cold, so I'd better go."

"Be careful Matt. I want you back in one piece." She gave him a warm kiss on the cheek, and ran back to the wagons in tears.

159

Chapter 16

Matthew Forbes rode up the hill, where Jacobs had viewed the slaughter below. He eased off of Chico and dropped the reins. He walked to the brow of the hill, still behind a heavy growth of trees, and located a spot where Jacobs had milled around. It was strewn with half smoked cigarettes. Moving in a wide circle, he finally located the trail, going down the opposite side of the hill. He quickly mounted up and headed along the trail at an easy lope. Since Jacobs had left at a run, his trail was easy to follow, as the horses shoes dug in to the loose soil.

"Looks like he's headed back toward Westport Landing, Chico." He picked up his pace. Somewhere along the way, he missed where Jacobs had changed directions.

"Easy, Chico. My trackin's gone to sleep, I've plumb lost the trail." He turned and quickly started backtracking.

He found the place where the tracks stopped, and he had milled around, as if checking to see if anyone was following. Then the tracks headed off to the right, toward the river. Matt wasn't sure that these were Jacob's tracks, so he stepped off Chico to have a closer look. At that instant, he heard a shot. A bullet missed, as it went over his head, followed by another that whizzed close by his ear. He quickly took cover behind a tree. He had drawn his Colt, as he scanned the area where he thought the shot had come from. About twenty-five yards away, he saw a fading blue haze from the black powder, where the gun had been discharged. No one was there.

He quickly mounted and headed in that direction, with his shotgun resting on his thigh, realizing he was closer to Jacobs than he thought.

Chico was a mustang with great stamina, and he was ready to move. Matt knew that he could move faster than Jacobs' horse, and could last longer.

He finally got a glimpse of Jacobs in the distance, moving in and out of the trees, trying not to be a target. Matt continued straight on, at a run. Before he realized it, Jacobs had stopped and taken a position behind rocks large enough to hide both himself and his horse.

Matt hardly heard the shot that caught his upper right side. It tumbled him into the bushes along the trail. He was still conscious, but he made no move. After a few moments, he eased his left hand to his revolver, and held it still, until he decided that Jacobs thought he was dead. Then he heard the sounds of horse's hooves as Jacobs hurriedly left the scene.

His side was bleeding but he didn't think any bones were broken. He took his neckerchief, and cleaned away most of the blood. He tore a string from the edge of the neckerchief, and tied it in place.

He crawled out of the brush and leaned against a tree, so weak that he passed out.

When Matt finally opened his eyes, it was late and almost dark. The bleeding had continued until the neckerchief had soaked, and dried, before the bleeding had finally stopped. His shoulder, on that side, was stiff and sore.

He managed to get to his feet and staggered to where Chico was standing. He reached into his saddlebags for his extra neckerchief, and made a sling for his right arm. He led Chico to a log, so that he could stand on it and roll into the saddle. He rode back to find the Jackson's wagons.

Matt rode for a long time, in and out of consciousness, until he could see the flickering light of the campfires and continued toward them. At camp he tried to dismount. But the pain caused him to lose his grip, and he fell from the saddle onto the ground near the fire, hitting a few pans that were near.

Jessica and Mary Ann were in the wagon next to the fire.

"Did you hear that?" Mary Ann asked.

"Hear what?"

"That noise outside. Something hit the pans and it sounded as if someone fell . . . I'm sure I heard a moan!"

"Mary Ann! It's just your imagination or some animal ran into the pots."

"No it's not! Hand me the lantern, I'm going to see what it was!"

Mary Ann grabbed the lantern, and eased carefully out the back of the wagon, with Jessica telling her not to go, "It' might be a bear!"

Mary Ann shouted back, "Jessica, it's Matthew! He's hurt!"

Jessica quickly jumped from the wagon and stood beside Mary Ann, looking at Matt, curled up in pain. She dropped to her knees, and tried to lift him up.

"Matt! What happened? Are you okay, Matt? Speak to me! Help me get him to the light of the fire, and bring the lantern."

"I'll get a towel and some water." Mary Ann cried, "Oh, Jessica, see if you can find out how bad he is."

The two of them cleaned and bandaged his wound, and placed Matt on his blanket. They bathed his face with cool water, and he began to revive.

Jessica, with tears in her eyes, asked again what had happened.

"I wasn't watching close enough, and Jacobs got the best of me. I wasn't able to follow." Matt gasped.

"And it'll be a while 'till you're able to do much of anything. A couple of inches lower and you wouldn't have come back." scolded Jessica.

Matt, weak from losing blood, was slow to respond. Finally he spoke, "Can you get your Papa? I need to talk to him."

Jessica answered, with the tears now running down her face, "Don't you think you should rest, and not worry now?"

"It's important that I talk to him now, before I pass out again."

"All right, I'll get him."

When Everett arrived, Matt could hardly speak. But he managed to ask, "Can anyone ride back to Westport to find someone familiar with the trail that would lead you to New Mexico? The blacksmith should know if there's someone reliable."

Everett looked at Jessica, and seeing her love for Matt, he answered, "Oliver's oldest boy could do that. But you should be up and around soon, and we can wait a few days 'till you're fit."

"Everett, I'm sorry, but when I can ride, I'll need to go after Jacobs. It's my duty. If I don't get him soon, he'll gather more men, and try again to get your gold . . . and we may not be so lucky next time."

Everett thought a minute. Then he answered, "I understand Matt. I'll get the boy started back to Westport Landing. Maybe he'll get back afore you leave, and you can talk to whoever he gets."

Everett saw that Matthew had gone to sleep while he was talking to him.

Three days passed, and Oliver's son Josh had not returned. Matt had been awake off and on, enough to take nourishment, and was getting stronger. As he sat in the shade of the wagon, he watched Jessica preparing dinner for the group. Her graceful moves, and beauty, assured him that he would return for her, as soon as he could.

In the quiet of the evening, Matt heard the sound of two horsemen coming toward the wagons. Out of habit, he reached for his Colt, only to find that it was missing. He turned to Jessica, "Someone's coming! They're a ways off, but you'd better get my gun."

The horsemen were about a hundred yards off when Jessica handed Matt his Colt.

"Can you see who it is yet, Jessica?'

She shaded her eyes, "Not yet, but I think It's Josh. It looks like his paint, and there is someone with him."

Matt stretched back against the log to see around the wheel of one of the wagons, "It's Josh all right. I don't recognize the feller with him, so he must'a found someone."

It was a few minutes before the riders rode up to the wagons. When they arrived, Josh came to Matthew, where he was sitting in the shade. "Matt, this is Thadious Hinds. The blacksmith introduced us, an' he says he's been to New Mexico territory before. Tad, this here's Matthew Forbes."

Thadious moved to the log where Matt reclined, "Good to meet ya, Mr. Forbes. Just call me Tad."

"All right, Tad, good to meet you too. We need to talk a while, and have you meet the Jacksons. Then we'll eat."

"Sounds good to me. I could eat a horse about now." Tad stood as he saw Jessica.

"Well, you've met one Jackson, and this is another, Miss Jessica Jackson. She's doing the cookin', and believe me, she does it well. Right now, we need to talk."

Jessica nodded acknowledgement of the introduction, then turned back to her cooking, leaving Matt and Tad Hinds alone.

"Tad, I understand that you've led trains before."

"Yessir, I've brought cattle up the Chisholm, and the Santa Fe trails too."

"You must be older than you look!"

"Well sir, I started pretty young."

"I guess you've dealt with a few rustlers and Indians in your time."

"Yessir, I done my share, I guess."

"Well, if you take these folks, you may run into a little different trouble"

"Oh, how's that?"

"Well, as soon as I can ride, I'm going after a man named Floyd Jacobs. He signed on to lead these folks, and then he tried to rob 'em. If I can't find him, he's liable to try again, and it'll be up to you to see that it don't happen! You'll have to scout out pretty far, and keep the Jackson men informed. They are all good shots, so you can depend on 'em. They've already had one run in with Jacobs."

Tad thought a minute and asked, "What are you planning? Are you coming back to join us when you're finished, or if you don't find him?"

"I've got to get where I can ride first. But you can take over, and we can get back on the trail right away. Have you thought about what trail you want to take 'em on?"

"Well, I gave that some thought while we were riding back here. I thought the best way would be to take the Santa Fe Trail, 'cause it goes north of the meanest tribes of Indians, and you got a fort or two on the way. We can break off the trail after Fort Lyon, when we get into New Mexico territory. There's a few mountains, but we can stay east of them, and go straight down to Roswell. It'll be further that way, but I think it'll be safer."

"Sounds to me like you've got it worked out pretty good."

"Only thing is, we pass right through Cheyenne and Arapahoe country. Now if'n I can scout it out, and there ain't much activity when we get there, I just might drop down and cut across them staked plains. It'll be a whole lot shorter. 'Course it'll have to uv rained to fill them buffalo wallers."

"Yeah, it will. I hope I can catch up before you get that far. I got grain in one of the wagons. Your horse'll need more than just grass, if you scout out pretty far, and you're welcome to use it. I reckon the extra shoes I brought won't likely fit your horse, but you might make 'em fit, with a little effort."

"Well, I'm much obliged Matt, and I hope you get back on your feet soon."

"Thanks Tad. I think I'll go back to the wagon and lay down. It's all yours, now."

Matt eased to the wagon, and stepped upon the log placed there so he could climb into the wagon easier.

Jessica saw him head toward the wagon, and decided to take him a plate of food and coffee. Her father joined the group of men to talk about the trip. Mary Ann was filling canteens at the creek.

"Matt, may I come in?"

"Yes, Jessica, please do."

Jessica sat close beside Matt, as the space in the wagon was small. Matt put his arms around her, and pulled her tightly to him and kissed her.

"Oh, Matt! I don't want you to leave."

He placed his finger across her lips to quiet her, and then kissed her again. "I won't be gone long. I have an idea where Floyd is, and if I'm right, and he *is* there, I'll be back soon."

She kissed him once again, and left the wagon with tears in her eyes, and fear in her heart . . . She knew that she wanted to share her life with him.

After a week and a half, Matthew Forbes decided that he had 'laid-up' long enough. He was up before dawn, and gathered enough provisions and extra ammunition for a few days. He headed back toward the little settlement that had sprung-up around Westport Landing.

He arrived on the third day, a short time after noon, and his first stop was the blacksmith tent, where he arranged to stable Chico. With that task completed, he headed toward one of the saloon tents, to find a meal. The first two that he checked were not serving food.

The next tent he entered, he noticed to his left, the bar was just boards held up by barrels. A few tables and chairs were crowded into the limited space.

When he finished his meal, he put his money for the meal on the table, and approached the bartender.

"I'm lookin' for a feller named Jacobs, Floyd Jacobs. He been in lately?"

The bartender, wiping a glass replied, "Yeah, he and a couple o' guys I ain't seen before wus in a few days ago, but I ain't seem 'im lately. You might try a bar down the street. They don't come in here much, unless they want to eat."

"Well, much obliged anyway, and by the way the food was good."

"Glad ya liked it. Tell your friends," said the bartender, as he continued to wipe the same glass.

Matt stepped out into the street. His thoughts were of Jacobs, and the fact that he was probably gathering men for another raid on the Jackson's gold. As he approached another saloon, the rowdiness from inside became louder. He hesitated at the entrance, to observe the men inside. He didn't see Jacobs, so he moved to the bar.

"What'll ya have mister?"

"Maybe a beer and some information." said Matt.

"Ain't got either. No beer's come down the river yet, and it ain't healthy to put out information."

"I was lookin' for a man named Jacobs, and thought maybe you'd seen him."

As Matt was talking to the bartender, a man stepped up by him at the bar.

"What you want with Jacobs?"

"Well, Sir, that's my business." answered Matt.

"Well, my name's Jacobs . . . Henry Jocobs, and I'm makin' it my business, if yore lookin' for a Jacobs!"

"I'm lookin' for Floyd Jacobs. You'll not do!"

"He's my brother, and I'm making it my business! What'a you want him fer?" replied Henry Jacobs, who obviously had too much to drink.

He made a move toward Matthew. He was immediately subdued, and marched outside with his arm twisted up behind his back.

"I believe you've had a little too much booze. If I can find somethin' called a jail, I think you better sleep it off. Now, have you seen your brother, or not?"

"He was here the other day, and asked where a couple of his old friends were. I told him I didn't know, and what's more, I didn't care!"

The man turned suddenly, taking Matt by surprise, and twisted out of his grip. As he came around, he knocked Matt back into the hitching rack. But Matt reacted quickly, and instantly had his Colt in his hand. The action stopped as soon as Henry Jacobs was looking into the barrel of Matt's '44-40'.

Matt called out to a black man standing by the water trough, "I reckon you can handle a gun, can't you?"

"Yas Suh, I'us in the army, and I shoots purty good."

"Hold this gun on this man, while I tie his hands, and if I can't control him, shoot him."

"Yas Suh! I can do that." He took the gun from Matt, and leveled it toward the man.

Matt took leather strings from his chaps' pocket, and tied the man's hands behind him. He asked the black man, "You know where the jail is?"

"Yas Suh, I does, jist foller me."

"Lead the way. I'll be right behind you."

"Yas Suh! You wont yo're gun back now?"

"No, you keep an eye on this man, and we'll put him in jail to sleep it off."

The man calling himself Jacobs turned to Matt, "You ain't gonna let that nigger shoot me, are you?"

"If you don't behave, I will," answered Matt as he turned to the black man. "Thanks for your help . . . ah . . . I didn't get your name."

Jim Bolin straightened up, threw out his chest, and with pride said, "My name is James Edgar Bolin. I got it when I was twenty-one, and going into the army." He thought a minute, "'fore that I was' 'Nigger Jim'."

"Well, I'll just call you Jim."

They walked on to the jail that looked to be made of railroad ties. They were often used for jails in the west, because they were hard to blow up. Jim waited outside, as Matt took Henry Jacobs inside. The Sheriff was seated behind a large desk, with papers piled high. On the wall were several yellowed 'WANTED' posters.

Henry Jacobs had been silent. But now he staggered to the desk and told the Sheriff, "I want'a file a complaint against this man!"

The Sheriff looked up, and realized the situation. He asked, "What'd he do?"

"He tied my hands, and had a nigger hold a gun on me, and brought me here against my will."

"You 'spose he had a reason?"

"I don't know, but I don't like it!" grumbled Jacobs, pushing the words around his thick tongue.

Matt spoke up. "Sheriff, I'm Matthew Forbes, Federal Marshal, and I think he needs to sleep it off."

The Sheriff rose, took a set of keys from a hook behind the desk, and unlocked a cell. "Right this way, Mr. Jacobs. You just take it easy for a while, and I'll get us both something to eat later." As the Sheriff locked the cell, he turned to Matt. "Now, what's this all about?"

I'm lookin' for his brother, Floyd. When I asked about him in the saloon, Henry got a little belligerent."

"You're lookin' for Floyd?"

"Yes, Sir. He's believed to be the one that's been signin' on to lead wagons. When he gets close to Indian Territory, he robs and kills them, and leaves signs that blame the Indians, not that they are harmless."

"I've heard about that. Ole Henry there is harmless, and is in here every once in a while. I'll keep him 'till he sobers up a bit."

"I don't 'spose you'd have an idea about where Floyd could be found?"

"Naw, I hav'n seen him lately."

"Well, thanks anyway, Sheriff. Say . . . you wouldn't happen to have a deputy badge would you?"

The Sheriff stepped behind the big desk, opened a couple of drawers, and pulled out a deputies' badge, and handed it to Matt, "It's one that just says 'Deputy' on it."

"That'll be fine. He *is* my deputy, but he won't wear it a lot, just if he needs a badge. How much do I owe you?" asked Matt.

"It's an extra. I got a couple of new ones a while back, then I found that one under stuff on this here desk, so, it's yours."

"Thank you, Sheriff." He pocketed the badge and walked toward the door.

"Let me know how your hunt for the other Jacobs goes."

"I will, Sheriff."

Matt squinted against the bright sun outside, and finally spotted Jim in the shade, leaning on the jail. Matt's gun was tucked in his rope belt. He walked up to Jim and leaned beside him. Nothing was said for a few minutes. They watched as a wagon passed, followed by a spotted dog, trotting with his tongue hanging out. It was beginning to get hot. "Well, we've got one Jacobs in jail . . . I wonder where the other one is? Seems nobody's seen him lately."

"Yas Suh, seem's so."

"Jim, what are your plans now?"

"I reckon I'll look for a little work down ta tha docks, so's to buy my supper."

Matt watched a couple of riders go by, then asked Jim, "If'n you got a notion, I can give ya' some work."

"Yas Suh? How's zat?"

"I guess I'm gettin' old, or shot too many times, but on days like today, I need a little help. I'm offerin' you a job as deputy Marshall. It don't pay much, but if you're where you can buy 'em, it'll pay for three meals a day, and a little left over."

"Yas Suh, but I ain't gotta horse or a gun."

"Let me worry about that."

Both fell silent, deep in thought. Then Matt asked, tongue in cheek, "You think you can break away from this wonderful little settlement?"

"Yas Suh, I think I can do that."

"All right then! Let's get you outfitted. Here, pin this deputy badge on and raise you right hand." He watched as Jim pinned the badge on his ragged shirt, and then raised his hand. "Do you, Jim Bolin, swear to uphold the laws of the United States of America and its Territories?"

"Yas Suh, I reckon I does."

"All right then, you're a deputy United States Marshall. Now take the badge and put it in your pocket. I don't want anyone to know our business. Let's find somethin' for you to eat."

None of the places that served food to the public would allow Jim to come in, and Matt would not eat without him. So Matt offered to pay the blacksmith for lunch. His wife wouldn't' hear of him paying, and offered them both a fine meal.

Matthew enjoyed the food, even though it had not been long since he had eaten. They didn't know how long it might be before they could eat again.

When they had finished the meal, he said, "We are much obliged for your wife's hospitality, and perhaps you can tell me where I might buy a good horse."

Later, they both sat on the sale barn fence, watching the stock move around in circles. "See one you like, Jim? The man tells me the horses are all broke to saddle."

"Yas Suh! I shore does. I always wanted one them Injun ponies, and that brown and white'n would be awful nice!"

"You didn't know it, but when we bought your clothes and tack, I got you a rope too. So here, take it and catch you that horse. Show me what you can do."

"Yas Suh. I'll do just that!" he replied, as he grabbed the rope, and jumped in with the horses.

Matt watched as Jim pulled his loop in the rope, and moved in slowly toward the paint. When he threw his loop, the move was so fast Matt could hardly see it skim over three others, and around the neck of the paint.

"Looks to me like you've done that before!" smiled Matt.

Matt spent the afternoon gathering as much information as he could from those who had seen Floyd Jacobs. They saddled up and packed the supplies they would need for a few days. Then they headed in the direction they thought Floyd Jacobs might have gone.

Matt watched Jim out of the corner of his eye, and noticed he had a big smile on his face. He said nothing, waiting for Jim to speak.

Soon the silence was broken. Jim Bolin swelled his chest and spoke, almost in a laugh, "Mr. Matt, I don't know how I'us gonna thanks you. This shore is a fine horse, jist 'zactly what I always want."

"I expect you to back me up if I get in trouble, Jim . . . just do your job."

"Yas Suh, I can do that . . . I can shore do that."

"Well, I'll depend on it. We better be lookin' for a camp. It'll be dark 'fore long."

A grove of cottonwoods gave them a good campsite, with a stream running as clear as glass. They posted their horses, built a small fire, and put on the coffee. As they both leaned back on their saddles, Matt asked, "Jim, tell me about your family, how many brothers and sisters did you have?"

"I don't know zackly. We all got split up and sold separately. I worked in the fields 'till I'us twenty or so, an' I runs away while the war was goin' on. That's when I run on to a all nigger regiment and I joined them. That's how I got my name. They tolls me I had to have a name to git my pay, and that's how I got it."

"That's where you learned to shoot?"

"Yas Suh . . . and trackin' too. They had me trackin' them patrols and all. I gots pretty good at it."

"That's good to know Jim. I s'pose we'll be doing a lot of that." Matt set the coffee pot to the side of the fire, and rolled up in his blanket. "Good night, Jim."

"Yas Suh, good night."

"An' Jim, stop callin' me Sir, we're not in the army here."

"Yas Suh, I do that."

After breakfast the next morning, Matthew Forbes and Jim Bolin mounted up and headed southwest. The sun was trying to rise behind them, into a clear sky. Jim was still smiling about his paint horse, and asked, "Mr. Matt, where we goin'?"

"From all the information I could gather from people, Jacobs and his bunch were headed for Lawrence, over in the Kansas Territory. That'd be about right, 'cause I figger he's gettin' men together, to make another raid on the Jacksons."

"Yas Suh, I thought ole' Quantrell and his men done sacked and burned Lawrence down."

"I think it's comin' back. I 'speck Jacobs is just usin' it for a gatherin' place. If they get together in Lawrence, a southwest trail will intercept the Jacksons."

"Yas suh . . . I reckon them Jacksons must have lots o' gold, if'n a man would go to that much trouble to get his hands on it!"

"Nobody knows for sure how much they might have. They sold everything to head west on reinforced wagons so Jacobs *thinks* they have a lot."

Matt and Jim rode along the north side of the Kansas River, staying close to the trees, watching for Indians or other riders. It stayed cool as they rode in the shade.

"Mista Matt, Just how far is it to Lawrence?"

"It's about forty miles, as the crow flies . . . it's a shame we're not crows."

"Yas suh." Jim agreed with a smile.

After they had traveled about twenty miles, Matt saw three riders in the distance. Jim lagged behind and quickly rode farther north into the thick trees.

As Matthew rode closer to the approaching riders, their appearance caused him concern. Their clothes were well worn; their horses thin and they had no supplies.

Matt spoke first, "Howdy, you folks live around here?"

The three began to spread out from each other, and the one, obviously the oldest, answered. "Yeah, just over the hill there. You alone? This ain't a good place to be alone."

Matt looked around for Jim, and found that he *was* alone. "That's right. I'm headed to Lawrence."

The leader spoke again, "Folks might think a traveler that's alone would be easy to take his stuff, seein' as how you got good clothes and tack. That horse ain't bad neither. Maybe you got a few gold coins too."

"Folks might think that, but they would be wrong . . . Why? Is that what you're thinkin'?"

174

"Why, no! We just want to see that you have a good trip, as you pass through our land."

Matthew watched as the fellow talked. The others eased out a little further. Finally he spoke up. "That's far enough gentlemen."

"Why? What seems to be the problem?" asked the older man.

"I don't have a problem, but you fellers move again, you'll have a problem!"

The rider on the left spoke to the leader, "Pa, we done palavered enough, let's get this over with." As he spoke, he was pulling his gun. It had not cleared the holster before a rifle barked, and he was tumbling over the side of his horse. Jim had been watching from cover and took the shot. Matt saw that the man had been hit, before he got his own Colt drawn. Immediately, he fired at the man drawing his gun to his right. As the young man fell from his horse, he shouted. "Pa?" But 'Pa' couldn't hear, since Jim had shot him as he was pulling his gun.

"I wondered where you got off to." Matt greeted Jim.

"Yas Suh, when I seen 'em, I got 'spicious and decided ta check 'em out, 'fore we got in trouble."

"Well, I'm mighty glad you did. For thieves, they didn't look like they had been havin' much luck."

"I think there's a wash there on the river where these men can rest in peace. I'll move them, and we can shove enough dirt to cover 'em. Just as well throw in their tack too, since it doesn't look like it would last long."

"Yas Suh, them horses need some grain. If'n they wus any poorer, them ribs 'd be on the outside."

"Bring 'em along anyway, Jim. We'll do something with them."

The summer sun had burned the grass even this close to the river. The dust rose up and seemed to settle on everything, as they rode on toward Lawrence. Soon the sun was drifting toward the horizon, and a slight breeze started to blow.

"Mista Matt? I 'speck we need to find a good place to camp, as they's a storm a comin'."

"Jim, I'm not going to argue with you, 'cause I'm beginnin' to think you've got a sixth sense."

"Yas Suh, sometime I think I do."

"Well then, let's get a move on, if there's a storm comin'."

They both eased a spur against their mounts. After a while, they slowed to rest the horses. Matt spoke up, "I smell smoke, Jim!"

"Yas Suh, I shore do too."

"Maybe there's some settlers around here close. Use that sixth sense to locate them."

Thunder roared in the distance, and a dark blue cloud formed in the northwest. They began to worry about a place to get out of a storm that might carry hail, this time of the year.

The trees had wisps of smoke gently drifting through them, as the air had become completely still. The trees seemed to part ahead of them, to reveal a small log house, the source of the smoke they had been following. Behind it, was a barn with a few stalls and a dog run.

Matt rode up to the house, "Hellooo, the house." He waited for a reply. The door opened and a tall thin man, in bib overalls, stepped out, gently holding his shotgun. He looked at Matt and then at Jim.

"Howdy, you fellers ain't carpet-baggers are you?"

"No Sir, I'm Matthew Forbes and this is Jim Bolin."

"Well I heard that most of 'em carpet baggers were a white man and a negro travlin' together."

"No Sir, I'm a United States Marshall, and Jim is a deputy. We were wondering if we could weather this storm that's coming, in your barn."

A short, gray haired woman appeared at the door, wiping a wooden spoon on her apron.

The man answered Matt. "You shore can. They's a few empty stalls and plenty of hay, 'cause we ain't got no horses . . . lost 'em a while back, so help yourself. There's some grain in there, too."

The woman spoke up, "Then you men come in here and eat, suppers gonna get cold, if you don't hurry."

Matt responded quickly, as the storm was rolling in, and lightening was dancing across the sky. "Yes ma'am!"

He and Jim hurriedly stabled the horses, pitched them plenty of hay and some grain. Then they returned to the house, and washed up.

A round hand-hewn table, loaded with hot steaming food, impressed them, as they entered the cabin.

The lady of the house directed Mat and Jim to their chairs and said, "You boys sit down and the Mister will ask the blessing."

Matt spoke up, "I'm sorry, I told you our names, but I didn't get yours."

"Hatton, Bonnie and Sam."

After the prayer, Matt asked, "Mr. and Mrs. Hatton, we thank you very much. You said you lost your horses. How'd that happen?"

"Indians! Our cow was in the pasture so they missed her, and we still got chickens." answered Sam Hatton.

Matt looked at the couple and smiled. "Those extra horses we brought in? Well, two of 'em are yours. They need some lovin' care, but I'm sure you can handle that. We'll take one, in case we have to pack."

"Well, young feller, I'm much obliged! Are you sure?"

"We are. They were only a burden to us, on the trail."

Bonnie Hatton got up to get the coffee pot, "You boys eat up, now," and poured each a cup full.

Outside, the storm was raging, and hail began to roar against the house.

"I say again, we can't thank you enough for giving us shelter against this storm."

"Mr. Forbes, looks like we got the best of this deal. I'll be able to plow again, and have a big garden. I've slowed down a little, and I've only been able to hand plow a small plot, since we lost the horses."

"I'm surprised you don't have more trouble than you do."

"It's Arapaho mostly, but we have six or seven different batches from other tribes that come by. They just come this far east ever once in a while, beggin' food and coffee. They don't usually give us much problems."

"Mrs. Hatton, we've not had good food like this in a long time."

"Oh, the Lord has been good to us, and we're happy to share with such nice young men," the woman answered.

When they had finished eating, Sam Hatton invited them to sit and visit a spell, "We don't get many folks coming through here.

After a while, Matt listened for a moment, "Sounds like the rain has let up. Me and Jim had better make a run for the barn. Again, we sure enjoyed the meal, Mrs. Hatton."

"I'm glad you did. Now you boys come in for breakfast before you leave in the mornin'."

They both nodded and answered, "Yes ma'am!"

Chapter 17

The two men continued on their journey, after a filling breakfast. "Jim, I think we should split up when we get near Lawrence, just to play it safe. That way we can ask questions in several places."

"Yas Suh, that'll be a good idea, since I best not go into them saloons."

"Check out the places you think are safe, and don't take any chances."

It was late in the day, when they arrived in Lawrence. The sun was setting beneath the clouds that hung lazily in the sky, and with no breeze, it was still a bit hot. They rode to a livery stable, and took care of their horses. Matt went east, toward the saloons. Jim headed west, toward what he called 'Shanty Town'.

No one knew, nor had seen, anyone with the name of Jacobs, or anyone that fit his description.

Matthew and Jim had agreed to meet later at the boarding house. Matt got their rooms, and arranged to get food to eat in the room, to avoid any problems with troublemakers that always seemed to frequent saloons and boarding houses.

While getting the food, Matt took a chance and asked the waitress if Jacobs and his crew had been in.

The waitress squinted, and then answered. "Jacobs . . . I think so, about two days ago, I was working the hotel side, and he signed the register for himself and three other fellers. They only stayed one night."

Matt thought a minute. "I don't 'spose you heard anything about where they might be goin'?"

"No, I didn't . . . uh . . . wait a minute! I did hear one of them ask Harvey Tyner, he's an old stove-up trail boss, how far it was down to the Santa Fe Trail, if that helps any."

"Yes ma'am, that helps a lot! They've headed right where I thought they would."

The next day, Matthew outfitted their extra horse with a small pack, gathered supplies, and then they headed southwest, toward the Santa Fe Trail. They followed a rough trail that they hoped had been taken by Floyd Jacobs and his men.

"Jim, the moon will be full again tonight, and we've not worked the horses too hard. I think we should make up some time by ridin' as long as we can see. If you get tired, just let me know and we'll pitch a camp."

"Yas suh, that sounds good to me. I'm ready and this ole paint's still a jumpin'."

Matthew and Jim rode into the night, stopping only long enough to let the horses graze and rest, and then moving on.

When the moon dropped behind the horizon, Matt reluctantly confessed, "Moon's gone, Jim. Guess we ought'a stop 'till we get a little daylight. The land around here seems to be risin' and fallin', and we might fall in a deep canyon."

"Mista Matt, if my hearin' is still good, I think I hear runnin' water not too far to our left."

"I can't see my hand in front of my face, so we can look when mornin' gives a little light," repliad Matt.

Jim loosened the cinch on his saddle, and put his reins around the saddle horn, then took hold of the stirrup to let 'Ole Paint' lead him.

Matt listened, and then asked, "What in the world are you doing?"

Jim smiled and said, "Come on foller us." It was still dark.

Matt led Chico, and stayed close to the paint horse. It was only a few minutes until they found the source of the rushing water.

"I knew this ole horse could find that water in the dark. He's mighty smart!" Jim was grinning from ear to ear.

"Yeah, and he could'a found you a deep hole to fall into."

They watered the horses, filled their canteens and leaned against a tree.

Soon, before the sunrise, they had enough light to see where to go, and they were on their way.

They had ridden for miles with each of them snoozing in their saddles. But Matt was wide-awake when he rode upon a recent campsite, and dismounted to study the area. "Jim, looks like we're not far behind anymore. I figger four men spent the night here last night. They haven't been gone long, 'cause the ash is still warm."

Matthew asked Jim, "You gonna be all right? We can stop for coffee, if you want."

"Nah Suh, let's us get closer. Then, we can stop."

Matt swung into his saddle, "I like the way you think."

Jacobs' bunch was not expecting anyone. So the tracks they left were easy to follow, and Matt and Jim made good time catching up.

"We're getting' close, Jim! We better leave the trail and move into the trees."

They rode parallel to where they thought the men were riding. Jim stepped off Paint, and lay prone on the ground where he could see beneath the low hanging limbs of the trees. "Mista Matt, I can see their horses' legs movin' from here. They's about even with us, and a couple a hunert yards away."

"Good, Jim, if they're that close, let's stop a minute and decide how we can do this. I have enough on Jacobs to take him in. But knowin' him, he won't go without a fight. Are you ready for that?"

"Yas Suh, I'm ready. How we gonna do it?"

"We'll need to think on that. Accordin' to the gal back at the diner, there was three that registered with Jacobs, and we could see that four were at their camp, so we know that there will be at least four. We'll watch 'em 'till they make camp. Then see what our odds are, then decide what we wanna do."

The sun, sinking behind the trees, cast long dark shadows over the area where Jacobs and his men had pitched their camp. Matt crawled as close as he thought safe, and counted the men with Jacobs. They totaled four, counting Jacobs. Matt backed out of his hiding place, and joined Jim.

"They've pitched their camp near the river, and the horses are tied to one rope, on the west side of the camp. Try to work your way around that side, and when you're where the horses are tied, give a little bird whistle. You can do that, can't you?"

"Yas Suh, I can do that."

"It don't matter what kind of bird, just give it twice, when you get both ends of the rope loose. If the horses cause too much commotion, I'll distract the men with a couple of 44's. If they go quietly, I'll wait 'till you give the birdcall again. Then you watch the back of the camp, and I'll move in on them."

Matthew crawled toward the camp, and took up his position where he could watch. He waited for the second birdcall, telling him that Jim had moved the horses, and was in position.

It seemed an eternity, waiting for the second birdcall. He watched to see if any of the men were aware that the horses had been moved out. They were talking and laughing, passing a bottle around, and they didn't notice anything unusual.

When the second call came, Matt rose up and walked toward the men. He was practically standing by the fire before Jacobs saw him, and jumped up, starting to draw his gun. When he realized that Matt had both his Colt and his small shotgun on them, he changed his mind.

"What's the deal Forbes? What are you doing here?" asked Floyd Jacobs.

"I think you're well aware what I'm here for. You're under arrest."

Hearing that, one of Jacob's men foolishly pulled his gun. Matt let the shotgun emphasize the need for cooperation. "Now, before anyone else gets gun happy, I don't know if you've broken any laws or not. I expect you have, but I don't know of it, so I only want Jacobs. Matt leaned his shotgun against a tree. He told Jacobs to move toward him, backwards, with his hands behind him. Matt slipped his gun into its holster, and started to tie Jacobs's hands.

Seeing that Matt had put away his weapons, one of the other men pulled his gun. Suddenly, a stream of fire exploded from the trees behind them, and the man went down.

"As I said, I only want Jacobs. If you keep insisting on taking on lead, we can oblige you." Matt then told the one man left, "You will have to walk a ways, but your horse will be tied near the river, and you'll be free to leave. Right now, just set down and wait a while."

Matt backed out, staying behind Jacobs, and headed toward his horse. He met Jim, who had brought Jacobs' horse to the same place, as they had agreed. Matt helped Jacobs onto his horse, and tied him to his saddle. Jim took one of the horses, and tied it by the river, for the only man left.

Jim had taken one of the better horses to replace the old 'crow-bait' as a packhorse. Part of the supplies was left for the lone rider. The rest were loaded on to their own packhorse.

The three riders crossed the Kansas River and rode south to join the Santa Fe Trail. They reached the trail four days later, and headed toward Fort Larned.

Several hours went by before they found a heavy grove of trees growing along the river. It looked inviting, so they decided to take time to rest and let the horses graze. Matt and Jim dismounted and tied their horses a few steps away. Before they could turn to take

Jacobs from his horse, he dug his heels in and the horse leaped forward into a run.

They were startled by the sudden rush, and it took a moment for them to get their horses to pursue Jacobs. A short distance ahead, they found Jacobs lying on his back under a tree. His wrists were bleeding from the leather tied to the saddle. He had not counted on his horse running under a low hanging limb. His hands were tied and he had no way to control the running horse. "Jim, it looks like a little fire might'a gone out of our prisoner."

"Yas Suh, shore does, don't it?" Jim smiled.

"Well, Jacobs, I reckon you'll feel the results of this little freedom try all the way to the Fort Larned."

Jacobs just glared at Matt, and spit dirt out of his mouth.

They found the horse he was riding a short distance ahead, contentedly grazing by the river.

After resting a while, and tending to Floyd Jacobs' wrists, they tied him again to his horse. The sun was well toward the middle of the cloudless sky.

A few hours later, Matt pulled up. "Well Jim, there's the Fort up ahead. It appears to be on the south side of the Pawnee River. Keep an eye out. There should be a place to cross pretty soon."

"Yas Suh. Boy, you can see plumb into tomorrow out here. What happened to the trees?"

"They don't many grow out here on the plains."

"Yas Suh, I reckon that's why they ain't got a tall fence around the fort. But they does have a gate" A gate had been erected with the fort's name across the top. When they arrived at the gate, Matt asked the guard at the entrance where he could find the commanding officer.

The Corporal pointed out the sandstone building where the Colonel's office could be found.

Matt and Jim tied their horses to the hitching rail. Jim sat down in the shade of the building. Matt stepped up on the board porch, lifted the latch and walked in.

The orderly was not at his desk, but the Colonel behind the large cluttered desk in the next office, looked up, "Come in. I'll be with you in a minute. All this paperwork has to at least make it into my 'out-box' . . . have a seat."

Soon, the Colonel tossed a pile of papers into the box on the desk marked 'OUT', and asked Matt "What can I do for you?"

Matt rose to shake the Colonel's hand. "Colonel, I'm Marshall Matthew Forbes, and I need to leave a prisoner with you until the circuit judge comes by here."

"What's he done, Marshall?"

Matthew explained the charges against Floyd Jacobs to the Colonel.

"If you're not going to be here, do you have proof for a trial?" asked the Colonel.

"Yes, Sir, I do. It's all here in my report. All his men were killed when he attacked a group headed to New Mexico Territory. He shot me and I was laid up for quite a spell. I just now caught up with him." explained Matt, as he dropped an oil skin packet of papers on the Colonel's desk, "It's all in there."

"You wouldn't be talking about the Jackson group would you?" asked the Colonel.

Matt looked up at the Colonel, "Why, . . . yes sir, I would! Do you know of them?"

"They came by here about a week ago and stayed a few days, led by a young fellow by the name of . . . Let's see . . . Hinds, yeah, Tad Hinds."

"That's the group that was attacked. We're trying to catch up to them."

"I see. Well we can put your prisoner in the billeting compound 'till the judge comes next month. I'll read your report and give it to the judge. I'll serve as a witness too, since the Jacksons explained to me about the raid."

"I thank you very much, Colonel."

"If you plan to spend the night, we have some empty bunks in the barracks you're welcome to use."

"If you don't mind, Sir, I think a short rest will do, and then we will move on to overtake the Jacksons."

"Well, you're also welcome to some food and supplies before you go. You're not likely to find much in these parts. Take on as much water as you can carry. It's dry 'til you get over the divide."

"I'm much obliged to you, Colonel! That will be a big help, as we're running short on most supplies. Did Tad give you any idea how he planned to go?"

"Yes he said they would head down to Doans' Crossing, once they hit the Western Trail."

"That means they will cross the 'staked plains', once they get into Texas. I only hope they'll find plenty of water." considered Matthew.

"I can't help you there. In April of this year, they established Fort Dodge, and they have water there. But you won't go that far north, if you're going to Doans' crossing. Anyway, it's good to know, in case you get into trouble."

The Colonel saw to it that they had plenty of supplies before they left.

Matt and Jim headed off toward the south. Floyd Jacobs yelled, as they led him to one of the buildings, "I'll see you in hell, Forbes!"

"I'm planning on the army hanging you, so tell the devil I don't plan on joining you there!" retorted Matthew.

As they rode from the fort, Matt spoke, "Well Jim, we kinda got a late start, but they said to travel along the Arkansas River, and we would hit the Western Trail.

"Yas Suh, that's just fine wi' me." Jim smiled as he patted his paint horse on the neck.

Matthew grinned and asked Jim, "I've not heard you call that horse you're so proud of, anything but 'Paint'. What is his name?"

Yas Suh, that *is* his name . . . 'Paint'."

"Well, that sure fits him." Matt smilingly agreed.

They rode south and west, across a barren plain that seemed to never end, with no trees except what grew along the river. Dust rose up and swirled around, and gently settled back over the prints left by their horses' hooves. Soon the trail started across the divide, and the going got slower.

With a full moon rising early in the evening, they rode well into the night, stopping only long enough to brew coffee, and let the horses graze and rest.

Jim was leaning against a tree, chewing on a string of jerky. You know Mista Matt, I shore am proud of that lil' ole paint horse. He doin' real good."

"Yeah, Jim, so you've been telling me. We were lucky to find him. As soon as he, and the other two, fill up and get rested, we'll catch up to the Jacksons."

"Yas Suh, I's ready for one of them dinners that you been braggin' about, that Miss Jackson whoops up."

"Well Jim, you won't be disappointed."

Chapter 18

They rode across the line into Oklahoma Territory, and soon came to the Canadian River. They took on as much water as they could, and turned south toward the Western Trail.

"The next stop is the Red River, and Doan's store at the crossing. Hopefully, we'll catch up to the Jacksons. I hate to say it, but we'll be crossing Indian Territory, where a lot of different tribes will be after our scalps. We better keep a sharp lookout. They can hit pretty quick."

"Yas Suh."

As they traveled south on the Western trail, Matt spotted a column of smoke, a couple of miles ahead. They had ridden far enough that trees and mountains blocked the origin of the smoke. So Matt rode to the top of a rise, to look down into the canyon ahead. He scanned the area with his field glasses.

Hurriedly, he rode back to where Jim was waiting, "Jim, lets move on down there. There's a wagon burning. I didn't see anyone around, but keep a look out for any movement."

Approaching the smoking wagon, Matt slowed to watch for anyone lurking about. Jim stayed back on the edge of the clearing.

Matt circled the wagon, checking for any bodies, or signs of life. Then he motioned for Jim to come on in, while looking for salvageable materials.

"What 'cha think, Mista Matt?"

"It's one of the Jackson wagons all right. No bodies of Indians or the Jacksons, so I 'speck they all carried their dead with 'em . . . Plenty of brass around, and arrows, so I reckon there was a hefty fight . . . Looks like it was Kiowa. I guess the Jackson folks took what they could from the wagon."

Matthew and Jim rode at a fast pace, pausing occasionally to rest the horses.

"That fight took a while, from the looks of the tracks that were around the wagon, so maybe if we ride hard, we'll be able to overtake them."

"Yas Suh, these ponies are doing pretty good, cause we ain't pushed too hard."

"Just lookin' at the wagon tracks we've been followin', I've not seen any sign that look like they're bein' followed, so maybe they'll be safe 'till we catch up."

The sun was sinking behind the hills, and it was beginning to get dark when they spotted a campfire, not too far ahead. "Jim, it looks like we may have caught up to the Jacksons."

Matt had just finished speaking, when a voice yelled out, "That's far enough! I got several guns on you. Now, you fellers move on in closer to the light!"

Matt spoke up, "That you, Everett?"

"Well, I'll be doggone! Matt? We never expected to see you again. Get down and come on in. Who's that with you?"

"This is Jim Bolin, Everett. He's my deputy. Jim, this is Everett Jackson, the head of the folks we been chasing all this time."

"Yas Suh, Mista Jackson, I's glad to meet ya."

"Well, you fellers come on in. Jessica's cookin' up supper now."

"How is Jessica, Everett?"

"She's fine, Matt. And she's gonna turn flips when she sees you! She's kinda been moanin' about never seein' you again."

We saw your wagon a ways back. Is every body okay?"

"We lost Howard's son, Warren, but the rest made it all right." We cut 'em down to size, and they grabbed their dead and took off.

"I'm sorry to hear that about Warren. As I recall, he was a good help on that Jacobs attack. I guess you'd like to hear that we got Floyd Jacobs, and left him locked up at Ft. Larned. I understand that Tad Hinds is still with you."

"That's good to hear about Jacobs, Matt, I reckon he'll get what he deserves, and yes, Tad is still with us. Quite a shot, that feller is! Kinda taken a likin' to our Mary Ann."

Matt was relieved that Tad's interest was in Mary Ann and not Jessica.

Jessica came around the wagon, near the cook fire. She found a gap in the harness on the tongue and stepped across. As she did, she looked up and saw

189

Matt. She dropped what she was carrying, and ran to Matt, threw her arms around him, and kissed him. She hung on his neck and began to cry. Between sobs, managed to say, "I thought you were dead, and never coming back."

Matt eased her back, looked into her eyes, "Why nothin' could keep me away, you know that!"

"I was beginning think that Jacobs had killed you, or you found some saloon girl"

"I did see a few of those." said Matt, laughingly.

"Oh . . . Matt!" exclaimed Jessica.

After a long embrace, Matt told her, "I want you to meet a feller that's been traveling with me, and all he can think about is eating one of your famous meals. Jessica, this is my deputy, James Bolin. I call him Jim."

'Hello, Jim, glad to meet you. And dinner will be ready in just a little while."

"How do, ma'am, and I'm shore lookin' forward to it," said Jim as he took a deep breath, to smell the food cooking.

Matt turned to Everett Jackson, "Have any troubles other than the Kiowas?"

"Wagons broke down a couple a times, lost a wheel, but I think we can have it fixed, or get another at Doan's. We only salvaged one from the burnin' wagon. We need to do a little work in the mornin', 'afore we get started."

"I'm a little worried about water across the staked plains. Maybe we can locate someone that has been through there to find out if it's rained. The buffalo wallers will be full across there, if they've had good rains . . . though they won't stay full long!" said Matthew Forbes.

"Tad seems to think that this time of year, it rains quite a bit, and if anybody's made a dugout and lived there awhile, they may have a well or cistern." answered Everett.

"We can only hope and pray."

Jessica started to bang on a pot with a spoon, "Come an' get it!"

No one needed a second call! Everett and Matt stepped closer to the fire, and sat wherever they could lean back. Tad Hinds, followed by Mary Ann and the other Jacksons, came around the wagon by the fire, and picked up their plates.

Jessica ladled food into plates and noticed that Jim had held back. "Jim you better get in here, or they'll eat it all up from you! By the way, you folks say, 'How do' to Jim Bolin! He's Matthew's deputy marshal. If you haven't noticed, Matthew came in a while ago."

After their greetings, Jim moved away from the fire, and sat next to a wagon.

Everett rose to ask the blessing. "Dear Lord, it's been a trying trip, this far. And we hated loosing Warren. Hold him in your hands, Lord. You've blessed us with a minimal amount of trouble, and we thank you for that. We thank you for bringing back Matthew to us. Lord, bless this food, and may we go on with your blessing, we ask in Jesus's name, amen."

Tad sat by Matt, and Mary Ann slipped in beside Tad. She looked toward Matt, and when she saw him smiling, she blushed and looked away.

"Tad, seems like you've done a good job, so far, and I thank you."

"Yes Sir, I've tried." answered Tad Hinds.

"Well, keep up the good work. Jim and I will trail along with you, just in case you need help." said Matthew.

"Thank you, Mr. Forbes, I appreciate that. We can use all the help we can get."

"I know you have some work to do in the mornin'. I'll ask Jim to stay here to help out, while I do some scoutin'. I need to see if the Kiowa went back to their camp, or if they're still roamin' this area. Then I'll join you later."

"Sounds like a good plan. I don't get a chance to scout much, for havin' to stay close to the wagons. I can't afford to lose another one."

Matt turned to Mary Ann, "How've you been getting' along, Mary Ann?"

She nearly choked on her food, and continued to look down at her plate. "I'm fine, Matthew."

"That's good. I'm glad to see you and Tad getting along so well." He silently wondered what had happened to Michael, the boy she had seemed so serious about. He guessed that the old adage,'Time changes everything', was true.

She hurriedly changed the subject, "Have you had a chance to talk to Jessica since you've been back?"

"Not much, yet. She's pretty busy cookin', I'll see her after we clean up the camp site."

When the dishes and pots were all cleaned and put away, Matt asked for another cup of coffee that was still heating by the fire. The sun was just about down, and the clouds that were still hanging above the horizon were shining bright golds and pinks.

Matt watched Jessica's every move, as she poured his coffee. "I think if we hurry, we can capture another sunset like the one we watched before."

"I'd like that, Matt. I've missed you more than I can say."

"The same here, I've thought of you every day."

Matt set his cup down, and took Jessica by the hand. They slowly walked away from the wagons. A cool breeze was drifting from the east, and the sunset reflected in the stream.

They watched the horizon a minute, and then Matt took her in his arms. "You can't imagine how much I've missed you." He drew her closer and kissed her. She placed her head against his shoulder, as they watched the sun sink behind the hills.

Next morning, the sky was still dark but filled with stars, as Matt saddled Chico. In the still of the cool morning, Matt's thoughts were of Jessica, and completing this trip so he could ask her to marry him. *"I'm not sure if she'll want to marry a U.S. Marshall and I'm not sure what else I could do. I gotta be able to take care of her. But, is it fair to ask her to wait for me, whenever I have to be gone?"*

Matt completely circled the area where the wagons had camped; looking for any tracks or signs. He was satisfied that no Indians had followed them.

It was still early in the morning, as he scouted further out from the group. He found a spring coming from beneath slabs of rocks. Time had loosened large pieces of sandstone, which had slid down the side of a tall butt. "Chico, we just as well try some of that cool, clear water. What'a you think?"

He lifted his canteen that was loopped over the horn of his saddle, and bent down to fill it. Suddenly, an arrow hit the water, and slid up on the grass with no force at all.

He turned, and saw five or six Indians riding fast toward him. They were still a good distance away. *"So that's why that arrow had no steam . . . they were too far away!"*

He quickly slid his Winchester from its scabbard, grabbed his saddlebags with his ammunition, and slapped Chico with his bags. He knew that Chico would head for the wagons. "That should get someone's attention, and maybe help will come."

As more arrows chipped away at the rock he was trying to get behind, he noticed an Indian riding to catch Chico, and fired from the hip. He watched the Indian fall, and then squeezed behind one of the slabs that stood near the spring.

The space behind the rock was tight, and he had trouble turning around where he could get a shot. When he finally managed to get in position, his rifle roared again, and another Indian fell. He kept firing, hoping that the shots could be heard at the wagons. He was worried, as no rifle shots came from the Indians, only a lot of arrows. The arrows were deadly, but his shots would be the only warning sounds.

After a few extra shots to alert help, he decided that he had better start making each shot count. Arrows were coming from everywhere, it seemed. His limited view made it hard to see from which direction they came.

As he leaned to his right to look around the rock, an arrow glanced off the rock next to him, and cut between his arm and ribs. Quickly, he untied his neckerchief, and stuffed it under his arm, while continuing to shoot at every movement.

By late evening, the Indians had apparently had enough. Only two were left, so he allowed them to place their dead on their horses and leave.

He waited to make sure they were gone before trying to leave his safe spot. When he finally tried, he found that he was too weak to move. The space was so tight, that when he finally passed out, he didn't fall, but was almost standing upright.

When he revived, the sun was dropping behind the hill. Shadows were long. He shook his head to get the cobwebs out, and tried to shift to a more comfortable position. But he was wedged tighter than his ebbing strength could move him.

He was unable to pull his neckerchief from his wound. He figured that the bleeding had stopped, as the blood dried. *"Surely Chico went to find help . . . they had to hear the gun shots . . . why hasn't anyone come? Maybe Chico's croppin' grass out there, waitin' for me."* He couldn't hold his head up, and passed out again.

* * *

When Matt awoke, he was lying in a bed, in one of the wagons. Jessica was applying cool spring water towels to his forehead. His wound had been cared for and was bandaged.

Matt asked in a slow halting voice, "Jessica? I thought no one would find me, unless I was awake and could yell to anyone that came for me. How did you find me?"

"Jim found you. When Chico finally caught up with us, we were miles down the trail, and then it took Jim a while to locate where you were. He said he back-tracked Chico, and when he got there, he could see part of your hat hanging out from behind the rock. He said if not for that he would never have found you!"

"Well, I'm glad he did, so you would have a chance to take care of me again."

"I like taking care of you! But you won't get much work done, being in bed all the time. What happened anyway?"

"I stopped for water, and about five or six . . . I think they were Kiowa, but I'm not sure . . . they started flingin' arrows a little out of their range, and it gave me time to get ready for them. They didn't have rifles. That seemed strange, but they attacked anyway. I think I got most of them, but I saw two gather up the others, and put them across their horses. I couldn't shoot any more. I'm glad they attacked *me*, instead of finding you and your family."

"You get some rest, Mr. Forbes! I'll see you in the morning."

"But I just woke up! Haven't I been resting?"

Jessica was leaving the wagon. "Yes, about two days. Now go to sleep and I'll see you in the morning. It's late!"

Matt stared at the canvas ceiling, *"Two days! How could I'uv been out for two days? She must be kiddin'."*

Tad Hinds came by and looked in the wagon. "Jessica told me you woke up. How are ya doing?"

"I'm not sure. Have I really been out for two days?"

"Yep, two days. You had lost a lot of blood."

"Well, where are we?" Matt asked.

"We should pull into Doans' tomorrow, if the ole Red's not floodin'."

Can you help me find my clothes? I feel like getting' up."

"You were in pretty bad shape, when they got you back here. You oughta take it easy for a while."

"I'll take it easy with my pants on a whole lot better."

Jim walked up, and looked into the wagon, "Think you'll make it, Mista Matt? I reckon if you don't, I can eat your share of the fine meals Miss Jessica puts together. You shore wus right about good cookin'."

"I'm beginnin' to think that food is all you think about, Jim!"

Chapter 19

The crossing of the Red River was uneventful, save for the fact that Jessica's Bible got a bit wet.

Jessica took her Bible and thumbed through it, "Why didn't you warn me? I had all our records in here."

Tad Hinds, riding by her wagon, spoke up, "I'm sorry ma'am but I thought you knew we were gonna cross the river, and things might get wet."

"I know, but I didn't think it would get up in the wagon!"

Matthew smiled, "Look at the record pages and see if they're smeared. You did them in pencil, so they should be all right Of course, the book'll be swollen after it dries, but you can still read it to me. If it's not okay I'll buy you a new one at Doan's."

"I don't want a new one. I want this one!"

She thumbed through the pages, and smiled a little, "You were right, the names and dates are okay. I'll carry it on the wagon seat, until it dries."

Everett Jackson walked up, "Bible get wet, Sis?"

"Yes it did, Papa, but it'll be all right. What did you find out about the wheel?"

"They had a new one, so we've got our spare back, and we can move on."

Matt had his clothes on, and was speaking as he was exiting the wagon, "Everett if they have another wagon, maybe a used one in good shape, and some water barrels that are not too expensive, I'll buy 'em. We still got that extra team, and we'll need to take a little grain and extra water, in case the plains are dry."

Everett answered, "I'll go check. I'm just glad we were able to save the team and harness from the wagon we lost.

"A man in the store, that just came across the plains, said it had rained 'pretty good', and the buffalo 'wallers' were full, and the grass is so high you could lose a cow in it. One thing though, he says we'll have to gather buffalo chips, 'cause there's no wood to burn."

"It'll be a good idea to carry as much wood as we can, and cut more when we find it," said Tad.

Outfitted again, and with an extra wagon, they got on their way. Matthew consented to ride on a wagon, until he got a little stronger. Jim did the extra scouting with Tad.

Two of the smaller boys had taken on an orphaned prairie dog to raise, and to scare the girls. That seemed to be their favorite game, while the adults were busy with their work.

The grass was tall, and it cut down on the wind flow. During the heat of the day, it made it even hotter for those that walked. Sides of bacon wrapped in brown paper, and tied to the side of the wagons, dripped fat, from the late day heat. Buffalo chips were plentiful, and gave them a source of fuel for cooking.

As all were gathered around having the evening meal, Tad volunteered, "I saw buffalo north o' here this mornin'. They wus purdy far up there, though."

Everett looked at Matthew, "We could use more meat. Reckon we could get one?"

Matt thought a minute, before he answered. "I might get one, but I'd have ta get awful close to get 'im with my 44-40 rifle."

"Indians ride close when they use a bow and an arrow. I reckon we could too." said Tad.

"If you'll haze for me, I'll give it a try," replied Matt.

Next morning, Matthew, Tad, and Jim were ready to leave before the sun turned the morning gray.

As they were riding out, Matt called to Everett, "We'll try to not be long . . . keep a sharp lookout."

They headed in the direction where Tad had seen the buffalo the day before. After an hour or two of scanning the area with his glasses, Matt spotted a buffalo hump of a lone grazing bull just above the tall grass and headed toward it. When they got closer, the bull was on a rise. The land dipped quickly on the other side, and in that low valley-like area there were what looked like hundreds of buffalo.

"Let's go after that first one we seen. We could gets run over if'n we gets down in that valley with all them others." analyzed Jim.

Matt smiled and answered, "Sounds about right to me, Jim."

He suggested to Tad, "See if you can circle around the other side, and we'll squeeze him a little, and Jim, drag back in case he turns."

"Yas Suh." Jim moved in the area behind, and stood by, while Tad made it to the other side of the animal that, so far, was more interested in eating than watching them.

Matthew started riding toward the buffalo. The big bull looked up, and started to move away, but Tad was there to make him go straight. When the bull noticed Tad, he began to run. Both Matt and Tad started running on both sides, and just as Matt raised his rifle to shoot, the bull turned quickly toward Tad. The massive shoulder and the weight of his large hump, hit Tad's horse, just as they were passing a muddy wallow. Both Tad and his horse slid down, and skipped across the muddy expanse. Tad came up spitting, and his horse came up shaking.

Matthew bit his lip to keep from laughing, "'Spose we try that again, Tad."

"Yeah, that's easy for you to say. I gotta find a waller that's got some sorter clean water in it first, and clean some of this mess off. You just keep your eye on that bull, 'cause that's the one I want!"

Matt rode after the bull, and kept him from joining the big herd.

When Tad was cleaned up a little, he shouted to Matt, "Okay, let's get after it."

Once again they managed to get the bull moving, as they had before. This time Matt was able to get a shot, and quickly jack in another shell then fired again. The buffalo began to slow from the shots, then finally dropped and was finished.

"Be mighty careful Tad. If he's like a deer, he may come up swingin'!"

"I will. Boy, Matthew! This thing will weigh over two thousand pounds if it weighs an ounce!"

"It does look like it. Jim, while Tad and I dress 'im out, it would be a good idea if you went back, and sent a wagon up here for the meat. We couldn't carry much on our horses. And Jim, let someone else drive the wagon. You best stay with the Jacksons. With this many buffalos around, there could be Kiowah or

199

Apaches huntin' this area. We don't want them to find the Jacksons."

"Yas Suh, I'll get 'em started this way soon."

When Matt and Tad rejoined the Jackson outfit, a lot of hoots and hollers greeted Tad.

"Hey Tad, I understand you went lookin' for fish, too while you wus gone huntin'." shouted Josh Jackson.

"Yeah, well I plan to use some of your drinkin' water to clean up with!"

With the wagons on the way again, Matt rode out for miles, scouting and watching for Indians.

Travel went well, with them encountering only a few rough spots, until they reached the edge of the Llano Estacado.

Matt came back to the wagons to let the Jacksons know that he and Tad had found a campsite. They had been traveling between two rivers and picked a site along the southern most river. It was decided to stop here, because they had reached the headwaters, and water was scarce. They dug holes in the bottom of the river that filled with water overnight. That gave them enough water to keep their barrels topped off, and to water the livestock.

Around the fire that night, they had everyone report on their rations and their water supply.

Matt summarized, "As I figger, we've got about two hundred more miles before we reach Roswell, in maybe a month or so. So we need to plan as to what we are goin' to need, and what we're goin' to run out of. I've seen some signs of Indians. They weren't fresh, but they were there. I also saw signs that the buffalo herds move the way we're headed. There are also some antelope, but they can outrun a horse, so I'm not sure if I can get close enough to shoot one. We needed to u've picked up a Sharps rifle, for these long shots here on the plains."

"Tad spoke up, "and I've seen a bunch of small game, and the birds are plentiful . . . everybody's got a shotgun, I reckon."

"We should do all right on food, since game seems plentiful. It's the water that we'll have to conserve, and scout for more," added Everett Jackson.

Josh Jackson poured himself more coffee, "Little Aubry has been drivin' the wagon for a while, and doin' just fine. I been just settin' the whole time . . . I could ride out in another direction, an' that would give four of us lookin' for water."

"That's a good idea Josh, but I want Jim to stay with the wagons. I don't want to leave them without protection. So far, the attacks have been without guns, only arrows, but make no mistake, the Indian ponies are trained to run right up against a buffalo, to give an Indian a better chance to kill it . . . and they can do the same to you! So don't' try to run away. If they don't have a gun, stand pat and shoot 'em." advised Matt.

Tad suggested, "We ought to be able to see 'em in this flat country, before they get within two miles."

"Don't bank on it! Somehow an Indian can just appear!"

* * *

Next day, they were on the trail well before sunup. The morning air was cool and refreshing, but they knew it would get hot later. The trail was dusty in places, and in others, the grass was tall. As they traveled, they continually gathered buffalo chips, and placed them in the skins hanging beneath the wagons. They collected some of the tall grass to use as starter for their fires when they camped where no grass grew.

Living conditions were getting worse, by the day, with increasing heat making them miserable. Lips split, and hands chapped during the dry times. And when it looked like a little rain might fall, they would each grab a corner of a clean tarp, and catch as much water as they could, and pour it in their barrels.

While scouting for water, Matt and Tad met near a small rise, and just sat staring toward the west, saying nothing for a while. Then after a big sigh, Matt spoke up, "Didn't see any springs, or any place that looked like a spring might be hidden. How 'bout you?"

Tad spit out the stem of grass he had been chewing on to hold back his thirst. "Nothin' yet, but we've not covered a lot of territory. I know there are springs somewhere not too far off. I can almost smell 'em."

"I've just been ridin' and lookin', but I guess I need to watch insects and animals a little closer. They may show us where a little water is. Then again, they may get enough from grass, like you been doin'. It would be good to find somethin' soon." As Matt spoke, he noticed in the distance, a puff of smoke rise slowly into the air. "Tad, I see smoke on the horizon! Go back and stop the wagons, and be prepared for anything! I can't tell if it's Indians sendin' signals, or some dumb white man a buildin' a fire bigger than he needs. Remind the Jacksons they need to be prepared. I'll get closer. There are a lot a washes and little canyons I can ride through."

"Right away, Matt. You be careful."

Tad jobbed his spurs into his mount, leaving a trail of dust as he headed back to the wagons. Matt eased down into a shallow wash, and started to make his way toward the smoke.

He wound his way through the little canyon, and when he rounded a turn in the wash, he heard a voice, "That'll be far enough, Mr. Forbes."

As he stopped and looked up, on the edge of the wash stood Floyd Jacobs! Matt was looking up into the barrel of a '45'.

Jacobs chuckled, "I told you I'd see you in hell!"

"Just how did you get away from the army, Floyd?"

"It's good to have friends, Matthew! Since the fort had no fence, it was easy for the man you let go to pull a window out of the building."

"What are you doin' out here? You been followin' since Fort Larned?" Matt asked.

"It'll be worth the trip. I saw how them Jackson wagons had been shored up underneath. They was carryin' a heavy load, not only their stuff, but gold. A lot of it too, I figger! Worth my while to look."

Matt knew he didn't have a chance to draw, and live. He noted that Jacobs had drawn his gun, but hadn't cocked it yet. So he watched, and listened for Jacobs to thumb back the hammer on the '45'. As soon as he heard the first of the four clicks that a Colt makes hammering back, he immediately piled off the opposite side of Chico, into the sand that covered the bottom of the wash.

Jacobs' shot went wild, and clipped the end of Chico's ear. The horse jumped back, giving Matt a clear shot at Jacobs. Instantly black powder smoke filled the air and through the smoke, he saw Jacobs falling, and then rolling down into the wash. He watched to see if Jacobs would move again. He then walked over to check him. He was dead.

Matt heard a rider coming, but couldn't see out of the wash. He was ready for the rider to come close to the edge of the wash. Then he collapsed, as he saw that it was Jim.

"Mista Matt, you all right?"

"Yeah Jim, I guess, another close call," he said, as he picked up his hat, and used it to knock off the sand he had picked up from the bottom of the wash. As he was looking down, he saw that where he had fallen into the sand was a darker color. He stooped down, and picked up a handfull. "Jim, this sand is wet under the top surface! We can get water here! But let's get it later. We had better see who's at that fire we saw."

"Yas Suh. I brung a shoval 'cause I figgered we'd need it. We's always buryin' somebody."

"Later, on both counts, Jim. Let's see how many men Jacobs had with him. I can't figger how they got ahead of us, and we never saw them."

"Well Mista Matt, they din't have no wagons to worry about!"

Matt and Jim continued to ride in the soft sand of the wash, toward where Matt had seen the smoke.

They rode up out of the wash, approaching the camp. Jacobs' men thought it was him returning, and were slow reacting. When they realized that it was not Jacobs, the three of them rose, and started firing. Matt and Jim were prepared, and began firing as they rode hard toward the men.

Two men went down immediately, and the third raised his hands in surrender. Matt stepped down, and disarmed the last man. He then began to check the others, to see if they were alive. When Matt turned his back, the man slipped a gun from his boot. There was a loud report from two guns. Jim's bullet penetrated the man, just as he got his own shot off, and he went down. His bullet knocked the heel off Matt's boot, as he went down.

"You all right, Mista Matt?"

"I guess so. Looks like he hit the heel of my boot. Dang, those are my best boots!"

Matt kept grumbling, and limped over to Jim, and took the shovel. "I'll start the buryin'. I shore hope the ground here's not too hard!"

"Yas Suh, I'll catch up the horses, and see what supplies they has. They won't be needin' 'em."

"Good idea, Jim. When we finish here, we need to dig some holes for water in that wash that looked wet." Matt looked up at Jim and grinned, "Guess we better bury Floyd Jacobs 'fore he wakes up and gives us trouble again!"

On their return to the wagons, Matthew stepped off Chico, and was limping toward where everyone had gathered. Jessica ran to him. "Matthew! Are you hurt? You're limping! Are you all right?"

"Yes, I'm fine, Jessica. I just lost the heel off my best boots."

As everyone gathered around Matt, he told them, "We need to move closer to the wash, before we camp. We should be able to fill our barrels, if the water turns out to be good. We'll have plenty for the livestock.

After the climb up onto the Llano Estacado, the trip across the plains moved well. The rather flat country was easier on the livestock, and they had no trouble with Indians. Jim Bolin had ridden toward the north and Matthew to the south. They were able to locate enough water each time they thought they were running out.

That evening, when the sun was resisting that last slip behind the horizon, and the sky was filled with the gold of another Texas sunset, Jim Bolin was the last rider to come in. "Well, I founds out why we ain't been attacked by Injuns. I found a lone dugout way up north. Fokes wus homesteadin' up there, and they tole me that the Injuns wus stayin' mostly in a canyon that's filled with buffalo. They said the Spanish called it Palo Duro."

Matthew listened, and then responded, "That means 'Hard Wood'. If it's anything like here, it means 'Hard to find Wood'. If the Indians are staying up there, maybe we won't have any more trouble."

After an early start, and miles of travel, the wagons heading west pulled the sun up from its eastern hiding place, to give a cool bright morning. The livestock were well watered, and given a little extra time to feed on the good grass growing in the area. Their destination was just a day or so further, if they had no trouble.

Matthew and Jim decided to move on ahead to ask about the exact location of the Cyrus Jackson place. They camped about a half a day's ride from the town of Roswell, and started early in the morning to reach the town about the time business would be starting up. As they rode in, the streets were still wet from the water wagon's early run to keep the dust down . . . at least for a little while. Kids were on their way to the school at the top of the hill, carrying their books. Some were chasing along behind a boy rolling a metal wagon tire, all the while his dog yipping at his heels.

Matt and Jim tied up in front of a boarding house where the sign read, 'Marsha's Rooms and Meals', hoping to get a good hot breakfast. "I's gonna go 'round back, Mista Matt," Jim decided, so as to not cause any disturbance, while trying to find the Jackson place's location. Matt stepped up on the boardwalk, and went in through the open doors.

Jim reached the back door, and stepped up on the small porch, and looked in through the screen door. The breakfast smells wafted his way.

As he looked in, a woman's strong voice came out, "Tell my eyes they don't see what I'm seein'! Come on in boy. Don't stand out there!"

Jim couldn't see who had spoken, but he didn't hesitate, and walked in to a warm kitchen. Jim gazed in disbelief. Before him was a beautiful young lady, wrapped in a white cook apron. He stood with his mouth open. "What's the matter with you, boy haven't you seen a colored girl before? And why are you coming to my back door? I own this place, and I serve *all* my customers in the front dining room, no matter what color they are! Go through that door and set yourself down."

The stunned Jim was speechless, and managed to get out a weak "Yessum," as he headed to the door.

When he entered the dining room he spotted Matt, and joined him at his table.

"Change your mind about eating out back?" asked Matt as he pulled a chair for Jim."

"I 'speck I had it changed for me . . . I'm not shore what happened. Have you seen da cook?"

The waiter interrupted their conversation, "I guess you'll be wantin' breakfast."

Then, directing his statement to Jim, "When you finish, the owner wants to see you in the kitchen."

Jim asked the waiter, "What's her name?"

"It's Miss Marsha Whitaker."

Matt just looked at Jim a moment, with a questioning expression on his face. "What was that all about? And no, I haven't seen the cook. Why?"

"She's da purdiest thing I seen in a long time. About like tha smoothest bar o' chocklate I ever seen!"

Matt smiled. "Reckon you've been hit hard. What's this about being called to the kitchen?"

"I don't know, but this Marsha Whitaker owns this place, and she say she serves all her customers here in the dinin' room an' for me not to come to tha back do'."

"I see . . . if you get a chance to ask, maybe she knows where the Jackson place is."

"I'll ast her, if I gets a chance. She a strong talker."

The waiter brought their breakfast. Matt added, "I'll ask around out here, after we finish."

"Yas Suh, I'll just meet you where we tied the hosses."

After breakfast, Matt went to find a land office, and Jim went to the kitchen. He looked in the kitchen door, and Marsha Whitaker looked up and saw him.

"Don't just stand in the door! Come on in, and have a seat. Breakfast is over, so we can take a little time and talk. There're no other colored folks in town, and you can see why I was surprised when you showed up."

"Yes'm, and you can see why I was surprised when you said 'come in'."

Marsha continued to do a little work, "How'd you wind up here, anyway?"

"Mista Forbes had a little trouble with a feller in Missouri. He's a United States Marshall, and he asks me to help 'im, then he made me a deputy."

"How did you wind up in Roswell?"

"It's a mighty long story, ma'am."

"Well, since I have someone to work for me tomorrow, 'spose you come by, and tell me about it."

"Yas 'um I'd like that."

"Just ask Harry, at the desk. He'll tell you where I am. I've gotta get back to work now, I'll see you then." She turned and went back to work.

Jim Bolin just sat there a minute, wondering what had just happened, rose from his chair and walked out the back door. He went around the building to where he had agreed to meet Matthew, and sat down on the bench in front of the boarding house.

He watched wagons and riders on horses going up and down the street, and was about half asleep when he saw Matt coming up the walk.

"What did your lady friend have to say, Jim?"

"She say come by tomorrow and talk. She had my head spinning so much I plumb forgot to ast her about the Jackson place."

"That's all right; I found out at the land office that Cyrus Jackson's place is southeast from here. The wagons should be showin' up pretty quick. 'Spose we head that way."

They mounted up, and headed to the south end of town. It was not long before the Jackson wagons came into view. Matthew and Jim rode out and met them.

"Everett, do you want to ride through the town that you've come all this way to be a part of?"

"Not if you found out how to get to my brothers place. We can see town later. It'll still be there!"

"All right then, just follow me. The place is just a few miles southeast o' here. It's on the Pecos River we crossed not far back."

The Jackson house was on the west side of the River, on a small rise that gave a view of a large part of the valley. Apple trees were planted all around, and they were loaded. The valley was a blaze of red, waiting for harvest.

On the porch sat a small Mexican, bent with age, with grey hair and a face creased from years in the sun. He sat watching, as they climbed down from the wagons.

Everett walked around to the porch, "Do you speak English?"

The man nodded. "Si Señor. I have lived here for many years."

"Is Cyrus here? I am his brother, Everett."

"Con mucho gusto, Señor Everett. Señor Jackson is in ze bed."

"I knew he was in poor health, from his letters."

"No, Señor Everett, he was protecting ze apples and was shot!"

Matthew looked at Everett, "Go on in, and see about your brother. I'll look into why he needed to protect the apples."

Outside, Matt approached the Mexican. "I'm Matt, ¿Como se llama?"

"Diego, Señor."

"Are there others working here?"

"Si, there are fourteen to help pick ze apples. Together, we hold off ze thieves. They did not know we were so many. After we shot ze horses that pulled their wagons, they tried to run."

"Sounds to me like you did okay." Matt headed toward his horse, "Can you let the others know that we want to ride down there, and take a look? I don't want to get shot."

"Si Señor." Diego rose and walked to the end of the porch. He took a large cow horn that hung from a nail, and blew three long blasts through it. "They will know we are coming."

"Good! Get your horse, and I'll get my friends to ride along. We'll pull those wagons to the barn, so they can be used again."

Matt and Diego met Jim and Tad at the barn, and let them know what was going on.

"Gather up some extra rope. We'll bring those wagons up here, so they can't bring more horses to hook up to 'em. Diego, do you have much trouble like this?"

"No Señor, I think they know Señor Cyrus does not feel well."

"It is time to pick them isn't it . . . the apples?"

"Si, that is why so many of us are here. The other families come each year to make ze money for ze families, I live here all ze time."

"Well, I know Cyrus Jackson is a lucky man to have you here." said Matt, as he tied a rope to the tongue of a wagon.

"Si, if ze thieves come last week, ze others would not be here, and we would have lost ze apples. We were just starting ze harvest."

Chapter 20

Everett came in and sat at the foot of Cyrus's bed. He thought that Cyrus was asleep, so he said nothing. Cyrus opened one eye, "Ain't you gonna say hello?" he asked.

"Dang you CY, I thought you wus asleep!"

"I wus, 'till I heard you come in."

"From the sound of your letters, I thought all this time you were dying."

"Well, I wus gettin' older, and this place can make a good livin' for all the family."

"You *know* there's four purdy good size families came here to help you, don't you?" said Everett.

"Yes, and I appreciate that. This place has really grown. I've built homes for all of you, and I also built a processing plant for the apples. There's a complete workshop, centrally located for everybody to use. Now I didn't buy no furniture, I knew how particular my Ruby was, so I hope you brought yours, or at least enough till we can order some."

"I saw the buildings when I drove up. Looked like a city itself. We got enough furniture for a while." said Everett.

"This mornin' I thought I'd lost this year's crop. If it hadn't been for Diego, and the other families being here, I guess I would have. That's another reason I needed y'all here, I kept buying more land for orchards, and it just grew bigger than I could imagine."

Everett looked at Cyrus with a squinted eye, "I *hope* it'll take care of us, 'cause I ain't goin' back! How bad you hit?"

"Ah it's just a scratch. I'll be okay in a day or so."

Outside, the men moved all of the wagons that thieves might use to haul the apples away, and placed them in barns around the compound.

"I guess these can be used as we harvest the apples, if we can find more horses." said Matt, as they pushed the last wagon in and closed the large doors.

As Matt turned around, he saw Jessica walking toward him. He just stood and watched. She removed her bonnet and her golden curls blew in the wind.

"Oh Matt, have you ever seen anything like what uncle Cyrus has built here?"

"No, but he didn't build one for us, I guess we can't get married . . . we wouldn't have a place to live. Oh, I guess we could stay in the bunk house with all the others."

"Oh, Matt, you tease! I bet there's a place we can stay 'till we can build. Where are Tad and Jim?"

"They've gone to check out that bunk house and clean up. That's where I was headed, after a little kiss, first!"

"I think I'll wait 'till after the clean up takes place," responded Jessica.

211

"Oh no you don't!" He grabbed her to him. They kissed and laughed at the same time. Then, they parted and went to their own plans.

That evening, Matthew and Jessica sat on the bank of the river, watching the sunset.

"Jessica . . . remember the plans I had for you that I said that you would agree with?"

"I remember, you wouldn't say what they were!"

"Well, I'm tellin' you now! I want you to be my wife, so we can sit like this, and watch all the sunsets that will take place, for the rest of our lives."

"Matt, you're serious about us getting married!" said Jessica as she snuggled closer.

"I am, if you can stand being married to a lawman," he responded.

"Do you have to keep being a lawman?"

"That's about all I know, Jessica. It's my life"

"Uncle Cyrus says that there's plenty to keep us busy here, and that we are welcome to settle with the rest. He also said he'd build us a house here, if we want." She then moved even closer, and put her arms around him. Then she began to kiss him on the neck and cheek, and finally on the lips, lingering with a long kiss.

He gently pushed her back, "You're unfair! How can a man say 'no' to that kind of treatment?"

He turned toward her, and took her in his arms. They sat silently beside the river.

The next day, Jim Bolin left before dawn to have breakfast, and to talk to the lovely Marsha Whitaker. As he rode along the main street, some businesses were already getting started for the day. Most paid no attention to him, but some gave a blank look. There was no smile or acknowledgement at all, as they went about their business. He tied up in front of Marsha's place, and stepped up on the boardwalk. He entered the lobby, and walked to the registration desk, "I'm 'spose to ask Harry the whereabouts o' Miss Marsha."

"I'm Harry, and I guess you're Jim Bolin. Marsha said you'd probably come by. She's in her office. Just go through those doors. It's the second door on the left."

Jim eased down the hallway, and gently knocked on the door.

Marsha opened the door, and with a smile, before Jim could speak, she asked, "What kept you? I'm starvin'! Let's go down and get some breakfast!"

Jim just smiled, and followed her back down the hall to the dining room, where they sat at a table in the corner. He finally got the courage to speak, "I told you how I got here, but you didn't say how you got this far out, and the only colored in the town."

"Well, it's a long story, but I think I can tell you before our breakfast gets here. I was nurse to a couple's baby, and they brought me here from N'Orlens, so they could take over this place from a cousin. After moving here they had more time for their boy, so I lived here in the boardin' house, 'cause I had to get up early to start breakfast. After about a year, the whole family died in a fire in the big house that belonged to the cousin. That ole house burned so quick we couldn't save a thing."

"How did ya wind up ownin' this place?"

"They had a will we found, here in the office safe that named the baby boy, or me, if I was the only one left. I've been here for four years. It's a whole lot better than where I lived in N'Orlens."

While Marsha and Jim were talking, a man came in and sat at one of the tables. He had the build of a blacksmith. His hair was long, and he had a short, full beard . . . and was fond of talking loud. After he sat down, he glanced across the dining room, and saw Marsha and Jim at the table in the corner. In a loud voice, he called for a waiter, and told him in no uncertain terms. "Where I come from, we don't have to eat with Niggers."

Jim rose slowly, faced the man, and replied, "Suh I guess this ain't where you come from. Now, enjoy yore breakfast."

The man stood up so quick his chair tumbled backwards with a crash,"You back talkin' me boy?"

"No suh. We both are trying to eat our breakfast, and since the lady owns the place, I reckon you should be quiet or leave."

The man rushed toward Jim Bolin with fists doubled and muscles rippling, "I'll show you where your place is." He swung a haymaker at Jim, who sidestepped and caught the man by the back of the neck. Jim used the man's own force to send him head first into the wall. The man crumpled and fell to the floor.

About the same time the local sheriff came to the dining room. "What seems to be the problem here?"

Marsha stepped up and explained what had happened, adding that Jim was a deputy U.S. Marshall. "I don't know who this man is."

"Don't worry about it, Marsha; I'll take care of it. He was causin' trouble at the livery a while ago."

Marsha returned to the table, and sat with Jim. He looked up and said, "Now, ya see why I always come to the back doe?"

Marsha smiled, "Well, you won't have to here!"

Matt came into the dining room and made his way to the table where Jim and Marsha sat. "So this is where you got off to, Mr. Bolin? And this must be Miss Whitaker. I'm Matthew Forbes, Miss Whitaker."

"Why don't you join us, Mr. Forbes?"

Matt nodded, and sat down. "Jim, here's a bank draft for your wages and expenses."

"I'm thinking about becoming an apple farmer, at least until I can buy some cattle and a little land."

"Well Mista Matt, I been sorta thinkin' about stayin' here too."

Marsha spoke up, "I've been need'n some help around here, and the sheriff's been sayin' a long time he needs help. Jim'll do all right."

Matt stood up, "I've gotta get back and start building a house. I'll invite you two to the wedding when I've finished."

Marsha asked, "Who's the lucky lady?"

"Miss Jessica Jackson. She came with the Jacksons to help her uncle. So, I'll see you two around."

Matthew headed back to the Jackson compound, and was met on the porch of the main house, by Diego, "Is Everett here in the main house?"

"Si, Señor, he is with Meester Cyrus."

Matt entered through the big door and continued into the bedroom where Cyrus and Everett were talking. "Could I see you outside a minute, Everett?"

"Why sure Matthew, I'll be right out."

Matthew walked out on the porch. Diego was gone, so he sat on the edge and waited for Everett.

The big door opened, and Everett stepped out, "What can I do for you, Matthew?" He took a seat on the edge of the porch, by Matt.

"Well Everett, I been thinkin' . . . since Cyrus offered us a part in the apple business, and I'm kinda tired of the Marshall business, I wus wondering if it would be all right if . . . well . . . if I sorta asked Jessica to marry me?"

"Well son, I don't think you can *sorta* ask her, you're gonna have to 'outright' ask her, and yes it'll be all right with me."

With tongue in cheek, Matt replied "That's all I wanted to know 'Pops'. I'm gonna do just that!" He grinned, knowing that Jessica had already agreed to marry him.

He slid off the edge of the porch and headed to the house where Jessica was staying. As he walked away, he heard Everett say, "And don't call me POPS!"

Bryan Forbes

Chapter 21

Bryan Forbes, the fourth son of Richard Forbes, traveling in the New Mexico Territory, has just come across the flatlands north of Aqua Negra Chiquita (Little Black Water), and later renamed Santa Rosa, New Mexico. He had camped by the natural lakes west of there, along his route. He traveled along the Pecos River, until Tecolte creek joined it, then on north, between La Mesita on the west and Middle Mesa on the east. He camped the previous night near Apache Springs. He was now entering the foothills of the mountains.

The day was bright, not a cloud in the sky. But it was early fall, and by afternoon you could always expect a shower. The appaloosa gelding he was riding was blue in color, with a good patch of speckled white on his rump. The bay, that was carrying his supplies, was marked with three socks and a dark mane and tail. Both horses were strong, and from good wild stock.

It was a couple of days past Bryan's twenty-eighth birthday. He was feeling good about the time he was making.

His blue-grey eyes scanned the horizon, in all directions, for Comanche that sometime roamed this area. Those eyes were in a well-tanned face, topped with light blond hair. It was covered with a well worn hat that *had* been white, and had seen cleaner days. Bryan Forbes was tall and muscular, from his hard work on a West Texas ranch. He wore a tan buckskin shirt he had made himself.

His saddle had a scabbard for his new 44-40 Winchester, model seventy-three, that he had won in a turkey shoot. He sported two frontier Colts, also 44-40s, slung low and held in place by leather thongs. He had had plenty of practice using them on coyotes, rabbits, snakes or tin cans. To date, he had never had to use them on a man. He felt ready for any attack, but had rather one didn't occur.

As he rode along, the trees became thicker . . . he slowed his pace in order to watch for any movement out of the ordinary. As he approached a broad valley, his first impression was that it seemed to be filled with smoke. He stopped, as he saw a small cabin on a rise, at the mouth of the valley, with a few horses standing around. He wondered if the cabin was on fire.

Then, he could finally smell black powder and knew it was the source of the smoke. He was confused, because he had not heard any shooting, though his approach had him riding through a deep valley. He guessed that the heavy air, and no wind, had kept the smoke settled in the trees.

As he watched, a Comanche rode across the front of the cabin, loudly yelling, as he loosed an arrow into the doorway. The Indian didn't get far before a shot rang out, from behind a large rock, about thirty-five yards in front of the cabin. Then he noticed the horses around the cabin were Indian ponies, with no riders.

Bryan Forbes hesitated to ride into the valley, for fear of being shot. He waited to make sure there were no more Comanches to show up. While he waited, a figure rose up from behind the rock from where the shot had come, and began walking toward the cabin. Bryan then rode on down slowly and sang out, "helloo, the cabin." The person walking toward the cabin stopped, and turned to look.

"Hello yourself! Where were you an hour ago?" The voice was that of a young woman, dressed in a man's clothes. She still had the rifle where she could use it. "Are you friend or foe?"

"I'm a friend ma'am, and I guess I was in a hole, 'cause I didn't hear any shootin'."

"We could'a sure used you, Papa and me. Seems like we been shootin' all afternoon long."

"I can see the results," said Bryan, as he indicated the Indian horses, standing around grazing, and bodies here and there, almost hidden by the grass. "You go see about your Pa, I'll take care of these horses . . . I'll put 'em in the corral. The burying may take a little longer."

"Papa was digging a hole to move the out-house . . . I guess you can just put 'em in there. We can dig another later." She went into the house. Bryan started leading the horses to the corral. He thought that she seemed to be a 'take control' girl, an attractive one at that.

He didn't get far, before he heard a scream from within the house. He dropped the lead ropes, and ran into the house. The girl was crying and holding her father in her arms. Her father had an arrow deep in his shoulder. She started to pull it out.

"Don't pull it out, ma'am!" he instructed.

"We gotta get it out to doctor him." she reasoned.

"Here, let me show you. The barbs on the head would cut too much coming out, because of the shape of it." Bryan carefully took hold of the shaft of the arrow, and pushed it on through far enough to get hold of the end. Then he broke off the shaft as close to the shoulder as he could, and pulled the shaft of the arrow out. "I'll help you get him on the bed, and you can doctor him up."

After placing her father on the bed, Bryan went back to taking care of the horses. He located the fresh dug hole, and started dragging the bodies of the Indians into it. He covered them, along with the blankets and anything else that would show that they were Indian.

When he went back inside, the girl looked up and said, "He is still unconscious. Do you think he'll make it?"

"Most likely . . . He looks pretty tough to me. Is he a drinkin' man?"

"I think he keeps some hidden from me somewhere . . . he says 'for medical reasons'."

"Well, I'd say this is a medical reason! Put some on his wounds, and I imagine he'll appreciate a little snort, when he wakes up! I think everything is taken care of outside. You might need to raise that corral fence a bit. Those mustangs the redskins were ridin' might jump out of there pretty easy, if they get scared. They're not used to being cooped up like regular horses.

"Oh, I found a couple of medicine bags on them fellers. The stuff inside looks like plants a friend of mine used to heal up cuts."

"You think it'll help?" she questioned.

"Yep, it sure helped mine heal up."

Bryan dampened a few leaves, placed them on each side of the old man's shoulder. Then he told the girl to tie them on, with clean rags, and wrap the shoulder.

"He should be fine in a few days."

"But he's still unconscious."

"More'n likely he's just sleepin'. He lost a lot of blood. Just let him sleep. He'll heal up better."

As he stood to head toward the door, the girl looked him over thoroughly, and then asked, "Who are you anyway, and where were you going?"

He paused, and turned back to answer, "Well my name's Bryan Forbes, and I guess I've been just a drifter. I got a feller in Santa Fe that's holdin' some cattle for me . . . Santa Fe, that's where I'm headin'."

"You got a ranch somewhere?"

"Nope . . . all my money's tied up in the cattle, but I don't have any place to put 'em. I had enough extra to get some land for a ranch, but that's gone now."

"What happened, gamble?"

"No. My cousin, his wife and kids, got burned out back in Virginia. I had to help 'em out. Like I said, I've got no place to put 'em, so I thought I'd get to Santa Fe and sell the cattle, if I can."

"I'm sorry about your cousin. You could put the cattle here, if you want to . . . We don't have any stock except those horses you put in the corral, the cow we're milking, and her calf. Indians killed our bull and ate him. Our land goes about as far as you can see in any direction."

"Wow, that's sure something to think about. I could pay you for the grazing by the head when I sell them." he mused.

"Right now, why don't you hang around, and I'll drum up some food and coffee?"

"You mean you can cook too?" he teased, tongue in cheek.

She looked at him pretty hard, and then they both laughed.

He watched her as she moved toward the stove, and put more wood on the coals. "You didn't tell me your name."

"It's Julie; Julie Harris . . . My papa's name is Paul. We've lived here for nigh on to seven years . . . and yes; we have young Indian bucks come by ever once in a while, when they get a little fire in their rears. But they don't usually hang around, and shoot up the place; like they did today . . . I hated what happened out there."

"Yes, but it comes to that once in a while." He watched her as she worked. She still had the old hat on that she was wearing outside. Her ponytail showed her light color hair. The jeans she wore fit pretty tight, causing Bryan to admire her figure. She had her papa's shirt on, with the tail tied in a knot in front. As she talked, she occasionally looked his way. Her bright blue eyes seemed to look right through him. Thoughts filled his head. *"I wasn't sure before, but I am now! She's mighty purdy!"*

After they finished eating, they talked a while about bringing the cattle back here. "I think that I can get more money if I keep them awhile, instead of trying to sell them at Santa Fe now." He rose, and started toward the door, "If it's okay I'll take a couple of those ponies for a little spending money."

"Yes, that's okay. Thank you for your help. Will you look in on papa with me, before you leave?"

"Yes, and if you will pack a couple of those biscuits, and a strip or two of bacon, I think I just might make it to Santa Fe. My supplies are just about gone."

He went into the room where her dad was, and checked his wounds. "Julie, the bleeding has stopped, and I sure 'nuff think he's sleepin' soundly, instead of unconscious . . . He don't have fever. You can put some more fresh leaves on tomorrow. I'll bet he'll wake up tonight, and ask for some of that soup you made."

Bryan tightened the cinch on the appaloosa, put the biscuits and bacon in the pack on the bay, then haltered a couple of the best Indian ponies, and rode off toward the west.

The sun was low, but he figured the sooner he got to Santa Fe, the quicker he could take care of his business. He followed a trail used by troops during the war. The going was still rough, because the land was rising as he moved west.

The sky had become overcast, but it didn't seem heavy enough to rain hard. He pulled out his slicker anyway.

The ground around the trees was covered with needles from the big spruce trees, so his hoof beats were quiet. He was traveling carefully, but he had almost nodded off when the appaloosa snorted, and brought him fully awake. As he looked around, he thought he saw movement to his right. He stopped, and held as still as he could. What he spotted was a band of about four braves, chatting in their tongue. Apparently the extra ponies had not picked up the Indians scent, as none whinnied.

"*I can't understand just what all these Comanche are doing so close to Pueblo country,*" he wondered to himself. He noticed that one had an old flintlock rifle. The others had bows and arrows. He knew that if he had to run, the accuracy of an arrow wouldn't be much less than the rifle.

Suddenly, one of the Indian Ponies whinnied, and the band came to a halt. He knew that they only had to look his way to see him, so he sunk his spurs into the appaloosa, and they were rapidly weaving through the trees. He could hear their 'yelps', and the arrows whizzing by . . . Then he heard the report of the rifle. The burning in his back, up under his shoulder, told him that he had been hit, but he continued to run. He fired at his pursuers, not sure he hit any, but it did slow them down. He hoped it was to retrieve their dead.

When the Indians saw that the mustang he was riding and the other ponies were moving very fast, with a pretty good lead, they lagged back and finally gave up the chase.

Bryan continued to open the distance for a while, then he slowed to a trot. The pain in his back grew worse. After another mile or so, he slowed to a walk, until he finally came to a stop. He had weakened, and knew that he must have lost a lot of blood.

He rolled slowly out of his saddle, and came to rest by a small stream. He removed his shirt and reached over his right shoulder with his left hand. He pushed on his elbow until his hand was as far over his shoulder as he could reach, where he could feel the wound in his back. As he pressed on the wound, the bullet fell into his hand. "How about that! I guess that brave was low on powder, since the shot just punctured the skin . . . probably a good thing too, that I had my slicker on."

He opened one of the bags he got from the bodies at the Harris' home, soaked a leaf, and placed it on the wound. *"Wish I could remember the name of that plant."* The leaf seemed to stick in place, so he put his shirt back on. After he drank, and watered the horses, he stepped up on a log, to make it a little easier to mount up. Then he continued on his way.

The elevation continued to rise as he headed on toward Santa Fe. He knew that the horses needed to rest and graze a little, so he began to look for a place to make camp. *"It can't be too far to the Pecos River . . . I'm feelin' stronger . . . I think I can make that okay."* He figured that once he reached the river, he would only be about forty miles from where he was going, in Santa Fe.

After a few more miles, he reached the river, and located an area where the river wash, in times past, left a slight overhang. After unsaddling, he staked out the horses, unrolled his blanket, and placed it by his turned up saddle. With his bed made, he gathered plenty of dry wood to build a small fire that wouldn't give up much smoke. He put on his coffee water to boil. *"These biscuits that Julie put in for me taste as good now as they did when she first made 'em . . . not hot o' course, but still good."*

After cleaning up, and getting his coffee pot ready for morning, he crawled into his blankets, and listened to the rush of the fresh, cool water in the riverbed. It sounded like music to him, as the water bubbled, rushing over the rocks. The smell of the tall Spruce trees drifted into his shelter, and he was soon wooed into a restful, and much needed, sleep.

Morning brought a dull gray to Bryan Forbes's campsite, as it was closed in on both sides, by the canyon walls. The cool breeze of the mountains drifted down the canyon. Bryan put on his hat and knocked out his boots, and began to stir a fire for the morning.

Hummingbirds were making 'screeching' sounds, unlike other birds, while flitting about looking for something sweet. A couple of chipmunks were also looking for breakfast.

He lingered over coffee, thinking how nice this place would be for a cabin. Lots of game to hunt, and plenty of wood to cook it on . . . but, no place to run cattle . . . and unfortunately a bunch of cattle was all he owned, right now.

"I guess I've sowed enough dreams for the morning. Better get to movin'."

The rest of the trip on to Santa Fe proved uneventful, but very tiring. Bryan rode in on the Old Pecos Trail, past the Palace of the Governors, and on to the yards where his cattle were being held. Daniel Brookings, owner of the yards, looked up as he heard the horses coming.

"Why . . . is that you Bryan? I thought you'd got yourself killed! I expected you three o' four days ago."

"I ran into a little situation with a few Comanches. A lady and her Pa were being attacked, and I couldn't get away, right off."

"Well at least you're okay, now. I reckon you came for your stock?"

"Yessir I did. Don't have a place of my own to put 'em, but the lady and her Pa have a place, and said I can keep 'em there, and pay them later when the stock sells. Let's go look at the cattle, I know you picked some of the best. Then I need to find a couple of hands to help get 'em back there."

Well, there's some good ole' Vaqueros that hang out by the ole' church south of town. They're good with a herd. They just don't want to go up that long trail . . . They may go to your place with you though."

"Good. I'll check them out, after I get cleaned up, and get some chow. Now, let's look at the cows."

Daniel Brookings was a large man, with stomach to match. He wore a blue cotton shirt that always had a button undone just above his belt, and a suit vest with a ribbon of a tie. He wore a wide brimmed hat that cast shade on a constantly red face, with a three-day growth of whiskers. Daniel owned a vast amount of holding pens, and land that would confine more than one good-sized herd that was being readied for the trip up the Santa Fe Trail.

Bryan and Daniel walked out the back door. Though empty now, cattle had been in the front pens for days, and when the wind picked up, it swirled dust into the air, thick and stifling.

They walked to the pens where Bryan's cattle had been held . . . but there were no cattle there!

Daniel shouted to one of his hands. "Harvey, where are the cattle that were in these pens?"

Harvey came over to where they were standing. "Well Boss, Cyril Hastings' foreman came out with his work order for the cattle in the front pens. He wus gonna join them to the herd he brought from the Hastings Ranch, and I tol' him where his cattle were. Then I went in to fix the water pump . . . I guess he took 'em all. It ain't been thirty minutes."

"I know Cyril had nothin' to do with this, but I'm not sure about Forest Bowman, his foreman. He may just 'uv intended to feather his nest with your cattle." said Daniel Brookings.

"Have you got a sheriff here?" Bryan asked.

"Yeah, but by this time o' day he would be too drunk to do anything."

"Where do you think this Forest Bowman is?"

"They take the herd out to the head of the trail, to see how they move. Then a bunch comes back into the saloon, usually. You might find him there, at the 'Steer's Head' saloon up on the north side."

"If I can't get satisfaction from this Bowman feller, I'll need a map to the Hastings' ranch."

"I can do that. Matter o' fact I'll go with you," replied Daniel, "and you can leave your extra horses here."

Bryan headed to the 'Steer's Head' saloon. When he stepped onto the walk, he first peered over the butterfly doors, to get an idea of what was going on. He wasn't sure how many hands would be in there. Two men stood at the far end of the bar, and three at the front. About six others sat scattered at various tables, playing cards. After locating everyone, he pushed through the doors, and walked up to the vacant part of the bar. He asked the bartender, "I'm looking for Forest Bowman. Can you point him out for me, if he's in here?" It was noisy enough that only the bartender heard the question.

He was polishing a glass. He nodded, and then tossed his head, indicating the end of the bar. Bryan went to the end of the bar where two men were standing, "I'm lookin' for Forest Bowman, and I understand that one of you gentlemen would be him."

The tall one on the end, with his elbows on the bar, leaned back and asked; "Who wants to know?"

"I'm Bryan Forbes. I want to know because he's taken an extra three hundred head of cattle that belongs to me!"

"Are you calling me a cattle rustler?"

"I take it then that you are Forest Bowman, and if the boot fits, wear it."

"And just what makes you think I've got your cattle?" asked Bowman, as he straightened up, and stepped away from the bar. As he did, the man next to him moved back away, and the bartender ducked down behind the bar.

Bowman was a big man, in a denim shirt, and leather cuffs. His gun was tied down, and as he walked, the 'jingle bobs' on his spurs rang out, just to let you know that he was there. He took a stance with his hands at his side.

226

"Well, my cattle left Brookings' holding pens when you did. I need you to get them back here, 'cause they don't go up the trail." Aware of the stance Forest took, he continued, "I don't want to kill you right here. All I want is my cattle out of Hastings' herd, and if you can't get them out, I guess I'll have to see Hastings." replied Bryan.

Forest knew that the man who had been with him at the bar, was fast, and had his back. So he moved his hand near his gun, "Them cattle's on their way up the trail, probably too far to bring back."

Bryan saw that Bowman's thong was still on the hammer of his six-shooter. "I don't think you're ready for gun play, Forrest. The thong is still on your gun . . . so just simmer down. All I want is my cattle."

The other man spoke up. "He may not be ready, but I am." He went for his gun, and almost got it out of his holster. Bryan's bullet entered at his shirt pocket, and kicked him backwards over a table. He rolled over onto the floor, dead before he began to fall. The two men at that table dove out of their chairs, and rolled clear.

Bowman stood dumbfounded, and didn't move. He had not expected Bryan to be that fast. "You have any idea who you just shot?"

"No, and I don't care. I think it's time you and I got on the road to the Hastings' ranch." Bryan said, as he removed Bowman's gun.

"He was Elton Kooch, supposedly the fastest man around here." marveled Bowman.

"I'm not impressed. He wasn't fast when it counted! Now let's go!"

He tied Bowman to his saddle, and walked back down the street to the pens, and met Daniel Brookings out front. Brookings had saddled himself a horse, and had Bryan's ready to go. He had penned Bryan's other horses, and they were taken care of.

"It won't take long. It's only a few miles to the headquarters," said Daniel. He started out, and Bryan followed, leading Forest Bowman's horse.

As they rode along, the horses' hooves raised small whirlwinds of dust that rose up over the road.

Bowman spoke: "Why am I going to the ranch? Shouldn't I be separating your cattle out? My men won't leave 'till I get there."

"My level of trust of you is not very high, right now. It would be easy for you to take that herd on up the trail, and I don't want to chase 'em."

They rode on toward the ranch house. Not much more was said. Just the steady clopping of the hooves on the trail, and a shrill scream of a hawk to his mate was heard. Soon, the ranch house was in sight. When they arrived, they tied up in front of the headquarters, and were met by Cyril Hastings.

Hastings was a man in his late fifties, with graying hair and a neatly-trimmed beard. He was well dressed, in pinstriped pants and matching vest. The sleeves of his white shirt were rolled up at the cuff, where he had taken out his cuff links. He looked very dignified, and spoke in a clear commanding voice.

"Howdy, Daniel, what brings you out this way?" he asked.

"Cyril, this is Bryan Forbes, and he has a bit of business with you."

"How do, Mr. Forbes. What can I do for you?" Then he noticed that the other fellow was Forest Bowman. "Well Forest, I didn't see that was you . . . what are you doing here instead of being with the cattle?"

Bryan spoke up, "That's what I wanted to see you about, Mr. Hastings. Seems when Forest got your cattle from Daniel's for the trail, he picked up about three hundred of my cross bred cows that Daniel was holding for me."

"Is that right, Forest?"

Forest shot a quick glance at Bryan, then looked at the ground, and answered, "Well, yes sir, I guess it is. I didn't know they wus his."

"Let's go inside, gentlemen. Daniel you and Mr. Forbes have a seat. I'll tend to this now." Inside, he called for his daughter, "Geneva, bring what we owe Forest. Mr. Forbes, do you wish to press charges in this matter?"

"No, Mr. Hastings. I just want my cattle back." Bryan answered.

"Forest, I supposed the references you brought me are 'shady', too, I won't be needing you any more."

Geneva Hastings, a tall, beautiful, red-headed young lady, with flashing green eyes, brought in some cash. She handed it to her father, and stood by his chair. The cash was given to Forest, "I think it would be a good idea if you, and your companions, left this country."

Forest moved to the door exiting hurriedly. Then he mounted up and left.

"Geneva, this is Mr. Bryan Forbes. Mr. Forbes, my daughter, Geneva."

Bryan swallowed hard. She was very beautiful. "I'm pleased to meet you, ma'am."

"And you, Mr. Forbes." she replied.

"Geneva, call Aledo in for me please. Mr. Forbes, we will get your cattle for you."

"Thanks, Mr. Hastings. I can't ask for more." said Bryan.

"We'll put them all back in the pens at Daniel's place, if that's okay with you, Daniel. It'll make it easier to separate them."

"I'm sorry. Won't that make your drive late, Mr. Hastings?"

"That will not be a problem, Mr. Forbes, after what we've put you through," said Hastings.

"That's fine with me Cyril. I've got nothing coming in for a while," said Daniel Brookings.

"Now, we have a big dinner prepared, and I'll expect you fellows to spend the night. We have plenty of room, and it's getting late."

"We don't want to put you out sir." answered Bryan, even though he had no arrangements to stay the night in town.

Aledo came into the room, holding his sombrero. He was dressed in the typical vaquero dress. A man of about forty-two or so, he stood straight and tall. His jacket was embroidered. His trousers had embroidered legs and were belled at the bottom. "You weesh to see me, Señor Hastings?"

"Yes, Aledo, take some of the men to town, as many as you think you will need, and tell Mrs. Tedford to put you up tonight. I'll take care of it later. That way, you can get an early start in the morning. Bring the herd back into Mr. Brookings' place, and we will be in tomorrow. Tell those men that hired on with Forest that we will not need them any more. You can take enough money to settle up with them."

"Si, Señor Hastings." He turned and left.

"Now, Geneva, I believe dinner is ready. Why don't we all move to the dining room, gentlemen," suggested Cyril Hastings, as he motioned them toward the room. "Mr. Forbes, where do you plan to move your cattle, since you're not going to send them to market?"

"I got the mixed bred stock to build a herd, and intended to buy a small ranch."

"And did you?"

"No, Sir. My cousin's family got burned out back in Virginia. At the time, I was the only one left with enough cash to help them. It took what I had to take care of them. I kinda have a herd with no ranch . . . that is . . . I had a herd. A friend east of here has offered their place to keep them, until I can sell a few. That's what I'll have to do, to get some expense money."

After washing up, they entered into the large dining room with its massive beams and large rectangular table, surrounded by heavy oak chairs. Cyril Hastings stepped to the head of the table, and motioned for Bryan to sit on his right. Daniel Brookings took his place next to Bryan, and Geneva Hastings sat across from them. The table was set with an abundance of food, and Bryan hadn't eaten a full meal in sometime. Even so, he watched his manners.

"Aledo and the boys should be bringing your cattle back soon, and if you wish, you can bring them here to the Bar H until you decide what you'll do with them. We've plenty of grass, and I'm sending a large part of our cattle to market."

"That's mighty generous, Mr. Hastings. I'll think on that."

During the meal, Bryan couldn't get over the change in Geneva. When he first saw her, her hair was pulled back in a bun. Now, her red hair fell over her shoulders, and the dress she wore was 'frilly', with colorful ribbons. And she floated, in high-buttoned shoes he had not noticed before. He was continually caught making eye contact with her piercing green eyes, and each time she smiled.

Cyril Hastings interrupted Bryan's thoughts of Geneva. "Where do you hail from, Bryan? It is all right to call you Bryan?" Cyril inquired.

"Why yes, certainly, Mr. Hastings. My folks came from Scotland, originally, but we wound up in Virginia. My brothers and I went out on our own when we were pretty young. If you don't mind my askin', how long have you had this place, Mr. Hastings? It's quite beautiful."

"Actually, this ranch is a part of the original Land Grant, and it's been in the family for many years."

"I'd a never guessed . . . what with Geneva's red hair and green eyes."

"That's because my grandfather married the heir to the grant, and Geneva's mother came from San Francisco. She was an Irish red-head also. Matter of fact, when you look at Geneva, it's like looking at her mother."

Geneva's face was flushed, but she remained silent.

When they had finished their meal, Cyril suggested, "If you gentlemen have finished, why don't we move into the parlor? It's more comfortable there." Geneva excused herself, leaving the men alone.

Bryan asked, as he rose from his chair, "And your wife, Mr. Hastings?"

"She died of the fever six years ago."

"I'm sorry."

"Oh, we had a good life together. I miss her, dearly." He looked at the floor, as they moved into the parlor, "Geneva has been a blessing all these years, but I think it's time for her to make her own home. Not many young folks around here . . . been thinking of sending her to a good school back east, where she could meet folks her own age."

"She's a beautiful young lady, Mr. Hastings. I know you're proud of her."

They sat and talked a while. Bryan looked at the clock on the wall. "I better get to bed. I plan to leave very early in the morning."

Cyril Hastings stood, "Our cook starts breakfast around four in the morning, to feed the hands. So, eat a good breakfast before you go. By the way, I expect you to come back by here, to let me know if your cattle have been taken care of."

"Yes sir, and thank you for your hospitality."

Daniel Brookings spoke up, "I probably won't go back to town until later in the morning. I want to enjoy Cyril's cigars and some of his good brandy"

"Well then, gentlemen, I bid you good night."

Geneva had stepped into the parlor. She had heard Bryan bid them goodnight. "Mr. Forbes, come with me and I'll show you to your room. Dad and Daniel will talk into the wee hours of the morning. You were smart to leave."

She picked up one of the lamps, and started down a long hall. The lamp threw dancing shadows into one doorway after another. When she reached the last room, she entered and placed the lamp on the table by the bed. She then started to light the lamp on the table. "Here, let me get that." Bryan placed a match over the chimney of the burning lamp, and it hissed into a bloom of light. He then removed the globe, and lit the lamp on the table. When he finished, he looked up and found Geneva watching him, with those beautiful eyes.

When she saw his gaze, she paused a moment, then turned and bid him "Goodnight."

"Yes, thank you and a very goodnight to you." He watched her 'glide' through the door, and out into the hall, until the light grew dark. He closed the door and thought to himself: *"If I don't quit thinking about her, I won't get any sleep at all."*

After Forest Bowman was fired by Cyril Hastings, he rode half way into town and dismounted. He tied his horse to a tree, intending to wait for Bryan to ride that way. He rolled a smoke, and paced around. His hatred for Bryan, for getting him fired, was building.

As the day turned into night, he moved nearer to the creek, and built a fire down behind the bank, so as to not be seen.

"Knowin' that damned Cyril, he probably invited them to spend the night!" He tossed his smoke into the fire, unsaddled his horse, and spread his blanket near the fire. *"Well, that ain't gonna get me to leave. I'll just wait 'im out."* He curled up into his blanket, and was soon asleep.

Bryan was up about the same time that the cook started the bacon. He washed with the cold water, combed his hair and put on his hat and guns. He started

233

down the hall, and had no trouble finding the kitchen . . . he just followed the smell of the bacon and coffee. When he went into the warm kitchen, the cook tossed a thumb toward the table, indicating the plate filled with bacon and eggs, with a cup of hot steaming coffee on the side. Bryan looked at the cook. "Many thanks, my friend! This should take me a long way, today."

The cook just nodded, and turned to his cooking. It would have been hard to carry on a conversation with the sizzling of several pounds of frying bacon.

Soon, other hands were coming in, saying their 'Howdys' to Bryan, as they moved to their regular seats. Bryan finished his breakfast, and had another cup of hot coffee. He motioned the cook thanks again, with a quick finger to the brim of his hat, and he was out the door.

There was a lantern hanging by the barn door, and he put a match to it. It gave enough light to find all his rigging. He saddled the appaloosa, and was soon trotting down the trail to town. The morning air was crisp and clear. He filled his lungs with it, and it put a smile on his face.

He could easily see the trail, as the soil was light and chalky, and was edged by grass on the sides that was much darker. It wasn't long before the soft gray of dawn shed even more light on the trail. As he rode along, his thoughts were of Geneva, and how she seemed to be looking at him, each time he looked at her.

Bryan didn't immediately notice the ears on the appaloosa standing erect, his head turned to the left, and when he did become aware, it was too late. The report of the rifle was loud, and the sharp pain in his side knocked him from the saddle. He reached for his gun, and looked all around, to find who had shot. Then in the dim morning light, he saw a figure mounting up. He rose up on his elbow, and fired. The last thing he saw was the figure rolling off his saddle. Bryan's appaloosa stopped, and stood over him.

Chapter 22

Bryan tried to open his eyes but the brightness of the sun streaming through the window caused him to close them quickly, and then slowly, try again. The first things he saw were lacy curtains that were strangely familiar, gently flowing back and forth in the breeze that came through the open window. His mind raced back to when he was a small boy. At his grandmother's house, her curtains blowing in the wind fascinated him. He then realized he was in the room where he had stayed at the Hastings. He heard footsteps, and turned to see Geneva coming into the room. She was carrying something but he couldn't make out what it was.

"Well, you're finally awake! Now I won't have to drip this soup into your mouth, as I've been doing for the past few days, to keep you alive. Let me help you sit up. I imagine you're pretty hungry. I haven't been able to get you to swallow much . . . just a few drops at a time."

"What do you mean, *past few days*?"

"That's just what I mean. You've been right here, for the past few days."

He searched his brain, until he finally began to remember what had happened. "I guess I was hit pretty hard."

"Not as hard as Forest Bowman! You apparently shot him before he could get away. He was found a few yards from where you were."

"Who found me? . . . Was I there long?"

"Daniel found you, when he was riding back to town. He came back; we got the buckboard, and brought you here. You lost a lot of blood, but Doc seemed to think you would live, so we didn't bury you."

"Well . . . thanks for nothin'."

"I knew you'd be pleased! Now take some of this soup."

"I will, if you'll give me some biscuits to sop in it."

Cyril Hastings came into the room. "I heard talking in here, so I thought I would see if it was our patient making all this conversation, or if it was Geneva still talking, while you were unconscious. How are you feeling, my boy?"

"I haven't had time to figure that out yet, but I'm working on it."

Cyril pulled up a chair, and sat beside the bed. "You had a pretty close call out there. It was Forest, he was laying for you . . . from all the smokes he'd stomped out around there, it looked like he'd been there all night, waiting. I'm just sorry he had me fooled. I should have known he was no good."

"I don't remember much. My mind was on something else . . . guess I wasn't paying attention." As he said that, he glanced at Geneva. Then he quickly looked away, not wanting to give away the fact that he had been thinking of her.

"I also have news about your cattle," Cyril continued. "Forest had told his men to go on up the trail, before he came back to the Steer's Head saloon, and that he would join them later. By the time Aledo caught up with them, they were almost to Fort Lyon. He fired the men that were with Forest, but then he and the rest of the boys had to stay with the herd. It would have been too hard on the cattle to come back. Once again I offer my apologies for what has happened."

"It was out of your hands, Mr. Hastings."

"I can tell you this: You can take what your cattle sell for, and I'll see that they sell at a premium: Or I can replace them with pure-bred animals that are in our south pasture, and you can keep them there, and be my new foreman. I need someone with cattle savvy to carry on around here."

"Wow, you hit a man hard, with decisions like that!" He tried to rise, but was overcome with dizziness and pain. "That hit pretty hard too!" He settled back and thought a minute . . . "I'll think on that. I guess since I have no money or cattle right now, I should go back to the Harris' place, and let Paul and Julie know of the situation, since their offer was first. That should give me time to decide, if that's okay with you, Mr. Hastings"

"It's Cyril, and yes, it's fine with me. You shouldn't leave them uninformed, since they made you a good offer. You certainly owe them that courtesy."

"A few days should help me get some of my strength back and clear my head. I can't thank you and Geneva enough. You've been more than generous."

Bryan took a few more days to recover. Then he saddled his appaloosa, and loaded his saddlebags with supplies. The morning was still grey before the sunrise, and it would probably stay that way, because of a heavy overcast.

He was saddling to leave, and was just getting ready to blow out the lantern he was using to get ready, when he heard the big barn door squeak. He turned to see the dim silhouette of Geneva standing in the doorway.

"Will you be gone long, Bryan?" she asked

"That I don't know, for sure."

She stepped forward, and pushed a cup of coffee toward him. When he saw it, he put both hands around the cup and said, "That will taste good, and give me a good start this morning." But Geneva still had her finger in the handle, and she slowly pulled the cup toward herself.

"Maybe this will help you decide. At least it will give you something to think about!" She stood up on her tiptoes, and gently pressed her lips to his. Then, before he had time to react, she turned to the door and was gone.

Bryan continued to gaze at the open door. He slowly took a swallow of coffee. "Dang! Women can sure make things complicated!"

After finishing his coffee, he mounted the appaloosa and headed east, retracing his route along the same trail on which he had come to Santa Fe, back toward the cabin of the Harris' in the valley. He made it a point to stop beside the Pecos River again, where he had camped before. It seemed to soothe his soul, and would help him figure out what to do.

He unsaddled the appaloosa, and spread his blanket on the grass and needles that covered the ground, under the large spruce trees. A small fire got his coffee going. Then he unrolled a couple of biscuits and some bacon. He leaned back on the saddle, waiting for the water to boil. He let his thoughts wander over the events that had taken place recently and all the offers he had. He soon began to think of Geneva, and the way she had made a move toward him. He briefly considerd that she might be playing games, but rejected the idea. He had to assume that it meant she cared for him.

After he finished eating, and getting his coffee ready for morning, he slipped off his boots, and listened to the river rushing over the rocks. The sound was so soothing that, even though he wanted to think of Geneva, and maybe even Julie, he was soon asleep.

The morning was still dark when he awoke. The air was full of moisture from the splashing river, and he felt rested. He slipped on his boots, after knocking them out. When breakfast was finished, he whistled for his horse, and was soon on his way.

When he had traveled to about where he thought the Harris' place should be, the sun was beginning to roll well past noon, and he could see smoke in the distance. He picked up his pace, as he continued toward the valley where the Harris cabin stood. As he reached the hill above the cabin, he saw the source of the smoke . . . the cabin, still smoldering, totally destroyed. Bryan felt sick.

He cautiously rode on down into the valley, and dismounted. He began looking to see if any bodies were in the fire. He found none.

"It seems this valley is destined to be filled with smoke, at least when I come here."

He began to look around the outside areas. The barn was gone, and the cow was dead. The Indian ponies were not there. There wasn't much left of the place, except for a small shed, that was away from the barn that had burned. He reached down, and picked up a moccasin from the *weeds. "Looks like a bit of a fight might have gone on here and at least one Comanche is either barefoot or dead."* He continued to look around the remains of the cabin.

Paul Harris had built the roof with small tree limbs, placed side by side, and then covered with sod to seal it against the rain. The roof had fallen in, when it burned, but the sod had kept one corner of the bedroom from burning completely. As he pulled away some of the roof that was blocking his way into the corner, he found a tin type of Paul and his wife, on a small shelf. He slipped it into his pocket.

As he continued to look through the ruins, he saw something under the debris. When he began to pull away the sod and timbers, he pulled a 44-40 rifle from the debris, which was the same caliber as his own . . . he decided that it might come in handy later. He returned to his horse, retrieved his cleaning equipment from his saddlebags, and put the rifle back in good condition. He used some of his extra strings of leather to tie it to his saddle.

Bryan thought, *"I guess I still have enough daylight left to track a ways."* He paused and surveyed

239

the scene once more. *"There's nothing I can do here . . . I can only imagine what's happened to Paul and Julie."*

He mounted up and decided first to make a wide circle around the place. When he reached the northwest corner, he found fresh tracks heading in that direction. He counted six or eight horses. Three of the tracks might have been made by the three ponies that he had put in the corral.

He rode on, following as fast as he could travel, and keep the tracks in sight. The Indians seemed to not care if they were followed. *"Unless . . ."* he looked around in all directions, *"they want to be followed, and then it just might be a trap."* He kept going anyway. He knew he had to find them.

The sun was hanging low in the west, dancing in and out, between the puffy white clouds, casting long shadows across the tracks, making them a little harder to follow. He slowed a bit, from time to time, then cantered on at a fast pace.

By late afternoon, Bryan was getting into the heavier timber. The years of fallen needles, from the evergreen trees almost obliterated the tracks. He had an idea, by now, the direction they were heading. The river was not too far away. He reasoned they would camp there, because of the water, and it was too far to return to their tribe.

He rode ahead, toward the river. After a while, he smelled smoke from a campfire, but he saw none in the area. As he continued on, he soon saw more smoke, just below the tops of the tall trees that gave protection from the gentle breeze, so that the smoke hovered overhead. He felt that he was close enough that he had best move forward on foot.

Bryan soon saw the source of the smoke, and crawled to the edge of the riverbank, where he could look down into the riverbed. He had brought the glasses that he had borrowed from Mr. Hastings, and he began to familiarize himself with the camp.

A very smoky fire was going, on one side of the camp, where green willow limbs had been erected to smoke strips of deer meat. He then spotted three white women, cutting strips of the meat, and hanging them on the green willow branches. Looking closer, he could see that one of the women was Julie! He looked, but could not find Paul. On the other side of the camp, eight young braves were starting another fire.

He crawled back from the edge of the riverbank, and decided to wait for night. He knew that the young braves would all eat together around that fire. That way they could tell each other how brave they had been, during the raids they had made. Also, how they would be praised among their tribe for getting more horses and the women.

Bryan waited until it was nearly dark. With the glasses, he knew that he could still see well enough to make out everyone's location. Then he crawled back to the edge. Just as he thought . . . they were hovered around their fire talking and laughing. The three women had been readied for a later rendezvous, and were tied hand and foot. They were by the meat drying racks, near where he had seen them before.

He muttered to himself, "Are you sure you want to take on this situation?" He contemplated the danger of what he was doing. He then moved farther down the riverbank, where he could ease down, through the brush and willows growing along the bank.

The sounds of the river rushing over the rocks, by the Indians' campfire, would cover the noise of his movements. Their staring into the fire would make their vision limited, in the dark. When he got close to the three women, he began to slowly crawl closer toward them. It suddenly struck him, *"They might think I'm some sort of animal, and start screaming."* So, he stopped. *"Now what?"* he thought. After thinking about the situation, he decided to throw a small pebble at Julie to attract her attention, hoping she would realiize that it was him. So, he tossed a small rock. She gave a muffled 'ouch'! He then rose up on all fours, where she could see him. When she recognized him, she nodded her head, to let him know. Then she told the others."Follow my lead. A friend is here to help us."

Bryan continued forward, crawling in the sand, until he was up beside Julie. He drew his knife and cut the bands from her hands and legs. She threw her arms around his neck, and kissed him. He quickly pressed his finger against his lips, and shushed her. Then he cut the bands of the other girls.

He whispered, "I'll stay here, while each one of you crawls back down the river, about thirty yards, and you'll see where I came down the bank. We can't all go at once. It would be too much of a commotion, and they might notice . . . but hurry before they check on you again."

Each woman crawled away, until only Bryan was left, and then he followed them. When they were up on top of the river bank, Julie grabbed him again, but he said, "It's not over yet. They'll want you any time now. While I wait here, you girls go straight down that hill. You'll see the appaloosa down there, and Paul's rifle is tied on the back of the saddle, Julie, get it and come back with it. I know that you're a good shot, and we both will have to be, to get out of this."

They ran down the hill to Bryan's horse, and Julie started to undo the leather strings. It seemed that it took forever to get the leather strings to cooperate. She jerked the rifle free, and as she started running back up the hill, she told the other girls to stay put.

When she got close to the top, she paused, and got down to crawl the rest of the way. She whispered, "Bryan, I'm here. What do you want me to do?" She crawled up beside him.

"They seem to not care about anything." Bryan mused.

"I guess not! They found papa's liquor stash, and probably others too. This is the first chance they've had to take a drink," she answered.

"No wonder they seemed to not have a worry. They've also stacked enough wood on that fire to light up this side of the Territory. We won't have any trouble seeing them."

She was on his left side. "Julie, you take the four on the left, and I'll take the ones on the right of the fire. We'll only have the first try. I doubt they'll do much chasing tonight. However, make each shot count! We'll need their horses to get the girls back to their families. If you're ready, we go on three. I hate to shoot them like this, but they would track us until they got us! Here we go . . . One . . . Two . . . Three!"

Bryan and Julie began shooting intantly.They both fired as fast as they could lever their rifles. It was over in a matter of minutes.

They paused and watched for a few minutes . . . nothing moved, so he slid down the embankment, and cautiously walked toward the fire. He checked each Indian, and determined they were all dead. He pulled them into a wash in the riverbank, and pushed the dirt in over them and their belongings. He then pushed both fires into the river. After that he removed as much as he could carry of the meat that had been smoking, and wrapped it in his neckerchief. Then he dismantled the drying racks, and threw them into the river. Finally, he went to their horses, and found them all tied to a rope stretched between two cottonwood trees. He took both ends of the long rope, leaving the horses tied to it, and led them up the bank, after locating a path where it was not so steep.

"I hope you girls can ride these Indian makeshift saddles. I think they'll work 'till we get you back home."

Julie spoke up, "That's just it, Bryan. They burned our place, and I don't know about the girls' homes. This is Katherine. We just call her Kathy." She referred to the leggy blond, with tear streaks down each cheek, "And this is Angela." She patted the slight framed brunette beside her. Together they thanked him for getting them out of this threatening situation.

"Good to meet ya. Now let's get started, we can talk about it on the way"

Bryan's head was floating. *"What have I gotten myself into now? Three homeless girls, with only the clothes on their backs."* he thought.

He let the two girls move ahead, and then he edged up close to Julie. "There's not much left at the cabin, Julie . . . I'm sorry. What about Paul? He wasn't at the cabin."

"Papa got blood poison from that arrow. He wouldn't take care of himself, and didn't last long after you left." She averted her eyes, so Bryan wouldn't see the tears in her eyes.

"You been stayin' there alone, all this time?"

"No place else to go. Besides I had the garden to take care of and the cow to milk."

"I didn't mean to be gone so long, but my cattle were stolen. Then, when I found 'em, they were half way to market. Finally, I was several days in bed after being shot by the man that stole 'em in the first place."

"I'm not sure that I understood what you just said, but did you bring cattle with you?" Julie asked.

"No. I don't have any cattle, or money either, but I've been offered a foreman's job and either the money my cattle brought, or some high-bred cattle to take their place."

"I guess I don't understand. I'm really confused!"

"Well, basically, I've got a job, and either money or cattle, when I go back."

"So, you're not staying here."

"Not much to keep either of us here." he said.

Julie looked at him a minute then, "You mean you want me to go with you?"

"Well . . . yes, like I said, there's nothing to keep you here. Your cow is dead, your house is gone and I didn't see any chickens. By the way, where'd these girls come from?"

"They lived a few miles down the road from us."

"Do they have any kin around here?"

"Kathy does, or did, but I don't know for sure about Angela. We'll have to ask her. Bryan, what about my land?"

"You do have a registered deed don't you?

"Yes I'm sure I do."

Then it will always be yours. And you may want to return some day, or you might rather sell it."

Bryan and Julie kicked a little speed into their mounts, and rode up beside the girls. Kathy still had tear streaks running down her cheeks.

"Do you girls know about your families . . . do they live around here?" Bryan asked.

Kathy spoke first, "Angela has an aunt and uncle not too far from our house, but I don't know about our home. I wasn't at the house when the Indians took me."

Angela spoke up, "I was ridin' a mile or two from the house, like I do ever so often, so I don't know, about my folks, either."

"So they could be all right then?" Bryan asked.

"Well, let's go to your house first then, Kathy." said Julie.

Kathy looked up at the sky, as if to get her bearings. She turned to the left, heading to the southeast. After they had ridden a few miles, a small house came into view. "That's it! It's not burned after all!" She kicked her horse, and ran up to the house. A man and woman, seeming much too old for a daughter as young as Kathy, had heard the horses coming, and were just stepping out of the house, as the group pulled up in front. Both gasped with relief, at the sight of the girl.

Kathy slipped off the horse and ran into the older woman's arms. They both warmly embraced, crying, and kissing over and over. The man hugged them both close, with tears running down his face, as well.

"Where were you? We were worried sick about you."

Kathy started telling her about being surprised, while looking for her calf that had wandered off.

Bryan smiled, and looked at Julie, "Well Julie, that's one problem solved."

Mr. Parker looked up at them and said: "Since you folks have been traveling all night, get down and we'll have breakfast, while you tell me just what's been going on with our little girl. I'm Joseph Parker."

They dismounted and followed them into the house. "I'm Bryan Forbes, Mr. Parker. I guess you know Julie Harris."

Parker nodded. "Shore, since she was knee high to a grasshopper!"

They had gone without good food for so long, that when they stepped inside the house, the smell of the food cooking almost made them faint.

Mrs. Parker was busy around the big open fireplace, with black pots hanging on swing out arms, Dutch ovens filled with biscuits, and a big skillet with steaks frying. She had added extra food and while it was cooking, the girls gave a complete account of their abductions.

Kathy told them about looking for her calf, and Angela said she was riding the creek, looking for plums, as she often did, when one of the Indians came from behind a tree and grabbed her. "I was scared to death until I saw Kathy and Julie! We had to cut up deer meat, and hang it, so's it could smoke and dry out, kinda like 'Gran' smoking hams out in the smoke house. When Mr. Forbes found us, we were tied hand and foot." said Angela.

Julie added, "They had papa's liquor, and I'm glad Bryan found us when he did . . ." She paused for several seconds, pondering . . . then, almost in a whisper, "No telling what might have happened when they finished all the whisky they stole . . . but Bryan got there in time."

Angela sat quietly listening, and also letting her imagination run wild about what the Indians would have done, when they got drunk enough. "I think we're lucky to be alive!" she blurted out.

Every one just fell silent and stared at her. They all knew she was right. It took the words, out loud, for the fact to settle in their minds.

The girls set the table, and gathered around. When the food was placed on the table, Mr. Parker gave thanks. "Lord," he said, in a loud voice, as if it was necessary to speak up, so the Lord could hear him up there, "We give you our thanks, for watchin' over these girls, including our granddaughter, Kathy. She's so young, and these other two ladies, and we thank you for sendin' Mr. Forbes to their rescue. And Lord we do thank you for these fixin's that Maw has put together for us, and we ask if you would bless them, and this house. Thank you, Lord, and Amen."

He then tucked a napkin into his shirt collar, and passed everything along.

"I can't thank you enough, Bryan, is it?" Bryan nodded, "for bringing our granddaughter back to us. You see, she lost her mama and papa to Indians when she was three, and she's been with us ever since."

"I'm just glad I came at the right time, Mr. Parker. I sure do thank you for the supper, Mrs. Parker."

After they had finished eating, Bryan stood up and suggested, "We really should find out if Angela's home and folks are all right."

Parker also pushed his chair back. "I've got the team hooked to the wagon already. We will see to it that Angela gets home. They've been friends a long time . . . You folks got plenty to do. You go ahead."

"Well, we thank you again. By the way, I'm going to leave all but two or three Indian ponies with you folks.

Directing his attention toward her, "Kathy, I'm glad you and Angela are okay."

Bryan and Julia went out, and mounted up. They took three horses, leaving the rest for the Parkers, as promised, and headed toward the Harris place.

It was getting late, but the sun was still shining brightly when they arrived at what had been the Harris' home. They pulled up in front, and just sat for a few minutes. Bryan could see the tears catching the sunlight as they ran down Julie's cheeks. He had seen her beauty before, but he sat quietly, and wondered why he had not seen that beauty, as it was at this moment.

"Part of a bedroom is under the sod of the roof, there in the corner . . . Oh and here's this," he pulled the tin type of her mother and father from his shirt pocket, "I found this in there. I saved it for you, in case the fire started again."

She took the picture, looked at it, and then she sat down on a large rock, and sobbed openly.

Bryan, not knowing what to say, just mumbled, "I . . . I'll see to the horses." He led the horses to the back of the burned cabin, where the barn had been. The corral was still standing strong, even though the barn had burned. There was enough collapsed debris left of the burned barn, that it filled in the rest of the corral. He put the horses there, and closed the gate. Then he began to look around.

A small shed, a short distance away had escaped the raid. He went out to it, and pulled the door open. Inside was dark, but he could see a hand pushed garden plow, hanging from the rafters, and a roll of wire by the doorway. When he could see inside better, he found hay, excess from a barn full, he guessed. He pulled out enough to feed the horses. Then he pulled out more, to make a softer place to sleep near the shed, in case it should rain.

After taking some hay to the horses, he came back to the shed, to see what else he could find. To his surprise, he found a saddle and bridle, not in too bad a shape. When he pulled the saddle out of the corner, he also brought out the wooden bench that had held the saddle. *"I believe I might just be able to make a packsaddle out of this."*

Later in the day, he went back and found Julie going through what was left of the cabin. "Not much left I'm afraid, Julie, though I did find a saddle in the shed."

"That was papa's. He hadn't ridden it in a long time. We didn't have horses until that day of the attack, when you put 'em in the corral, and he was never able to ride after that."

"I also found hay for the horses and for our bed."

"OUR bed? Aren't you moving a little fast?"

"I just . . . meant . . . ah." He blushed.

"I know what you meant. I was just kiddin' you."

Bryan changed the subject, "Did you find anything else worth keeping?"

She started to move boards and sod from in front of the fireplace that was still standing, "Not in that corner. Help me move some of this trash from in front of the fireplace."

They both began to pull at the limbs that had formed the roof. Ash and dust from the sod swirled around both of them.

"Just what are you lookin' for here?" he asked.

"The fourth rock from the left side of the hearth," she paused as she lifted the rock, "Papa's savings and they're still here." She removed a small metal box. Inside was a bag that jingled with gold coins, and papers that were scorched, but in fairly good condition. "This is the deed to the land. Here are some letters that momma wrote, and that's about it."

"The money will come in handy for you, since I don't have any yet." He moved out from the house, away from some of the flying ash. "I'm gettin' hungry again. Aren't you?"

"I am at that! You build a fire and I'll pull out some pots and stuff. At least, the pump on the well looks like it'll still works."

"What've you got in mind . . . cookin' a horse?"

"Well, suppose we have a look. Open up that cellar door. I've put up meat and a lot of vegetables, and I don't see why this isn't the time that we need them." As Bryan pulled the door open, she swung down into the cellar. Bryan heard her giggle, then yell, "Have you got that fire going yet?"

Once the fire was going, Julie placed a couple of the pots and pans on the fire, and dumped food from the jars into them. Bryan went to where he had left his things, and came back with a coffee pot and some coffee.

As they ate, the sun sank reluctantly into the west, leaving a glow of gold on the clouds that hovered just above the horizon.

"How about another cup of coffee?"

"Sounds good," She held her cup for him to pour, "Bryan, do you think we should tell the Parkers to come haul all the food to their place? They're getting on in years, and I imagine it would ruin before we get back here."

"Sounds pretty charitable to me. If you want me to, I'll ride over in the morning while you go through what's left here. I want to borrow some tools to build a packsaddle." They both fell silent for a few minutes. "Don't see any reason to put out this fire; it'll help keep the chill away."

She looked at him and smiled, "And I don't see any reason to wash any dishes, either."

"You mean you're not going to fix breakfast?"

Pretending to be miffed, she picked up a small stick, and made a motion to switch him with it. He caught her wrist to stop the swing. The unintended force caused both to fall backward, and roll down a small incline, laughing playfully. She landed on her back, with him holding both of her wrists down. The laughing stopped suddenly, and he was starring into her bright blue eyes. He paused, and then slowly leaned toward her parted lips, as she rose up to meet him. He quickly came to his senses, and broke away.

"Maybe we had better hit the hay."

She was still in a teasing mood. "And just what do you have in mind?"

Realizing what he had said, he slowly turned red and cleared his throat. "I . . . I just meant . . . well, we have a big day tomorrow."

They walked toward the pile of the hay. "I'm sorry but I only have one blanket."

She looked at him out of the corner of her eye, with a big mischievious smile, "There you go again."

"Now look! I didn't mean to infer anything, and if you don't behave I'm going to spank you!"

"Yeah? You and who else?"

With that, he pushed her down on the hay and gave her a few swats on her rear. "I don't need any help . . . Now, behave!" Bryan scolded.

She rolled over and looked at him. He watched her lying there, trying to be a gentleman, in spite of her making it difficult. Then she said, "Aren't you going to kiss me good night?" They both laughed and he kissed her on her forehead. He really wanted to kiss her again, as he had before. He was afraid that both Julia and Geneva's affections had just been a passing fancy. Julie was attracted to him because he had helped her. As for Geneva, it could be just because no one else was around. He felt that he should wait until he got to know both of them better, to let himself get close to either one.

Morning was dark and cold when Bryan stirred the fire back into life. He added wood, until it blazed high enough to light up the area, and warm the morning into life. Tiny sparks rose into the air, the pieces of cedar he added, popped and crackled. A small shaft of smoke went straight up with the sparks, and gave off a pleasent smell that filled the area.

Julia pushed up on her elbows, and saw that he had covered her with the entire blanket, "You're up awfully early, Bryan Forbes."

"I thought I would get an early start to the Parker's. I'm gonna borrow some tools, like I said. I'll come back and make that packsaddle to carry some of our things. I can probably have it finished by the time Mister Parker gets over here to pick up the canned goods. Then we can leave."

He dished out some of the smoked meat, and poured her a cup of coffee. "Here's your breakfast. I'll be back in a little while."

Joseph Parker and his granddaughter Kathy finally arrived at Julie Harris' place, and began loading the jars of canned food onto hay they had put in the wagon. They covered the jars with quilts that they had brought. "Here's an extra saddle blanket I had, to put under that packsaddle." Joseph said to Bryan.

Mister Parker loaded his tools that Bryan had used. He watched as Bryan loaded the supplies and some blankets that he had given them. Kathy had brought one of her coats for Julie. Soon, Bryan and Julie were ready to get on their way.

"Thanks for the supplies, Mister Parker. They will come in mighty handy."

"It's the least I could do, for you saving Kathy. Good luck to you, and Julie. I sure wish you could rebuild, and stay here."

"Well Mister Parker, I've got a lot waiting for me west o' here."

"I guess that's right. Now, you take good care of Julie."

"I'll make it a point to, Mister Parker."

Bryan looked over to where the girls were hugging, with tears in their eyes, saying their goodbyes.

He told Kathy, "You watch out for those Indians, young lady! I may be too far away to come and get you again."

She grinned, threw her arms around him, and kissed him on the cheek, "Thank you again, Mister Forbes."

Kathy jumped up on the seat by her granddad, and waved goodbye, as the team strained to pull the wagon up out of the valley.

"Well, Miss Julie, it's our turn to move out of the valley." He thought a minute, and noticed that their dying morning fire was putting smoke, once again, into the air. "I guess I can call this 'Smoky Valley,' 'cause I've never been here but what it was filled with it."

They mounted up, each taking lead ropes of the extra horses, and headed west.

Bryan felt familiar with the area now that he had been over it a couple of times. They had made good time, and had arrived at the river before the sun went down. "This is a good place to camp, plenty of wood and water. I wish I could take you up the river a ways where I usually camp. It's plumb beautiful up there."

"Why can't you take me, since we haven't set up camp here yet?" she asked.

"It would take longer, and there isn't enough grass for this many horses. They need to eat and rest. We can go next time we come by here. I'll tell you all about it over supper tonight."

"Okay, I'll hold you to that."

Bryan stripped the saddles and the pack from the horses, and made sure each got plenty of water. Then he picketed them where there was plenty of grass. In the meantime Julie had gathered wood to make a small fire behind the large rocks that had fallen from the cliffs. The surrounding boulders would shield the fire from being seen easily.

After they had eaten, they each leaned back and drank another cup of coffee. Julie finished, dumped out the grounds from her cup and stood up. "I'm going to

253

hold you to that story of your camping place. But first I'm going to the river and wash up a bit more." She pulled a towel from the packsaddle and headed to the river.

Bryan, afraid to move, as the river was close to the camp, sat still and looked forward. Many different situations passed through his mind. *"As sure as I look, whether I intend to or not, I know she'll be looking back at me! Doggone it, how do I get in these situations anyway?"*

He did manage not to look her way. When she got back to camp she spoke as she was drying her hair. "Thanks for the privacy. You have a strong will."

"No I don't . . . I just thought of another girl and that kept me occupied."

Julie took her towel in both hands, spun it round and round and popped him with it. He caught the towel, and pulled her down close with it. "I told you to behave yourself once before, or I'd make you wish that you had."

"Okay." She just looked at him with those bright blue eyes, waiting for him to make her wish that she hadn't popped him.

He pulled her closer. She fell into his arms and they kissed. She clung to him, until he gently pushed away.

"Really, Julie, we need to take it easy, I'm not as strong as you may think. I can't let us get too involved until we know each other better, and have some idea as to what's gonna happen."

"So, you were thinking about another woman, like you said."

"No, I wasn't. I was kidding you about that."

With that, she rolled up in her blanket and turned her back to him. "Good night." she said sharply, and became quiet.

This was a new experience for Bryan. He had no idea what to say, so he scooted down in his blanket and thought, *"Danged if I'll ever understand women."* He lay there looking up at the stars trying to figure out what had just happened . . . then Geneva popped into his mind. *"You 'spose she's why I hold back? I don't know if I can handle all this."* He didn't worry long before he was sound asleep.

Bryan was up before daylight. He stirred the fire enough to get coffee started. He wasn't sure whether to wake Julie just yet, so he took the horses to water them. He took his time, wondering how to handle the situation. Then, having waited as long as he could, he walked back to the camp. Julie was up, combing her hair. She had added the coffee to the boiling water and had beans out for their breakfast.

"Sleep good?" he asked. She didn't answer. "Honest, I really wasn't thinking of another girl, I wanted to watch you, but I knew it wasn't right, so I made myself NOT look."

She looked at him with an impish grin, "I was just washing my hair! You could have looked."

"I didn't know that. For all I knew, you was buck neked!" They both laughed, and the mood was light again.

Suddenly Bryan reached for his Winchester and stood up.

"What is it Bryan?"

"Man coming."

"I can't see anyone."

"He'll be here in a minute,"

After a short while, a voice came from up the trail, "Hellooo the camp."

Bryan answered. "Come on in, if you're friendly."

"I am that, and I hope you are! I could smell your coffee two miles up the canyon." the voice came back.

"She does make a strong cup! Come on down and I'll pour you one."

"Name's Will Taggley. Been up in the mountains a few months and decided to come down to see the changes that's been made in the 'civilized' world, as they call it."

Will Taggley was a rugged looking character, wearing a fur cap, and a buckskin coat with leather strings on the sleeves. He had a scraggly black beard with a few grey streaks, and heavy eyebrows that jumped up and down as he talked. He carried a .451 caliber Whitworth Confederate sharpshooter's rifle. He also had a Colt in his belt.

"From the looks of your rifle, you were a sharpshooter in the war."

"That I wus! General 'Little Billy' Mahone's brigade at St. Petersburg . . . Comes in mighty handy on long game shots."

"I reckon it's mighty pretty up there, isn't it?" Julie asked.

"That it is! Yes ma'am that it is. There's a right nice waterfalls a few miles up, worth a body's time to see."

"I wish we could . . . maybe next time." she said.

"You folks goin' fer?"

"Headin' for Santa Fe, as soon as we get loaded." Bryan answered.

"Mind if I ride wi' ya?" Will asked.

"Nope, not at all, I ran across a bunch of Comanche the last time through here, so you might just come in handy."

"That I can! Had some dealin's wi 'em myself, in the near past."

The three of them headed west on the old military trail that Bryan had traveled each time. They kept a close watch for Indians, since they were certainly noticeable on the trail with seven horses kicking up dust.

"Was the game as plentiful up high as it is down here?" asked Bryan.

"Even more so. That mule is loaded with skins. That's why I came down . . . gotta sell 'em and buy me some supplies. I got me a cozy lean-to up there, and it's like a little bit of heaven. I plan to build a cabin someday."

It was quite for a minute, and then Julie commented, "I'll bet it is."

The trip was uneventful, with no attacks. They rode into Santa Fe as the clouds lined up to be painted by the evening sun. The streets had been wet down to lessen the dust from the evening traffic, and there was a squishing sound as the horses slowly headed toward the boarding house. Bryan didn't notice the two men leaning against the porch posts of the Steer's Head saloon: Forest Bowman's men that had also been fired from the Bar H ranch by Cyril Hastings.

Bryan and Julie pulled up in front of the boarding house.

"I'll get us some rooms, and then take care of the horses. I'll be back shortly and we'll get something to eat." said Bryan, and Julie agreed with a nod.

Will Taggley was still mounted, "I think I'll find a place to get a bath and a haircut 'fore I stop."

"Kinda late for that, isn it? asked Bryan.

"Naw, you can go most any time 'roun here, in back of one of the saloons. Have 'em save me a room and I'll pay 'em when I get back," he answered.

Bryan went to the desk and arranged for the rooms, and carried what possessions that Julie had to her room. He headed to Daniel Brookings place, to care for the horses.

He walked into Brooking's office. "Daniel, I figgered you'd be gone home by now."

"Well, hello Bryan. I guess I let the time get away. You et yet?"

"Not yet, we will as soon as I wash up."

"WE . . . you not alone?"

"No Sir, there's a young lady whose home got burned out by Indians. I couldn't leave her alone. Then a man named Will Tagley came down out of the mountains to sell his skins. We invited him to join us for safety."

"Yeah, I know Will. He comes down ever once in a while. Why don't you go in there and wash up and let's go eat." Daniel motioned to the washroom.

"Sounds good to me."

They both washed up, and headed to the boarding house.

"Daniel, you go on in. I'll get Julie and meet you in there."

Daniel agreed. Bryan went to Julie's room and knocked on the door. There was no answer. *"Guess she went on down."* He went back down the hall to the dining room. He saw Daniel seated near the back of the room, but didn't see Julie anywhere.

"I thought Julie would be down here. I'll be back. I've gotta look for her. She wasn't in her room."

He went to the front desk and asked the attendant if he had seen her come from her room . . . he had not seen her.

"Has anyone come in, say, an old mountain man?"

"No sir, no mountain man, but a couple of cowhands came in right after you left, when you took the rooms."

"A couple of cowhands . . . did they come out?"

"No sir, they haven't."

"Did they get rooms?"

"No sir, they didn't!" The desk clerk answered with a surprised look.

"Is there a back door from the rooms?"

"Yes there is, now that you mentioned it! I wondered where those two cowhands went."

Bryan hurried into the dining room and told Daniel, "Julie's not in her room. The desk clerk said a couple of men slipped out the backway. For some reason, the cowhands may have taken Julie with them."

Daniel asked, "Do you want me to help you look for her?"

"No. You stay here until I make sure she isn't still here somewhere."

He went to the back door and studied the tracks. One man had held what looked like three or four horses, for some time. Small boot prints that might be Julie's and another man had mounted. They all had left heading northwest, away from town.

As he went back into the boarding house, he met Will Taggley coming in the front door.

"Will, is that you? I hardly knew you! You sure clean up nice." Will didn't look as old as Bryan had first thought. Bryan then explained what had taken place.

"It's pretty dark out. I don't think we can track 'em close, 'till mornin'." Will offered.

"I guess not, but I can't help but feel I need to go to her. Maybe they were someone she knew . . . nah, she wouldn't leave without tellin' us . . . besides; she's a long way from home."

They both went into the dining room and sat with Daniel. Bryan told them how worried he was, for her safety.

"I been seein' them two hands that worked with Bowman hanging around town for a while since you left." said Daniel.

Bryan thought a while, "That's who those two were. Sounds like they took Julie to get me to follow 'em. If that's the case, they may not expect me to follow in the dark, so I think I'd better try. I can tell the general direction they are going and move that way. The moon'll be up soon. From the tracks I saw, they were headed northwest where they'll run into the Rio Grande. I'll head that way. They'll camp where there is water and wood."

Will stood up, "I'm a goin' too, Bryan."

"Thanks Will. I might need your help. Daniel, I would appreciate it if you would get word to Mr. Hastings about what has happened, and that I will contact him as soon as I can."

"Why, I sure will, Bryan! Don't you worry."

"And Will, if you can shoot that rifle of yours as far as I think you can, better take it along."

"Wouldn't be without it!"

They went out the back door. Bryan held the lantern where Will could see the tracks that he was talking about.

Will examined the whole area. "Looks to me like two men and a woman like you said, and headed to the northwest."

"If we go straight west of here, and cross the Rio Grande, we can travel without running up on them. If they have a campfire, they'll be easy to spot. Not a lot of cover out there, a few trees right along the river and a lot of bushes."

"They can't be sure I'll come after them tonight, maybe they'll let their guard down."

"It ain't none of my business, but exactly what's going on here?" asked Will.

"Well, you heard Daniel say that Bowman's men had been hanging around?" Will nodded. "Bowman stole my cattle, and was headed up the Santa Fe Trail, to sell them along with the Bar H's cattle. I caught him. When I took him to the Bar H to see what they would have to say, they fired him. I guess these two pokes were expecting some of the money my cattle would bring them."

Bryan and Will rode toward the river. They arrived and found a good place and crossed. Then, they rode a distance on farther west, away from the river's edge.

The moon had risen about the time they crossed the river, and now was bright enough see by. They turned north again, and rode faster to cover more ground, carefully watching for any campfire on the other side of the river.

After a couple of miles, Bryan saw a glitter, well ahead of their position. "Will, I think I saw a fire up ahead where the river turns east. I think I should cross back over on the other side, and when I get close enough, I'll walk in to the camp. You ease on closer, where you can see their camp."

Bryan coaxed the appaloosa into the river, and headed toward the glow of the fire.

When he was close enough to see figures around the campfire he stopped, dropped the reins and eased on foot to the edge of the camp. He knew they were looking into the fire, and would not be able to see outside their camp. So he moved quietly and slowly to the very edge. When he was close, he spoke up, "Howdy fellers!"

They both jumped to their feet, and one said: "Doggone it man! You liked to have scared me to death!"

They were so surprised that neither of them had drawn a gun.

"Now, just stay where you are, and keep your hands clear of your guns, and we'll palaver for a while. When you left town, there was a young lady with you. I guess one of you dropped her off before joining here. I need to know her where-abouts."

"Why, I'm afraid we don't know what you're talkin' about." one responded.

"Let me jog your memory. I aim to find her, with your help . . . or maybe not. I came out here tonight because I didn't want to be bushwhacked like your partner Bowman did to me. I had to kill him, and I have no second thoughts about killing you. I don't plan to, but my plans have changed a few times lately.

"Since she's not with you, I guess you've put her somewhere for safe keepin', and if shes not safe, then I may have a problem lettin' you fellers go."

The quiet one began to slowly move farther to the side of the camp, and when he thought he was far enough from his partner that they could cover each other, he went for his gun. It was still only half out of his holster when Bryan's bullet knocked him on his back.

"Now, I still want to know where the lady is. Do you want to tell me, or try for your gun too?"

The remaining man stood staring at his friend. "I'll take you there and . . . and I'm not trying anything."

"Drop your gun belt, and put your friend across his saddle. Tie him on and let's get started."

About that time, Will Taggley eased up on his horse, "Don't look like you need much back up."

"Maybe not, but I'm glad you were there."

Bryan tied the hands of his prisoner, lacing the ends through the pommel and over the horn, tight enough that he had no slack. As he turned to mount, the angry man leaned back in the saddle and kicked his stirrup high enough to hit Bryan in the head, knocking him against his horse. He slid to the ground, shaken but not out cold.

Will's Whitworth boomed out. The bound rider had almost made it to the edge of the firelight. His horse fell and rolled over him. Will then checked on Bryan.

As Bryan was recovering, Will told him what had happened. "I only intended to stop his horse but it rolled over him. I doubt if he survived it. You gonna to be all right?"

"Not if he can't tell us where Julie is! We better look and see if he's got any thing on him that might help."

"Like what?" Will came back.

"Anything . . . a paper, map, address, anything!"

"Okay, I'll have a look."

Will helped Bryan stand and hold to his horse. Then he went to the fallen man to go through his pockets and saddlebags.

Bryan moved closer to the fire, and sat down on a log. He splashed a bit of water on his head, from his canteen, trying to recover enough to head back to Santa Fe. Soon, Will returned to the camp, "I didn't find a lot to help us, but I did find a key. All we got to do now is find a lock that it'll fit."

"No address or anything written down?"

"Nope, no papers, 'cept to roll smokes in."

"Well, I guess we better load him on with the other 'poke, and get back to town. If we can find out where they're stayin' maybe that's where we'll find Julie. I can't figure why they came out here, if they left Julie in town."

"They probably just wanted to get you out where they could kill you away from town." figured Will.

They loaded both men on the one horse, and headed back to Santa Fe.

When they rode into Santa Fe, the morning sun was just peaking over the hills. The streets were busy with the storeowner traffic, as wagons and buckboards were coming into town. Gentle columns of smoke rose from several chimneys, and the smell of coffee was in the air.

"I vote we give these fellers to the sheriff, and get some breakfast." said Will.

"We can get these fellers to the sheriff, but I'm hoping he'll know where they were staying." said Bryan.

They tied up in front of the sheriff's office and walked in. "Howdy Sheriff! We got a couple of fellers that kidnapped a friend of mine. They were reluctant to tell us where she was. They worked for Cyril Hastings until Cyril found out they were crooked."

"I been hearing about that. Seems they're saying you killed ole Forest Bowman . . . that right?"

"That's right Sheriff, after he shot me." answered Bryan.

"Now you done killed his friends, is that right?"

"Like I told you, they kidnapped my friend."

"It'll be kind'a hard to hear both sides now, won't it?" said the Sheriff.

"Well I have a witness to the one I shot in self defense, and besides they stole my cattle. I can get you all the witnesses you need! But what I need from you is where these fellers been staying, so I can see if my friend is there!"

"Okay, okay! They been 'a stayin' north of town, across the Santa Fe River in that little yellow shack on the creek. You can't miss it." As they walked outside the sheriff followed, and when he saw the two men draped across the horse he shouted to Bryan and Will: "Hey! What am I supposed to do with these bodies?"

As Bryan stepped up on his horse, he said, jokingly, "Put 'em under arrest." Then they rode off, hurriedly, toward the shack.

When they reached the shack, that had at one time been yellow, they were both off their horses before they were completely stopped. Dust engulfed them both, as Bryan put his shoulder to the flimsy door, and it landed flat on the floor inside.

"Dang, Bryan! I had the key I found on that feller!"

The shotgun style house had only two rooms, and there was very little in the first one, except a table and a couple of chairs, so they rushed to the next door.

Bryan opened that door a little easier, and there on the bed, tied hand and foot, was Julie. He quickly whipped out his knife, and cut the bindings. But Julie did not respond, "Will, get the Doc . . . Quick!"

Will jumped on his horse, and was gone in a cloud of dust. "Heck! I don't know where no doctor would be!" So he pulled up in front of the saloon, and ran through the butterfly doors. Everyone in the saloon turned to see what had burst through the doors. Two pulled their guns out of habit.

Will started waving out-stretched hands in front of himself, "Don't go off half cocked! I just need to know where the Doc would be."

"Well son, it so happens I'm right here!" An older gentleman stood up. He had the look of a doctor, with his tailored trousers and vest to match, over a white shirt with the sleeves held up with black garters. He had a stub of a cigar in his teeth, and gold-rimmed glasses half way down his nose.

"What can I do for you son? Are you sick?"

"No sir! There's a lady out cold, been tied up all night. A couple o' yahoos took her about suppertime last night, and she's been tied up ever since. You can take my horse."

"No need. I have my buckboard out back."

They both hurried out the back door, and Will jumped up beside the doctor.

When they arrived at the yellow house, the doctor grabbed his bag from under the seat, and sprung to the ground as if he was half his age. Then he ran into the shack. He looked at Julie and asked, "How long she been out?"

"I don't know for sure, Doc. She was out when we got here."

Doc opened his bag, and took out some smelling salts and fanned it under her nose a couple of times. She began to come around. "I reckon she fainted. Maybe when you came in, thinking it was the hoolagans returning."

"Could be, Doc. We did come in kinda forceful like."

"That's what I thought, by the looks of the door. How do you feel, dear?"

Julie sat up and said: "I guess all right. When I heard the door being knocked down, that's the last thing I remember."

"Just as I thought. Young lady, you need to get something to eat and get some rest! I think you'll be just fine. Lack o' food and all the excitement caused your system to take a rest. Now you do the same!"

The doctor and Bryan walked outside. "Thank you Doc, I'll come by and pay you later."

"No need son, no need at all. Glad I could be of help."

Bryan thanked the doctor, and went back inside. Julie was sitting on the edge of the bed. "Who were those men, and what did they want, Bryan?"

"They wanted me. And you became the bait," he answered. "I've got to go to the Hastings' ranch, so I'm gonna let Will take care of you. And please, try to stay out of trouble."

She looked around and asked, "Where is Will?"

"This is Will right here! Don't tell me you didn't recognize him just 'cause he's all cleaned up."

"Well, I'm sorry Will, I didn't . . . I thought you were some young handsome fellow off the street."

Will stepped closer and said, "I'm not sure how I oughta take that."

They had a laugh, and he said, "I'm glad you're feeling better. I'll see if I can catch Doc, and maybe we can ride back with him." He ran outside and yelled to Doc, "Can we catch a ride back into town with you, Doc?"

"You certainly can. Climb aboard and help that girl up here."

Bryan Forbes rode out of town feeling secure that Will would take care of Julie. Now all he had to worry about was Geneva, a job, and a herd of cattle or a wad of money, whichever he had.

"I seem to get more in trouble with every passin' day! What'll come up next?" he thought, as he eased along the dusty trail. *"Reckon I'll get there in time to eat. That cook 's one of the best and I shore been missin' a lot of chow lately."*

The trip to the ranch was easy. The land was flat and easy on the horse. A few trees along the way gave a little shade to rest.

"What am I going to say to Cyril? He may have hired someone else, since I've been gone so long. Will Geneva want me around, like she implied 'fore I left?

266

Foreman's pay is too good to pass up, if he still wants me.

"What about my cattle? Do I take the money, or should I take him up on his offer of replacing mine? I think the money might just be best, if I'm gonna stay on the ranch. I think I got more decisions to make than I had when I left!" So many thoughts ran through his head, enough that he was at the ranch before he realized it.

He could see Cyril leaning against a porch, post, and by the time he reached the ranch, Geneva was bringing a tray of drinks to the table on the big porch.

Cyril greeted him, "Saw you coming up the road . . . I'm right glad to see you! Hope you got the problem solved that Daniel told us about. I guess you did, since you're finally back. Get down, and we'll have some lemonade, and talk about your travels."

Bryan eased off his appaloosa, dusted himself with his hat, and stepped up onto the porch. "Howdy Miss Geneva," he nodded. Then, "Cyril, it's good to be back. Been a long time it seems, a lot has happened."

"Well then, sit down and tell us about it. We don't hear much news out here." said Cyril.

The two of them sat down and Geneva poured lemonade for each of them. Then she sat down by Bryan. "Yes, do tell us about your trip!"

He started first to tell them how he came to know the Harris family. "I just happened to ride up on the Harris place, during an Indian raid. Actually, it was purty much over by the time I got there. Anyway, that's how I met up with Paul and Julie. That's when Julie suggested I bring my cattle there. This time, their place was burned, and Indians had carried Julie off. I trailed them and found they had two other girls along with Julie." He continued his story, until he had explained why he was gone so long.

Geneva, with a tear in her eye, sighed, "Those poor girls."

He went on to tell them what happened when he got back to Santa Fe. "That about brings you up to date. I wasn't sure you'd still have a job for me, so I came to see."

"Where's Julie?" Geneva asked.

"She's at the boarding house. Will Taggley is taking care of her for now. She had a pretty good scare and was weak, but Doc said she'd be all right."

"The job's still yours, that is, if you'll still want it. We've been having some rustling going on, and Aledo and the boys can't seem to put a finger on where or when it's happening."

"I would like the job very much. Maybe the rustling will ease off since the two of Bowman's men are out of the picture. I'd like to do some wandering for a few days, but I'll need to get another mount. My ole appaloosa is kinda tired."

"Just tell Aledo what you need. I guess that you're hungry. Let's go in and see what the fare is today. Geneva, lead the way please."

"This will be the first real meal I've had since I been gone. Well, I guess that's not true. Mrs. Parker set a pretty good table"

Bryan followed Geneva and Cyril into the large dining room, and sat down at the big oak table.

"By the way Bryan, your cattle brought sixty five dollars a head, pretty good for the times. That comes to about nineteen thousand, five hundred dollars!

"That _is_ a pretty good profit, and I'm mighty thankful to you. Do you mind keeping the money for me?"

"No problem at all. If you need any, just let me know."

After their meal, Geneva volunteered to show Bryan where he would be staying.

They stepped into the bunkhouse and walked to a door that led into a private room. There was a bunk, stove and a desk. The desk contained the herd count book and the pasture rotation use, and other information about the various parts of the ranch. There was also a large map on the wall of the Spanish Land Grant. It showed the part of the grant that made up the Bar H Ranch.

"Nothing much is overlooked here. Seems I have what I need. I'll study the map tonight, and be gone a few days to see if I can find any leads on this rustlin'."

Geneva turned to Bryan, "I'll have Aledo get your lamp filled for you."

She moved close, pressing against him, "I missed you while you were gone, I wasn't sure you were coming back."

Bryan wasn't sure whose heart he felt. Was it his, or hers? It didn't matter! He put his arms around her, drawing her even closer, if that was possible, and kissed her. Then stepped back and gazed into her eyes, "You're so beautiful . . . are you telling me you don't have a half dozen cowboys around here a chasing you?"

"I honestly don't . . . Oh, Lawrance Davis over on the Flying A thinks he's got his rope on me, but he's crude and overbearing. He has a fair size spread, and runs a lot of good stock, so he thinks I should be taken with him."

"The Flying A, mmm . . ." He studied the map on the wall. "Does it join your father's grant?" he asked.

"Yes, look here on the map, his is the other half of the grant." She points to an area on the map, "This canyon is the line. It runs for miles east and west forming the border of our ranches."

The question crossed his mind "I *wonder if he's losing cattle too*" . . . Then he said, "So that I'll know, show me what his brand looks like."

Geneva took a pencil and began to draw. "The A has a bar across the middle, and the ends of the cross bar have a short bar pointing up at a forty five degree angle like this, like little wings. Thus, the Flying A."

Bryan asked, "Is the top of the A always pointed like you have it here?"

"No, now that you mention it, it's sometime rounded. Why? What are you thinking?"

"Well, it's just *that*, a thought . . . but I'm thinking how easy the Bar H can become the Flying A. I like to study brands and it just kinda . . . jumped out at me"

She looked at him in deep thought. "You don't think a longtime neighbor would do something like that, do you?"

"He might, if he's in trouble, and if a little more money would solve his problems."

"But he wants to marry me! He wouldn't steal from me, would he?"

"Look at what he would get, if he did marry you." Bryan said, as his hand circled the Bar H ranch on the map.

She moved close again, "You might say the same thing about you." Her eyes sparkled as she reached out for him, pulled him close and squinted an eye at him, "How about it? Are you just interested in what I might inherit?"

"I might be." He held her close and kissed her again, "I can't keep doing this, and get out early tomorrow. I better say good night."

As she turned toward the door, "Okay then, but you don't know what you're missing! Goodnight."

Bryan followed her to the door, kissed her once more, and closed it. He went back into the room to study the map, thinking: *"how do I get myself into all these situations? . . . I need to be thinking about tomorrow, not what I might have missed tonight . . . hmmm . . . I wonder what she meant by that!"* He forced himself to concentrate on the map.

He drew a smaller, less detailed map to carry with him. It would help him recall the features on the main map. He studied it a while longer, then lay back on the bunk and fell asleep.

Bryan awoke early, as usual. But what was unusual was that he was still fully dressed. *"I knew I was tired, but I didn't know I was that tired!"*

He left quietly, as the other hands in the bunkhouse were still asleep. He quietly made his way to the kitchen. By the time he finished his breakfast, the other hands were drifting in.

"As soon as you've finished, Aledo, I'd like to get another mount and pack-horse. I'm gonna see if I can find out where these cattle are going."

"Si Señor, I weel be right out. Do you weesh me to go with you, Señor Forbes?" asked Aledo.

"No, you have plenty to do here. Take your time. I've a lot to get ready yet."

The sun was well into the sky by the time Bryan left the ranch. There was still a chill in the air and the smell of fresh rain on the soil. "Must'a rained during the night," he commented out loud. His mount's ears moved back and forth as he talked. "I like to see those ears movin' like that, and I'll expect you to keep me aware of any surprises. Papa told us to always watch the ears."

The land was rolling with hills and valleys, and some rising buttes formed at the same time the Rockies were. It was hard to see long distances, so Bryan stayed alert to any strange moving in the distance. So far, he had only seen a coyote and a hawk diving for the same field mouse.

Reaching the canyon that divided the Bar H and Flying A ranches, he was surprised to find that it was very deep and wide, with steep sides lined with rocks. "Nobody'd drive cattle across that . . . It's way too steep! It's gotta be a lot more shallow somewhere, if they're taking cattle to the Flying A or anywhere else south of here."

Bryan rode another mile and a half to a butte where he could ride up to have a better view. He took the glasses from his saddlebags and scanned the area, looking for crossing places. Not seeing any likely places for anyone to cross with cattle, he decided to look for a spot to camp for the night.

Riding off the butte, and back one more time along the canyon, Bryan examined the walls and the floor of the canyon. The sides were of sandstone and the bottom was sandy. *"Doesn't look like any water's been through here lately. Better look for another source to pitch camp."*

He rode on for a few miles, and finally came upon the Rio Grande, as it wandered its way through the foothills of the Rockies. The place he picked for a campsite was quiet, and had enough trees for shade.

After he watered his horses, he located them where they could get plenty of grass. He then gathered wood to build a fire. He tossed his saddle on a grassy spot, and spread a ground cloth for his bedroll.

He leaned back and studied the map he had drawn, while listening to the birds and the water moving by. The sun in the west was flashing golden spotlights on the whole area as it pushed its way through the cottonwood trees. *"Guess I better get a fire going and some coffee on before it gets too dark."*

When the sun had gone down, he sat by the fire drinking another cup of coffee. He listened a few minutes then said aloud, "Will, I been wonderin' why you didn't come on in when I first heard you."

Will rode in and dismounted, "I wasn't sure it was you, 'cause you never let me see your face, and them ain't the clothes you was wearin' yesterday. How'd ya know it was me?"

"By the way that ole mountain horse of your's drags his hind leg!" Bryan's careful listening had taught him to distinguish the sounds of familiar riders.

"You got another cup o' that mud?" Will asked.

"Help yourself. Then tell me what you're doing out here."

Will poured himself a cup, "Ain't you got no sugar?" He asked.

"Sugar's for sissies, but I'll stick my finger in it if you want. By the way,what about Julie?"

"No thanks! I don't use sugar anyway. Well, I tell ya, it's like this: Your *ranch girlfriend* came to town and invited your in *town girlfriend* and me, to come to the ranch. When I found out you wus out here lookin' fer rustlers, I just figgered you might need some help . . . 'sides Mr. Hastings offered to put me on his payroll fer a while, and I can use the money."

Bryan looked at Will for a long minute. Then he asked, "Geneva invited Julie to stay at the ranch, didn't she?"

"Yep! Seems Geneva was fascinated with the story you told about Julie and all her problems. They seem to hit it off real good."

"I hope they don't hit it off too good! It might get me in trouble."

The next day, Bryan Forbes and Will Taggley rode along the border of the Bar H, looking for likely places where cattle could be moved. The canyon that divided the two ranches ended at the river. The upheaval that blocked the river from the canyon continued on the other side, and was too steep and high for cattle to climb.

Having no luck finding a crossing place, they returned to the camp they had made along the Rio Grande.

The sun was hanging low in the west as the two began to prepare their evening meal. Coffee was brewing on the fire, and Will was frying bacon. When he looked up through the smoke, he saw a rider approaching.

In a low voice, Will alerted Bryan, "Rider coming."

"I saw 'em a while back. Don't look like a cowhand." answered Bryan.

"He shore don't," Will responded. "Dressed a little too fancy, I reckon."

They kept on with their cooking, keeping an eye on the man riding toward their camp. Soon the rider hailed them to come into camp.

"Ride on in, if'n you're friendly."

The response came at once, "I'm friendly! The name's Russell Culp. I'm cattle detective for these parts." He rode in and dismounted.

"We're just getting ready for supper. Will you join us?"

"Don't mind if I do."

"My name's Bryan Forbes and this is Will Taggley. What are you doing in these parts?"

"Well, this, and other ranches, are in my territory. Several have been loosing cattle lately, and they asked me here to check on it. Been watching you fellers yesterday and today, and finally decided if you were rustlers, you weren't having much luck."

"We both ride for the Bar H brand," said Bryan.

"If you don't mind my askin', how come your ridin' the Bar H and the Flying A line?" asked Culp.

"You ever notice how easy the Bar H brand could be blotched into a Flying A brand?" Bryan responded.

"I never noticed."

"Those folks are so close, I kinda figured nobody ever paid attention. Here, let me show you." Bryan took a stick and drew in the sand as Russell watched.

"Well, I'll be . . . it sure could! I never thought of it. They been neighbors for years," said Culp, "I suppose you've got a plan."

"I guess you've seen that we're lookin' for a place where cattle could be driven across. That's a pretty deep canyon to the east, and pretty high hills on the west, so we've come to the conclusion that it's here." said Bryan.

"Now how's that? I don't see what you mean," admitted Culp.

"Me and Will have ridden this whole area, and we've decided that they cross right here. Take a look: the river is blocked from going into the canyon by an upheaval in the past, and that continues on the other side of the river, clear to yonder. It's way too much of a hill for cattle to climb. I think that canyon may even be where the river changed course when all those rocks got pushed up there.

"Take a look back there a ways. The riverbank is cut pretty low . . . low enough that cattle could be driven into the river and swum past the canyon and then out the other side. It may not even be deep enough to make them swim. We decided to give it a try tomorrow, and make sure it's possible to get out on the other side, 'fore we do any accusin'."

"That sounds plausible to me. I just might as well ride with you," said Russell Culp.

"Why don't we eat? I'm starvin'!" said Will.

"You're always starvin', Will."

After breakfast the next morning, the air was heavy with moisture stirred up out of the river, but the wind was light. Will stretched and shivered, "Say, don't you think we ought to wait 'till it warms up a little?"

"A little cold won't hurt ya, Will. It'll do a right smart of good," said Bryan.

"How far do you think we'll have to swim, before we can get out on the Flying A side?" asked Culp.

"Not too far, if this is where they cross. Too many cattle would drown, if they had to swim long . . . IF they had to swim at all."

"If there are cattle there, I want to examine some brands." said Russell.

"Will, we'll leave our supplies here. No use our stuff gettin' wet and . . . listen!" Bryan stopped what he was doing.

"What is it, Bryan?"

"Listen . . . I hear cattle bawlin'! Everybody into the rocks . . . Quick! Hide the horses . . . and Will, get guns ready. And you too, Russell."

They were leading the horses into the large rocks that had caved off the side of the hills and scattered along the river. "Will, when you get that rifle of yours, get us plenty of ammunition out of the pack. I'm going a little higher with the glasses to see what's comin'. I'll be right back."

Russell Culp cupped his hand behind his ear. "I still haven't heard any cattle yet."

Will was pulling at the ropes on the packhorse to get to the ammunition, "Sometimes I think Bryan's got hearing like an old jackrabbit! Let's get the horses hidden."

Bryan came down from the hill and explained the situation. "About five men with a small bunch of cattle, too dusty to know exactly how many, but I'd bet money they are coming right here to cross. If they do, we'll be ready for them. They are on Bar H land and they are not Bar H hands. Russell, I'd also bet you get your chance to check out some brands!"

The three of them stayed well hidden behind the rocks until the riders were close to where they would drive the cattle into the river. Bryan then stepped out where the riders could see him and asked in a loud, booming voice, "You gentlemen headed far, with Mr. Hastings cattle?"

The rider heading the drive reined up quickly, and his hand dropped close to his gun. A voice came from the rocks, "I'd move your hands a bit higher, if I was you!" Will made himself known to the riders, and they raised their hands up higher.

The rider that seemed to be in charge spoke out, "You'll find the cattle belong to the Flying A!"

Bryan turned to ask the rider his name. Out of the corner of his eye he caught the sun reflecting off the barrel of a rifle from up on the hill, where he had first observed the riders. He drew his gun and fired. Bryan's bullet hit its mark, and the shot from the hooligan's rifle, as he was falling, kicked up the dust between Bryan and Russell. They watched him roll down the hill.

The others didn't move. Bryan made them lose their guns and get off their horses. "On your bellies . . . now! Will, if you'll do the honors, these men are ready to be tied, while Mr. Russell examines the cattle they were driving."

Each man was bound hand and foot, and then leaned against the rocks while Russell Culp and Bryan started to examine the cattle.

"I believe you're right, Bryan. The brands have been blotched to the Flying A."

One of the men shouted to them, "What makes you think they've been run?"

"Well, for one thing we can see where the runnin' iron has made fresh burns, and the other thing is they're on Hastings's range." answered Bryan.

"Why, they just strayed over here, and we're takin' 'em back home."

Russell laughed, "Strayed across that canyon?

"You seem to be in charge. What's your name?" Bryan asked the man talking.

"Not that it's any of your business, but it's Lawrance Davis!"

"The owner of the Flying A Ranch, I take it?"

"That's right, what of it?"

"I think Geneva Hastings will be a little disappointed in you, is all."

"What do you know of Geneva Hastings?" asked Davis.

"I work for the Hastings, and their concern is my concern."

"What do you mean you work for the Hastings? Where's Forest Bowman?"

"So . . . you and Forest Bowman were in this together? I figured as much. Bowman rustled cattle from the wrong person, and now he's dead, along with a couple of his cronies. We've talked enough! Will, let's get these fellers mounted and start back to town. It may take awhile to convince that sheriff that these men have been doing the rustling."

"Russell, do you have enough to make sure these men will spend time in jail?"

Russell yelled back, "I do indeed!"

Will Taggley cut the leg ties on Lawrance Davis and helped him on his horse. As he turned his attention to helping the other rustlers on their horses, Davis clamped his spurs into the sides of his horse, and sped off into the river.

"Want me to shoot him, Bryan?" Will asked as he raised his sniper rifle.

"No, let him go. I want to follow him to see where and how he took the cattle across. You can shoot any of the others, if they take off. I think you and Russell can take them into town."

Will placed the butt of his rifle on his thigh and answered, "I think we can handle it! What about the cattle?"

"They will be fine here; there is plenty of water and grass. Aledo and the boys can come back later and put them on the best pasture. Take the pack horse with you. I'll go back to the Bar H by the main road."

Bryan let a few minutes go by to make Lawrance Davis think he had gotten away. Then he rode into the shallow river and headed through the gap. He watched carefully to see where Davis had come out of the river.

The river bottom was hard stone, and that made it easy to move through the gap. Once he reached the other side, Lawrance's tracks were easy to follow. He rode up out of the river and followed at a distance to see where Davis would go. According to his hand drawn map, it looked to him that Lawrance was headed to his ranch house.

When Lawrance Davis reached his house, he rode directly to the woodpile near the kitchen door. He was looking for the double bited axe that he knew was there. When he saw the axe stuck in the chopping block, he rolled off his horse and quickly used the upright sharp blade of the axe to cut the bindings from his hands. He then ran into the house.

His first stop was to strap on another gun belt, and retrieve a rifle from the gun cabinet. He loaded as much extra ammunition as he could into his saddlebags, and ran to his safe. It contained a few stacks of money and some papers. He stuffed the money into his pockets, but left the papers. He didn't bother to close the safe, as he rushed out the door, mounted his horse, and rode toward the southwest.

When Bryan arrived at the Flying A ranch house, he approached cautiously, not knowing if Lawrance Davis was still there. He eased off his horse and dropped the reins. His horse was breathing deeply from the brisk run from the river, and his hot breath made puffs of steam in the cool air. Bryan stood still and listened. He looked around at the tracks. When he was satisfied that Lawrance Davis had left, he went to the house to make sure no one else was there.

Inside the house he found the empty ammunition boxes, and the empty space where a rifle had stood in the gun cabinet. Just as he was ready to leave, he noticed the safe with the door still ajar. He saw that it still had papers and a few dollars in gold coins. He removed the papers and studied them. Apparently one was a deed of sorts where Cyril Hastings' grandfather had sold this ranch house and acreage to a Mason A.

Davis. *"Maybe this was the great grandfather to Lawrance Davis."* Bryan placed the papers in his inside pocket, and went out to trail Davis for a while. He tracked him long enough to let a lawman know which way he had gone. After a few miles of tracking, he headed back to the Bar H, and crossed the bridge that joined the two ranches.

Bryan arrived at the ranch, and went directly to the bunkhouse. The sun was beginning to sink below the mountains in the distance. As he stepped up on the porch, he paused long enough to light the lantern hanging by the door before he went inside. Instead of going directly to his room, he walked in where he saw Will Taggley sitting on his bunk. "Did you have any trouble, Will?"

"Nope! The boss man sent Chico and Josh to help Russell take them into town. They wus calm as lambs all the way." Will answered.

With a chuckle Bryan commented, "Careful, Will. You're in cattle country now! We don't speak of lambs."

"Okay then, they wus calm as fillies on a green grass pasture . . . say, speaking of fillies, what are you going to do about those two gals?"

Bryan dropped his head, and didn't say anything right off. Then he looked Will in the eye and said: "I just don't know. What would you do?"

"Me? I have no idea. Ain't never been anywhere close to a situation like that." Looking down at the floor, he continued, "If ya don't mind me sayin' so, I've kinda taken a likin' to Julie. We sorta got acquainted after you left. I hope you don't mind."

"Why should I mind? I got no ropes on either one 'em. To be honest, as much as I like Julie, I just can't get Geneva outta my head! They are both kind'a purty aren't they?"

"That they are! Yes sir that they are." Will answered. "I hate to change the subject, but what did you do with ole 'Lary' Davis?"

"He rode off into the sunset. I trailed him awhile, enough to know where he was headed. I'll let the sheriff chase him, 'cause I'd likely kill him, if I caught up to him."

Chapter 23

This time of the year the sun doesn't bother to get up as early as a ranch hand has to, so it was still dark. The stars were so bright Bryan could see his shadow as he walked to the main house for breakfast.

Aledo and some of the other hands were already at the large table just off the kitchen. "Sorry to be so late, but yesterday was a rough day."

"Señor Weell told us about your day. I would have never suspected Señor Davis of such." Aledo replied.

"Aledo, if you don't mind, I would like for you to check to see if the cattle need to be moved from where we left them."

"Si Señor, we weel go this morning, Señor Weell told us where they are."

"Good! Muchas Gracias, Aledo."

Aledo, with a smile, answered, "De nada, Señor Bryan."

Bryan wanted to talk to Cyril Hastings, but he hesitated because he knew that both Geneva and Julie were in the house. He wanted to avoid seeing them together for a while, if he could. Finally, he moved through the hallway from the kitchen and entered the large dining room. At the table were Cyril and two of the most beautiful girls a man would want to see. They both smiled, and together said: "Good morning, Bryan." He blushed and responded quietly.

"Bryan is it?" Cyril turned to see, "Sit down my boy and have your breakfast."

"Thank you, Cyril, and later I have a few questions to ask you."

Bryan sat across from the girls, and helped himself to breakfast. Each time he looked up, the girls were smiling at him. He tried to make small talk, but finally said, "I think the rustling should stop now."

Cyril paused eating, with his fork half way to his mouth, and looked at Bryan. "So soon, you've taken care of it?"

"Well, yes, I guess so. Things just seem to fall into place."

"Do we know who was responsible?" Cyril asked.

"Yes, we do. Besides your late foreman and his men, it was ramrodded by your neighbor, Lawrance Davis." He glanced at Geneva. She showed no response.

"I find that hard to believe! Is he in custody?" Cyril questioned.

"He was, but he managed to get away. I know the direction he's headed, so I'll let the sheriff handle it. The others are in custody, Aledo and the boys have gone to bring the cattle they were rustling back here. That batch of cattle had the flying A brand, changed from your brand of course."

The room fell quiet, and they continued to eat. After a few minutes, Geneva asked, "How do you know he was rustling instead of moving some cattle?"

"Russell Culp came up. He's the cattle detective for this area. While we were trying to figure out how they would get cattle across the canyon, Davis showed up with a bunch of cattle that he had just blotched the brands on. They were your cattle, on your land, with the Bar H changed to a Flying A."

"I would never have thought it of him." said Cyril.

"Cyril, what do you know about your grandfather selling the Flying A house and land to Lawrance Davis' great grandfather?"

Cyril was thoughtful for a moment, and then answered, "I didn't know that he did. I thought the Davis family had always owned the Flying A."

"Do you have a signature of your grandfather?" asked Bryan.

"Yes, I think so. Why do you need that?"

"With the other problems you've had with them, I guess I'm just suspicious."

"If you're finished, Bryan, lets move into the den. I have some of his papers in there."

"If you ladies will excuse us," Bryan followed Cyril.

Cyril went to the large oak mantle over the fireplace, and opened a rosewood box, and removed a yellowed paper from it. He checked to see if it had a signature. It did, and he handed it to Bryan.

Bryan studied both papers. After a minute he said, "Cyril, what do you make of this, these signatures I mean?"

Cyril took both papers and examined the signatures. "Well, what jumps out at me is, they are not the same!"

"That's what I think too. Do you have any other signatures of his?"

"Yes, let me look." He went back to the rosewood box, went through several papers, and came up with another. He handed it to Bryan.

Bryan examined this signature and compared all three. "Looks to me like this deed I got from the Davis' safe is a forgery!"

Cyril looked at Bryan, "What does this mean?"

"I'm not sure yet, but I'll go into town and see how and if this is registered. I'll need to take these other two papers with me."

Cyril nodded. Then Bryan left the room. As he stepped into the dining room to go back through the kitchen, he saw Geneva. His eyes quickly scanned the room.

"She's not here, Bryan. She's outside with Will."
She walked in his direction. "I haven't had a chance to
welcome you back yet." She moved in close to him, and
looked him in the eyes. "What does she mean to you,
Bryan?"

He had expected a kiss and this question took
him by surprise. He thought, *"How do I answer this?"* . . .
"As I've said in the past, I think we all need to get to
know each other better. I've had a lot on my mind lately."

"You mean I haven't been on your mind?"

"Oh boy, I'm afraid you have."

"That's all I wanted to know." She slipped her
arms around him and kissed him.

Changing the subject, Bryan spoke quickly, "I
need to go into town to check out something, I'll see you
later young lady."

It was approaching noon when Bryan Forbes
rode into Santa Fe. A few wagons were backed up to
store fronts, and supplies were being loaded. A couple of
kids were pitching a ball to each other down the edge of
the street, and an old yellow dog followed, barking all the
way. Bryan rode up to a false fronted building identified
by a sign as 'BRENTWORTH LAND & ASSAY'.

He dropped the reins over the hitching post in
front of the building, and stepped up on the walk. He
paused long enough to look up and down the street.
"The town is sure growin'." He lifted the latch on the door
and went in.

There behind the waist-high counter, stood a
man with a green eye shade over a pair of gold rimmed
glasses that had inched their way nearly to the end of a
slightly hooked nose. He looked up when Bryan reached
the counter, and asked if he could help him.

"Yes, you can. I'd like to know if this deed has
been registered."

"Let me see." The man studied the deed and
said, "1760 . . . Let's have a look." He went to the back

of the shop and pulled a big book from the upper shelf. "If it's been registered, it'll be in here." He plopped the big book on the counter with a 'bang'. Dust rose in little whirl winds from beneath each end, and he blew the rest of the dust off with a big puff. As he opened the book, he reared back enough to let the large binding clear his hooked nose.

He then thumbed through the huge tome. Page after page, he looked at the names. "Danforth, Danzig, Dalton," His finger moved up and down the pages. "Denny, Devlin. Nope! Never been registered. If it had, it'd be in this book. Folks used to not record it right away, and then they forget about doing it."

"One more thing, if you don't mind."

"I don't mind, if it don't take long. I haven't had my lunch yet."

"It shouldn't take but a minute. The land grant that's the Bar H, has it ever been split up or any sold off."

The little old man walked back to shelves, pulled out another book, plopping it on the counter with the same routine. "Nope, never been split or sold, and that's according to the book!"

"I'm much obliged to you." Bryan turned and walked out. *"I guess the whole Davis family worked a little outside the law.*

"Well Mr. Cyril Hastings, I think you have a little surprise coming."

He gathered up the reins, and tightened the cinch on the appaloosa. He was on his way back to the Bar H when he saw the sheriff walking along the walk. "Howdy Sheriff! I was just coming to see you."

The sheriff paused, and then stepped out into the street." You're the feller that left me with a couple of stiffs."

"Yesser, I'm afraid I am, but I had to save my friend. If I'd waited any longer, she would'a died."

"I reckon then she's okay?"

Bryan nodded.

"What'a you need now?" the Sheriff asked.

"You know a Mr. Russell Culp, the cattle detective for this area?" The sheriff nodded. "Well, we caught a few rustlers west of here on the Bar H, and they will be bringing them to put in your jail until the judge comes this way again."

"How many you bringing?" he asked.

"There's five of 'em. The head man got away and is headed southwest toward the Pueblo reservation, if you want to take a posse and go after him."

"I don't have enough money to feed five men till the judge comes, much less to pay a posse."

"Well, Sheriff, I'll see that you get money to feed them. If you decide to go after the leader, you know him. He is Lawrance Davis, and rustling is not the only law he's broken."

"Lawrance Davis! . . . Are you shore?"

"I'm sure! We caught him red-handed, but he managed to get away. Be on the lookout for him. We will too."

The ride to the ranch was uneventful, as far as events go, but Bryan's mind was filled with all kinds of self induced problems. There were the two girls, and overseeing the ranch that may have just doubled in size. *"Maybe I should take my money and head on down the trail, like I started to in the first place."*

When he arrived at the ranch, the sun was already down. He took care of his horse in the last few moments before losing daylight altogether. He went straight to the main house. A lamp was shining by the door. He stepped up on the porch and knocked. Geneva came to the door.

"You're a little late, aren't you?" she asked.

"It's been a long day. I just need a minute with Cyril, if it's all right."

"You know it is! Come on in, I'll call him."

Bryan entered and sat down. After a few minutes, Cyril came into the room, "You wanted to see me, Bryan?"

"I'll only take a minute. You still ride don't you?"

"Sure do, most every day." answered Cyril.

"I guess I haven't been here on the ranch long enough to know. I need for you to take a ride with me in the morning. It may take most of the day. Is that okay?"

"Sure, I'll be ready."

"I've had a long rough day, so I think I'll hit the hay, and explain what's going on in the morning. Good night."

"Yes, good night, Bryan."

Bryan was up early, so he used a lantern to give light enough to get his appaloosa and Cyril's palomino ready. He led them to the rail in front of the main house, and then went in for breakfast.

When he and Cyril finished eating, they mounted up, and headed for the Flying A ranch. As they rode along, Bryan spoke up. "Cyril, I've checked the registry in town and found that your grant is still intact. No sale has been made and the deed to the Davis family is a forgery. Your great grandfather didn't sign it. I thought you may want to examine the place, and we need to see if any livestock needs care."

Cyril rode along in silence, taking it all in. Overnight he had almost doubled his holdings. "Bryan, I won't begin to be able to take care of all this with the men we have. It'll be like caring for two ranches."

"I know, Cyril. We'll manage. It'll just take us a while to see what we need."

As they rode up to the headquarters, it looked deserted. No dogs, no chickens, nothing in sight that would show that it had been occupied.

"Cyril, since I have a gun, I'll check the house, if you'll check to see if any livestock's in the corral. They may have left some horses penned up."

"All right and Bryan . . . be careful!"

Having been in the house before, Bryan had an idea where things were located. He stepped up on the porch and pushed the door open. It squeaked slightly on its hinges. It was dark inside, regardless of the bright sunlight of the morning . . . He paused, then entered. He gave a quick look around the room, before moving on to check the rest of the house, which was also deserted.

Cyril saw that a couple of cows were in the corral. Seeing him, they started to bellow. He used a can of water left by the pump to prime it, and drew a trough of water. Behind him, he heard Bryan approaching,

"Better get ready to milk one of these cows. If we don't, they'll likely burst. There were no horses penned up." Cyril advised.

By late afternoon they had ridden out the area around headquarters, and were satisfied that they had taken care of everything. Cyril mounted up and took a last look around. "I'll send one of the boys over to stay to milk and take care of the place, 'till we decide what we're going to do."

They headed back to the Bar H. It was mostly a silent trip, as each had a lot on his mind.

It was late when Bryan and Cyril arrived at the Bar H. Julie was there by the corral. "Mr. Hastings, you go on up to the house, your supper is ready. I'll help Bryan take care of the horses. We'll give 'em a good rubdown."

Cyril replied, "Thank you Julie, I can use the help. Not as young as I used to be, and it's been a long day." He went on to the house.

Bryan and Julie led the horses into the corral, and began to rub them down. Julie spoke first. "Bryan, I'm going back home, and Will's going with me."

Bryan kept brushing the appaloosa.

"Well, aren't you going to say anything?
"You're not through brushing Cyril's horse."
"Bryan Forbes! I'm gonna hit you with this brush!"

Bryan laughed, then grabbed her by the arm, pulled her close and gave her a big kiss. Then he stepped back he asked, "Now do you still want to go?"

"YES! I'm sorry, Bryan. I don't think you are serious about me, anyway. Will and I have gotten to know each other the last few days and we do pretty good together. We talked about rebuilding father's cabin and running some cattle there. We may go up to Will's lean-to in the mountains; I'd like to see that."

"Sounds like you have given this some thought."

"We have."

"If that's what you want, then that's great. You like Will a lot?"

"Yeah, he reminds me of you."

"Reminds you of me? That's a heck of a thing to say about a feller you're gonna ride off into the sunset with!"

With a giggle, she replied: "I was just playing with your ego, silly! I really think I'm in love with Will."

"Time will tell. I know that the two of you will be happy. But I could sure use Will around here right now since this ranch has doubled."

"The ranch has doubled?" Julie was surprised.

"Yes doubled!" He explained what he had found.

They both went up to the main house to join Cyril and Geneva at dinner.

Geneva, holding a coffee pot over a cup, paused and looked up, "What have you two been up to?"

"Just taking care of the horses," said Bryan.

"Yeah, I'll bet!" she teased.

Julie laughed, "I told him about what Will and I were planning to do, so he knows." She looked at Bryan, "I think she wanted you to squirm a little."

Bryan's face was red; as he sat down to eat. "Well, good riddance! I couldn't get any work done around here, with the both of you jokin' all the time. Cyril, you're the head of this household. Can't you make them behave?"

"I'm afraid it's a little late for my control. That's why I hired you, to pass the reins to someone else. Looks like you're it!"

Bryan grinned and said, "Well, sir, I guess I'll have to learn to handle your daughter. Maybe Will can handle the other one!" It was the girls' turn to blush.

After dinner, Geneva and Bryan went out on the porch to sit in the swing. Geneva folded her arms together and shuddered. "Winter's coming on. You can feel it in the breeze."

"I had hoped Will could stay on a while. We need him here, and I'm afraid if they leave now, they could run into some really bad weather." Bryan put his arm around Geneva. "I don't know if your dad told you or not, but the Flying A belongs to you and Cyril."

"What do you mean?"

"Just that, the deed that Lawrance had to the house and land was a forgery. Cyril didn't know otherwise, until I checked the records."

"What about Lawrance?" she asked.

"Don't know. Last I saw of him, he was headed southwest toward the Pueblo reservation."

She put her head on his shoulder and he held her closer. "What happens now?"

"I think I'll talk to Cyril in the morning. I'll ask him if it's all right to try to get Will and Julie to stay on the Flying A until spring. I think it would be foolish for them to go back without a house there. Besides, it would be hard to find someone to take on a big spread this time of year. It would be a big help to Cyril if they stayed, and I think they will."

"So, you just want it to be easy on you and Dad! Is that it?" she joked.

"Someday your 'catty' little remarks are going to get you in trouble!"

"As long as it's with you, I can handle trouble!" She smiled and snuggled closer.

He grinned "I might even ask him for your hand. Just hope I can handle you!"

Benjamin Forbes

Chapter 24

Richard Forbes' youngest son, Benjamin, was also the last to leave their home in Virginia. Only a daughter, Mary Elizabeth, remained at home.

He was a handsome young cowboy, who had been traveling from ranch to ranch, taking on work when and where he could find it. He stood six feet two inches tall. Unlike his brothers, his skin was swarthy and his dark eyes seemed to be smiling, whether he was or not. The ringlets of dark wavy hair peeked from beneath his sweat-stained hat . . . His strong physique came from working hard, and using every muscle in his body, on those ranches.

Benjamin was presently riding in the 'Hill Country' of Texas, toward a campsite just west of the town of Fredericksburg. The sunrays flickered through the trees as it dimmed in the late afternoon sky.

He was upset that he would have to go back into town tomorrow for supplies. He could not understand enough German language to communicate adequately with the storeowner to make his purchases before closing time. He later found that the population of Fredericksburg, Texas refused to learn or speak English.

Ben, as he liked to be called, stepped down near a spring that ran into Baron's creek, and began to set up camp. He gathered wood and started a small fire to make one last pot of coffee. His last two corn pones completed his evening meal. Then he sat back, and enjoyed the cool breeze from across the spring.

Next morning, Ben was up before light. Since he had no food, he didn't bother to start a fire. He rode on into Fredericksburg to try again to buy some supplies.

Stepping inside the general store, he could see most everything he would need. He managed to do a lot of pointing, and using signs to get the reluctant German storekeeper to fill his needs. He loaded up on German sausage he had loved so much as a boy.

Once his supplies were loaded onto his pack animal, he headed southwest to a town he thought was called Brownsborough.

Benjamin rode for two days, and missed the town he was looking for. He landed a few miles west, along the Guadalupe River.

The sun moved slowly toward its nightly home in the west, as he rode in the canyon along the Guadalupe River. The walls were already bringing dark shadows to the trail, and Ben looked for a good campsite. He soon settled for a stream that wound its way around the Cyprus trees, and dropped into the Guadalupe River.

After a meal and a couple of cups of coffee, he leaned back on a large tree and watched the water bubble in the spring. Mixed with the gentle sound of the spring, he thought he heard a faint reed whistle, far in the distance. He listened a while, and the tune reminded him of a death song of the Comanches that he had heard years ago . . . or maybe not.

"Why would I remember that? I only heard it once," Ben reflected. Sundance, his bay horse, stood nearby cropping the lush grass that was growing around the spring. "You keep nibblin' grass. I think I'll walk down the canyon and see if I can find where that music's comin' from."

The sound was farther away than he thought, but his determination to find its source kept him going. "It's gettin' louder, so I must be gettin' closer."

As he continued along beside the river, the walls of the canyon rose higher. The upper edges of the yellow and white sandstone reflected the sun enough to illuminate the high walled valley where he was walking.

The shrill reed whistle, with its mournful tune, seemed to come from higher up. He carefully scanned the upper walls of the canyon. A bit of movement caught his eye, and beside a scrub of a tree growing out of the canyon wall sat a figure balanced on a narrow ledge . . . a ledge so high a fall would be fatal. What little clothing he had on said 'Comanche' to Ben.

"Ho Comanche, how did you get up there?" No reply came back. "Don't tell me I'm gonna have more language trouble! Do you understand Texican?" Still no answer so he walked closer until he was right underneath the Indian on the ledge.

He called again, "Ho Comanche!"

The Indian stopped playing the reed whistle and looked down at Ben and called out, "Ne bahito'!"

"Do what?" questioned Benjamin.

"Ne bahito', I fall."

"Okay I understand that. You fell."

"Jaa, ne bahito'!"

"I don't know what the sam hill you could'a been doing to fall down there!" exclaimed Ben.

"Ma quena'bunit."

"There ya go again. What's that?"

"It dark . . . horse turn when he see cliff, I sleep, go over horse's head, then cliff."

"Okay. Now I can understand _that_ talk."

"Jaa, kammah-kantyn, omo-camacat!"

"Dang it! I can't understand that jargon."

"I have hurt in leg," the Comanche replied.

"Well, hold on! I'll go get my rope and see if we can get ya down . . . How long you been up there anyway?"

"I see taabe . . . sun, three times."

"Dang! I reckon you are hurtin' after three days! No wonder you was playin' that tune, hang on, I'll be right back."

Ben headed back down the trail to his camp, and rode back with his rope.

"Okay, see if you can catch the rope, if I can throw it that high. Tie it around that bush . . . tie it short, 'cause we gonna need all of it, or you'll have to drop on that bad leg."

Ben threw the rope up three times before he got it high enough for the Comanche to catch it. With it tied securely, the Indian started to let himself down. When he reached the end of the rope, there was still about a ten-foot drop to the ground. Ben rode under him, and he was able to drop behind the saddle. Then he eased to the ground, where Ben handed him his canteen, and examined his leg.

"Don't look broke, guess you just jammed it good when you hit that ledge," Ben looked up to where the rope was tied to the bush, "Now, how in blazes am I going to get my brand new rope back?"

"I know junubi . . . you say . . . arroyo, can go on top where horse stands."

"Now how do you know he'll be standing up there after three days?"

"He always wait for me."

"What's your name anyway?"

"Toaui-Piajuhtzu'."

"Uh Hu . . . Now tell me your name so's I can understand."

"I sorry, I think Comanche, you say "Silver Eagle!"

"Okay, that's a good name. You can call me Ben. My name's Benjamin Forbes.

294

"Now get on, and we'll go up that arroyo and get your horse. What were you doin' ridin' out at night anyway?"

"I not have good medicine . . . no magic dream . . . try three times, others laugh, make do woman's work, I go away."

"Did ja plan to go back?"

"No . . . you call . . . 'outcast'. I no can go back."

"They must'a been rough on you, from the looks of the scars on your back." said Ben.

Silver Eagle's face twisted, questioningly, "What scars?" Ben pointed to a scar on his arm, "That's a scar, and you got 'em all over your back."

"Yes, many scars." After Silver Eagle answered, he sat in silence.

"How'd ya learn to speak Texican?" asked Ben.

"Mother white woman. She not live long, so learn little."

Ben wondered, how the Indian knew about the arroyo, "Tell me, how did you know about this arroyo . . . you been here before?"

"Jaa, rode with Apache here before."

"Did they know you were Comanche?"

"They no care. They steal horses."

"You may be good to have along, if we run into any Apache."

When they reached the steep grade near the top of the arroyo, Ben spoke up, "I better walk from here. It'll be easier on ole Sundance if there's just one of us the rest of the way up. It's purdy steep."

Ben dismounted and led the way. When they reached the top, there standing on three legs, with his head down in sleep was the Indian's paint pony.

"See, him always wait for me."

"By golly, that's a trick I wish Sundance knew! He's always wanderin' off a' eatin' grass. That's a good lookin' horse."

They took Silver Eagle's rope, and tied it to Ben's saddle horn. Ben took hold of the rope, and stepped over the edge of the cliff, and let himself down to retrieve his rope from the bush. He slipped his toe into the loop of the rope, and then shouted, "Silver Eagle, back ole Sundance up, and pull me out of here." As the Indian led Sundance backward, Ben managed to find an occasional foothold to help his ascent. He reached the top, and rolled his rope. "We better get a move on, or it'll be so dark I won't be able to find my camp."

"Silver Eagle go with you. Maybe leg be better when sun come back."

"I wouldn't count on it. But a little coffee and some sausage right now might help, since you haven't eaten lately." said Ben, as they started back down the arroyo.

Once back in camp, Ben gathered wood and started a fire, and put coffee water on to boil. "You're pretty far south, aren't you? I thought Comanche stayed up around Palo Duro area."

Not sure what Ben was asking, Silver Eagle answered, "Follow buffalo. Need coat for to'mo."

"Who's Tomo?" asked Ben.

"To'mo not who, is first of cold!"

"Oh . . . You mean winter! You won't have to worry about that for a while." Ben paused, as he thought about traveling with an Indian, and what he might run into. Then he asked, "Did you do much traveling with the Apache?"

"Not long . . . no like kill whites."

"Did you kill many?"

"I not kill, I leave when they kill."

Ben thought, "*He don't seem like much of an Indian.*"

They both fell silent and stared into the fire, each taking a sip of coffee now and then. After a few minutes Ben asked, "How's that leg doin'?"

Silver Eagle pointed to his leg, "Hurt no so much now. Have yocoro'."

"Have what?"

Silver Eagle used his fingers to indicate limping.

"Oh! You got a limp. Well, take it easy. I'm leaving the first thing in the mornin', to try to locate the little town of Brownsborough again. I guess I rode by it yesterday. They's a banker there named Billings that raises cattle, and he may need a couple o' hands . . . what would you think about becomin' a cowboy?"

"Silver Eagle looked at Ben with an amused expression, "You think white man hire Indian?"

Benjamin Forbes looked at his newly acquired acquaintance. He had long black hair, folded and tied in the back with leather strings. His dark skin, darkened even more by three days in the sun, was smooth and his eyes were like two chunks of volcanic basalt. He certainly didn't look like a cowboy!

"Why, we'll just tell 'em you're a cowboy," answered Benjamin with a big grin on his face, "I got some extra clothes in my pack, except boots and a hat, but I can get them in town when I go. You think you can handle that?"

"Death came on ledge to me. You gave new life. I try your way. Where he raise cattle?"

"They told me he had land close ta here, and was lookin' for more west of here a ways."

Ben walked to his packs and began to pull out clothes, "I betch'a these'll fit like a glove." He handed them to Silver Eagle.

Silver Eagle took the clothes and asked," What glove?"

"Glove? Oh, that's just a sayin'! Here, I'll just give you a pair. I can git more. They pull on your hands and keep the rope from burnin' 'em, when that ole bull runs away from you. In the winter, what'd you call it to'mo? They'll help you stay warm."

"Silver Eagle had to smile as he pulled them on, "Gloves good!"

"Another thing, we got ta give you a cowboy name. I can't keep callin' you Silver Eagle all the time. They shore 'nuff wouldn't hire us. I'll come up with somethin'."

Ben wrapped up in his blankets, "reckon if I'm gonna git up early in the mornin' I'd better git some shut eye."

"You not afraid Silver Eagle take scalp while you sleep?"

"Not after you tole me about why you left the Apaches."

Ben rose in the darkness of early morning. He paused and looked at Silver Eagle, still in his blankets, and thought, "I trusted him last night with my life. I guessl can trust him with my stuff 'till I get back."

Benjamin decided to backtrack on the Guadalupe River to locate the town that he had missed by riding too far to the north.

"Sundance," his horses' ears shot back toward Ben, then forward again, as if to say 'I'm listening', "I don't know exactly what I got us into, by savin' that Indian . . . It sounds to me he ain't welcome by any tribe . . . but if I can make him into a cowboy, maybe he can take another shot at havin' a good life."

As Ben rode along the Guadalupe, he started seeing signs of life. Trails got wider and a house or two showed in the distance. Arriving at the edge of the settlement he saw the sign, 'Kerrville, Texas.' "Well whad'a you know! I've missed Brownsborough again. Don't matter, they'll have a store here I reckon, and I can ask somebody."

As he continued on into town, he noticed many riders and wagons moving in the dusty streets. Large gingerbread houses popped up occasionally like those he had seen in Fredericksburg. He soon found a little store that had items on the porch, like he was looking for, and he tied up in front. He took a moment just to watch the people moving about. He was surprised by the large population.

After taking it all in, he turned and stepped through the large open door.

In the far corner of the store, a grey haired man with a bushy mustache looked up, "Come in young man. How can I help you?"

Ben squinted toward where the voice came from, as his eyes adjusted to the light, "Yes Sir, I'm lookin' for a couple o' things, and I'm shore glad you speak my language. First of all tell me what happened to Brownsborough? I rode all 'round here and I haven't found it yet."

The little man chuckled, and walked up close to Ben, and pushed up the small gold-rimed glasses. "Well Sir, you found it! It's called Kerrville now, and has been since it became the county seat of Kerr County, way back in '58."

"So . . . that's why there's so many people out there."

"Yes Sir, it's a busy place around here, off and on. Now, what can I do for you?"

Ben's eyes moved along the tables, "Well, I need a hat and a pair of size ten boots, not too high priced, I reckon."

"I think I have just what you want right over here." The little man moved quickly through the tables that were loaded with goods. He turned and handed Ben a hat that had not been shaped. It had a wide flat brim and a high round crown. Ben took it, and tried it on.

A muffled snicker came from across the room. Ben turned to see who was laughing. He saw a young girl quickly dart back through the doorway to the back.

"Don't mind her, mister. It's just my daughter, and I'm afraid her manners are not quite what I'd like them to be. Here are the boots you wanted."

"You have a mighty pretty daughter, Mister? . . .

"Hanner, George G. Hanner," the man answered.

"I'm mighty glad to meet ya, Mr. Hanner! I'm Ben Forbes. OH! I reckon I better get a couple o' slickers and a pair of gloves. If you don't mind, I'd like to leave my horses tied out front a while."

"Don't mind a' tall. It'll just look like I got business."

Benjamin placed everything in his pack except the hat that had been placed in a box, and he carried it as he walked down the boardwalk to find the bank.

As he approached three men on the walk, making small talk about the weather, he spoke up, "Excuse me fellers. I'd like to make one of you an offer. I got a brand new hat here in this box, and I'd like to trade it for one of yours that'll fit."

The men just stared at Ben for a minute then one man spoke, "To tell you the truth I'm kinda attached to my hat. Are you offering any cash too?"

"No sir, I can't do that. You see my friend lost his hat and we're lookin' for some cattle work. A new hat might look like he ain't ever worked cattle before."

"It might at that, le'me see your new hat."

Ben pulled the hat from the box and the man looked it over. "Well that's a good brand . . . and it's my size," he pulled it on and turned to the others, "How do I look?"

They made the trade and Ben put the old hat in the box, and tied the string back around it. He went back to his horse, hung it on his saddle horn and proceeded to find the bank.

Ben entered the building that he heard was the bank, removed his hat, and approached one of the ladies. "Ma'am I was told that this was a bank, but it looks like another mercantile store. I was lookin' for a Mr. Billings. I understand that Mr. Billings has some cattle he needs worked, and I'd sure like to talk to him. My name's Benjamin Forbes, ma'am."

The lady looked up and smiled, "You're in the right place, cowboy. Have a seat Mr. Forbes, and I'll see if Mr. Billings can see you." She walked to a large door, said a few words and returned, "You may go in, Mr. Forbes."

"Thank you, ma'am." Ben entered the office and was bid to sit down. ""If you don't mind, Sir, I'll just stand. I won't take much of your time. I'm Ben Forbes. Me and my friend heard that you need hands to work some cattle, and we need the work. We've worked cattle before and will make you good hands."

Mister Billings looked Ben over, "I do need hands, and you look like you would be a good one. If you can show up in the morning, I'm willing to give you a try. I'll draw you a map, and expect you to report to Tucker Johnson. I'll meet you there."

"Thank you Sir. You won't be disappointed!"

The two were hired to help move a small herd to North Texas, and join them with a larger herd coming from Ft. Worth. Other cowhands would drive them up the Western Trail to Dodge City. Ben and Tom were to meet the crew the next morning, to start moving the herd. The man in charge would be Tucker Johnson.

When Ben returned to the store, where he had tied the horses, the pretty young girl was sitting on the porch. He didn't notice her there in the shadows. As he was untying his horse, he heard, "Aren't you gonna wear that new hat, Mister Forbes?"

Ben turned and asked, "How'd you know my name?"

"I heard you tell papa."

"Well, the hat's not for me. It's for a friend."

"A girl friend maybe?" she asked, as she rose and walked toward him.

"Ben looked down at the reins in his hand, "You sure do ask a lot of questions."

"Well, do you?" she asked.

"Do I what?"

"Have a girl friend."

"I'm not sure that's any of your business."

"Well, I heard you tell papa I was pretty, and they're havin' a dance tonight, and I thought you might just ask me to go."

Ben was almost tongue-tied when he finally turned toward the girl, after tossing the reins over Sundance's head. His mouth dropped open, as he saw her close for the first time. She looked at him with a big smile. Her blond hair was pulled back, and her blue eyes sparkled from a face as smooth as glass. He was finally able to speak, "You know my name. What's yours?"

"Grace Hanner. What about it, are you taking me to the dance tonight?"

"Does Mr. Hanner know you're asking me out tonight?"

"Yep, I told him I was going to ask you, when you got back."

"But you don't know anything about me."

"Don't need to know you! I just want to dance with you, not marry you!"

"What time does it start? I gotta go out to my camp first."

"Oh . . . about sundown, I guess. You're not trying to run out on me are you?" she teased.

As he mounted, he looked down into her blue eyes and smiled, "I wouldn't miss it for a gold eagle." He turned the horses and rode out of town. She stood and watched him disappear, thinking she would never see him again.

When Ben returned to camp, Silver Eagle was sitting by a small fire, turning a roasting rabbit on a green stick.

"Boy, your leg must'a healed fast for you to chase down a rabbit!"

"No chase. Have bow and arrow and he come close," answered Silver Eagle, as he removed the rabbit from the fire.

Silver Eagle pulled some of the rabbit meat, and Ben reached down to take it. "I got us that job with Billings. We join a couple o' guys of his to drive some cattle up to Red River. He may have some work for us when we git back." Ben paused a while, "I thought of a cowboy name to call you, if that's all right."

"Is good name?"

"I think it is. Since you went over that cliff lookin' fer a coat for the to'mo, I figgered I'd call you Tom Coats, so it'ud be easy for both of us to remember."

Silver Eagle chewed on a chunk of rabbit, and said the name over a couple of times, "Tom Coats . . . Tom Coats! That be good cowboy name."

"Well Tom, I'm glad you like it. Now, I gotta go back into town tonight, ta do a little dancin'! I hope you won't get lonesome. I didn't think you could dance on that bad leg." Ben said smiling.

"Smile mean you find squaw?"

"Actually, she found me! But that's all right. I'll get to dance anyway. 'Fore I forget it, you need to try on these boots and hat. See if'n they fit and if you're goin' to look like a cowboy. I traded a new hat for this one, so's it'ud look like you been wearin' it."

Silver Eagle pulled on the boots and limped around the fire, satisfied that they fit. Then he put on the hat. "How Tom Coats look now?"

"By golly, you do look like a cowboy! Better wear those boots a while, make sure they don't hurt your feet. If they do git to hurtin', go stand in the stream 'till they stretch to your feet. I gotta wash up and change my clothes. Don't know for sure when I'll be back, but I won't close the town down."

Benjamin put on some of his better clothes, wet his hair down, combed it carefully, and put on his string tie, "Well Tom, what do you think?"

Silver Eagle didn't respond, so he asked again, "Hey you, Tom Coats! I asked you how I looked."

"I forgot name! You look like search for squaw."

"I ain't searching for no squaw! And you'd better practice your name, 'cause that's what everybody's gonna call you while we're working."

"I remember is Tom, Tom Coats. Like you say, see you later!"

"Right, I'll see you later, Tom!"

Ben mounted Sundance, and headed to Kerrville. His heart seemed to be beating a little faster than usual.

When he arrived at the store, there on the front porch was the most beautiful girl he thought he had ever seen. He sat on his horse taking in her beauty. Her blond hair hung down past her shoulders in long curls, and her white dress, with small ruffles at the bottom, had little blue ribbons laced in and out of the ruffles.

He stepped off of Sundance, and she met him on the street. They were face to face. He watched her eyes sparkle, as she told him that she really hadn't expected him to show up.

"Hey, I said I would, didn't I?"

"Yes you did, and I'm glad! Let's move on to the dance."

She caught his arm and they walked toward the fiddle music that was drifting through the streets.

When they arrived at the temporary dance floor, couples were already dancing. Others clapped, keeping time with the music. Benjamin and Grace Hanner stepped up and began swirling into the crowd of dancers.

Laughter, and a little dust, filled the air as the fiddle player's tunes pushed the couples around the floor.

They were well into their second dance when Ben felt a heavy hand on his shoulder that spun him around, and a big hand smashed him in the face. He was thrown off balance so much that he kept stepping back to get his feet under himself, until he crashed on top of a table loaded with a full punch bowl and glasses. When Ben was able to look up, he saw the one that hit him. Grace was running toward him.

"Benjamin, are you hurt?" She turned to the offender, "Jesse Fenton, you shouldn't have done that!"

Jesse looked at Ben, then at Grace. Sweat was running down his red face, and he weaved from having had too much liquor. "He had no business dancing with my girl!"

"I've told you before, I'm not your girl!"

She turned to Ben and saw only a blur, and felt the wind as he pushed passed her. He dove headlong into Jesse's middle! Soon, cries came from the crowd, 'Fight . . . Fight'! But the blow to Jesse's midsection had been well placed, and Jesse was out like a lamp.

Ben got up and dusted himself off, pulled his hat on and took Grace by the hand.

"Come on Grace, I've had enough of your boyfriend!"

"I tell you, he's not my boy friend!"

"Well, he thinks he is, and I don't want to hang around 'till he comes to." By this time Ben was practically dragging her by the hand.

"Where are you taking me?"

"Somewhere I can stop this nose bleed."

"Then you are hurt! Let me see. Oh, Ben let's go behind the store. There's a pump there and a wash basin."

Grace took a washcloth from her father's store, wiped his face with the cool water, and held it against his nose, until the bleeding stopped. Then she rinsed it, and placed the wet cloth on his forehead. He stared into her eyes, as she came close. He moved a little closer, she didn't move back. So he gently kissed her, and she kissed back. The wet cloth slipped down between their faces, and they began to laugh.

"I better go, I gotta get ready for the drive and I might just stay too long."

"Do you have to? We're just getting to know each other?"

"I won't be gone long. Then we can get to know each other . . . unless . . . "

"Unless what?" she asked.

"Unless you get sweet on Jesse while I'm gone."

Grace grabbed the wet cloth from his forehead, and started hitting him. "Benjamin Forbes, I told you there's nothing between Jesse and me!"

"Okay, Okay, I believe you! Stop hittin' me!" He reached out, pulled her into his arms, and started kissing her. She relaxed and put her arms around him.

"Ben, are you sure you'll come back?"

"I came back tonight like I said I would, didn't I? I'll be here, I promise!"

"I'm holding you to it." She reached up and kissed him again, then went inside and closed the door.

Ben stood there a moment, thinking, *"You can bet, little lady, I'll be back!"* He turned and went around the building, and rode back to his camp.

Inside the store Mr. Hanner heard the door close, and asked, "Is that you Grace?"

"Yes, Papa, it's me."

"You're in early, dear. Are you all right?"

"Yes, Papa I'm fine. Ben had to leave to get ready to do some work for Mr. Billings."

He studied her expression. "Well, it looks like he made an impression on you."

"Yes he did, Papa, and he said he would be back, but I wouldn't blame him if he didn't."

"Why's that, Honey?"

"Oh that Jesse Fenton was drunk, and he attacked Ben!"

Mister Hanner was talking as he walked off, "I never did like that boy. I don't think that Ben Forbes is the type to let that bother him . . . I bet he'll be back."

Back at the camp, Silver Eagle, now called Tom Coats, was leaning against a tree. His blankets were ready for bed. A small fire gave light to the camp.

When Ben finished taking care of his horse, he placed his saddle by the fire, spread his blankets and changed from his good clothes.

Tom watched him. "You not talk, squaw run away?"

In a low voice Ben answered, "I think I was followed from town. I'll put out the fire and when it's dark, move behind the rocks."

Ben scattered the coals and poured the rest of the coffee on them. When it was out, they broke for the rocks.

It took a few minutes for their eyes to adjust to the darkness. But when they did, they saw three figures with their guns drawn, walking toward Ben and Tom's beds.

They waited to see the intruders' intent. When they heard the clicks of Colt hammers being cocked, Ben spoke up calmly, "I'd thank you to not shoot holes in my blanket . . . best you drop your guns or be buried right here!"

The men dropped their guns and raised their hands. Ben advanced to see who was ready to kill them in their sleep.

When he was close enough, he recognized the leader. "Well, if it's not our friend, Jesse Fenton!"

Jesse snapped back, "I told you to stay away from my girl!"

"I reckon it 'ud be a good Idea to talk to Grace about that. By now, Tom has your horses. To give you time to think about what you intended to do, take off your boots now, and start walkin' back to town! We'll send your horses and your boots along later. Now move!"

As Jesse hopped toward the river he yelled back to Ben, "You ever show up in Kerrville again, I'll kill you!"

"Jesse, you look for me after we get these cattle up the country, 'cause I'm a comin' back!"

"About an hour later, Tom Coats showed up at camp. "Where ya been Tom? I thought you'ud left."

"Watch men, so they no come back."

"Thanks Tom, I reckon they've walked enough. Go ahead and send their boots and horses back. They may be able to catch them and ride a while."

Tom tied their boots to their saddles, and turned the horses loose. Then he picked up his gear. "I sleep away from camp and watch if they come back."

"I don't think they will . . . I hope not, 'cause we don't need to be fightin' if we're gonna work cattle tomorrow. See you in the mornin'."

Morning came wrapped in a grayish white fog that was even thicker over the river. Benjamin could see a flicker of a blaze and the shadow of a man through the haze. Tom Coats had water on for coffee, and Ben could hear the sizzle of the bacon in the skillet, "Man, you get up early, don't you?"

"Tom Coats get hungry, so fix breakfast."

"Sounds good to me, and I'm glad you're remembering your name. I'm gonna make a cowboy out of you yet."

After breakfast and packing, the two of them headed to the north side of Kerrville to meet the riders that they were to help move the cattle.

As they joined the men that were beginning to arrive at their designated meeting place, Captain Billings drove up in his buckboard. He was dressed in a coat and tie, since he was on his way to work. He had a round face, strong jaw and eyes shaded by heavy brows. One would not think of him as having been a distinguished Texas Ranger.

"Mornin' gentlemen. I see everyone is here. You can get to know each other later. Tucker, I want the cattle in the north pasture to go up to Dodge. The army's anxious to get 'em. Then I want you and . . . What are your names again?"

"Benjamin Forbes, Mr Billings, and this is Tom Coats."

"Okay Tucker, these two will come back with you from Red River. I have things for all of you to do here."

"Yes Sir, Mr. Billings." answered Tucker Johnson, who had been his foreman for several years. He was a tall lean man, with a heavy mustache streaked with grey, as was his thick brown hair. His voice commanded respect.

"Tucker, I sent Ole Billy Watley and the chuck wagon on earlier, and he ought to have some breakfast a few miles down the trail." said Billings.

"Thanks. We should be back in a month or so, if them ole longhorns don't get too wiry." said Tucker.

"Fine, I'll see you then." Billings got into his buckboard, and opened up a cigar box. Billings was known as a banker, even though he ran a mercantile business. That cigar box was THE bank, wherever he conducted business. He handed money from it to Tucker. "This ought to take care of you 'till you get back." He headed back to Kerrville.

Tucker Johnson turned and mounted his horse, "Well, you fellers heard, so lets get started! Ole Billy'll be waitin' for us, and I can smell them biscuits from here. You boys can put your things on the wagon when we get there. You can alternate your horses with those in the remuda."

The men started to push the herd of longhorns north. It took a lot of fast riding to work some of the vinegar out of the determined mossbacks in the herd that had been roaming free.

Tom Coats turned out to be a fast learner, and was in the swing of the roundup quicker than Ben thought he would.

The herd rumbled past Billy Watley and the chuck wagon. The men took turns dropping off for their breakfast, and the herd kept moving.

Tom and Ben's soogans and other needs were loaded into the chuck wagon, and the packhorse was turned in with the remuda.

The herd moved well, and at sundown on the fourth day the cattle were bedded down near water and plenty of grass.

The sun eased down behind the horizon and filled the sky with a rosey red sunset. All but the first night riders gathered around Billy's cooking fire, finishing the last of the beans and biscuits.

Tom Coats joined Benjamin after pouring a cup of coffee and sat beside him. "Ben, I see signs of Apache at start of day."

"Are the signs recent or old?"

"They new. Watch to take cattle from herd and steal horses."

"You're sure it was Indians?" Ben asked.

"Ponies not have white man shoes."

"Okay Tom. I'll alert Tucker to watch, especially the horses, I doubt he'll mind loosing a cow or two if they take 'em and run."

Ben got up and joined Tucker, who sat puffing on a smoke. "Tucker, Tom said he saw signs of Indians today, he thinks they may be after our remuda."

Tucker looked at Ben and asked, "Is he sure?"

"He's sure. He's seen what these renegades do, so he knows the sign."

Tucker Johnson pulled on his boots, and walked to Edgar Hinds, "Edgar, we need to alert the night riders to watch for Indians in the early mornin'. They're roamin' these parts and may take after the remuda, and we can't spare no horses."

About the time Edgar Hinds got up, bullets started zinging in from all direction! Everybody scrambled and fell flat on the ground. Billy Watley had a tub of creek water heating on the fire, and he quickly grabbed the handle and dumped it on the fire. In the darkness every man in camp shot at the invaders muzzle flashes.

Ben and Tom ran rapidly away from the chuck wagon. As their eyes adjusted, rider silhouettes made it easier to make shots that counted. It was over as quickly as it started, and the shooting stopped.

Night-riders had heard the shooting, and came to the chuck wagon. Tucker saw the men and asked, "How'd these Indians get past you?"

The one named Pat Mitchell, dismounted and declared, "Tucker, they waren't no Indians! They wus boys from town! Said they had a message for Benjamin Forbes, so I said ride on. Hell, I didn't know the message wus gonna be so final. Did anybody get hit?"

Tucker looked around, "I don't know . . . if Billy hadn't dumped that fire out when he did, we could 'uv all been killed . . . Where is Forbes, anyway?"

Edgar Hinds spoke up, "He and that Indian went out to see if'n anybody got killed!"

As Ben and Tom returned, Tucker approached them, and asked, "Ben, why'd these boys from town want a piece of you . . . is it 'cause of the Indian?"

Ben walked over close to the fire. "No Sir, they never saw Tom. A feller named Jesse Fenton claimed I stole his gal, and he started a ruckus. Then he came to our camp and tried to shoot me. We made 'em walk back to town barefooted."

"Sounds to me like he aims to end his competition," commented Tucker. "I'm not sure we need this kind of problem, Ben."

Ben looked up and answered, "Yes Sir, I understand. We won't have any more trouble from him. I found Jesse and a couple more out at the edge of the herd. I just came back to get a shovel . . . figgered it's the least I can do." Ben paused, then turned to Tucker, "By the way, Tom said we need to stay alert. These men were not the signs he saw this mornin'."

"I see! Well, take Edgar and Tom with you. Then you better turn in, we got a long day tomorrow."

Chapter 25

No rain had fallen since the drive started twenty-five days ago. The last few days of traveling along the dry Lipan creek had yielded little water, and when the cattle smelled the water from the Colorado River, they ran the last half-mile.

Tucker, reading the situation, yelled, "Ben, you and Tom get to the river and make sure they don't cross! We'll hold 'em on this side for a while!"

Ben acknowledged, and spurred Sundance into a run for the head of the herd, with Tom following close behind.

At the river, Ben and Tom rode out into the water far enough to make sure the cattle only drank, and did not cross the river.

As they sat there catching their breath, Ben looked at Tom, "Well whatda ya think of cowboyin' now?"

"As Edgar Hinds says, I getting' hang of it!" answered Tom Coats.

Ben laughed, "Sounds like you're getting the hang of the talk, too."

After watching the cattle drink, Tom Coats rode up beside Ben. He leaned close, "Apache across river."

"Can you tell how many?"

"Not sure. Think it Grey Feather. Grey Feather ride with ten, fifteen braves. You ride tell others, I meet with him."

"Are you sure?"

"Jaa, I sure."

Ben rode easy, as if checking the cattle, until the brush thickened enough to hide him from view. Then he rode hard for Tucker and the other men. Tom rested easy, as if nothing had occurred.

Soon Grey Feather, seeing that Tom was alone, crossed the river. He and his horse were painted as an Apache brave. Tom turned to face him.

Grey Feather spoke. "Does my Comanche brother Silver Eagle travel with the white eyes now?"

"Jaa, life better than travel with Apache butchers."

"You didn't talk that way when you drank our whisky and ate our beef!"

"You kill for no reason, not my way. I left your ways, and now eat, and drink, and get money. I not have to kill as Grey Feather. Why you here?"

"I'm here for the white eyes horses, and beef for my braves. Do not get in way, or I kill you, Silver Eagle."

"I have new name with this work. I now called Tom Coats, and you no take from white man."

"If you try to stop my braves, you die with Indian name or white man name. I not care."

Grey Feather turned and rode quickly to where his braves waited. He gave a shout and they were all in the river, moving fast. The meeting between Tom and Grey Feather was just long enough for Ben, Tucker and the rest to come racing to the river.

Shots rang out from the brush where Ben had disappeared. Two of the Indians fell into the river, but the others kept coming.

Tom rode to the edge of the brush and dismounted. He began firing from behind a rocky outcropping. The other men rode toward the river firing, as fast as they could.

When the Indian's number dropped to six, they retreated across the river, and disappeared.

Tucker shouted to Ben. "Bledsoe was hit, and's in the river! Check on him 'fore he drowns, if'n he ain't dead already!"

Ben rode into the river, rolled off Sundance, and held Tim Bledsoe up out of the water. He yelled, "Throw me a rope and pull us out! I think he's still alive!"

Edgar Hinds tossed a loop over both men, and took a dally around his saddle horn, and pulled both men out of the river. Tim's wounds seemed to be a glancing blow to the head that just knocked him out. He bled so much that made it look worse than it was.

Ben checked him out and when Bledsoe started to wake up he asked, "Am I gonna be all right?"

Ben told him, "You'll probably live to get married!"

Old Billy got some coal oil from the chuck wagon, wet a rag with it, and then tied it around the wound on Tim's head.

Tim Bledsoe looked up at Billy and smiled. "Dang Billy! That smells as bad as some o' your cookin'!"

"Watch it Bledsoe! Or you'll be doin' the cookin'!" Billy walked over to the river to wash his hands.

Tucker rode up to Tom Coats. "Tom, I want 'a thank you for givin' us the warning. That gave us enough time to get here, 'fore they could get a start on the herd."

Tom nodded to Tucker. "I glad you come fast. Grey Feather not friendly to Tom Coats."

"We'll keep watch in case he comes back."

The cattle were pushed on toward the Red River Crossing, with stops along the Colorado River. Then they moved on to Fort Griffin where they planned to take on supplies.

With the cattle bedded down and camp made, Billy was filling plates by firelight. Oliver and Tom Coats were filling their second cups of coffee.

Tim Bledsoe, even wounded, wouldn't have it but that he pulled his own weight. So he and Pat Mitchell were saddling up to night ride. Edgar Hinds slicked his hair down, and retied his neckerchief. "Ben, you coming in ta Fort Griffen with us? I hear it's mighty wild 'bout now!"

Ben reached for the coffee pot. "Nah I ain't much for drinkin' an whoring . . . I'll go in in the morning with Billy, to get supplies."

"All right, but you gonna miss a lot o' fun!" replied Edgar.

Ben looked up and smiled, "Reckon I might come in later. You better watch yourself! Them army boys are trained tough and the Masterson brothers have the badges in Flat!"

"I'll keep a watch, 'sides Martin's comin' too."

"Okay, I may see you later."

Edgar and Martin rode into the town between Fort Griffin and the Clear fork of the Brazos River called Flat. Most trail drivers and trouble-makers gathered there to 'cut the dust' from their throats.

Back at camp, some were sleeping to relieve the night-riders later. Others were staring into the coals left from Billy's' cooking fire.

Ben threw the grounds from his cup. "Tom, you wanta go into town?"

Tom Coats looked at Ben with a big grin, "Indian have to fight too many white eyes! Best stay here."

"I see what you mean. Well, I think I'll ride in for a while. See you later."

Ben saddled up and headed toward Flat. Arriving in town, he noticed a large tent on the corner with a banner proclaiming a revival. He could hear the preacher shout, "Let's all stand and sing." When the congregation started to sing, some were off key and others were just loud.

Ben listened to the singing, as it blended with the 'rinky-tink' piano music emitting over the bat-wing doors of the Elk's Head Saloon. That was just one of many saloons in Flat. Ben smiled, with memories of his Christian raising, and moved on toward the saloon where Edgar and Martin's horses were tied. He stepped up on the boardwalk and paused, trying to decide whether to go to the revival or into the saloon. He chose the latter.

As he pushed through the doors, he saw a full house. Edgar and Martin were standing at the bar. Edgar elbowed Martin and indicated the door, "I figgered he 'ud show up."

Ben made his way to the bar and stepped in beside the two. He turned his back to the bar, and leaned on his elbows as he surveyed the house. "I allow as how trouble should be limited here tonight."

Edgar turned and asked. "Oh? How come?"

"That's Bat and Jim Masterson in the corner wearing the badges, and John Selman is with 'em."

"That don't mean nuthin'," spoke up the bartender, as he moved opposite Ben and the others. "If there's a fight, they are likely to join right in . . . What'll you have?"

"Sorry. Liquor don't agree with me." explained Ben.

"I got sarsaparilla. How 'bout a bottle?"

"Now that sounds good. I think I will."

As the bartender sat the bottle on the bar, loud cursing came from across the room. As Ben turned to see what was going on, a chair flew toward him. He managed to catch it. Then the whole place erupted into a free-for-all. Men from at least three camps joined in the ruckus. Bat and Jim Masterson eased their chairs against the wall, and watched.

As fighters struggled past the men at the bar, blood spattered in all directions.

Ben grabbed his bottle of sarsaparilla as he, Edgar, and Martin darted behind the piano to watch the show. They dodged bottles and chairs, but then someone pulled a gun and started shooting.

"Let's get out of here!" shouted Martin. They slipped out the back door, through the alley and around to their horses in front of the saloon.

"Dang it Ben, I was lookn' forward to a date tonight!"

"Were you lookin' forward to getting' shot?"

"Nah, I reckon not." said Martin, showing great disappointment.

"Well then, consider yourself lucky."

As they mounted up, a body rolled out the doors of the saloon. An angry man followed, with his gun drawn. He fired at the man on the ground. Then, for no apparent reason, he fired at Martin. The shot hit him in the shoulder, as he was mounting. Being off-balance, he fell backwards into the dust.

Ben's revolver was instantly in his hand. He shot the gunman, as he was pulling down on Edgar. The shooting brought the Masterson brothers out of the saloon. Ben piled off his horse quickly, and checked out Martin's wound.

Bat Masterson looked at the man on the ground, then at Ben.

Ben spoke up, "Seems this feller had some problems, and he came out shootin'. He hit my friend, and started to shoot the other. I just couldn't let him do that!"

Bat Masterson holstered his gun. "He deserved what he got! He already killed a couple of men inside.

Sorry I didn't get out here sooner. I thought he was one of the men that got killed. Your man going to be okay?"

"I think so . . . I've got the bleedin' stopped. I think we can get him back to camp."

Ben and Edgar helped Martin onto his horse. "You gonna be able to make it?"

Martin nodded his head, "I think I'm all right . . . it was the fall that I didn't like."

As they rode out of town, they passed the tent meeting. The congregation was singing 'Shall We Gather at the River'. The three couldn't help but smile.

It was beginning to get light by the time they reached camp, and Tucker hurried to meet them. "Ben, them Indians made a raid on our horses! Tom just left out tracking 'em."

Edgar stepped off his horse, then helped Martin down, and got him closer to the fire. "Billy, tend to Martin. He took one in the shoulder. I'll go with Ben to catch up to Tom."

Edgar and Ben headed in the direction that Tucker pointed out. "Ben how we gonna be able to foller Tom?" asked Edgar.

"He'll leave signs along the way . . . easy to see, that don't take much of his time."

After a couple of hours, Tom was in sight, a few hundred yards ahead of them, so they picked up the pace, and before long the three of them were riding together.

"Tom, do you think this is Grey Feather's work?"

"Jaa, he know I chase. He think this get me and get horses too."

"He may be right, if we don't find him soon. Do you have any idea where he might take them?"

"He go by Brazos River, follow canyons. He find deep canyon to hide horses."

Ben noticed that Edgar had crossed the river and was checking the other side. "See anything Edgar?"

"Nope, I guess they are still on that side."

Suddenly an arrow buzzed between Ben and Tom, and stuck in the mud at their feet. In response, a shot rang out from Edgar across the river, and the Indian lookout rolled down the side of the breaks.

"We must be close. They've started dropping lookouts," said Ben. "There goes our chance to check them out before they know we're here. I reckon they're runnin' by now, so let's go!"

Ben thought they had the advantage, because Grey Feather had been pushing the herd hard. The older cowponies resisted running that much without a rider, and they had slowed down.

When Ben and Tom rode up out of the river bottom, they saw horses not too far ahead. They started moving quickly toward them, with Edgar soon joining them.

"Tom, if you can ride to the point and turn them, I'll shoot at everything I can to keep them busy along the flank. Edgar, take those on drag and be careful!"

The three split up and rode hard to their assigned areas, then began firing. The Indians continued running with the horses, and when they hung low on the side of their ponies, it was hard to tell which were the remuda horses, and which were the Indians'.

Tom rode hard toward Grey Feather, who was concentrating on trying to keep the horses running faster. When Grey Feather finally realized that Tom was riding right up close, he turned and slowed to defend himself. But he was rolled backward off his horse by the slug from Tom's revolver.

Once Grey Feather was down, the others turned away from the herd, and allowed them to be stopped. Tom, joined by Ben, began to turn the horses back toward the river.

"That was easier that I expected." admitted Edgar.

Tom wiped his brow with his neckerchief. "Only four. They'll come back for Grey Feather when we leave."

Ben asked Tom, "How long you knowed Grey Feather anyway?"

"Long time, how you call . . . scars? Some from him."

"You sorta came even today, I guess."

With the horses returned to camp once again, Tucker sent a man into Flat to hire a couple of hands to help keep an eye on the horses.

Tucker Johnson started the herd moving early in the morning on their push to the Red River crossing, because the days were getting hot, and the cattle would be loosing a lot of weight. From Ft. Griffin, the next stop for a few days would be Oregon City, where the Western Trail crosses the Brazos River. The town would later be named Seymour, when it became the County Seat of Baylor County, Texas.

Camp was made near the Brazos, as heavy clouds were forming in the north. Everything was waterproofed, as much as possible. The storm hit around midnight, long after Billy had things tucked in for the night.

Morning brought a welcomed freshness to the air. After breakfast, Billy moved the chuck wagon out as soon as he could, to get ahead of the herd. Two of the night-riders, Simon Dority and Arnold Stanton were flanking the chuck wagon when Billy hollered, "Creek up ahead! Looks like a deep one, purdy muddy too." Simon and Arnold rode up to examine the muddy creek that carried water into the Brazos.

"I guess this is still the best place to cross. Reckon we'ud better cut the team loose, and rope the wagon down one side and up the other." analyzed Arnold.

"If we wait to cross where the herd is, it would take too long, and you wouldn't get anything to eat for a long time!" commented Billy.

Simon surveyed the scene and agreed, "Just as well take the tongue out, too. Don't want to break that."

Billy unhitched the team. They removed the tongue and tied the ropes on the back of the wagon, then to the front. The wagon was pushed over the edge and gently eased down into the creek. Then, all they had to do was take the team to the other side of the creek, and reverse the procedure to pull the wagon up the other side.

"It don't look as steep comin' out this side. Let's see if we can get the wagon out with my horse. If not, we can pull it with the team," suggested Arnold. He crossed the creek and Simon tied the rope to the front of the wagon, and then moved to the back with Billy, to push on the wheels, while Arnold pulled from the front.

As the wagon eased up the other side, it appeared to be going well. Suddenly, without warning, the knot in the rope, covered with slick mud, slipped loose and the wagon started slidng back down the side. They were not able to hold the heavy wagon. Billy managed to side-step the wagon, but Simon's boot was caught. He was pushed down into the mud and was unable to get free before the wagon wheel rolled onto his chest.

Billy shouted for Arnold to pull, as he couldn't budge the wagon himself.

"The rope came loose! Nothin' I can do!" shouted Arnold. They tied the rope again, working as quickly as they could to get the wagon off Simon's chest. It was too late! His chest was crushed, so that he couldn't breath.

Some of the other hands heard the yelling, and came to help. The wagon was pushed up the side of the creek.

The men cleaned the mud from Simon's body. He was buried near where he had died. The brief service was held, as the cattle slowly moved on their way.

After the rain of the previous night, Benjamin Forbes, riding point, was glad to be out of the dust. It was easier to think when you were not breathing Texas dirt. All he had to do was pick a good trail, and think. He had been doing a lot of thinking about a little blond girl in Kerrville, Texas.

"Sundance," his horse's ears popped back, then forward to acknowledge hearing his name, "we're gonna have to move fast goin' back to Kerrville, 'cause I shore want to know that Grace Hanner don't fault me for Jesse's death."

After an overnight at Oregon City, The herd was pushed across the clear fork of the Brazos, and on to the last forty miles to where these cattle were to join the other herd near Doan's crossing. Ben and Tom, along with Tucker, would return to work for Billings at Kerrville.

Tucker watched Ben dismount, and approached him. "Ben, you and Tom did well to help get us here, and I know the Captain will appreciate it. Get your soogans off the chuck wagon, and here's a little cash to pick up what else you might need at Doan's. I'll be ready to head back as soon as I talk to the other trail boss about all these longhorns."

Ben and Tom bought a few things from Doan's store, and then got their things from Billy's wagon. They pulled out extra horses, made one a pack horse, and loaded the supplies. Ben saddled a big roan that he had ridden a lot during the drive, to give Sundance a little time off. Soon the three headed back south, along the same trail on which they had come.

While they had traveled several miles down the trail, Tom Coats had been scanning the sky. "Looks like storm coming."

"Dang Tom, I don't see no clouds . . . you sure?" asked Ben.

"Wind stop . . . horse jumpy . . . winds start again stronger. It rain soon."

Tucker twisted in the saddle, looking for clouds. "It does look like there is a streak of dark grey in the North West I never noticed before. We better find some shelter. On our way up, I saw a shack with a barn and a corn crib just north of Oregon City, on the Wichita River," he said thoughtfully.

"Man, that's miles away! We better apply the diggers, and let your horse do the thinkin'."

A quick kick, and all the horses were stretching as if they knew for sure the weather was turning. Benjamin was in the lead, with Tom and Tucker just behind him, jumping over rocks and limbs. Just before they were getting ready to stop for a breather, Ben's horse stepped in a hole, and tumbled head first into a shallow ravine, tossing Ben about twenty feet ahead and to the other side of the ravine. It looked like he would never stop rolling.

The other two pulled up, and both jumped off in a run, to see if Ben was still alive. Blood was everywhere. Ben was out cold! At first, they couldn't tell if he was dead, or just unconscious. Unfortunately, the big roan's neck was broken when he went into the ravine.

"What are we gonna do? I'm afraid to move him! He may be all broke up inside!"

Tom looked around the area. "We move horses in dry creek, and Ben to where rocks stick out for cover."

"But Tom, if it rains, that ravine'll likely fill up with water."

"Rocks cover Ben, if it hails. We move if water get high."

"Okay, let's do it."

They moved the horses first, and then gently eased Ben onto a shelf just beneath the outcropping of limestone, that was large enough to shelter all three. The horses stood together in the ravine below them.

"Tom, can you tell if he's all broken up?"

"Can not tell. He skinned good, will have many scars. I get cloth from pack. Be right back."

Tom jumped down from the ledge, and hurried to the packhorse to get what he could find to stop the bleeding. He knew that Billy thought coal oil would cure anything, so he took the small can of lantern oil, a torn shirt, and returned to the ledge. Tom and Tucker washed Ben's wounds and wrapped them as best they could. "I make travois. We need get Ben to Shamus."

"You mean a doctor?" Tucker asked.

"Jaa, doctor. Not know how far we need go, but must hurry."

"I agree with you, there. The rain is not hard. Let's get this thing built."

It took awhile to cut the limbs long enough to have a little spring in them, so as to not jar Ben too much. He was laid on the ropes wound between the two long poles, and was covered with his slicker. The three rode on in the rain.

"Boy, this is a heck of time to break the drought!" commented Tucker.

A few more miles down the road, Tom scouted out the area around the trail, and spotted a house in the distance, and to the right of the trail. So they picked up the pace as fast as they felt it safe to pull Ben.

Upon reaching the house, Tucker called out, "Hellooo the house!"

Almost immediately an elderly man came to the door. "What can I do fer ya, strangers?"

"We got a man bad hurt! We'd like to get him out of the rain, and see how bad hurt he is. Is there a doctor around here?"

"Bring him inside! We kinda do our own doctoring around here, since it's maybe forty miles to the doc I know of. What brings you fellers to these parts?"

Tucker and Tom carefully placed Ben on a daybed near the fireplace. Tucker answered, "We just finished takin' some cattle up to the Red River crossin', and was headed back to Kerrville when this storm came up. We were tryin' to outrun it. Ben here, his horse stepped in a hole, and threw him across a ravine. He's got a lot of scratches and bruises, but I don't know if he's busted up inside."

The old man moved toward Ben, "Well, 'spose we take a look." He checked Ben's head first. "He's gonna be out fer a few days." Then he started to feel along Ben's collarbone, and down his arms then his legs. "I don't feel any breaks in his bones, and his belly's not swellin'. So I reckon we'll just have to wait 'till he wakes up, and ask him about his insides."

Tucker thought about what the man said, then agreed, "I reckon so. By the way, do you mind if we stay in your barn?"

The man looked at Tucker a moment, then told him, "I built extra rooms on to this place, 'cause I had my wife and seven kids here. They all died of the fever. So ya just as well stay here in the house, 'cause they ain't nobody here but me now."

Tom had stood back, feeling a little uneasy, until the old man spoke up, "I noticed your beads young feller. You're Comanche ain't ya?" Before Tom could answer, he continued, "My wife was Comanche. She'uz taken by a bunch Kiowas, 'till I took her away from 'em . . . that 'uz back in my younger days. Reckon we had a good life . . . I hated to lose her . . . my kids too. I shore miss 'em . . . I don't know why I didn't die too"

Tom nodded to the old man, but said nothing. Then the old man turned to Tucker, "I know you fellers are gittin' anxious to move on, and I've seen fellers in this shape be out fer a week or two. So if'n ya needs to be movin' on, I reckon I can take care of him. 'Sides, my niece will be comin' to check on me in a day or two, like she always does, and she'll hep too."

325

"How'll he eat or drink in that condition?" asked Tucker.

"Fer some reason they'll swaller liquids, like water and soup, and it'll be enough to keep 'em alive. I got plenty o' both."

"I hate to leave him on your shoulders, but I can't do anything with him in that shape. I guess if you're sure you don't mind, Tom and I will be movin' on in the mornin', 'cause the Captain will be expecting us. We'll come back as soon as we can get away. His horse and an extra, and his soogan we'll leave, in case he needs 'em. I guess I need your name, so I can tell folks where he is."

"Pleas Beavers, that's short for Pleasant . . . my momma said I was always pleasant."

"Yes Sir. I'm Tucker and this is Tom," he pointed to the bed, "He's Benjamin Forbes, goes by Ben. We'll be back when we can."

"I know ye will. Now I reckon I'll turn in right here close by. You fellers know where the beds are."

After breakfast, Tom and Tucker started home. The morning was filled with fresh clean air as the two men reluctantly rode back on the well beaten-down trail where cattle had moved north.

After twelve days, Tom and Tucker arrived in Kerrville, tied up in front of Captain Billings's mercantile, and reported in. They explained to the Captain about Ben's accident, and how Tom had saved the horses.

"I'm not sure we could do anything, if we went back right away. He's out cold, and Mister Beavers has taken care of men in this shape before."

"Well Tucker, if you think we should wait to check on him, I guess we can do a little work before you go back," said Captain Billings.

Tucker turned to Tom, "What'a you think Tom?"

"Must wait. But not good!"

As they came out of the store, Grace Hanner caught Tucker's arm and ask, "Didn't you take a herd of cattle to Red River, and didn't Ben Forbes go with you?"

Tucker turned to her, "Yes he did ma'am, but he ran into a little trouble on the way back."

"He's not dead, is he?"

"No ma'am, he just . . ." she cut him off.

"Where is he? Can I see him?"

"Ma'am, he's twelve or fifteen days from here. He's being looked after all right, and he should be comin' back in a few days."

Grace started to walk away, and then turned, "You sure he's taken care of?"

"Yes'm, the feller has experience with Ben's type of injuries."

"What kind of injuries?" she asked.

"Well ma'am, we don't rightly know. But Mister Beavers seemed to."

She looked Tucker in the eye, "Tucker Johnson, if you go where he is, I'm going with you, you hear!"

"Yes ma'am."

Chapter 26

Pleas Beavers had just finished getting as much soup and water down Ben as he could. He just sat and looked at the injured man. "Well feller, it's been three days and ya ain't moved. So I reckon it's time to start movin' your arms and legs to keep 'em limber, or you won't be able to walk 'fore long."

A call came from outside the cabin, "Uncle Pleas are you in there? You're going to be surprised, when you see what mama sent to you!"

Pleas Beavers called out "Come on in, Margie."

When she opened the door, she saw Pleas sitting on the bed, working on Ben. "Who's that, Uncle Pleas?"

"Feller named Benjamin Forbes. He ran into a little trouble on the trail."

"From the looks of him, trouble ran into him. You sure he's not dead?"

"Yep, he's breathin'. 'Sides I been getting' soup down him for three days. You be able to stay a few days, and hep get 'im up and around?"

"You think he'll ever get up? He sure looks bad!"

"Shore he will! His mind is just lettin' his body recuperate!"

"I planned to stay a while. Brought you a slab of bacon we smoked last week, and a few things momma put up from the garden. But best of all, your favorite, a pecan pie"

"Your mama's a jewel, Margie! I appreciate it, and I can shore use yer hep. Maybe I can get a little sleep, if ye relieve me."

"Of course I will, Uncle. You look like you're about to drop!"

Pleas went into the adjoining room to lie down, and quickly fell asleep.

Margie Beavers took warm water, and began to bath Ben's wounds.

Margie was eighteen, tall and slender with dark eyes, and long brown hair that tumbled over her shoulders and down her back. She spent her time helping her parents with the farm, and occasionally taking care of her uncle, since his family had died. She and her parents had tried to get Pleas to move to their home, but with no success.

After a few days of feeding Ben, and caring for his wounds, Margie observed that he seemed to move once in a while, when she talked to him.

"Benjamin Forbes, you need to get up! I'm getting tired of feeding and bathing you!" Ben turned on the bed and moaned but his eyes never opened.

"That's it . . . rouse a little more . . . we want you to wake up and talk to us. You've been here a week now. Time to stop free loading. Make yourself useful."

Margie thought that talking rough to him might make him mad enough to wake up. She turned and walked to the stove where she had coffee heating.

Ben finally opened one eye to a narrow squint, "Who are you, and where am I?"

She turned with the pot in her hand, "Oh, so you decided to come alive, did you?"

"Yeah . . . and if that's coffee you have in your hand, I could sure use some."

"Coffee it is, but you should eat something first."

"I'd rather have the coffee." He lifted the sheet and asked, "Where are my pants? I can't drink coffee without my pants! You never did say who you are, and how I got here?"

"It's a long story. Uncle Pleas said you were running from the storm, and your horse fell." She handed him a cup and poured him a little coffee. "Don't get excited about your pants. You haven't had any on in a week and half. I'm Margie Beavers."

"I guess you know who I am . . . now how did I get here?" he asked.

"Uncle Pleas said two men brought you here after you fell. This was the first house they found, lucky for you! You've been out since then."

"And . . . and you've been takin' care of me that long?"

"Well Uncle Pleas and I, we've taken turns."

Pleas came out of the bedroom. "I thought I heard answers to your talkin', Margie! I guess our boy has come back to life. Howdy son. I'm Pleasant Beavers, and I'm glad yer doing a little better".

"I reckon I am, if I've been here as long as this little lady says I have! But . . . I can't seem to find my pants!"

"Well, ask Margie what she did with them after she helped me take 'em offa you!"

"She helped you take 'em off?"

"I couldn't bathe you with them on, could I?" Margie asked, with a mischievous smile.

Ben's face got red, and he tried to sit up, but the pain caused him to lie back down.

"Dang, I ain't never been bathed by no woman before, 'specially as purdy as you."

Margie smiled, "Not even by your mother?"

"Mothers don't count! They seen you as God made you anyway."

"Well, now I have too!"

"Ah dang it, you didn't have to tell me that!"

After a few days of eating solid food, Ben was able to get up on his feet, and was getting his strength back. He and Margie began walking together in the evenings, and watching sunsets come and go.

One of those evenings, Ben and Margie were quietly sitting on a log over looking a small pond, with little diver ducks skimming along the surface. Ben finally spoke, "My memory is still a little hazy. I mean how I got here, and who brought me to your house, and as a matter of fact . . . who I am."

"Oh, it's not my house. It's Uncle Pleas' house. I just came over to see about him, and you were here. He said a man named Tracker or Tucker . . . I can't remember which, and a Comanche Indian, brought you on a travois. That's all I know."

"They just dumped me here and left?"

"I guess they had to get somewhere, and they didn't know when you would wake up."

"Ben shook his head, "I reckon it'll all come back some time. Enough about me, what does your husband think about you being gone this long."

"Silly! I'm not married. There's nobody around here to marry."

"Don't you go into town ever once in a while?" asked Ben.

"Town's too far away, and besides, we have everything we need here, and at our place. What we don't have, Daddy goes in to get it."

"Boy, I sure hate to think such a pretty girl as you is all hid out here where no guys can find you! On second thought . . . maybe that's not so bad."

Margie blushed and turned away, "Thank you for saying so Ben, but I know I'm kinda plain."

Ben moved a little closer. "I don't think you're plain. I think you're purdy!"

"It's getting dark, Ben. Maybe we better go in."

"Don't you want to watch the moon come up? I been watching it lately, and it should be comin' up real soon now."

"I guess so . . . if it's not too long."

She shivered slightly, and Ben put his arm around her, and pulled her close. She didn't pull away.

They sat and watched the moon rise from a reddish glow to a full silvery ball. Margie felt him looking at her, and turned to look at him. When she did, he kissed her. It was a brief kiss, and they looked at each other for a moment, and kissed again . . . this time, lingering.

Margie stood up, "I had best go in now. I've probably stayed too long." She turned and walked to the house. Ben continued to sit by the pond for a while.

When he finally went in, he paused at her door and gently knocked. After a few moments, Margie came to the door.

"Margie, I just wanted to apologize for my forwardness earlier tonight. I shouldn't have taken advantage of the moment like that."

"Ben, it wasn't all your fault. After all I was there too."

"Well . . . I just wanted you to know, that's all."

"Okay, Ben, I'll see you tomorrow."

"Yeah, goodnight."

Ben's thoughts as he walked to his bedroom, were mostly of Margie, and the kiss, because both were fresh on his mind. But everything else was a jumbled haze. *"I still can't remember how I got here and who were the two men that brought me here? Am I married or have a girlfriend? Should I get involved with Margie? I wish I could remember!"*

He had a disturbing night trying to sleep, but old habits are hard to break, and he was up before dawn, stoking wood into the kitchen stove, getting the coffee ready.

Soon Pleas came into the kitchen. "I see you got the coffee on, and I thank ya. A feller can't get that first cup too soon."

"No Sir, he can't"

"I brought in some eggs yestiddy evenin', and a side of bacon that Margie brought. How does that sound?"

"That sounds mighty good, Mr. Beavers. Seems like I can't get enough to eat lately."

"Call me Pleas. Bein' hungry is a good sign you're getting' better. You just set there and drink your coffee, and I'll have this breakfast goin' in a wink."

"I think I'll see if I can ride a little today, Pleas. I think I just might be strong enough to handle it."

"I speck that'ud be good for ya."

Ben stood as Margie came in. She busied herself helping her uncle. They exchanged "good mornings", and then they all sat down.

When Ben finished breakfast, he went out the door, saying over his shoulder, "I'll see you both later."

Margie looked at Pleas and asked, "What did he mean by that?"

"Oh, he felt like he could ride, and that it would hep him feel better."

As Ben went into the barn, Sundance saw him, whinnied and ran to meet him. He rubbed Sundance's nose, and led him to where he could saddle him.

"Sundance, I'm sure glad I wasn't ridin' you when we hit that hole, or it would have been your neck that was broken." He continued to saddle his horse, and then he stopped and looked Sundance in the eye. *"Now how did I know that?"* He thought. *"It may be comin' back to me after all."*

He rode for hours, up along the Wichita River and then back again. Bits and pieces of memories kept flashing through his mind.

"Sundance, we about wasted a whole day. I reckon we better head back." Returning to the house took some time. Without paying attention, he had covered a lot of territory, just riding and thinking.

When he got close to the house, he heard gunshots, and kicked Sundance into a run. He didn't have his Colt with him, but he unsheathed his Winchester as he rode toward the house. He found Kiowa Indians shooting and circling the house. He fired, and the closest one fell. He continued to hit one after another, until only one was left. That one started to run. Ben stepped off his horse to aim better, and the last Indian dropped.

Ben quickly ran to the house. Pleas met him at the door. "Ben I'm shore glad ya made it back when ya did!"

"Where's Margie, Pleas?"

"Why, she's in the bedroom, shootin' towad's the back."

Ben hurried into the bedroom, "Margie, you all right?"

Margie was sitting by the window, her rifle barrel was resting on the sill, but she didn't answer.

Ben rushed to her side, and discovered an arrow in her chest, and blood covering the front of her body. She had been dead for a while.

Ben hurried out, grabbing his Colt from the hat stand by the door, as he ran outside. Pleas heard a loud cry, and Ben's Colt, as he shot each Indian again and again! When he had emptied his revolver, he sat down by the woodpile, and buried his face in his hands, "Why wasn't I here . . . why?"

Pleas guessed what was wrong, and looked in the bedroom to be sure. Then he walked to the wood pile, his eyes filled with tears, and put his hand on Ben's shoulder, "Wasn't your fault boy, so don't be so hard on yourself."

"I should have been here, Pleas . . . she was so young, I should have been here!"

"Gotta take things as they come, boy. They just don't always happen the way we think they ought."

"But she never had a chance to go nowhere, or do anything like other folks . . . it just don't seem fair."

"Life ain't fair. Ye gotta quit blamin' yaself. She wouldn't blame ya. Now come in, and help me take care of her. I'll take her home to my brother's in a little while, and let them know how it happened."

"I'll go with you, Pleas."

Pleas and Ben took Margie home to her parents, where they buried her under her favorite tree, her swing still hanging from the limbs. When they returned, they both sat and stared at the walls.

Next morning after breakfast, Ben broke the silence. "Pleas, I can't thank you enough for takin' care of me, and thanks to Margie, I'm getting' my memory back, a little at a time. I'd shore like to see you go stay with your brother and his family. You could help take care of them if the Indians come back, and they probably will. And you know . . . I hate to say it . . . but you don't have Margie to come by anymore."

"I'll consider it Ben. I kinda hate to leave a place where my wife and family was with me so long . . . it kinda sounds like ya may be leavin'."

"Well Pleas, I probably over-stayed my welcome long ago. I know where home is now, so I 'spect it's time to get back there. I want to leave a little cash with you, to help take care of all that grub and coffee I been takin' in."

"Naw sir, Ben! Ya don't owe me nothin'. I was just glad to have ya."

Ben saddled up Sundance, and readied the pack on the other horse. As he mounted he looked at the house, then with a little gig of his spurs, he headed toward Kerrville.

He by-passed Fort Griffin, *"I don't feel like all that rowdiness, and besides I have all the supplies I need."*

Ten days later, it was evening when he reached Kerrville and rode directly to Captain Billings's place. Tucker saw him coming. He knocked on the bunkhouse door and shouted, "Tom! Ole Ben's comin' up the trail!" Soon they both watched as Ben rode into the ranch yard.

Ben rode up beside them, looking down with a smile, "You fellers got anything to eat?"

They laughed as they pulled Ben from his horse, and all three headed to the cook shack where Billy had things on the table.

"Ben, if you know what's good for you, you'll get on ole Sundance and get into town as soon as you can, 'cause there's a little blonde girl a chompin' at the bits to see you. By the way, me and Tom never got to see Pleas' niece. How wus she?"

"I 'spect she saved my life, her and Pleas, 'cause when I came out of it, I didn't know nothin'. She kept after me and 'fore long, I started to remember."

"Was she purdy, Ben?"

"To me she was everything a man could want!"

"And you came back without her?"

"While I was out recollectin', Kiowas shot up the place. I managed to get all of them when I come back, but they shot her and she didn't make it."

"I'm shore sorry, Ben. That must'a been hard to take. Anyway, you better go see Grace. It 'us all we could do to keep her from ridin' up there after you."

After supper, Ben headed to town. He didn't know how she found out he was back, but he looked up and saw Grace riding hard toward him. She jumped off her horse and started running. He stepped down from his horse, and collided with her as she jumped up on him with both legs and arms, and gave him a flurry of kisses.

"I thought sure you weren't comin' back." she said, interrupting her kisses.

"Well, for a while I didn't know where to come back to."

"They told me they left you with an old man to take care of you."

"That they did, but his niece helped too."

"Oh, she did, did she? I think I'm jealous! Should I be?"

"No Grace, you shouldn't be! She was killed by Indians."

"Oh Ben, I'm sorry! I didn't know."

"I know you didn't. You didn't have anything to be jealous about, once I got my memory back."

"What if you hadn't got it back? Would you have stayed there?"

"I don't know . . . I might have."

"You mean you didn't even remember me?"

"Don't matter! I know who I am now, and it was you I wanted to see!"

They led their horses to the side of the creek, and sat down on the grass next to each other. The sun had gone behind the hills, and evening was loosing its glow.

"Ben, I missed you terribly! Don't go off and leave again."

"Gee, Grace, I'm sorry, but I didn't miss you at all."

She glanced at him, shocked by what he said, then he grinned, and she realized what he meant. She put hands on his shoulders and pushed him backward on to the ground, and piled on top of him.

"Your kiddin' is liable to get you shot one of these days, and I just might be the one to do it!" She started kissing him again.

They lay there with their arms around each other, looking up at the early stars, "Ben, do you ever wonder how many stars are out there?"

"Nope! When I realized there was more'n I could count, I'm satisfied to just look at 'em."

"That's not very romantic."

"Well then, how about this?" He pulled her into a close embrace and they kissed warmly.

"Grace, we oughta get moving! Moon goes down early, and it's gonna get darker soon, and your pa will worry about you."

"Okay Ben, but you will try to come in tomorrow night for supper won't you?"

"I promise, I will."

"And Ben . . . It's good to have you back."

Ben watched as she rode away. Then he mounted to ride back to the ranch. He had just gotten started when a voice out of the dark said, "Hold up right there!"

Ben couldn't see who it was but stopped anyway. "What seems to be the trouble?"

"I figgered if I follered Grace, I'd find you. You were told that if you came back to Kerrville you'd be killed!"

"I was told that by a man that's dead now."

"I was with Jesse when he told you that, and you made us walk back to town. Now lose your gun belt and let it drop."

"What I did, you deserved, since you were trying to kill me," said Ben to the unknown man.

"Well, you deserve to die for killin' Jesse!"

"What did you expect me to do? He was trying to kill all of us!"

"Get down off'n that horse, and let's you walk a while."

Ben eased down, all the time squinting to see the figure silhouetted against the starlight, and watching for any movement. The man rode in behind Ben, to make him walk a little faster.

"We're gonna walk 'till your feet are good and sore. Then I'm gonna shoot you, a little at a time, so's you know you're dying, a little at a time."

"What's the point of this? I did nothin' to you except make you walk a ways, and that was because you tried to kill us."

"You killed my friends, and we had big plans together!"

"What kinda plans that you can't still do?" Ben wasn't sure how well the rider could see, as dark as it was, but he felt that if he could fake a fall, he could reach his gun hidden in his boot. He continued talking to the man, thinking his attention would be more on the conversation, and less on his actions.

A quarter mile or more from where they first started, Ben began to hobble as if his feet were beginning to hurt. He pretended to stumble, but got right back up and continued to walk.

"How you like this walkin' since the boot's on the other foot?" the man asked with a synical laugh.

"Well, these boots are getting' a little tight!"

"Thanks for reminding me! Lets stop and you can take them off and walk barefoot a while, before I kill ya."

Ben sat down. He could see the man's outline against the starry sky. He slipped off one boot, then carefully eased the other off. The hidden gun slipped into his hand. He kept it hidden behind the boot he had taken off.

"Hurry up! We ain't got all night!"

"You're right, we don't have all night. I gotta get back to the ranch.

His calm comments confused the man. "What are you talking about?"

Ben lifted the gun, and shot. The wounded man rolled off his horse.

"I need to get back to the ranch. That's what I mean!"

After he put his boots back on, Ben placed the man on his horse, securing him so that he wouldn't fall off. Then he gave his horse a good slap on the rump to head him back to town. After Ben located his gun belt, he whistled for Sundance. Again in his saddle, he continued on back to the bunkhouse at the ranch.

When morning came, Ben was up early, as usual, enjoying the cool morning. He walked slowly toward the cook shack, and stepped inside to see Billy Watley.

Billy looked up. "You're sure up early, what can I do for you, Ben?"

"Nothin', I was just checkin' your water and wood, and looks like you got plenty."

"I thought you were going to move cattle today." said Billy.

"Naw, that's tomorrow. I got a little work here, then I got a big date for supper tonight."

"Good! You can sit right down and finish peeling these potatoes!"

"Okay, but if anyone comes in, I'm leavin'!

Later that morning, Ben was saddling up when Tom came riding up.

"You not forget Tom Coats, Ben?"

"I did for a while there, Tom, but not now. How's things goin' as a cowboy?"

"Silver Eagle glad Ben not forget."

"I only remember Tom Coats!"

They both laughed, and Ben mounted up. As they rode along, Tom asked, "Squaw glad you home?"

"She seemed ta be. I was sure glad to see her!"

"What about girl that take care of you?"

"That's right, you don't know, since you went back to the bunkhouse when I told Tucker. While I was out rememberin', a bunch o' Kiowas raided the house, and Margie was killed."

"Bad thing Indian do sometimes."

Ben agreed. "Maybe some day we can live together like me an' you . . . 'till then we just have to watch out. Hang on a minute, Tom." Ben stepped down to tighten his cinch. At the same time, Tom stood up on his saddle. "What ya see up there Tom?"

"Much dust . . . something or somebody move fast."

"Are any of the hands out there workin' the cattle today?"

"No, not think so."

"We better have a look."

They rode toward the dust until Tom said, "It Apache, ten maybe fifteen, with many horses."

"Tom, the direction they're headed will take them right into old man Ingram's settlement. They've got a lot of canyons and the river to cross before they get there. If we don't warn those people, the Apaches can run the horses through town, killing folks and burning it down. We've gotta beat 'em there!"

The two rode as fast as they could toward the little settlement of Ingram, just northwest of Kerrville and even closer to their ranch. They arrived well ahead of the

Indians, and were able to get the settlers into position to fend off an attack. They got behind anything they could for protection.

Tom and Ben were crouched behind a wagon. "Ben, they are close." said Tom.

"Okay, Tom." Then he shouted to the others. "Here they come! Wait 'till they get closer before you fire!"

The Apache came riding in fast behind about fifteen stolen horses, but the Indians were taken by total surprise. Gunfire came at them from all directions and they were dropping quickly. The few Indians not hit turned, and headed west along the Guadalupe.

Ben saw the herd of horses begin to settle down, after the Indians were cut off from chasing them. He leaped on Sundance, and cut them back toward the livery at the end of the street.

After containing the horses, Ben rode down the street to see how many people might have been injured. Only two had sustained injury, and it appeared that neither was going to be fatal.

Ben and Tom were told that no one in the settlement had seen these animals before. The people were anxious for them to take the horses, since they had saved them from certain distruction.

They started the horses back toward the ranch. "I see a few brands, but I haven't been around these parts long, so I don't recognize any. You don't 'spose they drove these all the way from Mexico, do you?"

"They not run horses that far. Tucker know brands around here."

"Yeah, reckon you're right. I'll let him sort 'em out, 'cause I got a big date tonight."

Ben's heartbeat quickened as he rode to the Hanner's home, anticipating the evening with Grace.

When he reached the house, George Hanner was on the front porch.

"Howdy, Mr. Hanner."

"Hello, Ben. Not much use to get down. Grace says she don't want to see ya tonight!"

"What seems to be the trouble, Mr. Hanner?"

"Bob Simmons came by and told her that you killed Jesse Fenton in cold blood! You didn't, did you, son?"

Ben was worried, because he had had to shoot Jack Harris, another of Jesse's friends, after Grace rode home last night. He thought, *"She won't believe I had to do that, either!"*

"NO Sir, Mr. Hanner it ain't so. I need to talk to her, to tell her what happened."

Hanner moved to the edge of the porch, "It won't do no good, Ben. Bob told her you'd make up a story about killing him."

"Tell her she can ask Tucker Johnson or Tom Coats. He tried to kill us all on the trail. An' tell her too, I'll be back tomorrow, and I'll expect to see her when I get here!"

"I'll tell her Ben," said George Hanner, as he walked back into the house."

Ben sat a few minutes, blankly staring at the house. He snapped back, as the door closed, and then he headed back toward the ranch.

Thoughts ran through his mind as he rode along, *"how am I goin' to convince her that any killin' I did was because I was on the way to bein' killed? 'Specially since I had to kill Jack right after she left for home."*

The more he thought about it, the angrier he became. "Well Sundance, what a fix I'm in . . . well, I'm not gonna lose another girl. She's just gonna have to listen to what I say!" He had not gotten far when he turned Sundance on the spot, and headed back to the Hanner's.

When he arrived at the Hanner's, he rode around to the back. He eased Sundance close and stood up on his saddle, and found the window to Grace's room on the upper floor open. He could hear sobbing coming from the room. The sun was down, but with the glow of the sunset, he could see her lying on the bed. "Grace?" he whispered.

She raised her head, "Go away! I don't want you here!"

"Grace, please don't shut me out . . . let me explain."

"Why should I listen? Bob told me what you did. I can't listen to a killer!"

"You listened to Bob's story that wasn't true, and I'm comin' in to tell you mine!"

Ben climbed in the window and moved to the bedside.

"How could you think I would do what Bob said?"

"Jesse is dead, isn't he?"

"Yes, but nobody knows who shot him!"

"What do you mean?"

"Jesse and a bunch of others, probably Bob was with 'em, attacked us in camp. We were all around the fire, and if Cookie hadn't dumped water and put the fire out, we would be the ones that are dead! Everybody was shootin' . . . so we don't know who shot Jesse."

"Bob didn't tell it that way."

"Well that's the way it happened. And I gotta tell you something else . . . when you rode off last night . . . Jack Harris ambushed me on the trail, held me at gunpoint, and said he was gonna kill me."

"I suppose you killed him, too."

Ben looked at her a while, wondering what he could say that would make things okay with her. He decided to just tell her the truth, and trust her to understand. "I had no choice, Grace. I'm sorry, but that was all I could do. I hope there are no more out there that wants me dead."

"Bob did say that 'we' would take care of it!"

"Then, there are more lookin' for me."

She melted into his arms, "I'm sorry I believed the worse about you, but I thought Bob was a friend. We've known each other so long . . . I just didn't know."

Ben smiled and said, "Don't let it happen again!"

"I won't . . . I promise." They kissed, gently, both relieved to have the matter settled between them.

"I better go . . . before . . . dang I hope ole Sundance hasn't wandered off or I can't get back down from here!"

At breakfast the next day, all the hands were sitting around the table when Tucker Johnson spoke up, "Ben, I looked at those horses you and Tom brought in, and I didn't recognize any brands. As far as I'm concerned, they're your's and Tom's."

"Well, Tucker, if you're sure, me and Tom might just sell 'em, and buy a little spread to raise a few head of cattle, sometime down the road."

"I'm all fer a feller getting' ahead if'n he can, so good luck. Don't forget, we move cattle today."

"No Sir, I won't."

For several days, Ben thought about the chance they had to buy a place and some cattle. Finally, he discussed it with Tom.   "Tom not know what cattle cost. Land not cost. It everybody's!"

"Well . . . it don't work like that for white men. You gotta have a title to the land."

"What title?" asked Tom with a confused look on his face.

"That's a piece of paper that say's you own what land, and how much of it, and where it is located."

"Where paper come from?"

"You get it from the feller you buy the land from. I'll ask around to see if any land is for sale near here. It's gotta be close, so's we can work to pay for what the horses won't cover.

"Tomorrow is Sunday, and I'm goin' into town early enough to see if there is some land we can buy." said Ben, as he was brushing the dust off of his boots.

"Will Ben Forbes have time for land, or for squaw?" asked Tom Coats, as he turned so Ben couldn't see his teasing smile.

"I'll have time for both, I hope, 'cause they're both important! Since it's Sunday I don't reckon any business will take place." Ben kept brushing.

"When you bring squaw home, no time then for land." said Tom with his twisted grin on his face."

"Well then, I'll just let you do the work!" Ben turned and brushed a little harder on his boots.

Ben Forbes was up early and had on his best pants and new shirt. His hair was slicked down as much as the bulk of it would allow. He pulled on his hat, saddled Sundance, and headed to town.

As he rode the trail, his senses seemed to be sharpened. He noticed the birds flitting from one tree to the next, all the time chattering away. A cool breeze gently flipped his neckerchief and an occasional cloud brought temporary shade, then passed on.

When he arrived in town, the church on the hill at the north end of town was belching forth a crowd of well-dressed citizens. No stores were open, so Ben stopped in at the Sheriff's office. He eased his reins over the log hitching post, and entered through the arched adobe door. In the office was a large desk, placed to the right of the room, where Sheriff Vandergrift sat with his feet propped up, eating a sandwich and drinking his coffee. He looked up as Ben approached. "Howdy, Ben! It is Ben isn't it? I remember. Pull up a chair and have a cup 'a coffee."

"Don't mind if I do, Sheriff." Ben walked to the big stove where the coffee warmed.

"What brings you to town?" asked Sheriff Vandergrift, between bites of his sandwich.

"Sheriff, I'm lookin' to buy a little place to raise a few cattle, and maybe build a house."

"You aimin' to get married, Ben?"

"Not sure. Have thought on it, though." said Ben, as he poured his coffee and sat down across from Sheriff Vandergrift.

"You know Ben, seems that several places might go up for sale, since some of the folks around here are getting' older and are ready to hang it up."

"Have any Idea who that might be?"

"Not off hand, but ole Zeb Ekhart over to the land office would probably know. He's up at the church right now."

"I saw them lettin' out at the church, when I was ridin' in."

Sheriff dropped his feet to the floor. "Ole Zeb Ekhart'll be comin' to his office pretty soon. He always does, since his wife died last year. He's almost livin' there."

Ben stood and set his coffee down. "Thank ya Sheriff. I'll move on and see if I can catch him."

"I bet you can. Come back when you can, and set a spell." Sheriff Vandergrift rose as Ben walked out the door. Ben sat on the bench out front to watch for Zeb Ekhart to come to the land office.

He didn't have to wait long. Zebulon Ekhart exited the diner and proceeded to the land office. Ben caught him at the door of his office. "Mister Ekhart, mind if I talk to ya a minute? I know it's Sunday, and a lot of folks don't like to talk business on Sunday, but I don't get into town often, and I'd like to know if'n there's some land I might buy kinda close to town here, to raise cattle on."

Zebulon Ekhart lowered his glasses so that he could look over them. "Young fellow, you sure talk fast. Come inside, and say all of that again. What's your name, boy?"

"It's Benjamin Forbes, Sir. They just call me Ben."

"All right Ben, tell me again, what you said at the door."

"Yes Sir. I was wonderin' if there's some land kinda cheap near here for sale. You see my friend and me want to raise a few head of cattle, and we don't have much money. So we will have to work to pay for any land we can buy. That is, if we can pay for it a little at a time."

"I see! Well, young fellow, you've come to the right place. 'Spose we have a look. Folks usually let me know when they want to sell out. I think the old James place is one of them that hasn't sold yet."

Both Ben and Zebulon Ekhart turned toward his office door as Grace Hanner floated through it. "Benjamin Forbes, I thought that was you I saw coming in here," she tipped her bonnet in mid sentence, "and good morning again to you Mister Ekhart. Ben you were supposed to come tonight. What's going on?"

"Oh, I'm comin' tonight, but I wanted to ask some questions today."

"What kind of questions could you possibly ask of Mister Ekhart?"

"Well now Miss Hanner, aren't you getting' a little nosey?"

"I guess I was, Ben. I'm sorry."

"Don't be sorry . . . I was just jokin'. What I was askin' about'll effect you, too."

"What do you mean by that?"

"Well, Mister Ekhart was about to see if there was any land for sale that Tom and I might be able to afford."

"That old James place. What does that have to do with me?"

"I swaney, Grace! For a girl so purdy, I just can't see how you can be so . . ." he quickly checked himself, thinking he was about to get in trouble, "How could you not know? I want you to be a part of anything I do."

Grace pretended surprise. "How sweet, Ben. All right, I'll leave you two alone, and I'll see you tonight!" she said, as she drummed her forefinger on his vest.

"Well Mister Forbes, while you two were courtin', I found that acreage up the hill a ways, toward Junction. I think it's about a hundred and twenty or thirty acres. It has a house of sorts, and corral and a small barn . . . and it says here the barn's full of hay. The whole place'll go for seven hundred and fifty dollars."

"Mister Ekhart, we've got horses that we can sell for maybe half of that, and maybe more, but I'll have to see if'n I can borrow the rest. Meantime if you can hold on to it 'till I can see, I'd appreciate it."

"Son, it's been for sale for four years! It's not likely to sell in the next few days."

"I sure do thank ya, Mister Ekhart. And thank ya for the little map you drew for me. Me and Tom'll ride out there when we can. I'll let you know soon."

When Tom and Ben finally had time to check out the land, they rode up out of the valley on the road to Junction. The sun was bright, not a cloud in the sky. "You know Tom, I think we just might make a go of it. Ranchin' can support us pretty well, if we can get it goin', and I think we can . . . don't you?"

"Tom think what you think, Ben."

"Now Tom, you gotta be for doin' this too! You never know, you just might find that squaw of your dreams one of these days."

Tom, trying not to smile, answered, "Tom not lookin' right now."

"I know, but you might, someday. Ole Zeb said there's a barn and a house already there."

The two rode on, with thoughts only to themselves. As they topped the hill, they could look down into the valley, where smoldering ruins of buildings were giving off their last whisps of white smoke! They rode quickly toward the dying embers.

"Tom, acordin' to the map Zeb drew, this is the place that was for sale!"

"Maybe price be less with no house or barn," said Tom with a straight face.

"Somebody had to 'a set these fires, for the house and the barn both to burn."

Ben rode a circle around the smoking ruins. "Tom, I smell coal oil! Somebody has set this fire, and I'm gonna find out who and why!"

They turned and headed back to Kerrville.

The first place they stopped was the land office. Ben dropped his reins and stepped up on the boardwalk. The big door to the land office was open, and Ben barged in.

"Mister Ekhart, did you let anybody know we were buying that place out west o' here?"

"No Sir Ben, not a soul knew. Why?"

"The house and barn have been burned. Somebody set it."

"Reckon it was Indians?"

"Indians don't use coal oil when they burn a place! Thank ya anyway."

Ben stepped outside and told Tom that he was going to see Grace. Tom headed back to the ranch, and Ben walked to the Hanner's store.

"Howdy Mister Hanner. Grace here?"

"She's upstairs, Ben. Go on up, just let her know you're coming."

Ben bounded up the stairs, "Grace, I'm comin' up!"

"In here, Ben."

He opened the door and Grace pounced on him, and put her arms around him, "I missed you, you know!"

"I missed you too, Grace. But right now we need to talk."

She moved back, and looked into his eyes. "Sounds serious, what is it Ben?"

"When I was talkin' to Zeb about a place to buy, did you know it was the James' place he was talkin' about?"

"Yes Ben, I heard him say that it had been for sale a long time, and the James' place has."

"Well, did you mention it to anyone else?"

She turned and thought a minute. "I might have mentioned it to Bob Simmons. He asked about you and we talked awhile. Why?"

"I don't understand why you would even speak to that guy, after him lying to you about me." Ben was irritated. "He told you they were going to get me!"

"I'm sorry, Ben. I just wasn't thinking. I guess it's hard to think that I can't trust him. I've known him all my life. Why does it matter?"

"Did you know that he ran with Jesse?"

"I knew that he and Jesse went to school together . . . when they went to school. I don't understand, Ben. What's going on?"

"Somebody burned the house and barn on the James' place last night."

"It might have been Indians, Ben."

"No, whoever burned it used coal oil to make it burn good and fast. I reckon it had to be Bob Simmons, 'cause you and me are the only ones that knew about it. Zeb said he didn't mention it to anyone."

"What are you going to do?"

"Have a little talk with Bob Simmons, I guess!" Ben went back down the stairs.

Grace called after him, "I'm sorry Ben . . . please be carefull."

Ben walked across the street to the Sheriff's office and walked through the open door, "Sheriff y' got a minute?"

"Shore, Ben. Come on in. What can I do for you?"

"Me and Tom are tryin' to buy the old James's place, and when we went out to look at it, the house and barn were burned down."

"Indians, huh?"

"No sir, they wus soaked in coal oil, and one of Jesse's friends was the only other person that knew we intended to buy it . . . name of Bob Simmons."

"Now, Ben, what makes you think it was him?"

"Well, you know about the trouble Jesse and me had about Grace. Jesse tried to kill me twice 'till he got hisself killed, shootin' into the camp fire on the Colonel's trail ride. Then one tried to kill me after I got back from that trip. So it stands to reason. If you don't feel you can look into it, I reckon I'll just have to."

"Ben, I ain't got no eveydence to confront him with."

"Well, Sheriff, I'll go out there and see if I can find some. I'll be back."

"Ben, you want to be careful and keep your eyes open! Bob Simmon's got hisself a reputation fer gunplay over in the Mills valley."

"I'll stay alert, Sheriff."

Ben turned and walked out. He headed back to Grace Hanner's place.

"Grace, do me a favor: when you talk to Bob Simmons, drop a little hint that I've heard that something of value was beneath the floor of the James house, and that I'm hopin' that it didn't burn. Not knowin' where it might be, I'll camp out 'till I find it."

"Ben, you're convinced Bob did it, aren't you? Okay, he comes by the store most every afternoon. I'll drop a hint as subtle as I can. But don't be surprised if he doesn't show up, because I don't think he would do a thing like that."

"Grace, he's the only other one that knew about it, and the Sheriff said he has been building his reputation as a gunman, which tells me he might do anything."

"Then, you be careful," she snuggled close, put her arms around him and kissed him, "I want you to be around to rebuild what burned."

Ben Forbes melted at her touch, returned the kiss, then left. He rode to the ranch to let Tucker Johnson know what he had in mind.

Tucker listened to Ben's story. "I guess we can handle things here. It's kinda slow right now. You be careful. Do you think you can handle this by yourself?"

"I think I can, Tucker. Right now, I'm gonna tell Tom what I plan, and then get my stuff together. I'll ask Billy to put together some eats for a day or two. This Bob Simmons is likely to come this evening, if Grace gets a little misinformation to him."

"Good luck to ya, Ben. Hope whoever it is that you draw him out."

Ben placed everything he would need into his saddlebags and blanket cover, rolled it up and tied it on back of his saddle. Then he headed toward Junction on his way to the James place. It would take him an hour to get there and set up camp.

The up-hill terrain out of Kerrville was a good pull for the sorrel, 'Luke', that he had chosen to ride, so he stopped half way up to let his horse take a breather. Looking back into the valley, he could see many of the houses and the Guadalupe River. I hate to say it, but I reckon we better get on, so's to be there before dark."

Before long the James place was in sight. "Well, Luke, the well's still got water in it and the grass wasn't burned. So how 'bout we make us a camp right here? We can be stirrin' ashes all day tomorrow, 'till Bob or someone comes to take us out."

With camp made and bedding spread, Ben started a small fire to make coffee, and warm a couple of Billy's biscuits in a can he brought along . . . a trick all the Forbes boys learned from their father . He sat sipping the coffee for a long while, thinking that he might be attacked before dawn.

Luke's munching on grass was so consistent that it sounded like footsteps, causing Ben to have chills all over. Soon he grew sleepy, so he put out the fire, rolled up in his blanket and was quickly asleep.

About two in the morning, Luke's snorting and pawing woke Ben. He rose up, gun in hand, and quickly looked around. He heard the growl, and saw a large coyote, bristles up and teeth bared. It was between Ben and Luke. As he started to move toward Ben, Luke began to stomp the ground and whinnie. The coyote squatted low with his tail between his legs, and disappeared into the darkness.

"Thank you, Luke! I see you hate coyotes as much as I do. I know that Billy's biscuits are good, but I never thought of using 'em to bait coyotes!"

Ben's eyes had adjusted to the darkness, and he could see well, so he decided to look around. He rolled his saddle blanket, and other supplies in his blanket, and placed them by his upturned saddle, "That ought ta look like I'm sleepin' here, Luke, I'll be back after I look around a bit . . . for some reason I don't think we're alone, and I don't mean a four legged coyote either."

Ben slipped on his boots and walked away from his camp. The further he moved, the better his view of the general area.

Something in motion in the distance caught his attention. He couldn't make it out at first, but continued to keep an eye on it. Because little else moved, he decided that it was a rider. The movement of the figure became more evident as he rode closer to the camp. Ben continued to watch, as the man stepped off his horse and tied it to a scrub oak. Then he sat down, and removed his boots, and slipped on moccasins. *"I reckon he expects ta slip up on me,"* his thoughts brought on a smile, *"he might just be surprised!"*

Ben started to slowly step back closer to his camp. He moved with short, light paces, so as to not draw the rider's attention.

The intruder could see the blanket that Ben had propped up on the saddle. So he continued to move slowly toward what he thought was the sleeping Benjamin Forbes.

"BLAM! . . . BLAM! . . . BLAM!" Three quick shots from the gunman's Colt echoed through the nearby canyons. Luke reared his hobbled front legs, and moved backward. The coyote, which had been hiding behind a small bush, ran for his life, with his tail between his legs! Ben watched the white cloud of smoke rise into the starlight.

"You must be Bob Simmons. I've been expecting you!"

The startled man turned toward the voice, and shot again. Still blinded from the flash of the first shots, he missed Ben.

"Get rid of the gun and get on the ground, Simmons, or you're a dead man."

Knowing he had no other choice, Bob Simmons pitched his Colt away and lay down.

"I know why you're here tonight. You thought I was gonna find something valuable. But I don't know why you burned this place, or why you're trying to kill me. Several of Jesse's bunch have died trying to kill me. I'd think you're 'bout the only one left. You wanta join the others?"

Bob Simmons looked up at Ben, "We all swore to Jesse that we'd get you."

"How many swore?"

"The ones you killed on the trail drive . . ."

Ben interrupted, "Lots of other men's bullets went into that crew!"

"Anyway, Jack Harris, who I guess you killed. He came in on his horse, dead. And there's me. That's all I know of."

"If you're lucky you may be the only one that lives, out of that whole bunch. My Papa told me the Bible says 'Vengeance is mine, says the Lord!' I reckon it looks like that's true. A body ought not do vengeance on his own, 'cause he's liable to die. Now, I'll expect you to be payin' for a bunch o' lumber, and help get a house and barn on this place! Otherwise, I'm liable to let the Lord and Sam Colt finish this vengeance thing!"

Bob Simmons glared at Ben, "I ain't planning ta do nothin' of the kind!" He turned and leaped for his revolver. Ben fell and fired at the same time, to throw Simmons' aim off. When he hit the ground, he rolled over and fired again. The shot was unnecessary, because his first bullet caught Bob Simmons under the chin.

Ben was slow to get up. When he finally rose to his feet, his boot was filling with blood. He sat back down, removed his boot, and found that the blood was coming from his leg. Bob Simmons' bullet had gone in just under the skin above his ankle, and came out just under his knee. *"I hate to think where that bullet might'a gone if'n I hadn't fell and rolled!"*

He pulled Bob Simmons away from the fire pit, and started a fire so he could see. As Ben examined his leg, he found that the bullet traveled under the skin without damaging the muscle, so he bandaged it with his neckerchief to stop the bleeding.

"That oughta take care of that, and I reckon the shots took care of Mister Coyote." He pulled his saddle and blanket closer to the fire, looked to see that Luke was doing all right, then crawled into his blanket and collapsed into deep sleep.

Ben slowly opened his eyes, as he awoke to the crackle of his campfire blazing higher than it was when he went to sleep. He raised his head slightly and gripped his 44-40 revolver under his blanket. He squinted to make out the figure on the other side of the fire.

"I thought maybe Ben Forbes dead too! He not move," said Tom Coats, as he was lifting a coffee pot, and pouring Ben a cup, "Tom saw boot with hole in it, and blood on leg sticking out of blanket."

Ben took the cup of coffee, "Well Tom, it was just like we thought. Bob Simmons came last night and shot a couple of holes in my blanket, Later got a shot off that hit me in the leg. I guess the boot top slowed the bullet down, but it still moved up my leg. I think I stopped the bleedin' last night, but I didn't feel like ridin' in after all that happened. How long you been here anyway?"

"I find good shovel in shed that burn, buried man you shot, then build fire."

"I thank you for that, Tom! Now I gotta see if I can get on ole Luke. By the way, he chased a coyote off last night; right when he was gonna take a bite of me. The critter high tailed it later, when the shootin' started."

Ben started tying his gear on Luke. Tom untied Bob Simmons' horse, tied the reins around the saddle horn, and gave him a good swat on the rump so he would return home.

"I think maybe that's the last that swore to kill me . . . at least I shore hope so."

After taking another ride around the land they had bought, Tom and Ben rode back to the ranch. Ben went in to the cook shack, and got Billy to fix up his leg.

Billy cut the leg of Ben's pants, and examined the wound. "I can't rightly figure just how you did this. The bullet ran right up under the skin. I'll wrap it and put a little coal oil on it, and it'll be as good as new in a day or two."

"Do you have to put coal oil on it, Billy?"

"Why, that bullet put a lot o' dirt under your skin. You don't want to get blood poison do you?"

"I reckon not, but I'm not sure which is worse."

The next Sunday evening, Ben rode into town to have supper with Grace and her dad.

"Grace, Bob Simmons was the one that burned the house and barn on the James place. Your clue about me lookin'for somethin' o' value' brought him right out to the place."

Grace sat a pitcher of water on the table, and sat down. "Well I wasn't sure but I thought he asked a lot of questions."

"I think he was the last of Jesse's friends that were out to get me."

"I hope so, and when I see Bob Simmons again I'm going to give him a piece of my mind!"

Ben sat staring ahead, without saying a word. Grace, studying his face, asked, "He's not . . .?"

Ben faced her, "I'm sorry, Grace. There was nothing I could do to prevent it."

"That's what you meant, when you said he was the last."

"I really am sorry! Four times Jesse and his friends tried to kill me, and I was lucky enough that they didn't. If that bothers you . . . I'll leave, if you want."

"NO! I don't want you to leave. I hate that you had to kill them, but they meant nothing to me. You're the only one I care for."

"Do you mean that, Grace?"

"Yes, I do!"

Ben took Grace by the hand and led her out on the veranda. He took her in his arms, looked into her eyes, and asked her to marry him, if her father agreed.

"OH yes, Ben! I will! I'm sure Father will agree."

"OH? He wants to get rid of you does he?"

"Oh you . . ."

He pulled her closer and kissed her, a long lingering kiss. Then he held her quietly. She nestled gainst him, feeling happy and secure.

357

"Grace, we'll have to wait 'till I can do some rebuilding."

"That's all right, Ben. We can work together."

Reluctantly, Ben pushed back. "I better go now. I'm only human! I'll see you tomorrow."

As they passed through the dining room, Grace's dad looked up. "You two get things settled?"

"Yes, Father, Ben asked me to marry him."

"That's if that's all right with you, sir." Ben injected.

"That's fine with me son, and I'll kick in for the lumber to rebuild what you lost."

"I can't thank you enough for that, and we'll get started as soon as we can."

Ben finally told them both goodnight, and left for the ranch.

On his ride home, Ben whistled, sang and talked to the birds, as he thought about his future.

Tom was waiting on the porch of the dining hall.

"Tom, you can't guess what happen at supper."

Tom smiled and leaned against a post, "Tom thinks you get in trouble."

Ben stepped off his horse, and tossed the reins across the hitching rack. "What do you mean?"

"You get self tied to woman!"

"Now, just how did you know that?" Ben laughed.

"Tom see smile on face, not there before."

"Okay, you're right! Not only that, but Mister Hanner said he'd furnish lumber for us to rebuild."

"Tom glad, will help Ben with house."

"You'll need a place too."

Tucker Johnson walked out of the house, "Howdy Ben. Did you have a nice Sunday at Grace's?"

"I shore did Tucker! I asked her to marry me, and she said she would! Her Pa said he'd help with the lumber to put the James place back together."

"Well Ben, that sounds good. But you better plan on two houses, 'cause Tom here's been courtin' a dark eyed beauty over in Ingram, every time you go to town! By the way, you two can take Mondays off a while to get started buildin' . . . that is, if you can get your work done here."

Tucker went back into the house. Ben turned to Tom. "So the Silver Eagle flies again . . . I thought you told me you weren't lookin' for a squaw!"

"Tom not lookin' then . . . had already found."

Benjamin Forbes smiled and shook his head. "Why are we standing here? We've got tomorrow off. Grab a hammer and let's get started!"

Mary Elizabeth Forbes

Chapter 27

Two silhouettes stood at the track rail, at the Virginia home of Richard Albin Forbes, father of the Forbes Clan. Richard and his daughter, Mary Elizabeth, discuss their plans. The early morning has wrapped them in a thin haze, and you can hear the hoof beats in the distance approaching fast, and passing in front of them.

The sound of a stopwatch clicks, "Well, Lizy, we've sold all the horses except Mister Spencer, and according to my watch, Spence is still the fastest around this part of the country. I'm glad we decided to take him with us to Charles' place in Texas. I'm takin' Farley's Folly to Eldon Potts in Galveston. I expect him to pay the balance on him when we get there. I hope they can stand the trip to Texas, 'cause before we get to Charles' place, we cross a lot of territory."

"They'll make it all right, Papa."

"I hope I can! The ole ticker isn't what it used to be. I'm just glad we were able to sell the place so quick."

"Ah, Papa, you'll do okay too."

"Lizy, we better get started for Memphis. I figger it'll take us a month and a half if we don't have trouble. That is, if your little mules can hold to the trail. That's a long way."

Don't worry so much! "They'll make it, Papa. They're strong as oxen."

The two of them turned and headed to the house. "We can only hope so."

The travel would be hard, first to Memphis to catch a boat to Galveston, where he would deliver Foley's Folly, the last horse to be sold.

The journey had been tiring, but eventually Richard and Mary Elizabeth arrived in Galveston. They were met by an excited Eldon Potts, who had seen Farley's Folly at the Forbes place in Virginia, and had paid one third of the price, with the agreement for him to be delivered to Galveston. The remainder was to be paid today at his delivery.

Potts was all smiles and hand shakes, as he checked out the horse, "Looks like he came through fine."

Mary Elizabeth spoke up, "They all did fine . . . didn't have to do much aboard ship, but eat."

While Richard Forbes and Eldon Potts finished the paper work on the sale, with the transfer of registration papers, Mary Elizabeth walked Mister Spencer, and two little mules they brought to pull the wagon north. After exercising them, she harnessed them to the wagon and prepared for the trip to her brother Charles' place in North Texas. They didn't travel far before making their first camp.

The weather was pleasant, and they had a good meal. Richard wrapped his blanket around himself. "Lizy,

I'd help you clean up, but I'm all in. I'm surprised we made such good time to get this far!"

"Don't worry Papa, it won't take but a minute for me to get things taken care of. You get some rest!

Lizy was up before the sun. The morning was cool, and a little fog nestled in the low places. When she had breakfast ready she called, "Papa, rise and shine! We got a long way to go!" She dished up eggs for Richard, and then became aware that he had not stirred, and given her the usual "You fix it, and I'll eat it!"

She called him again. When she didn't get a response, she went to him. Her father had died in the night. "Well, Papa, I guess in your sleep, was the easy way to go! I'm sorry, we should have stayed home!" All the while, she packed, harnessed, and cried.

In the wagon, she carefully spread a blanket, and wrapped her father. She remembered an abandoned cemetery, just north of Hitchcock, Texas, so she turned around, and took her father there, where she buried him, herself. "At least, Papa, we'll know where you are." Once again, she continued north on her journey, alone.

At the evening campsite, Mary Elizabeth rearranged her bedroll, and fluffed her heavy coat she had placed beneath her head for a pillow. She needed sleep, but the thoughts of having to bury her father by herself, and memories of her mother, brought on emotions that had been denied too long. She stared at the stars that peeked through the umbrella of tree limbs over her camp. Silent tears rolled over the sides of her face, into the hair she had just brushed.

"I miss Mama so much! She shouldn't have died when she did! I was too young to become a grown up. Yes, Papa was always there. But his attention was with the boys, 'till they left home. He never knew the needs of

a little girl . . . I shouldn't have insisted that we make this journey . . . Now, he's dead.

I dug the grave by myself. I wrapped my Papa in that blanket, and rolled him into the ground, by myself. I shoveled the earth on top of him, by myself. And here I am, by myself, completely alone.

Well that's enough sniveling! I'm not alone at all! I have the Lord, two little mules and Mister Spencer! Now, Lizy, tomorrow, you're on your own! You're a big girl now!"

Some distance on further north of their location, a young man by the name of Hank O'Neill, a tall, handsome and tanned young cowboy, had just finished eating. He didn't know that his life, and that of the Forbes family were destined to come together in the near future.

His meal had been served in a saloon filled with buffalo hunters, in a little southern Texas town. He watched a man at the next table as he rolled a smoke, then twisted the end so the tobacco wouldn't fall out.

Loud voices came from across the room. Without warning, a man quickly stood, knocking his chair over backwards, and firing across the table. "Damn you, Murray!" Exclaimed the shooter, as he waved his arm to fan away the smoke, to get another shot.

Henry O'Neill, with gun in hand, jumped toward the man and came down hard on his gun arm with his Colt. The man's heavy side arm spun across the floor, cutting its way through the sawdust. Hank then bent the man's arm up behind him and pushed him down on the table.

O'Neill leaned close to the man's ear and said, "Now, I don't know but what that feller might just deserve gitttin' shot, but let's not be shootin' in here. Somebody might get hurt!"

The shooter, with his face pushed against the whisky covered table, screamed out, "You broke my arm! When I get up I'm gonna kill you!"

Hank held the man down, and asked, "Has anyone gone for the sheriff?"

The bartender said, "Yes, I sent my floor sweeper to find him."

As the bartender finished his reply, the butterfly doors swung inward. The sheriff stood and looked around the room, and the bartender nodded toward the problem.

The sheriff walked to the table where Hank held the man down, "What seems to be the trouble here?"

"Well Sheriff, seems this feller thought he had the right to do a little target practice on the man across the table. I just convinced him that it shouldn't be done inside."

The man across the table had removed his coat, and checked to see how badly he was hit. Luckily, he was only scratched.

The Sheriff took hold of the gunman's arm, and jerked him up from the table. "I'll take him off your hands, son. You did the right thing. This is Harv Coffman, and he's been nothin' but trouble since he hit town, again."

"Thank you Sheriff. I was afraid this feller might shoot somebody . . . like me!"

As the sheriff took Coffman out, Hank O'Neill flipped a couple of coins on the bar, and pushed through the doors. While he stood on the porch, the man who had been shot came out, holding a towel to his arm. "I wanna thank you fer stoppin' ole Harv, cause he'ud killed me if you hadn't."

"My pleasure! I was afraid he might shoot someone else, or me. It was crowded in there. I just hope you weren't cheatin'."

The man looked Hank straight in the eyes. "It was an honest game. He was just loosin'. Keep an eye out for Harv! He can hold a grudge!"

"I don't plan to hang around long, but I'll watch out for him."

Hank took the reins from the hitching post, and mounted his brindle dun that he called 'Tiger', because of the faint dark stripes across his hindquarters.

As he rode down the dusty street, it was beginning to get dark. The buildings along the streets looked like giant ghosts hovering over him as he rode. He headed to the livery, where he placed Tiger with Whiffel, his other horse. Then he walked down an alley, and headed toward the little abandoned shack where he had put up for a night or two.

Henry O'Neill entered the shack and struck a match to check if any oil was left in the old lamp. After lighting it, he settled into the rocking chair by the table, and began to clean his revolver. It wasn't long until he began to doze off.

He woke himself by cocking his 44-40 Colt that was still in his hand. Having been only half asleep, his mind was alerted by the crackling of fire and the smell of wood burning just outside the window. He quickly grabbed his soogan and other gear from the bed, and hurriedly tossed them out the door. He quickly stuffed a shell into his 44, and ran to the back of the house. There he saw the shadow of a man still pouring coal oil on the fire.

When the arsonist saw Hank, he threw the can at him, and started to run. He pulled a gun and fired as he tried to escape.

Hank dropped to his knee to skylight the running figure against the darkening evening sky, and fired. The shot hit its mark.

Hank heard footsteps running behind him, and quickly turned. "Don't shoot! It's me, the sheriff!" came a voice out of the dark.

"Sheriff, I did nearly shoot you! Do you know who that is . . . is it Harv?"

"Yes it's Harv. I was taking him supper when he slammed me, and ran out. I've been looking for him for over two hours."

They both turned to look at the burning shack. "We can't do much about that, I guess," mused the sheriff. "Did you salvage your gear, before you had to get out?"

"Yes I did. It's out front. I reckon I better move it, 'fore a cinder flies in it. I wonder how he got coal oil that quick."

"I'm sorry, young feller. He got my can and a pistol at the jail. If it won't bother you, you're welcome to sleep in the jail tonight. I suppose you won't mind a great breakfast in the mornin', cause Sarah, from the boarding house, was gonna bring it to old Harv anyway."

"Sheriff that sounds like somthin' I just can't pass up. Thank you."

"It's the least I can do, since I feel like it was my fault anyway, a lettin' Harv get to me that way. Is your horse here? I'll put him up for you."

"Nah, Sheriff, Tiger is over at the livery with Whiffel, my pack horse. I left my pack there with the horses."

"All right, then. I'll see you in the mornin'. Now I better see to Harv."

Henry, 'Hank', O'Neill, an early riser, had washed up and was strapping on his gun belt when a pretty girl with a covered tray came through the jail door. "Good mornin' ma'am! You must be Sarah. Sheriff said you would be bringing breakfast for Harv."

The girl, still holding the tray, looked around and asked, "Where is Harv?"

"I'm afraid that Harv passed away last night," said Hank, as he took the tray from Sarah, "and the Sheriff said that I could have his breakfast."

The girl smiled and gave up the tray to Hank.

365

* * *

Henry O'Neill rode out of the little town and headed north. The morning was overcast, giving a cold somber feeling. He was headed toward a gap in the far distant hills where the buffalo came south by the hundreds.

Hank had watched the buffalo in the past, slowly moving south with their bushy heads hanging down, making their way slowly toward the 'Gap'. They were never suspicious of the hunters who were ready and waiting.

O'Neill rode slowly, as he had no particular place in mind that caused the need to hurry. By the end of the day, he had made little progress. Looking for a place to set up a camp, he began to look for water, an item in short supply in these parts.

He rode through the breaks, searching for game trails that often led to a water source. He finally gave up and decided to use the water he carried on his packhorse.

"Well, Tiger, you and Whiffel will have to do with a hat full of water tonight. And maybe . . . just maybe we'll come across a source tomorrow.

Hank rode along the edge of a sandstone wall until he came upon a broad slab that was flat and broad enough to set up his camp for the night. When his horses were picketed on a small stretch of mesquite grass, he gathered buffalo chips and started a fire for his coffee, and to cook a bit of bacon.

He had just gotten his meal started when gunshots began to echo off the rock walls surrounding him. He quickly stood, gun in hand, and moved out away from his campsite, where he had a better view down the draw. He saw three riders being chased by another.

The rider in pursuit was firing when his horse stepped in a hole. His head went down, and both rider and horse rolled twice. Neither moved, until Hank arrived on the scene. The horse got up and shook hard. The man groaned and tried to sit up. Hank saw the badge on his vest.

"Just sit easy for a bit. You took quite a tumble."

The man spit dirt and shook his head. "Did you see which way they went?"

"Nope, I was watchin' you." Hank answered.

"Dang it, that's the second time I've lost those varmints!"

"What did they do?" Hank asked.

"Well, some time back they robbed the stage that comes out of Fort Chadbourn. Today they took a payroll headed for a small mining camp."

"Well, Sheriff . . . I reckon you are the sheriff," Hank addressed the stunned man, who nodded yes, "Those fellers are gone, and from the looks of 'im, your horse is lame."

The Sheriff picked up his hat and shook the dust off. "I got a small posse coming soon that can give me a ride. I just as well call off the chase 'cause if I chased them, in about a mile, I wouldn't find them anyway. They always seem to just disappear."

"See if you can stand, Sheriff. If you can, I'll lead your horse over to my camp. We'll have some coffee and a strip of bacon."

"I can sure use the coffee, thank you. My name's Parsons, Ed Parsons."

"I'm Henry O'Neill. Folks just call me 'Hank'."

At Hank's camp, he poured him coffee. "Sit back on that taller rock, Sheriff. That a'way you won't have so far to get up. I've got some bacon cooked. All I have to do is warm it a little."

The sheriff sipped his coffee, and watched Hank as he prepared the bacon. "You headed anywhere in particular, son?"

Hank looked up. "No sir . . . man I worked for up and died. So I thought I'd see what was goin' on out this way."

"I see . . . Well, not a lot goes on, I guess, except when we git a robbery like this morning."

"I guess that is some goin' on! Anyone hurt?"

"Naw, They wus in 'afore anybody got to work."

"How's that leg doing, Sheriff?"

"It's a little stiff, but I can git around on it. And I thank you for your help, young man, and for the coffee."

Long shadows were cast by the time the Sheriff's men came. They wasted no time visiting before they gave him a ride back home. Hank watched them leave, and then rolled into his blanket. He was tired after the episode, and was soon asleep.

Light was creeping into the morning sky when Tiger's pawing the gravel woke Hank. "Need a little more water, boy?" He poured another hat full of water for each horse, then fixed his breakfast, packed up, and was on his way.

The sky was blue, a slight breeze was blowing and the ride was pleasant. Before long, he came upon a creek with good water. He drank deeply, filled his water jugs and let the horses get their fill. He discovered good grass and shade, and decided to stay there a few days to repair his tack, think about where he wanted to go, and what he wanted to do.

After resting a few days longer than he planned, he began riding again. The trail dropped down into a small valley where a wagon was stuck in the mire of a drying pond. There was no team hooked up to it. He began to circle the area carefully, as to not get bogged down, also. When he paused to continue his examination of the situation, a woman's voice came from a large rock to his left. "Well, what do you think?" His hand was automatically filled with his Colt.

Looking her way, he thought he saw a man, but no woman. Then she spoke again, "Hey . . . take it easy! I've got my hands up . . . 'sides I could'a shot you several times over, if I'd a mind to . . . Well, what do you think? Can we get it out?"

"Dang! I thought you was a man sittin' there!"

"Well, I'm not!"

"I see that now! Where is your man?"

"Haven't got one and not lookin!" She eased down from her perch on the large rock, and walked toward Hank. "What can I call you, besides stranger?" she asked.

"Henry O'Neill," he replied, as he stepped down from his horse.

"I have a brother named Charles. We call him by his nickname, 'Chuck'. Henry is usually called 'Hank'. Mind if I call you 'Hank'?" she asked.

"Nope, I don't mind at all. 'Cause that's what everybody calls me . . . and you ought not tell a stranger that you're alone."

"I didn't tell you I was alone! I just said I didn't have a man! Henry O' Neill is it? Then you're an Irishman. My name is Mary Elizabeth Forbes. My folks originally came from Scotland, but they lived in Cork, Ireland before coming to America."

"Well, what d'you know? My folks came from Waterford, a long time ago though."

Henry, gesturing over his shoulder toward the wagon, "How'd this happen, anyway?"

"Winds been blowin' and the muck was covered with so much dust, it looked solid. Once the team got started down the side, it was so muddy they just kept sliding." she replied, placing her hands on her hips.

"Yep, I can see that. Where's your team?" he asked.

She started walking back toward the rock where she had been sitting. "They're back here." They both walked behind the rock, and there were two little white mules working on the short grass that was growing in the shade. Behind them was the most beautiful copper colored thoroughbred stud he had ever seen.

"How'd you get 'em out?"

"Once I unhooked 'em, they came right out. They just couldn't pull the load."

"Well, why didn't you get that big old horse there to help 'em pull?"

She turned toward him, with a frown on her face. "Are you kidding? That's Mister Spencer! He's worth over fifteen thousand dollars. We brought him from Virginia, where we used him to breed horses for racing.

"Well, pardon me! He just looked like a big long horse to me! Let's hope these little mules don't mind going back in. Sometimes mules can be a little stubborn."

She answered quickly, "A little? These little buggers can make you cuss the day they were born!"

"Okay, let's see if we can convince them." Hank replied, as they tightened the collars and straightened the harness. When they got the mules ready to go into the mud, Hank stopped, removed his boots and rolled up his pant legs. "I don't need a boot full of mud," he mumbled, as he eased out and hooked up the team, "Hand me the end of my rope that I hooked to my saddle."

Mary Elizabeth Forbes tossed the rope to Hank. When he had it secured, he mucked back through the mud, picked her up and carried her to the wagon. Then he realized that her clothes gave a false impression of her body. She was actually very trim and firm. He eased her onto the wagon seat and got back on dry land. He led Tiger forward until the slack was taken out of the rope, and then gave the signal to move out. She popped the reins, and the little team strained against their collars. Tiger pulled hard at Hank's coaxing, and soon the wagon moved.

When it was clear of the mud, Hank suggested, "We better ride on to the creek, and get some of the mud washed off before it dries." When they got to the creek, Mary Elizabeth slipped off her overalls to her long handles. Hank turned away, trying to keep from looking. Noticing his shyness, she asked, "What's the matter Hank? Haven't you seen long handles before?"

"Not on a lady . . . I wasn't sure you had any on."

She laughed, "I guess I've lost a little modesty. I lived with five bothers before they all came out here to be 'cowboys'!"

Hank watched as she removed her hat and her red hair fell around her shoulders. The water rippled, flashing light on her face, and he could see her bright green eyes.

Soon the team, wagon, and Hank's feet, were all cleaned and cooled from the water splashed on them. Hank built a fire, and put on some water for coffee. As he sat back against a wagon wheel, he asked, "Now 'spose you tell me why a purdy gal like you is off out here by herself."

"I wasn't by myself at first . . . my Papa came with me from Virginia. We were headed to my brother Chuck's, since Papa got too old to fool with the horses. But the trip was just too much for him." She took a deep breath, "He's buried some miles back."

"I'm sorry about that, Mary Elizabeth. Didn't any of those brothers come along?"

"That's where we were headed. My brother Charles settled on a fairly large ranch up close to a little town called Henrietta, and he told Papa that they have plenty of rooms at the ranch house for Papa and me. My other brothers are scattered all over, and didn't have room for us. Now that it's just me, I guess it doesn't matter that much, but our plans were already made.

Hank picked up a couple of cups and poured the coffee. "Mary Elizabeth . . . doggone it, isn't there somethin' I can call you besides all that name?"

"Sure, the family all calls me Lizy."

"Well that's good! I was afraid they just called you Mary."

"Now what's wrong with Mary?"

"Nothin', but when your name is Mary Elizabeth you just gotta say 'em both, and that's a lot of name to be sayin' all the time!"

"I guess that's why they call me Lizy."

"Well I saw a feller in Ft. Worth that had one of them big fury dogs he called "Lizy", so I'll just call you Liz."

"Well, Hank, I'm glad we finally got the name business settled."

"I'm sorry. They tell me I think on things too hard. Now, are you still planning to go up where your brother Charles and his family are?"

"Yep, I thought I would. Where are you headed?"

"I'm sorta between ranchin' jobs; just driftin' . . . I love to see the country."

She took a sip of the coffee then asked, "Why not trail along with me? They tell me there are several ranches up that a way. Maybe you could hire on one of them . . . you never can tell, my brother Chuck might need some help. His ranch is pretty big."

"I reckon I'll have to think about that." He wasn't sure what to think about traveling so long with a woman. "You know you're a couple o'months or more away from there, don't you? Providin' you don't run into some Kiowa or Comanche."

"I don't care. I got plenty of time and you don't have a job to go to!"

Hank stared at her, taking in her raw beauty. "Do you have any idea what Indians 'ud do to a woman if they catch 'er?"

"Hank, I've got three loaded rifles, and four of Mister Colt's equalizers, and plenty of experience using them! You can bet I don't miss very often!"

"Maybe if'n we're careful we can avoid any contact with 'em."

"So it sounds like you're going with me."

"I reckon I might . . . for a ways. We have a good bit of sun left, so let's get on down the road."

Hank got up, and kicked out the fire, and poured the rest of the coffee on the coals. Then he tied Tiger and Whiffle to the back of the wagon with Mister Spencer, and crawled up beside Liz. She popped the reins and they headed north.

Chapter 28

Henry O'Neill eyed a gathering of dark blue storm clouds rising in the northwest. "Liz we'ud best start lookin' for some shelter. Those clouds may hold a lot o' storm."

"Just what do you suggest, Hank? These hills don't look like they're holding any homes or barns."

"I'm still lookin'."

"And what are you looking for?" she asked.

"I don't know exactly: clam shells maybe, piles of shells where Indians have camped. There may be an outcropping or something near those areas. Hank jumped from the wagon, and started to search the area near the cliffs they were traveling through.

He could hear thunder in the distance, as Mary Elizabeth called out, "Hank, come look at this!"

He ran to the location where Mary Elizabeth had driven the wagon. "Liz you may have just saved us from the storm!" He investigated an area where the dirt on the sides of the cliff had slid out from under a large outcropping of sandstone, leaving a shelf large enough to cover the wagon and team. "Pull the wagon under here Liz."

"You don't think that'll fall on me, do you?"

"Nope! Looks solid to me. I bet it's been hanging like that for years."

Liz set the wagon brake and Hank tied a lead rope to a large rock to hold the team in place. Then he tied the other three horses to the wagon before they both moved farther back into the dug out area.

They hadn't yet seen, back in the shadows, a large slab of sandstone had sometime in the past, broken loose from the ceiling, and now stood vertically on its end. It was in front of a small opening that turned out to be a cave entrance, large enough to walk into, if you bent down.

Hank tried to see into the opening. "We need to make a light . . . no telling what might be in there."

Mary Elizabeth thought a minute, then volunteered, "There's a strip off a gunnysack and some coal oil in the wagon, enough to make a torch if I can find a stick.

Thunder roared louder, and the wind began to pick up. Tiny droplets of water were blown in every direction. Hank, moving well back into the dry, tied the coarse cloth around a limb that he found in the back of the wagon, and drenched it well with coal oil, and started toward the entrance to the small cave.

"Liz, you might oughta stay out here, and let me check it out . . . not many bears around, but there could be a big cat a hidin' back in there." He struck a match to the soaked cloth. Bright yellow light filled the shelter. Hank, with gun in hand, held the torch forward and moved carefully into the opening. The darkness peeled away on the sides of the cave, as he raised the torch high, and looked as far as the light reached. He started to slowly move forward. As he advanced, the floor angled downward slightly The farther he went, as his eyes became used to the dark inside, he began to observe water dripping from the ceiling, that flashed like bright jewels as they fell.

Muttering to himself, he became afraid that his torch might burn out completely before he could return to the entrance. The coal oil had burned out, and the cloth began to smoke. The edges of the cloth had little orange coals that blinked on and off as the cloth tried to burn. He could see the light from the entrance, so he turned and moved quickly in that direction.

As he exited, Mary Elizabeth greeted him with: "I thought maybe you weren't coming back!"

"It gets mighty big in there, and I was running out of light."

The rain came down in sheets, blowing in every direction, and occasionally reaching into their sanctuary. The horses and little mules turned their tails toward the rain. "Hank, it's a good thing you gathered up those buffalo chips, and dry limbs, 'cause it looks like we won't be finding any dry wood for a day or two."

Hank agreed. "I'll get a small fire started so we can eat. Later, I need to make a good torch 'cause a lantern just won't make enough light. I want you to see the inside of this cave. You won't believe what you see!"

"It's that good, is it?"

"It's that good!"

After they finished eating and were drinking coffee, Hank began thinking of something to use to make a torch that would last long enough to explore the cave further.

He dug through his pack. "I've got an old pair of britches in here somewhere. I could split 'em and then have enough to make two torches, so when one goes out, the other would be ready to light."

"I have an old dress, too. That ought to make a couple if we need them." Liz volunteered.

"Good! We can save those 'till later, in case we need to go back in. We can take the lantern, too. That'll give us enough light to come back out." Hank took the old worn pants and split them down the middle. He secured them to limbs from the firewood that he had gathered earlier along the trail.

He took the utensils used for the meal they had just finished, and placed them in a sack he found in the wagon.

"What are you doing, Hank?"

"There's water inside. We can wash these things in there, and save our water. Here you take the bag and I'll get one of these torches going."

The sun had set and it was getting dark in the camp. The air was wet and cool, but the rain had stopped. Hank struck a match to the end of a torch. The silky flame fluttered, and slowly moved down the soaked head of the improvised torch. The yellow glow once again engulfed the darkness, and Hank led the way into the small cave entrance. Liz followed close behind . . . very close!

As they moved further into the cave, Liz spoke, "Chuck you didn't tell me that it was so beautiful . . . I've never seen anything like this."

"Yeah, it is kinda purdy."

Hank lifted the torch higher to illuminate a larger area. "Hank, what's that?" Liz asked.

He turned to see what she was asking about. "What's what?"

"Over there by that column . . . someone's lying over there!"

He eased toward the direction she had pointed, and raised the light higher. She had seen a partially mummified body, half buried in the sand that covered the floor of the cave.

"Well, what do you know? I guess we're not the first to find this place!"

Hank moved closer, and held the torch over the shrunken body.

"Some of the bones have been scattered, some varmint I reckon."

"Hank, look at this!" A small chest-like box, also half buried in the sand, was lodged under the left arm. Liz retrieved it from the sand and opened it. Hank held the torch, so they could see what was in the box. "There're jewels, and gold coins, bank notes and a couple of watches . . . all sorts of valuables!"

He moved back to examine the skeleton. "Liz, there is a bullet hole through one of his ribs. It looks to me like this feller was a thief. He probably held up a stagecoach, and got his self shot, then made it back here to die."

"Why do you think he held up a stagecoach?"

"Cause the stuff in that box is like a collection from a lot of people. The ladies had jewelry, others had money and watches . . . things from different folks. Also a sheriff I ran across a while back told me he had wounded one of the thieves in a stage hold-up a long time ago, and I'll just bet this is the feller he was talkin' about."

Liz stared into the box. "I guess so. Sounds logical to me. I 'spose we oughta take this stuff to the sheriff, and maybe he can find out whose it is."

"It wouldn't take long to take it to him." Hank quickly placed his arm in front of Mary Elizabeth. "Shhhh! Listen." They both listened quietly. "I hear hoof beats!"

"Yes I hear them, but there is so much echo in here I can't tell where they are coming from."

"Must be another way in, 'cause the sounds are not coming from our entrance."

Inching further in, Hank discovered the room got larger, and had a slight glow of light coming from the right. He quickly pushed the torch into the sand to extinguish the flame. Then he blew out the lantern.

"Hank what are you doing? We can't see without the light!"

"Give your eyes a minute, and you'll see that a little light is coming from somewhere."

Soon they could see well enough to move. Once they entered the room, they could see on their right was another entrance, opening to the north, large enough to bring horses in, one at a time. They settled behind a large rock and waited.

Three men rode in and dismounted. The one that appeared to be the leader, telling the others what to do, spoke up, as he lit a torch that had been placed in a hole in the wall. "Travis, let's have that stagecoach schedule you got last week. Don't get it wet! And Jonas, you better be damn sure that it'll come out'a Fort Chadbourn. That sheriff got too close the other day, and I don't want that to happen again."

Jonas volunteered, as he removed his slicker, "Hawk, they told me it stopped at Fort Chadbourn every week, on the same day, unless they have Indian trouble. They said that it sorta ran along the old Butterfield Mail line that quit running back in '61!"

"All right, then! Let's look at that map. They ain't a lot of ways they can take!" determined Hawk.

"They said they always take the same road, and I could catch it most anywhere 'long the route, if'n I wanted to ride," reminded Jonas.

Hawk looked up and sarcastically replied, "Well, did they tell you the best place to conduct a holdup?"

"No Hawk, they didn't."

"All right, then. Shut up and let me think!"

"Sure Hawk, sure."

Silence hung heavy in the cave while Hawk studied the map. "Looks to me like, when the stage drops into Rock Canyon, we can cover it from above, and move in on them from the front. That way we got 'em covered two ways."

"We'll need at least one more man to pull it off." suggested the one called Travis.

Hawk looked up from the map, "I got a man in mind."

He had hardly finished speaking when a rock rolled from under the foot of Mary Elizabeth. As small as it was, the sound it made in the cave was loud.

"What the hell?" exclaimed Hawk.

"Ah Hawk, you know there's all kinds o' varmints in this cave!" said Jonas.

"I still don't like it! Go see what it was and kill it!" said Hawk.

Jonas and Travis pulled their guns, and started climbing over the slabs of limestone that had fallen from the ceiling over the centuries.

Henry O'Neill motioned for Mary Elizabeth to hide behind the rocks, and he went the opposite direction.

"Jonas, I think I saw somethin' up on the left."

"Can't see anything. It's so danged dark in here!" replied Jonas. "Where are you anyway, Travis?"

No answer came from Travis. Hank had intercepted him and knocked him out. Then he waited for Jonas, who was stumbling in the dark.

"Gol dang it, Travis where are you?"

A firm blow to the head put Jonas in the same place as Travis.

Hawk's loud voice came from the floor of the cave, "Can't you two do a simple thing? Where the hell are you?"

"Hank answered, "They're busy right now, Hawk."

"Who's that? . . . Where are my men? . . . Step out here, so I can see you."

The echo from the cocking of Hawk's revolver filled the cave.

"Not planning on a little shooting, are you Hawk?" taunted Hank.

"Come out where I can see you!"

"Drop your gun, Hawk."

"Why you bothering us?" asked Hawk . . . "We ain't done nothin' to you."

"Just drop your gun, or I'm liable to have to shoot you. I'm tired o' talkin', so I may shoot you anyway."

"Now just hold on a minute! I'm . . . I'm dropping the gun. What'a you done with my men?"

"They're resting right now! Back away from the gun."

Hawk complied with the order, and Hank holstered his Colt. He grabbed the two men by the collars and started dragging them down to the floor. "Keep a gun on 'em, Liz."

Hawk couldn't see Liz, and thought Hank was bluffing. He started for his gun but backed off quickly, when Liz placed a shot at his feet.

After Hank took all their ropes, he made Hawk lie on his stomach by the others. He tied them all hand and foot, then separated them, and looped each rope around a large rock, to keep them from getting together and freeing themselves.

"Just what are you planning to do, stranger?"

"Well I haven't decided yet . . . thought I might just ride off and leave you here all tied up."

"Now wait a minute! You can't do that! We ain't done nothin' to you, and we ain't done nothing wrong Why you doin' this?"

"We listened to your plans, and all the time I served with the Texas Rangers, I didn't hear anything that would make those plans sound law abidin' . . . 'sides, I was close by, when the sheriff was chasing you. Since you seemed at home here, we aren't sure you didn't shoot a feller we found farther back in the cave . . . took him a while to die!"

Hawk just looked blankly at Hank as if in thought. "We ain't shot nobody lately."

"This wasn't lately! It was sometime back."

Hawk thought a minute, and then asked, "What was this feller wearin'?"

"Hard to tell since he dried out pretty good, and he had a hole in his ribs."

"Doggone!" Hawk began talking without thinking about what he was telling. "I bet that was Shorty! We always thought he run off with the loot from a hold up we did . . . did you find anything else with him?"

"Yeah. Not that it will do you any good . . . we found some coins, watches and stuff like that, and some papers that looked like rats had chewed on to make a nest."

"Well I'll be . . . I was sure he run off. I knew he was shot, but he wouldn't stop and let us look at his wound. Them papers was worth a lot of money, and they was a deed to a ranch in there . . . did you find that?"

"Nope! We may look later, I'd like to have a ranch, but I reckon we'll give it all to Sheriff Parsons.

"What are you gonna do with us?"

"Well, I'm sure the stage line and the Sheriff will be glad to have you fellers to visit with a while . . . maybe a few years at Huntsville."

Hank moved back among the rocks where Mary Elizabeth was holding a rifle on the group. "If you'll keep an eye on 'em, I'll go around and get Tiger. Then I'll put them on their horses."

"What ARE you going to do with them, Hank?"

"I'm gonna take 'em back to Sheriff Parsons, and let him deal with 'em. You can either stay right here 'till the weather clears and the mud dries a bit, or head on north, and I'll catch up to you later."

"How long do you think it'll take you?"

"I reckon a day or so."

"Okay. I can do some mendin' on my harness. I noticed yesterday that some stitchin' had pulled out. I'll be right here 'till you get back."

Hank eased up on Tiger and led the string of crooks south. His heart thumped in his chest at the task he had taken on. It was hard to lead them, and to look back to make sure they stayed tied. His thoughts ran the gamut, *"Thieves, stranded woman, dead man and loot! These are things a ranch hand just don't have to worry about! And I don't know how I get myself into stuff like this!"*

"Hey . . . hey you!" It was the man called Travis, "my head's bustin' where you hit me. How 'bout some water?"

Hank kept on moving, "You'll have to wait!"

"But I'm getting' sick at my stomach!"

"All the more reason to wait. You drink water now and your guts'll turn wrong side out! We'll stop later."

Hawk's face was turning red, and he gritted his teeth, "What kinda man are you any way? The man needs water!"

"We'll all get water when I tell you we'll get water! You chose this way of life. Now ride with it!"

They were quiet for a while, only griping and mumbling to each other. Hawk had been working the ropes since they had left. Hank had the men tied so that the lead rope continually pulled their bindings tight, and each time Hawk thought he was getting slack, it was jerked tight again. He shouted to Hank, "I get out of this consider yourself dead."

"You get out of this, and you and the one that gets you out of it are both dead!"

Jonas got Hawk's attention and whispered, "What are we gonna do, Hawk?"

"Shut up, and let me think!"

"Okay, Hawk."

They rode along a while contemplating how they would escape. Finally, Hawk eased back and quietly told Jonas to fall from his horse.

Jonas replied almost out loud, "In these rocks?"

"Yes, just do it! That a way, it'll seem more like an accident. It'll give me a chance to try somethin' I been thinkin' about."

"All right . . . but I don't want to!" He watched for a chance to fall on the trail where it wasn't so rocky. When he decided on the best spot, he kicked his stirrup and eased off as if he was asleep.

He hadn't counted on the way the rope was tied around his hands! It tightened, and he was dragged along behind.

Hawk yelled at Hank, "Hey cowboy my man fell we gotta stop and help him!"

Chuck continued on, dragging Jonas. Jonas' horse, half asleep, continued to follow as if nothing had happened.

Hawk shouted again, "What kind of guy are you? . . . you gonna kill him, if you don't stop."

"Let this remind you, stay awake and you ride! Try to buffalo me, and you'll get the same thing."

"Nobody's trying to buffalo you! He just went to sleep."

"He's awake now, isn't he? We'll stop 'fore long. Then he can get back on his horse . . . that is if his horse keeps followin' us."

Jonas realized that Hank wasn't fooled. He jumped to his feet, and began to trot along behind.

The task ended for Hank, when he reached town. The Sheriff was glad to receive delivery of the outlaws, as he had several counts against them. "Mr. O'Neill, I'm sure there's some sort of reward from the stage lines."

"Well, Sheriff Parsons just you hang on to it, and I'll pick it up when I ride back this way. I'll probably be needin' it by then! By the way, the reason these fellows were able to disappear, there's a cave a few miles north of here they can ride right into."

Mary Elizabeth Forbes picketed Hank's horse Whiffel, Mister Spencer, and the little mules on grass away from the cave. When she returned to camp, she went into the cave to get water. While she was inside, two Kiowa Indians rode up, and saw the wagon under the shelter. They stopped to look around. One dismounted, and carefully walked around the wagon. Not seeing anyone, he walked back to his horse. He told his companion that no one was around. They decided to take what they could find.

While they were talking, Mary Elizabeth came from inside the cave and was standing by the wagon, with a rifle trained on the two. When they turned toward the wagon, they heard, "If I were you, I'd get back on your horses, and leave!"

The first Kiowa had walked all around the wagon and had not seen anyone. Thinking that she was an apparition that had just appeared out of thin air, he froze in fright! Then he shouted to his companion, "Spirit man that talks like woman bad medicine! We go!"

They both ran and took a leap onto their horses and left in a hurry. Their fear left Mary Elizabeth laughing, "I'll have to tell Hank about this!"

A short while later, Hank hurriedly rode up to their camp, dismounted and called out, "Liz! Where are you?"

She came from behind the wagon, and answered his call, "What's the hurry, Hank?"

"Are you all right? I saw a couple of Indians coming from this direction, and they weren't lettin' the grass grow under 'em! They shouted to me that they saw a man spirit that talked like a woman."

She smiled. "That's what they said, a 'Man Spirit that talks like a woman.' At least that's what it sounded like, as he high tailed it out of here."

"I guess you scared the livin' daylights out of 'em. Those two hang out at the back door of the saloon down south of here, moochin' drinks from anybody they can. They speak and understand a little Texican. We won't have any trouble with them, or the cahoots I took to the Sheriff."

She laughed again, as she described how she just 'appeared' with her rifle trained on them. "One of them came up and circled the wagon. I could hear him, but I couldn't see much of him, just his feet go by. I was glad that I had taken the rifle in the cave with me. When I heard him talking to the other Indian, I just stepped out and held my rifle on them, and told them to leave.

Mary Elizabeth went to get the mules. "Time we got under way! I'll hook 'em up."

The land was cut with creeks and shallow canyons, and rising slopes that made the little mules tire quickly. This caused Hank and Mary Elizabeth to stop more often. To lighten the load, Hank rode Tiger, rather than ride on the wagon. He scouted for water and campsites at closer intervals than they wanted.

Hank came back from one such excursion, and eased Tiger up beside the wagon. He decided to ride there a while, beside Liz. Neither spoke for what seemed to be an hour. Then Mary Elizabeth spoke, "Hank, I know we're holding you back. If you don't feel like you can stay with us going this slow, well, I wouldn't think anything of it, if you left right now."

Hank didn't answer right away. "You think you're going to get rid of me?"

"No, I just thought . . ."

"You just thought did you?" he teased.

"I mean . . . we've not been making much time and I thought . . ."

Hank interrupted her, never looking directly at her, "Well don't! I'll let you know if I want to leave. Besides . . . I like to see you work, you do it so well . . . and I kinda like your cookin'"

"Yeah, that's the trouble with you men. You like to see us girls work and cook!"

"I like to watch you sleep too! Even if I can't see those green eyes of yours. And I like takin' it easy. It gives me a chance to see the country . . . and to get to know you better."

Hank couldn't see the smile on her face, "Henry O'Neill, you may be far removed from the 'Emerald Isle', but not far enough from the 'Blarney Stone'."

Later, Hank returned from another scouting trip. "I found a spot about a mile ahead, up by those trees, that you can see on the horizon. There's water in a little creek that's as clear and cool as you 'ud want. We can fill our supply and maybe take a bath."

"Oh? You don't have it in mind to take advantage of me, do you?"

"Now, you take things the wrong way! I just meant we could clean up there."

"Are you trying to tell me I smell like my mules?"

With that, Hank kicked Tiger, and rode on well ahead. He never looked back, so again he missed the smile on Liz's face.

By the time she pulled in to the campsite that Hank had selected, he had wood gathered, and was laying a fire for the evening meal.

When the horses and mules were watered and picketed nearby, Hank finally spoke to Mary Elizabeth for the first time since they had stopped, "You were kinda rough on me back there. Did it make you happy?"

"No Hank, it didn't . . . I'm sorry if I hurt your feelings, but you shouldn't have such thin skin! I was only teasing you."

"Ah, it was all right. I guess I deserved what you said. Maybe it was payback time! Anyway it's still light enough to take a swim or bath . . . whichever. So you go ahead, and I'll fix us something to eat."

Mary Elizabeth, with washcloth and towel in hand, asked, "Do we have enough water? I would hate to soap it up before we know we have enough."

"Where you'll be is just a wide spot in the stream. The soap will move right along . . . anyway, there's a spring feeding into it too, so we can have all the good water we need. Better move on! The grub'll be ready 'fore long."

Hank's back was to the stream where Mary Elizabeth was bathing. The willows were thick all around the water, but he could hear her singing, and he liked it. "Hey there Liz, your dinner is about ready. Better move along." Then he added, "You can keep on singing though."

He heard her coming up behind him. "Better grab a plate or everything will get cold."

He looked up as she moved beside him. She was wearing a red dress, and her hair was still a bit wet. She was rubbing it dry, as she sat down close to him. She smelled like spring flowers.

He couldn't take his eyes off of her as he handed her a plate. She took it and said, "Maybe I'll get to liking *your* cooking. I already like your work."

He continued to stare at her, not saying a word. "Hank, close your mouth, or say something!"

"You look . . . clothed . . . I mean . . . that's shore a purdy dress . . . I never seen you in a dress before."

"That's because I haven't had a chance to clean up. I'll be back in my work clothes tomorrow! Now, how about some of that coffee?"

As he poured coffee into her cup without looking at her, he mumbled. "You don't smell like the mules either, you smell like flowers."

"Why, thank you, Hank . . . I think."

The evening sunset was as colorful as one could imagine . . . the entire sky was a firey red and little clouds that were left in the sky were a bright pink. Soon all the colors began to fade, as they sat around the fire that had burned down to the coals.

"Tell me Hank, do you ever think of the old country?"

He hesitated before he answered, "No Liz, I don't really have anything to remember on my own, since I've never been there. I do remember my mother telling me about the birds and other animals that lived along the River Suir, and the old Waterford glass factory where my dad worked . . . the factory was close to the old home where they lived. I kinda know what she meant, 'cause it's the same way along the rivers here in Texas. I doubt the animals are too much different."

Liz looked into the coals, "I wasn't born then, but I can remember the things mother told me about Ireland, before they came to America. It was so vivid it was just like I had been there! I would really like to see it."

They sat quietly together, and Liz stirred the coals with a stick, just to watch the small lights of the embers rise into the night sky.

On the distant horizon, a flickering glow followed by a deep rumble drew Hank's attention. "That little rumble may mean rain, later. It often comes from that direction. When you want to turn in, you get in the wagon, and I'll stretch the wagon sheet over the ends, just in case it does rain."

Liz stood. "I'm about ready now. Been a long day, and I feel like I could sleep for days."

Mary Elizabeth Forbes climbed into the wagon. After Hank tied the sheet to shed any rain, he unrolled his bedroll under the wagon, and slid between the blankets.

It wasn't long before gentle drops of rain on the wagon woke him. He reached down and pulled the soogan canvas over his head. The rhythmic sound of the drops soon lulled him back to sleep.

Henry O'Neill woke before the gray of morning, and tossed the canvas cover off his bedroll far enough back to keep any water from getting on his blankets. He had covered enough wood for breakfast, so it was quickly under way.

"Rise and shine my fair lady! The air out here is cool and pure after that rain last night, and your breakfast is ready."

He watched as she stepped from the wagon. Her red hair hung loosely around her shoulders, and a smile was on her face, "You could spoil a girl . . . having breakfast ready when she gets up."

Without a smile he turned the bacon sizzling in the pan, "Tomorrow's your day!"

Uneventful days passed as the little mules struggled with their load, causing them to make camp often. One stop was Valley Creek. Then they journeyed east to pass through the hills before they camped on the Spring Creek.

"Liz, I'm worried about the little mules. They seem to get slower every day. Maybe we should look for some bigger stock."

"Aw, Hank, I couldn't part with Lacy and Lucy! They are like family."

"We could bring them along, if we can get stock cheap enough . . . but that'll depend on the grass, and we'll need to get feed, just in case. It's still a long way to your brother's place."

"I guess it's something to think about."

"I'll scout out from here, and see what I can find. There's good water here, so we can stay for a few days. I'll take Whiffle and a pack too, to see if I can shore up our supplies. Keep an eye out for Indians"

Henry O'Neill rode out to the east. Mary Elizabeth Forbes watched as he turned toward the north, weaving his way through the thick growths of trees, cedars and scrub brush.

Later, when he stopped to get a drink from his canteen, he thought he heard chopping sounds. Speaking out loud, to the horses, "Boys, it looks like we might 'a found some signs of life." He continued to ride toward the sounds, and soon saw the man chopping wood, "Helloo the house."

A bearded man paused, and turned toward Hank. "Come on in if'n you've a mind to."

"I will thank you sir. My name's Henry 'O Neill, folks call me Hank"

"Well Hank 'O Neill, ride on in to the humble home of Lester Stiles, and get down awhile and stretch your legs."

"Where IS that home, Mister Stiles?"

"It's kinda hid. If you look close just below that bluff . . . "

"Why yes, I see it now. With a dugout that hard to see, I bet you don't have much Indian trouble!"

"Matter o' fact, I don't, 'cept to bum coffee and sugar. An' that's from regulars that don't cause no trouble."

"Mister Stiles, I was wonderin' where I might buy a couple stout horses, trained to harness."

Stiles scratched his head, "Well sir, Jacob Schwartz, about a mile or more along the creek there, can probably fix you up. He's got good stock, but you'll have to haggle with him."

"I can do that! Any place close, where a feller could get supplies?"

"Yes sir, so happens he has a store too. Got good wagons and makes regular trips to Fort Griffin selling to folks around here. I got coffee on the stove if you'ud like a cup."

"Don't mind if I do."

"Come on in and sit. They's a cup on the table and the coffee's hot, 'cause I just finished my dinner a while ago."

Hank picked up a cup and sat on a chair made of bent cedar limbs, "How'd you come to settle here, if you don't mind my askin'?"

"Well sir, I like to study plants and trees and animals. Have since I was a kid, and when I broke down and spent quite a few days here, I discovered there was lots of all kinds of both, right here, so . . . I just stayed and have loved it more the longer I'm here."

"So you're kinda homesteadin' this area."

"I reckon I am! It's been a good home. I may even build me a house someday."

"Well Mr. Stiles, I got a young lady a waitin' for me to locate some good strong horses to pull her wagon. So I guess I better be movin' along. I thank you for the coffee."

"Glad to have you. Don't get many folks by here!

Hank followed Stiles direction to Jacob Schwartz's place. He was able to acquire a pair of part Belgian horses trained to harness. He also got most of the supplies that they needed. When he completed the transaction he returned to their camp, where he had left Mary Elizabeth.

As Liz saw Hank coming, she hopped up on the tailgate of her wagon, and watched him across the field, trailing Whiffel and the two red horses he had bought.

"Well, looks like you did all right! Took you long enough, I thought you had danced out on me."

"When are you going to believe in me? I told you, you weren't getting' rid of me that easy. Well . . . what do you think of the horses?"

"They ought to be big enough to pull my wagon, but . . . what are we going to feed 'em?"

"The man said they were used to grass and they're big enough that they won't be workin' too hard. So grass should be enough, but I bought some feed from Schwartz, where I got the supplies, to kinda supplement it. I imagine Mister Spencer could use some too."

"Hank, do you think my harness will fit? I'm pretty sure Papa used them on bigger horses."

"We'll see. It's almost too big for the little mules, and it has several holes to let out. Let's try it."

They expanded the harness, and were able to make a comfortable fit. Once the horses were harnessed, the group traveled at a much faster pace.

"Liz, are you sure you want to keep the little mules?"

"Hank, they've been in our family ever since they were born!"

"Okay, but we'll have to stop longer to let them all graze, and buy some more feed before too long."

Two hours later, Hank asked, "Liz where are your guns?"

"Under the seat. Why?"

"I've notice a lot of tracks, and they're not too old . . . keep on lookin' forward, but be ready to get the guns."

"What are you thinking?"

"With all these horses, we're prime targets for a raid. Indians would have a pretty big coup . . . my scalp, you and six horses."

"You think there are Indians near?"

"I do, at least four by the tracks I've seen. Fortunately I think they are traveling the same way we are, but they check back-trail often, and if they see all these horses, they may turn back on us.

"When we get to those trees, we'll set a spell, and let them get further ahead. When we get the horses staked out, I'll ride ahead to see where they are. They may not be too far."

They reached the trees, and found that they were near a small stream trickling between the rocks. "This looks to be a good campsite. Overnight will give us a safe distance. I'll still ride out to see if I can find them."

While Hank was removing the pack from Whiffel, after he had picketed the other horses, he heard a shrill yell coming from behind. He turned to see an Indian riding full speed toward him, with his bowstring pulled to its limit.

Hank dropped the pack, and slapped Whiffel across the rump to move him out of the way! Then he crouched and drew his colt and fired. The arrow missed him, and he missed the Indian.

He stood his ground, then at the last second, side-stepped. At the same time, he reached for the Indian's leg, pulling the invader from his horse.

The force caused both to roll, and the Indian came up first, with knife drawn. He leaped toward Hank, slashing in both directions. He caught Hank's arm with one slash, and drew blood, setting him back a step. Hank then drew his own knife, and the fight became a closer contest.

Mary Elizabeth, in the wagon with her rifle, shot one Indian approaching from the west, and swung her rifle to shoot a second that came from the opposite direction. Hank had told her to watch the horses. "They will send one man to steal them, while the others keep us occupied."

Another Indian, unseen by her, jumped from his horse to the back of the wagon. The springs on the wagon flexed under the sudden impact. Liz grabbed her revolver that was in her lap, and fired under her arm. The bullet caught the man in the chest, and pushed him off the back of the wagon. He didn't move again.

Henry O'Neill and the Indian were locked in combat. Once in a while, a hand would come loose, and both men slashed the air, until finally Hank moved in quickly, and his knife plunged into the mid section of the Indian. As if in slow motion, the man sank to his knees, and then toppled over dead.

Henry turned quickly toward the wagon, where Liz sat watching the fight, "You did good, Cowboy!" she commented.

"Looks to me like you did all right, too." He picked up his revolver, and began to load it again.

"Hank you're bleeding pretty bad! Let me look at that arm."

He pulled the split sleeve up to see a gash about three inches log.

"Let me get my needle and thread. That needs sewing up."

Hank leaned against a wagon wheel and watched as Liz washed the wound and threaded a needle. "I just hope you've done your sampler." he chided.

"All girls do their sampler, don't they? Anyway I did mine, but that don't mean I'll get this sewed straight."

"As long as it'll grow back together, I guess it'll be all right."

Hank looked down as Liz sewed his arm. Then he finally spoke, "Liz, when that Indian shot at me and missed . . . well, I'm afraid he hit one of your mules . . . I'm sorry."

Tears welled up in Liz's eyes, but she continued to work on his arm. When she had finished, she fell across his lap and cried, "Oh Hank, so much bad has happen on this trip . . . I wish I had stayed in Virginia."

"If you had stayed in Virginia, I wouldn't have met you, so I'm glad you didn't." He gently consoled her, by patting her shoulder.

Liz turned her face, so he couldn't see her tears, "Thank you, Hank."

Hank spent the rest of the afternoon taking care to erase all evidence of what had happened. He dragged Lacy, the little mule that was shot, to a small canyon. They reluctantly agreed that it would be too hard to try to bury her. He then made camp.

"Liz, I think that those were the only Indians traveling here. At least that's what the tracks showed, before they attacked . . . but we had better be alert. I'll watch for a while, but I don't think any would attack us at night."

Chapter 29

After a late supper, Hank let the fire die down, and was drinking a cup of coffee, when Liz stepped down from the wagon and sat beside him.

"Tell me about yourself, Mister Henry O'Neill. Where are your folks? Where did you live before you started to wander?"

Hank stared into his cup for a long moment. "Lost my folks to Indians down on the Rio Grande. We had a store there. We served ranchers mostly, around those parts . . . We had heavy wagons for freight; hauled ore and equipment for mercury mines in that area. When I lost my folks and my brother, I just didn't want to stay there any more."

"What about the store? Didn't you want to stay with it?"

"They burned everything . . . I was away hauling to the mines and found them when I got back . . . I moved on to a friend's ranch, and worked there for a year or so. Folks kept talkin' about better and bigger places 'till I just decided to see for myself, and here I am, nothin' bigger . . . but so far it's a lot better right now. What about you?"

"I've told you about me. My brother Charles, that's where we are going."

"You said you had other brothers. Where are they?"

"My oldest brother Delbert married Belle Haskell, whose father owned the Box RH ranch in Montana.

When Mister Haskell died, the ranch went to Belle and she wanted Dell to run it. It wasn't long 'till they were married.

Charles got a ranch and three partners kinda by accident when they found the deed. Indians had killed all survivors.

My brother Matthew settled near Ruidosa in New Mexico Territory. He and his wife Jessica have apple orchards there.

Bryan and his wife Geneva live south of Santa Fe on the Bar H ranch.

My brother Benjamin and his wife Grace settled west of Fredericksburg."

Hank thought a minute. "I haven't been there but I've heard of it. We're not too far from Fredericksburg."

"Yeah, I know. I think we're going to try to get together before too long."

"I bet that'll be fun."

"I hope so!" She stood, "I think it's time to turn in. Let's not have another day like today."

"That sounds right to me."

"See you in the morning."

Hank O'Neill continued to lean against the wagon wheel, finishing his coffee, feeling the movements of the wagon as she prepared for bed and thinking about the things that had happened during the day.

From inside the wagon, Mary Elizabeth called out, "Hank, I can't thank you enough for deciding to come along with me. I really couldn't have made it without you."

He smiled to himself, and said, "Goodnight Liz, so far it's been fun!" He crawled into his blankets.

* * *

As the morning began to gray with light, Hank was pouring coffee, when the big stud picketed nearby started snorting, stomping and tugging on the rope.

Hank stood up and listened, then reached for his rifle. "Liz," she answered yes, "better get your guns ready! Mister Spencer is restless!"

The wagon rocked as she hurriedly put on her clothes. She was muttering, "Not again! He's the nervous type, I hope it's a false alarm. Anyway I'm ready, and I'll watch from the wagon! " She pitched the wagon sheet back, and sat where she could see.

Hank looked all around. "If it was one of my horses, I'd worry more, 'cause I'm not sure your fancy horse could smell an Indian."

"Oh you don't think so, do you? Well, we had Indians in Virginia too!"

"Hello the camp!" A voice from within the trees called out.

"Come on in slowly, if you might." Hank answered.

"I'll do that, and I thank you, Sir."

A tall man on a roan gelding rode in and stepped down, dropped his reins and eased toward the fire where Hank stood. "Mind if I have a cup of that coffee, Sir? I haven't had a cup since yesterday morning."

Hank got another cup and poured it for the man. "Didn't catch your name, I'm, Henry O' Neill." He intentionally didn't mention that Elizabeth was with him until he found out more about the man. "Where you headed?"

"The name is Allen Fisk, and I'm headed to Louisiana, a gamblin' house down there needs a dealer . . . say . . . I was noticing that big stud you have picketed over there . . . you ever race him?"

"Don't belong to me, belongs to my traveling companion and she never mentioned racing him . . . she said he was for breeding."

Elizabeth climbed down from the wagon, "Morning gentlemen."

Hank looked to Liz. "Elizabeth Forbes, this is Mister Fisk."

"How do, Ma'am.   Are you the owner of the stud?"

"I might be. Why do you ask?"

"Well, there is a little town about six more miles or so on north of here, and they are having an anniversary or something. Anyway, they are having a big race this Saturday, and the pot is pretty high, like $200 or $300 dollars or so. There will be gambling on the side I'm sure. Thought you might be interested in the pot . . . that is if your horse is pretty fast. He would be running against a couple of those quarter horses that are real fast for a quarter mile or so, some even farther than that."

Elizabeth acted a bit unsure. "He used to run a little . . . he might be able to still run."

"Ma'am, if you think he can, I might just go back into town and put in a bet or two."

"Mister Fisk, I'll think about it. I sure could use the money."

"I like the look of your horse. I'm going back and see if I can find a room. And then I'll make a few bets."

"You would bet on a horse you don't know if he can run?"

"Ma'am, I've seen a few horses in my time." Mister Fisk mounted his horse and headed back the way he came. As he was leaving, he called over his shoulder, "I don't think they will let a woman ride."

"What do you think of that, Hank?"

"You really plan to run him? You heard what he said. They won't let a woman ride, and I don't think Mister Spencer likes me too much."

"Hank, the reason I plan to breed him is because nothing has been able to beat him yet. They won't know I'm a woman! After all, I'm the man sprit with a woman's voice."

Hank smiled, "Have you ever thought there might be a first time for a horse to beat him?"

"Let me worry about that! As far as they will know, I can't talk, so they will think I'm just a boy you use to ride your horse."

"You better work him a little. We don't have much time 'till the race. I'll ride on ahead and get him entered."

Mary Elizabeth Forbes stepped up into the wagon, and was moving things around. Finally she located a sack and reached in, "Ahhh, here it is!" She pulled out a racing saddle.

"Here what is?" asked Hank.

"My racing saddle!"

"Your racing saddle? Why, there isn't enough leather in that thing to make a holster!"

"That's right," she explained, "You don't sit on it anyway, you ride over the withers."

"I'll be doggone! I never seen anything like that before."

"It's real light weight. I'll bet the horses of those fellers at the race will be toting heavy saddles like yours."

"You're probably right! I'll go on and register, and see if we can buy supplies there. We're far enough from the town I doubt anyone will see you work Mister Spencer."

When Hank arrived at the community gathering, he realized that it was folks from all around, and not really a town. But there were a few buildings in the area where the people gathered, and put up banners and posters announcing the race and celebration.

An older man, sporting a well-groomed beard with a corncob pipe protruding from it, approached Hank. "Howdy, young feller! You here for the celebration?"

Hank eased off of Tiger, and dropped the reins over the rail. "I thought I'd find out what's going on and maybe join in."

"Well, Sir, Folks'll be bringing food and drinks come Saturday, ta watch the big race."

"What's the celebration about?" asked Hank.

The old man took his corncob pipe out of his mouth, and used it to point out features of the small town. "Anthony Slocomb come here to settle down seventy five years ago this Saturday. Lived at the end of the street. 'Course his place burned years ago, but his place of business still stands. It's that building right over there. I don't know what his business was, and not sure anybody else does, but we celebrate every year 'cause it's just the thing we do to get together, I guess. Like I say, we only come here once a year and now is the time."

Hank looked up and down the street and concurred with the man, "I must agree, it sounds like the thing to do! You say they have a race Saturday?"

"Yes Sir. Starts at tuther end of town, at that big tree, then around that little butte way down yonder at the tuther end, and does that twice and finishes where it starts."

Hank studied the route a moment. "Looks like about three quarters of a mile or more."

"That's about right, likely more." agreed the old man.

"Can anyone join in this race?"

"You shore can, if'n you got a couple a double eagles."

"Forty dollars! That's a pretty high entry fee," said Hank.

"Consider if'n you win, how much you git. We usually have fifteen ta twenty entrees . . . you could win up ta $400 or $500. That's a lot o' money."

"You can say that again! And if I lose, I'm out forty bucks! Where do I sign up?"

"See that big banner over yonder? Right underneath is a table, an' them folks'll take your money, and sign ya up."

"I thank you Sir, and I'll see you Saturday."

Henry O'Neill paid the money, got a receipt and a number for the rider to wear, and was on his way back to their camp.

The camp was empty. Neither Mister Spencer nor Mary Elizabeth was anywhere in sight. Hank muttered half out loud, "Well Liz, give him a good workout!"

He built a fire to start dinner, and soon Liz came riding up on Mr. Spencer. "Well Mister O'Neill, what did you find out?"

"We are entered! They had sixteen entered when I signed up, but there will be others. Four brothers that always enter, and usually win, hadn't arrived yet, so the pot looks good. How was Mister Spencer?"

"Great, as always! Another day and we'll be ready."

"Why do you have his legs wrapped? Did he hurt 'em?

"Nope! I wrap them to protect the tendons during workout, and to keep them from swelling.

"Sounds good to me. Let's eat, and I'll tell you about the route."

"Okay. I'll join you as soon as I rub Mister Spencer down, and walk him out."

Saturday dawned clear and warm. There was no wind and Mister Spencer was ready to go. Hank saddled Tiger and Whiffle, so that Elizabeth could ride Whiffle and save Mister Spencer for the race.

"Liz, one reason these Barnfield boys win is the distance is good for their quarter horses, and they tell me they have the best around here."

"Well, then I guess it's time they had a new winner!"

Hank and Mary Elizabeth rode into the little town leading Mister Spencer. He was dancing a bit sideways with excitement, as other horses were milling around the starting area of the race. Liz had her hair tucked under a six piece cap, and with her loose britches and shirt she looked like the boy next door.

The Barnfield brothers were in town and ready to race. "Hey boy, is your horse scared or somethin'? He's shore dancin' like he is."

Another brother snickered and quipped, "Maybe he needs to go to the privy."

"What's the matter boy? Cat got your tongue?"

Mary Elizabeth circled her mouth with her forefinger to indicate to them that she couldn't speak.

When she turned to walk away, they could see the number on her back, "You ain't plannin' to race that ole long legged plow horse today, are you?"

Without stopping, she turned her head and nodded yes.

Josh Barnfield turned to one of his brothers, "Hey Jimmy! This kid's gonna run this old long legged plow horse against us! What'a you think o' that?"

Jimmy answered, "As long as he puts up the double eagles, I don't mind takin' 'em from him."

Mary Elizabeth was close enough to hear them, but paid no attention.

"Hey Kid, we ain't lost a race yet, so you just as well set and watch us!"

It came time to line up for the race. Liz sat on Mister Spencer with her knees even with her saddle, and she was leaning forward as a Jockey would. The boys began to laugh at her.

"Ain't you got no saddle, kid? You liable to fall off half way 'round."

She ignored them.

"I reckon he can't hear, neither."

All of the horses were in a line. With the large number of horses entered, it was very important to get out front as quickly as possible. By taking the lead, it would help to avoid having to contend with bumping, and hand to hand combat that Hank had told her usually took place in these races.

Unfortunately, the Barnfield brothers and their quarter horses managed to get in the lead.

Three riders were unseated before they got to the first turn. When the group of riders became visible, having made it around the small butte that was the first turn; the quarter horses had taken even a greater lead over the group. Liz and Mister Spencer were in about fifth place. Several riders began to drop out, having competed against the Barnfield brothers in previous races.

As Hank watched Liz so far behind the quarter horses, he could feel his double eagles disappearing in the dust stirred by many horses.

Liz moved up a little by the time they reached the starting point, which was the second turn of the race. The crowd was yelling for their individual entries, and it all blended into a loud drone, as the horses passed by each part of the crowd.

Liz edged close to the Barnfield who was bringing up the rear of the four brothers. He stopped beating his horse, and slashed Liz across the face with his quirt. When Hank saw it, he entered a protest to the judges. They didn't seem to be interested in what he had to say. It was made clear that this was just a part of the race.

When horses could be seen after rounding the butte, Liz had moved even with the third brother, and stayed far enough away from him to not get hit again. All that was left was the final sprint to the finish. The Barnfield horses began to tire. Liz gently rubbed Mister Spencer's neck, and squeezed him with her legs. As if he knew how important it was, Mister Spencer opened up and left the remaining brothers in his dust.

Mary Elizabeth won the race by at least four lengths and the noise of the crowd died quickly. Allen

Fisk, with a handful of bills, nodded 'thanks', as Hank proceeded to the judge's table to collect the winnings.

The elder Barnfield, Joseph, walked close to Hank. I guess you lucked out today! People don't usually beat my boys."

Hank looked at the man and asked, "Is that because they are afraid to? Or are your horses actually that fast . . . that is to win every time?"

Not catching the sarcasm, Joseph Barnfield continued, "I take pride in my horses, and I want to buy that horse of yours."

"I'm sorry Mr. Barnfield. He's not for sale."

"I'll give you two hundred and fifty dollars for him right now!"

"I'm sorry . . . not for sale."

Getting a bit agitated, Joseph Barnfield came back with, "Nobody gives that much for horses around here! You're just missin' your chance!"

"Maybe I am, but he's not for sale! But I'll tell you what I'll do: for three hundred, I'll breed him to your best mare."

"I wouldn't give three hundred to buy that crow bait!" Barnfield turned and stomped off.

The old man that Hank had talked to before entering the race heard Barnfield, and he approached Hank. "Better watch out for him! He's a purdy bad hombre, and he don' like nobody beatin' his boys!"

"Thanks, ole timer. I'll be alert." Hank placed his winnings in his saddlebag.

Liz had left quickly on Mister Spencer, for fear of trouble. Hank gathered the reins of Whiffle and Tiger, and mounted and left for the camp.

When Hank rode into camp, Mary Elizabeth was rubbing Mister Spencer down. He sat and watched her move about, making long strokes, all the while softly singing to her pride and joy.

He realized that he was staring, so he dismounted and walked up to her, "You did all right out there today . . . and you sure got old man Barnfield stirred up! He's achin' to buy Mister Spencer . . . even offered two hundred and fifty dollars for him."

"What did you tell him?"

"Not for sale . . . but I did offer to breed his best mare for three hundred dollars! He left real mad."

"For three hundred dollars you would have to breed her yourself! 'Cause Mister Spencer gets a thousand dollars!"

"Dang Liz! You're not pullin' my leg are you?"

"No Sir! That's why we brought him along."

"Well, I'll be dogged! Who in the world would have that kind of money for a horse?"

"Probably nobody around here, but back in horse country, racing was a way of life, and a good horse could win you a lot of money. Mister Spencer had the body, the stamina, and he won all his races! So he could bring top dollar, and not have to race any more."

As he took the saddle off Wiffle, he said, "Ahhh! But he raced today, didn't he?"

Liz looked at Hank and smiled, "Yes he did, didn't he? By the way, how much did we win?"

Hank looked down, "One more thing . . . the old man I told you about . . . he warned us to be on the lookout for the Barnfields. They could mean trouble since you beat them so bad."

"Okay! I think it's time to get on our way to Chuck's place anyway. Maybe we'll lose the Barnfields if we move out tomorrow. I've got a feeling some of those folks were just a little glad Mister Spencer beat them! You didn't tell me how much we won!"

Hank went to his saddlebags and pulled out the money. "Your share, plus a couple of side bets I made for you, you came away with eight hundred and eighty dollars! It's enough for a disappointed racer to come and try to take it away. I managed another two hundred from a couple of unfortunate gentlemen."

When Mary Elizabeth Forbes awoke the next morning she noticed that Hank O'Neill was already cooking breakfast. She could hear and smell the bacon frying. She decided to get the two work horses harnessed up to get moving as soon as breakfast was over. When she went out where all the horses had been picketed, she discovered that Mister Spencer was not among the others.

She brought Tiger and Whiffle to be saddled, "Hank! Mister Spencer is gone . . . taken during the night! I don't know what they were thinking, because there are tracks everywhere."

"You don't think he might'a just wandered off?"

"No way! Mister Spencer's racing shoes make a pretty distinctive track, and he's making them right behind a couple of other horses."

"Dang! How'd they do that without me hearing? Here! Take some of this bacon and we'll get right after them. They shouldn't be hard to track with him in behind, since his tracks will be on top of the others."

Liz was shaking her head, "I can't understand. Usually, he would put up a fight if a stranger appoached him."

Hank slipped the end of the last cinch into the slot on the saddle and mounted. "If one of Barnfield's horses was in season, he wouldn't put up a fight against going with them."

"I guess you're right about that. I never thought of that possibility."

"You don't think like a guy!"

The tracks stood out and were easy to see. Before long they were in front of the Barnfield's house.

Hank yelled, "Barnfield, we've come for our horse!"

The door opened and Barnfield stuck his head out. "I don't know what you're talkin' about!"

"We just followed his hoof prints and probably a couple of your sons' here."

"Well, if you did, he must'a follered 'em here."

"That's likely so . . . anyway we come to take him back."

As Hank spoke, a shot came from the window beside where the elder Barnfield stood and the bullet whinned by Hank's ear.

Instantly Elizabeth drew and fired at the shooter. A moan came from inside. "I wouldn't move, Mister Barnfield! We'll just get Mister Spencer, and leave. Hank, can you make it back to camp? Did he hit you?"

"I'll be all right, Liz. Let's just get the horse and leave before we have to kill all of them. Barnfield . . . you better watch your boys, if you want them to stay alive! They may have all been drunk, but that's no excuse."

Barnfield stood amazed at how a woman could have drawn and fired so quickly. "You better tie your horse better, so he won't stray agin."

"Yeah, we'll do that!" Sarcasm dripped from Hank's voice. "Liz, you go get the horse, and I'll keep and eye on the house. And watch out! There's still three other brothers! From the looks of the way they handled this theft, they were mighty drunk, and probably still are!"

Chapter 30

When they arrived back at camp, the bacon was cold, but the coffee was still sitting on hot coals. So they placed the skillet back on the coals just long enough to get the meat hot. Then they proceeded to have thier delayed breakfast.

Elizabeth harnessed the team while Hank saddled his horse. Then he helped her with the wagon.

"Liz, when I went back to check on the races, I took a little time to ride on north a ways, to ask questions of people that knew the land. We're not far from a little town called Palo Pinto, and they said there's a branch of water running near there. I think we should head there, and plan on spending a few days to rest up, and take on a few supplies. They said there's a deep canyon west of town, so we'll keep to the east. We won't be too far from Fort Richardson, at Jacksboro . . . sounded like maybe forty miles or so."

"Reckon there's deer there? We're getting low on meat."

"Yes . . . lots of deer. I'll see if I can get one."

"Hey! What am I? A lump of coal? I can get a deer myself!"

He grinned, "Well, excuse me!

"All these towns in this part of the state have had their share of Indian trouble, burned out several times. So we can take the time to clean and load the weapons."

Elizabeth looked at Hank and smiled, "Except the clean one that I'll use to get us a deer!"

The brush thickened, and the terrain continued with its ups and downs. Hank rode ahead to scout out trails and roads that might be cut for access to homes in the area.

On his return he reported to Liz, "I've found an old Indian trail we can get to the higher land around Palo Pinto. It's east of here and it goes right along a westerly bend in the Brazos River that winds north toward Jacksboro. We can stop any time we want, because the river has a lot of water in it."

"Sounds good! The horses can't keep climbing these hills the way we've been doing. You go find a camp site and I'll head toward the river."

When the camp was set up and a fire started, Liz picked up her rifle. "Hank, it's late enough the deer ought to be up. I'm going to see what's out there."

"Fine, I'll get supper started and if you're lucky we may have steak tonight."

"Lucky? You just get the stuff ready! I don't have to be lucky to bag a deer. If there's any here, I'll bag one!"

"IF, huh? Sounds like you're protecting yourself."

Without another comment, she mounted and rode off. She came to the edge of a canyon, and marveled at how much territory she could take in from this point. Along a stream in the bottom, she saw several deer grazing together.

About a quarter mile down the canyon, she found a place where she could take an old deer trail to the bottom, and move closer toward the deer. "Whiffel, you stay right here! I'll be back in a little while." She began to stalk the area where she had seen the deer grazing.

She eased toward the site, sat down beside a large log and took inventory of the group. She wanted to pick out the largest she could take, just to get back at Hank.

While watching the group graze, she could see several bucks of considerable size. Then a very small motion to her right caught her attention. She slowly turned toward the movement. A very young Kiowa boy was stalking the same group of deer. He had sneaked up from the south, and had not seen her there behind the log. She watched him move slowly, noticing that he was rather young, and seemed to have only one arrow.

He pulled an arc in his bow, and let loose the arrow. It missed its mark, and slid along the grass, hardly noticed by the deer. The boy sat down, disgusted that he lost his last arrow.

Liz raised her rifle, fired and instantly, fired again. Two of the largest deer fell on the spot. The Indian boy sat as if petrified, until Liz motioned for him to take one of the deer. At first, he didn't understand, but she indicated again, and the boy ran and began dragging the smaller of the two.

As she walked up she motioned for him to take the larger one, because he looked as if he needed food worse than they did.

He smiled, but took the smaller deer on his shoulders and disappeared into the woods.

Liz retrieved Whiffle and placed the nice eight-point buck over the saddle, then climbed on behind.

As she rode back into to the camp, Hank joked, "Took two shots to get one, huh?"

"Not hardly! I gave one to an Indian."

"You WHAT?"

"Gave one to an Indian boy . . . he shot his last arrow and missed. The least I could do is share! He looked awfully hungry."

Hank stared, as she hung the deer in a tree to dress it.

"You may have just put us in good with the Indians in this area. Was the kid horseback, or walking?"

"Don't know. He could barely carry it . . . walked into the woods and disappeared . . . had tears in his eyes when he took the deer, so . . . so I guess he appreciated it."

"He may be a shunned kid, or he may be looking out for an abandoned old person . . . hard to know for sure."

"Well, whatever, he's fixed up for a while." She cut a couple of pieces of meat and handed them to Hank, "These should be good. I like mine well done!"

After supper, as they finished their coffee, Hank sat quietly stirring the coals with a stick. "I think I'll ride out in the morning to see if the boy was with someone that needs our help . . . If that's okay with you."

"Sure. I'll go with you, Hank. You don't think he might be with a war party?"

"If he looked as pitiful as you said, he's probably not with a bunch. If he had been, they would have come after us by now."

"I guess they would have. Well, good night Hank."

Early morning was crisp, and light dew made itself known on saddles and other things around the camp. After a wipe down, Liz and Hank were on their way down into the canyon, by the trail Liz had traveled yesterday.

"Where did you shoot the deer, Liz?"

"I got down and made my way about fifty yards to that fallen tree. The boy went into the woods about there too."

Hank stepped down, dropped his reins and walked to the edge of the woods. Liz moved silently behind him.

Bits of smoke wafted around the tops of the trees. As they walked farther into the woods, they saw a small figure wrapped in a blanket, obviously the boy Liz had seen. Strips of meat were hanging over the smoking fire. His back was to them, so he didn't realize they were behind him. Hank and Mary Elizabeth took the opportunity to pause, and look for other Indians.

"Looks like he's alone," observed Hank. "What do you suppose he's doing here?"

"More important, how are we going to communicate with him? Do you know any Kiowa talk?"

Hank looked at her and admitted, "Very little."

They turned to the left into the trees, circled around, and came out in front of the boy, so as not to scare him. Then they moved toward him.

He was dozing and when they woke him, fear filled his eyes. But when he saw Liz, he smiled and relaxed.

"He recognized you, Liz."

"Sure he did! We're friends," she boasted, as they stood in front of him.

The little Indian looked up at them, smiling. "I know what you're saying."

Hank and Liz were silent, as they were shocked at what they had heard. Liz was the first to speak.

"You understand?"

"Yes. My mother's father and mother took me when my mother died. I lived with them, and learned English from them. My true father was a great warrior that was killed in battle with the blue coats."

"What is your name? I'm Henry, they call me Hank and this is Elizabeth. I call her Liz."

"They called me Johnny, but my true name is Yellow Bird."

"Well, Yellow Bird, how did you get out here alone?" Hank asked.

"I tried to go back to my tribe after my grandparents died, but Dancing Shadow would not let me. He dropped me off at the green river, and I walked here looking for food."

In a low voice, so the boy could not hear, Hank ask Liz, "What do you think . . . should we take him with us?"

"Why not? We have room, and it's not too much farther to Chuck's."

"So, Yellow Bird, how about you riding along with us?"

"No horse!"

"You can ride on the wagon with me." said Elizabeth.

"I can take my jerky?" The boy asked, "The rest can feed my friends, the coyotes."

They gathered up his things, put out the fire and returned to their camp. Soon they would be on the road again, to the ranch of Charles Forbes.

"Can Johnny ride the white one?" Johnny asked when he saw the little white mule.

Hank laughed, "She's about your size! We'll have to ask Liz about that."

Hank and Johnny brought all the horses up to the wagon where Elizabeth was straightening harness.

Johnny asked again, "Miss Liz, do you think Johnny can ride the white one?"

"Lucy? I think you probably can. Lucy had a sister, her name was Lacy, I think Lucy misses her a lot, so she might be glad to have someone close to her again. We can give it a try, anyway. I bet she'll like it, but let's give her some time to get to know you."

Johnny handed her a handful of grass, "I will, she'll like me, I know."

Johnny and Lucy got along fine! He soon was riding along with Hank, as he searched for an easy trail to their final destination, the Charles Forbes home called The Branding Iron Ranch.

After miles of twisting and dodging hills and scrub oaks toward the north, Liz yelled out to Hank and Johnny, "There they are!"

Hank looked but saw nothing, "There what are?"

"The blue oak trees! Chuck said they all looked blue in the sun. That's got to be what he was talking about . . . we must be close."

Hank studied the trees. "Yeah, I see what you mean. They do look kinda blue. What's that got to do with your brother?"

"He said that we would know that we were close when we began to see them."

"Boy, I guess so. But I sure don't see nothin' that looks like a ranch."

"Ah Hank, don't be such a dummy! It just means it's not too much farther. Anyway, start watching for a little town or settlement when you scout out, because it's south of the ranch."

They rode on for a few miles, never seeing the settlement. They later learned it was to the west of their trail. But it wasn't long before they saw the gate to Chuck's Ranch.

"Guess we missed any town they were talkin' about, 'cause the sign on the gate says 'Brandin' Iron'. So I reckon we're here." commented Hank.

They pulled through the gate and stopped. "Hank, isn't that a thing of beauty? The house looks so clean and white."

"And big!" observed Hank.

They proceeded to the house, and pulled up to the hitching rack. "Wonder if anyone's home."

Hank stepped down from his horse. "There's a dog headed this way"

"I bet that's Chip! Chuck told me about him."

"Someone's comin', Liz."

"That would be Chuck! He walks like Papa!"

As Chuck approached, he began to walk faster, "Is that you, Mary Elizabeth?"

"It's me all right! We finally made it."

Chuck picked her up, swung her around, and kissed her. "Where's Papa?" he asked.

"Chuck, I want you to meet Henry O'Neill. He came with me, almost all the way."

They clasped hands. "Just call me Hank."

"Glad to meet you, and thanks for traveling with my little sister."

Chuck went to the wagon and lifted little Johnny down, "And who is this fellow?"

"That's Johnny Yellow Bird. He just joined us a while back."

Chuck kneeled down, on the boy's level. "Welcome, Johnny Yellow Bird. We're glad to have you! Then he looked up at Liz. "You didn't say where Papa was. Did he not come?"

"Yes Chuck, Papa came. But his heart wasn't too good and . . . he's buried north of Houston, in a little cemetery close to a town called Hitchcock. After that I was all alone, until Hank came along."

"I was afraid that might happen. I guess it was his time to go. But it's a hard thing to accept.

"Well Hank, I thank you again for helping my little sis."

"Not at all, Chuck. She's quite a perfectly capable woman, and it was my pleasure! We had some exciting events I wouldn't have experienced if I hadn't decided to ride along with her."

"I'll bet that's true. Y'all come in! I want you to meet Emilia. Chan's fixin' dinner, and he always fixes too much. He and Cecil Johnson, and of course Emilia and I are the owners of the ranch. I want you to meet everybody! The boys have already had chow, so I'll have Raymond take care of your stock. I'm glad to see that you brought Mister Spencer. Papa said in his letters that he had big plans for him, when he got here . . . come on, Chip. It's time you ate, too."

While everyone was visiting and getting acquainted, Liz pulled Chuck off to a corner of the room. "Chuck, I was hoping that you might have work for Hank, so he could stay around."

"Kinda grown sweet on him, have you?"

"Well, yes, but he doesn't know it. He's been really good to me, and he just might be a good husband! I'd like to see what blooms."

"Okay then, he's hired! Anything for my little sis . . . and Lizy, you see that hill right out there? Take him riding out to watch the sunset there . . . that's what got Emilia for me!"

"Thank you, Chuck!" She hugged his neck. He's a good hand. You won't be sorry!" And if I'm the woman I think I am, he won"t be either! It's going to be a good life!"

Epilog

Delbert Forbes continued to live on the Box RH ranch with his wife Belle. He managed to conquer his problems with the cold Montana weather, by layering his clothing, and of course, using her father Raffe's heavy winter coat that Belle had promised him!

They had three sons, Troy, Raffe and Richard. Raffe and Richard joined their parents helping to manage the ranch. Troy went to California and became a Veterinarian. He raised and trained horses for the Western movie industry of the time.

Charles Forbes, and his wife Emilia, along with Chan and Cecil Johnson, welcomed Mary Elizabeth, Henry O'Neil and Yellow Bird to the ranch in North Texas. After the railroad was completed, Chuck built a gun repair shop there on the ranch, and continued repairing guns, and supplying ammunition. He taught Yellow Bird the trade, and they worked together for years. Charles and Emilia had a son, Charles II and a daughter, Imagine. Emilia nursed the fruit trees, that John C. Bekendorff had planted, back to health.

Matthew Forbes had four sons, Jacob, Matthew Jr., Walt and Everett, with his wife, Jessica. When Matt's four years as a United States Marshall expired, he chose to stay with the apple business. Jacob, his first son, went on to law school and opened an office in Albuquerque, New Mexico. Matthew Jr. also studied law, but served in the State Senate in Santa Fe. Walt and Everett stayed in the apple business and were able to improve the production with special seed selection.

Jim Bolin and Marsha Whitaker married and continued operating the boarding house.

Bryan Forbes and his wife, Geneva became the parents of four sons. They were Cyril, Richard,

Daniel and Jeremy. Geneva's father, Cyril lived long enough to see his grandsons. Cyril and Richard, the two oldest sons, took over the flying A Ranch. That gave Julie and Will Taggley the chance to return to Eastern New Mexico, to rebuild on her father Paul's land, where they would raise cattle. Julie finally got to ride up into the mountains, to see the land that Will had told her about . . . Land that later became the Pecos Wilderness. Daniel and Jeremy stayed with their parents on the Bar H Ranch.

Benjamin Forbes and his wife Grace rebuilt the home that burned. They were eventually financially able to leave the Billings Ranch, and acquire their own stock. They became the parents of twin girls, Hailey and Hanna. Like their mother, the girls loved to ride, and during their high school years, they developed skilled trick riding and roping routines. They later moved to White Plains, New York, close to the headquarters of the Wild West Shows that were touring the country at the time. All of the Forbes families were able to visit together at their home.

Tom Coats, Silver Eagle, and his wife, Margarita, built on the land by Ben and Grace. They had no children. Tom raised Hogs to supply the sausage industry.

Mary Elizabeth Forbes O'Neil and Henry stayed on at the Branding Iron Ranch. Charles soon asked 'Hank' to take over the duties of foreman of the Branding Iron. In addition to Yellow Bird who was like a son. Liz and Hank had three sons, Charles, Richard and John. They were attracted to thoroughbred horses, and both studied animal husbandry. Together they promoted the breed the ranch was known for, the offspring of Mister Spencer.

The Forbes Family . . . just ordinary people who lived their dreams, settling the West.